mk

Island of Passion

Here is a tale of Jamaica with its beauties and its brothels, its slaves and freedom, its arrogant, uneasy ruling class and the girl from Galway whose lust for power, money and men led her to practice the island's black art of voodo.

DARK DRUMS

"probes the nature of a mysterious woman and black magic in colonial Jamaica: violence and intrigue hone the story to taut-edged turbulence."
—*Philadelphia News*

"is an exciting story about the kind of woman who provides legends, who held the love of a man even while she destroyed him."
—*Springfield Republican*

"is a stirring, action-packed novel in a land that has been known since its discovery as a land of violence and uncontrolled passion."
—*Montgomery Advertiser*

"is an intense story filled with all the emotions and passions of unrestrained and comparably unconventional living . . . the story of a woman who knew what she wanted and defied any odds to get portrait of a country and a people of ng removed."
—*Durham Herald*

DARK DRUMS

Wenzell Brown

WARNER BOOKS

A Warner Communications Company

WARNER BOOKS EDITION

ISBN 0-446-89292-0

Published by arrangement with the author

Cover are by Lou Marchetti

Warner Books, Inc., 75 Rockefeller Plaza, New York, N.Y. 10019

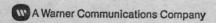 A Warner Communications Company

Printed in the United States of America

Not associated with Warner Press, Inc. of Anderson, Indiana

10   9   8   7   6   5   4   3   2   1

Dedicated to

BELLE CAMPBELL HUFF

ACKNOWLEDGMENTS

ALTHOUGH DARK DRUMS is completely a work of fiction, it was suggested by several parallel legends found in the West Indies. Its characters, except those well known in history, are purely creations of the imagination as are Rune Hall and other points mentioned in the book. However, the author has utilized source material in order to re-create Jamaica of about 1800, and he would like to make special reference to three specific sources. Katherine Dunham's fascinating and beautifully written book *Journey to Accompong* (New York: Henry Holt & Co., 1946) has been most useful in giving verity to Maroon dances and certain other aspects of life in the Cockpit country. Richardson Wright's *Revels in Jamica* (New York: Dodd, Mead & Co., 1937) has been invaluable in portraying the theatrical life of the period. J. Antonio Jarvis' chapter on superstitions and witchcraft contained in his *Brief History of the Virgin Islands* (St. Thomas: Art Shop, 1938) has been most useful as a check against the author's own observations in these fields.

W.B.

BOOK ONE

Jamaica, 1794

1

Two cocks glared at each other across the littered deck of the *Liza Mae*. The yellow one jumped up and down on thin claws like a ballet dancer, then stuck out his tawny neck and gave a raucous cry of defiance to the black bird perched on the lap of Captain Jabez Lunt.

Lunt chortled and stroked his bird with a pudgy, grimy hand. "Ay, Cousins, ye dinna think that cock o' yourn can beat old Brassie-bones here, do ye?"

Cousins held the dancing cock securely by its tail. His thin, sallow face held no trace of humor. His voice was low, metallic and harsh. He leaned forward, hovering over his bird. "Ay, that I do, Captain Lunt. Your Brassie-bones is filled with blood and thick with fat. Me bird may be scrawny but he's a fighter. Dare ye pitch Brassie-bones against me Blonde?"

Lunt roared with laughter, his huge belly bouncing up and down in scornful mirth. "Brassie's killed a round score o' birds in his day. 'Tis time he took a rest and put on a layer o' fat to warm his bones. But that bird o' yours, Cousins, he wouldn't last a minute with me Brassie. Where'd ye git the stringy beast?"

Cousins spat and viewed the skipper of the *Liza Mae*, his eyes beady with hate. "It's big talk you're a-making, Captain. Ye come into me house and slap ye guineas down and shout for rum and lay ye hands upon me wife like she was from the Christian Steps and we were all dirt beneath ye feet."

"Ay, Cousins, you're a ruddy mad mon. That woman o' yours is like a plucked bird indeed. Me, I've no use for a scrawny woman nor a scrawny cock. What ye need's

11

a good gal with some flesh upon her to bring the boys their tote. Now I've a gal here on board what will do fer ye. A gal from Galway she is, wi' papers for three years. And a daddy hanging high from a beam at Galway Crossing. How much'll ye bid on her papers, Cousins?"

"I've no guineas and well ye know it, Captain Lunt. But I've a pipe o' wine that says me Blonde can beat ye Brassie-bones. Will ye wager the girl's papers agin' that?"

"A good wager, Cousins," Lunt roared, "but I've not tasted ye wine."

"Nor I laid eyes upon ye wench."

Again Lunt laughed, his fat belly straining against the twisted top of his breeches. "Right ye are, Cousins. Never buy a pig in the poke, nor a wench ye've not seen." His voice rose in a sudden roar. "Kate, where be ye? Come here, Kate."

A girl came to the doorway of the Captain's cabin. She was tall, big-framed, and seemed deliberately awkward in her movements. She kept her head bent low so that only the bronze hair, pulled straight back from her forehead and knotted in loose braids, could be seen. The ring of bare-chested seamen, and the hangers-on about the dock who had clambered aboard the deck of the *Liza Mae* when news of the impending cockfight had been passed about, fell silent and turned to look at Kate. There were murmurs and guffaws among the men, for despite the girl's ragged clothing and sullen manner, her body was firm, strong and well shaped. Even now as she stared down at her hands and shuffled her bare feet, there was a sense of latent power about her, a litheness of movement that gave away in part the careful masquerade of slatternliness by which she sought to protect herself from the too-open gazes of the coarse men who surrounded her.

Lunt extended a pudgy finger. "There she be, Cousins. What do ye think o' her? Is she not a more tasty piece than that Mannie o' yours?"

Cousins scowled and his thin lips drew back to show yellow, broken teeth. "Leave Mannie out o' this, Lunt. I'm no whoremonger like ye used to be before ye grew too old and too fat for the game." He looked sharply at Kate. "What's the matter with the gal? Why will she not raise her face? What have ye done to her?"

Lunt's pendulous cheeks were splotched with purple. "Take care of ye tongue, Cousins, or I'll have ye thrown off from me ship and a rope to ye back to boot. Ye boarded me ship with your mangy bird and wanted to pit him against me Brassie here. Ye say ye've no money—only a pipe o' wine. All right, I say I've a gal with three-year papers on me hands. I'll wager ye a look at the wench. If ye want to go on with the game, say so. If not, get off the *Liza Mae*. The likes o' ye's not welcome here." He shifted his weight heavily and shouted to the girl. "Look up, Kate. Think ye ye're worth the risk o' losing for a pipe o' wine?"

Kate only bent her head still lower, until they could see the nape of her neck. She folded her arms across her breasts and leaned her weight against the open door.

"Look up, I tell ye," roared the Captain, "or are ye a-wishing another taste o' me belt?"

Kate straightened slowly. She had smudged her face with tar and her skin was coarsened by the salt wind and the sun, her lips bruised and puffed from a blow of the Captain's fist. She tried to assume a look of dull stupidity, her green eyes half-closed, masked against expression. Yet something of her inner pride and defiance reached the ring of gawking men.

"Ai, she's like a spittin' cat," a man murmured, but Captain Lunt's taunting voice cut across his words.

"Speak up, Kate," he bellowed, "be ye worth a pipe o' wine?"

Kate's eyes blazed with a sudden anger that she could not restrain. She glared defiantly at Lunt and then she turned slowly, taking in the ragged men, one by one, who surrounded the crude cockpit. The men lowered their eyes as her gaze fell upon them and a few mumbled beneath their breaths. Only Cousins remained unperturbed, stroking the tawny head of his cock. The girl's voice was unexpectedly soft when she spoke, yet it rang with a clear, sharp timbre. She addressed herself to Cousins, not to Lunt.

"I'm a bound girl," she said, "indentured for three years. I'll not run out on my articles. What else do you need to know?"

Cousins grunted but gave no answer. Lunt was shaking

13

with anger. "Ay, it's a proud one ye are, Kate. And proud ye were the day ye watched ye daddy dangling from a yardarm at Galway Crossing. Ye're not forgettin', be ye, Kate?"

The girl flushed scarlet with the taunt. Her eyes fell again to her bare feet and her shoulders drooped. She shuffled over to the rail and her hands clenched the wood until the knuckles showed white against the coarsened skin. The glistening water was crystal blue beneath her and, beyond the docks and warehouses, there was a strip of white beach with palms casting slanting shadows upon it. But she saw none of these things, for in her mind's eye the red sun crept again up Galway Mountain and, in the dim morning light, a man—her father—mounted the steps to the gallows.

One of the cocks gave a harsh cry and Kate swung about, suddenly frightened. The preparations for the fight were going on and none among the men paid further attention to her.

Lunt spoke to Cousins. "Well, mon, be it a wager?"

The innkeeper's taut face gave no inkling of his thoughts. "I've given ye me answer, Lunt. Me Blonde'll fight ye Brassie-bones—a pipe o' wine against the gal's articles."

"Right," boomed Lunt. His thick hand flicked out close to the black cock's eyes. The crouching bird's head, with its comb cut flat to form a bloody line, lashed out like a striking serpent. A spot of red appeared on the Captain's wrist and trickled in a tiny rivulet across his palm. Lunt clamped his lips to the wound, sucked out the blood and spat it into the grimy circle. "So ye think old Brassie-bones is slow, do ye, Cousins? He's not lost his speed."

Then he raised his voice: "Hi, Morgan, where be ye, lad?"

"Here, Captain." A young man stepped out from the shadowed recesses behind the Captain's cabin. He was tall and slender. Dark hair hung in close curls about his forehead and formed shaggy sideburns. His skin was darkened by the sun until it was the color of copper. His brown eyes sparkled and the teeth glinted, unnaturally white, in the bright light. He wore a close-fitting jersey with vertical stripes of blue and yellow, and stained blue breeches.

"Ye say ye've handled cocks in London, Percy lad?"

14

"Ay, that I have, sir."

"Then ye'll handle Brassie for me."

"Ay, sir."

The cock was struggling now, and it raised its voice in sharp challenge to the dancing bird across the ring.

Young Percy Morgan took a stained, red bandana from his pocket and fashioned a crude hood for the black bird. He scooped the cock up in his arms and slashed the thin rope that bound its legs. He spat into his palm and pressed down the ruffled feathers until they glistened black in the sunlight.

"Who's handlin' ye Blonde?" shouted Lunt at the innkeeper.

"None but meself shall touch 'im," retorted Cousins dourly. He had the yellow bird hooded, too, and it was resting quietly against his body. The crude circle that marked the pit was formed of tar which was melting under the hot Jamaica sun. The odor of sweating flesh and the sickening stench of rotting muscovate mingled with the tar and the salt water. At Lunt's orders, a sailor whisked a broom across the open space on the deck. The men busied themselves laying bets but the odds were heavy on the black cock, for most of the sailors had seen Brassie-bones fight before and knew the lethal swiftness of the big bird's beak and spurs.

Young Percy Morgan handed his charge to a nearby seaman and crossed the pit and crouched beside Cousins. In low voices they discussed the terms of the fight. Neither bird wore metal spurs, but the natural spurs of each were sharpened to needle points. Rounds were to be two minutes with a minute's interval between.

"Gard, mon, what sort of sashaying be ye up to?" lamented Cousins' companion. "When our cock goes in, it's to the death."

Morgan shook his head, smiling. "London rules. That's the way they fight in Old Trelawny Block."

Cousins scowled but shrugged his shoulders in assent. Morgan stepped back across the ring, but as he did so, looked for the first time straight at the girl by the rail. She stared past him, out over the shimmering bay toward the nearly hidden town of Port Royal. Morgan took Brassie-bones up in his arms again and ran his hands

15

across the hard, almost metallic feathers that had been clipped to prevent flight. The girl's eyes caught his for a moment and a brief glance of understanding passed between the two. Kate's sullen lips quirked into the suggestion of a smile and she gave a scarcely perceptible nod in the direction of Cousins, indicating that she wished his cock to win. Then she turned and stared down at the shabby gray docks of Kingston.

The hooded cocks were quiet, but Lunt's voice was raised to a bellowing scream as he ordered two blackamoors to move his chair to the edge of the ring. The Captain, it was agreed, would give the signal for the contest to begin.

Morgan withdrew the red bandana from Brassie's head and prodded the black bird with his fingers until the cock jumped in anger and threw out a challenge to the yellow bird. The Blonde needed no prodding; it strained against Cousins' encircling hands.

"Go in!" boomed Lunt.

The black bird catapulted from Morgan's hand. The two birds met in the exact center of the ring, nearly two feet above the deck. They seemed to remain suspended there endlessly as the clipped wings flapped and the raking spurs sought out vital spots and the heads darted backward and forward as each cock tried to fasten to the throat of its adversary.

The cocks fell back to the deck, both staggering from the force of the impact. A spray of carmine spurted from above the Blonde's right eye and turned into a thin streamer of blood. He pitched backward, leaving his breast exposed. But Brassie-bones moved too slowly and the Blonde was ready for the next attack. As Brassie's vicious beak darted out, the Blonde took to the air and raked the black back with his spurs. Again Brassie came in, moving stiff-legged, approaching the Blonde from the blind side, waiting cautiously like a stalking hunter to get in the fatal blow. The Blonde circled and then exploded into action, flying at the larger bird, raking with his claws, pecking. Brassie waited but, as the Blonde withdrew, got in a single telling blow at the yellow neck. Again there was a spurt of blood and the yellow bird staggered backward. Brassie moved in swiftly, but the Blonde met the attack. The

16

ellow head struck at the black throat, but the half-blinded bird missed and the head was caught beneath the upraised black wing.

The two cocks sprawled together in a flurry of feathers. "Separate!" screamed Lunt. "Time!"

Morgan and Cousins moved swiftly toward their cocks and each raised a bird in his hands. The innkeeper spat in his palm and rubbed the saliva against the Blonde's wounds. He wiped off the blood with his sleeve and then mopped sweat from his own face, leaving a grotesque smear across the bridge of his nose and on his cheek.

Morgan's skillful fingers pried at the black cock, but he could find no injury save for the superficial gashes on the back. He glanced about quickly to make sure that he was not being watched, then his hand tightened against the muscle of the right leg. Slowly he pressed, twisting hard until he felt the tenden snap beneath his fingers. Brassie gave a startled squawk and struggled against the restraining hands. Morgan quieted him with the hood. Again he looked sharply about to see if his trickery had been noticed. Lunt was leaning forward in his chair, chuckling with self-satisfaction. Cousins was intent on the Blonde. Only Kate Donley's eyes were upon Morgan. They were level, unchanging, but Morgan knew that she alone had been aware of his action.

Lunt raised his voice in raucous jeering. "Ye canna expect to fight a gamecock with a stewing chicken, Cousins. Why do ye not give up and spare the poor bird his life?"

Cousins' face was set and he did not look at the man who mocked him.

"Do we go on, Cousins?"

The innkeeper nodded.

"Go in!"

A second time the two birds catapulted across the ring and met in mid-air, the struggling bodies joined together by a murderous hate.

Percy Morgan glanced away from the struggle to seek out Kate. She had left the rail now and was standing behind a giant blackamoor who crouched beside the ring. For the moment she was intent on the fight and had forgotten to preserve her pose of sullenness, the heavy aloofness

17

which had masked her actions on the ship. Her face was flushed with excitement. Her green eyes sparkled and her full lips were open to show strong, even teeth. The sun changed her bronze hair into a crest of flame. She was breathing hard and her firm breasts strained against the thin fabric of her dress.

"My God, there's the making of a beauty in her," Percy murmured to himself. He thought of the nights when he had talked to her on deck. It was queer that she had let him, for she had refused to speak to any of the others. The moon had etched her face in pale light that last time and for a brief hour she had forgotten the need for concealment. Her voice had a gentle Irish lilt, and a haunting beauty came into her eyes. She had gone on talking for a long time, telling him of Galway, speaking of love and fear and ambition. He had had the idea she wasn't really talking to him, but to someone else in her imagination.

That a bound girl should have ambitions had struck him as a bit ridiculous. Still, he had ambitions too. She had been so absorbed in what she was saying that she had not heard Captain Lunt until he was almost upon them. Morgan had managed to slip away, unrecognized in the darkness, but Lunt had seen that Kate was with a man and that night he had beaten her in his cabin. After that, Morgan did not speak to Kate again, but there was an understanding of sorts between them. If Kate stayed here in Jamaica, he would skip ship. He was bound he would see her when both of them were free.

The roar of the crowd on the deck interrupted his thoughts and drew his eyes back to the ring. The black cock was down, floundering, one wing dragging in the melting tar. The Blonde strutted above him, pecking at the helpless bird but not delivering the death blow.

"He's done for," roared Lunt. "For God's sake, mon, put an end to it."

Percy stumbled toward the black bird but Jabez Lunt was ahead of him. The Captain whisked the yellow cock aside and with his pudgy fingers snapped the neck of Brassie-bones.

He tucked the dead bird beneath his arm. "Ay, me poor cock, I shouldna a-let ye fought. Ye were too old." Tears stood in the Captain's eyes, then he turned to Cousns and his face was livid with rage. "You, Cousins, ye filthy swine, take the gal and git off me ship. I see ye face here again, I'll rip ye apart and feed ye to the sharks. Git off, I say, git off the *Liza Mae*. Take the gal and never either of ye show agin."

He whirled and strode toward his cabin, still carrying the dead cock.

The men left on deck were silent save for Cousins. The innkeeper chuckled. He snatched up the triumphant Blonde and started for the gangplank. "C'mon, gal," he called to Kate over his shoulder. "Ye'll be a-comin' wi' me."

Kate's mouth opened as though she were about to protest but no word came. She looked pleadingly about the circle, but all eyes were averted. Percy Morgan walked toward the rail swiftly. As he passed, he whispered, "I'll come for you. I will come." Kate gave no sign of hearing. She assumed the slow, awkward walk she had always used on the ship. Her head bowed and she obeyed the innkeeper's command. She followed him down the gangplank, across the splintered docks to the cool shadows of the warehouses. Only at the doorway did she stop and look back at the seamen who were now formed in an uneven line along the deck of the *Liza Mae*.

Percy Morgan was leaning far over the rail. He raised his hand in a little salute. Kate stared at him for a few seconds, then her lips parted in the tiny, twisted smile he had seen but once before.

"C'mon, gal, quit danglin'," came Cousins' sour voice. He seized Kate's wrist and pulled her roughly into the darkness that lay beyond the warehouse door.

2

THE LIGHTS of the Laughing Donkey were dim. A soot-coated lantern hung at either end of the bar of rough-hewn lignum vitae wood. Blue smoke curled about the low rafters. The skirling of a bagpipe mingled with the rough voices of sailors. Every now and then the hoarse squawking oaths of a parrot pierced the confused din of the room.

Mannie Cousins stood on tiptoe behind the bar, her chin just even with the flat board. Mannie's face was pinched, narrow querulous. Skin, hair, and lips were all gray. Her colorless eyes were rheumy and the uneven lines of her nose ended in a pendulant lump. When she spoke, her voice was thin and nagging. She pushed two glasses of rum across the counter toward Kate Donley.

"For God's sake, gal," Mannie whined. "Act like ye was alive. Anyone ud think ye was a jumbie. The boys as come in here ain't got much chance to see a pretty gal. Give 'em a smile and make 'em happy."

Kate rested her arms for a moment on the scarred wood. "They can go to the Christian Steps, can't they?" she retorted.

"Mind ye tongue, gal, or maybe that's where ye'll be going. Lord knows you're little enough use round here. Can't see why Gabe keeps ye."

Kate shrugged and picked up the heavy glasses. Life here at the Laughing Donkey was not so hard as it had been aboard the *Liza Mae*. In the afternoon, there was the tiled floor to be scrubbed and the glasses to be polished. Mannie Cousins stood over her, watching, lashing out at the girl with her sharp tongue. Kate had learned to hate Mannie, but she was not afraid of the little woman, for she knew in her heart that Mannie was more frightened of life than she. Gabe Cousins was seldom about in the daytime, and when he was, he was dour and silent. One afternoon he had come in and perched on the bar and watched Kate as she knelt on all fours cleaning the tiles. He had said nothing and Kate had not turned, but she had sensed his eyes upon her. Mannie had appeared unexpectedly at the door and taken in the scene. Her face had filled with venom. "Git out o' here, Gabe Cousins," she had screamed. "Git out, I tell ye." Gabe had grunted and, without answering, moved slowly to the door. When he had gone, Mannie came to where Kate was crouching. Slowly, in a monotone, Mannie began to speak the coarse words of the London slums from whence she had come. Kate worked on, pretending not to hear. Then, in sullen rage, Mannie had kicked over the scrubbing bucket. Grimy gray water had splashed over Kate's face and arms, soaked the front of her dress and trickled down her breasts. Mannie had run away. Kate had listened to the click of her heels on the stairs and her harsh, strangled breathing. Then Kate got up, smiling a little, and went to the bar and poured herself a glass of whisky. "Mannie Cousins," she said softly to herself, "Mannie Cousins, you're right to be afraid."

Nights were better at the Laughing Donkey. There was music and laughter and the talk of the sailors. The tavern was not so different from those which she had known in Galway, for sometimes in the evening Mullen, her father, had taken her with him when he slipped away from the cottage and they had gone together to hear the wild music and the lilting Irish tales told by the Galway fishermen.

Here at the Laughing Donkey she liked to listen to the conversations, though she pretended not to hear lest her interest draw the unwanted attention of the men. She clung to the habits she had formed on shipboard, walking flat-footed, bending forward a bit to keep her face concealed. Even so she felt the eyes of the seamen upon her. However, there was little danger. Mannie was always near at hand, not to protect Kate but to make sure that she had no respite from work.

Mannie presided over the bar, measuring out each dram of rum or ale as though it were some precious fluid that never could be replaced. The coins she stored in a tin box concealed beneath the counter, fondling each one as though she hated to take her fingers from it. When the tavern closed for the night, Mannie counted the money with endless care, made notations in the red ledger she kept beside the box, then toted the coins upstairs where she spread them out on the bed and counted them again. Then she would get down on her knees and crawl halfway beneath the bed. Here a large strongbox of carved teakwood bound with brass was screwed solidly to the floor. Mannie undid the lock with a huge brass key and got up again. She stacked the coins taken that day and carried them beneath the bed and placed them one by one beside those already there. Once Mannie had forgotten to close the door to her bedroom and Kate had watched the ritual from the dark corridor. Mannie had not seen Kate until she crawled out from beneath the bed. Then she had screamed and rushed to the door and flung it shut. Kate heard the scrape of the bolt as Mannie slid it home. Mannie slept alone in the huge valanced bed and would let no one else enter the room, not even Gabe.

Kate seldom spoke to the men whom she served at the Laughing Donkey. She slid full glasses in front of them and took the glasses away when they were empty. She did not laugh at the rough jokes but kept her face sullen, without expression. Only two men attracted her among those who came to the tavern. There was the Scot who played the bagpipes, and the old colored man who came here often with him. His name was Koshi, she had learned, and he was a freeman. There was something about Koshi that reminded her of Mullen. The way he sat, listening to the others, smiling but seldom speaking. It was as though he were above them all and knew it, and still could be gentle and understanding. Kate wanted to talk with Koshi but dared not do so in the crowded tavern. Still, she felt that there was a kinship between them and that the key to her future rested, in some inexplicable way, in his hands.

One other stood out among the crowd, forcing himself upon her attention. This was Sydney Brandon, a hulking man with a mass of black beard, coarse of feature and obscene in speech. Brandon was the owner of a large plantation, yet he always dressed in working clothes. In a booming voice, he roused the hangers-on to discontent. He railed against the Governor, taxes and the low prices of sugar; but his loudest complaints were about the in-

22

creasing number of free Negroes on the island and the fact that they were allotted land. Cleverly he pitted white and black against one another. Although he appealed to the rabble. Kate sensed his insecurity and his lust for power at any cost. Whenever she heard his voice she tried to keep herself busy elsewhere. Yet she knew Brandon's words were affecting some of the seamen for, from time to time, she heard rumbling against the blacks and complaints that freedmen were admitted to the tavern.

Five weeks had passed since she had first come to the Laughing Donkey. The day after her arrival she had watched the *Liza Mae* sail out of the harbor and she had waited, hoping to hear from Percy Morgan. There was no word from him. She wondered if she had misunderstood the whispered promise, "I'll come for you." There had been no chance for her to make inquiries about Percy, for Mannie Cousins had kept her virtually a prisoner within the tavern, not even permitting her to go up the alleyway to Harbour Street. But this afternoon the *Liza Mae* was back and she had learned from the talk at the bar that it had only gone as far as Montego Bay to take on a cargo of muscovate. Men from the *Liza Mae* were in the Laughing Donkey now, but Percy Morgan was not among them.

Kate took the two glasses that Mannie had pushed toward her and moved to the table where Gabriel Cousins sat with two men in sailor's garb. As she slid the glasses before the sailors, a hairy hand reached out and touched hers. She drew away and the man laughed. "A high and mighty wench ye are," he called, "for one as was lost in a cockfight."

Kate swung about and went to the table where the Scot was playing the bagpipes. The three men watched her. Kate sensed their ugly mood and was glad that Brandon was not here to set off the spark of violence. The sailor who had spoken turned to Cousins. "I dinna come here to be insulted by ye serving-wench, Gabe. 'Tis time ye learned the gal some manners."

Cousins jerked his eyes away from Kate. "She's all right, Bard," he mumbled. "Just feared up a bit.' '

"You a-keeping her for ye'self, Gabe?" the sailor laughed. "What's Mannie got to say about that?"

"Shut up, Bard. Mannie will hear you."

Bard rocked with laughter. "Ye're a-scared o' that plucked chicken of a wife of your'n, Gabe. Scared as Hell."

"All right, let it be," growled Cousins.

Kate had crossed again to the bar and brought back two thick mugs of ale to the table where the bagpipe player sat. Her eyes lost their sullen quality as she looked down at the little Scot. His was a round, humorous, puckered face and, though he wore a stained blue shirt and smallclothes, a tam-o-shanter was cocked at a jaunty angle on his bald head. "Ay, lassie," he greeted her, "I'm a-thinkin' it's my skirling you're a-liking. 'Tis a Scottish pipe, yet it knows some tunes of old Galway too."

The Scot began to play the pipes softly. The din of the sailors broke off and the room grew quiet. It was an old Irish ballad that the Scotsman played, filled with the voices of the little people, the wail of the banshee, the lament for the dead.

Bard plucked at Cousins' sleeve. "The Scottie," he whispered. "Who is he?"

"Name o' MacFeathers," returned Cousins. "A lawyer he is, and they say he's a smart one—a bit too smart if what they tell be right, for he left Glasgow a jump ahead o' the bailiff. He's been to court only two times in Kingston, but each time he's plucked a mon from the shadow o' the gallows."

"And the black devil with him," growled Bard. "What's a nigger doing here?"

Cousins switched his gaze to Koshi, who sat with MacFeathers. This Negro was of medium height, with jet black skin and a fringe of white hair. His face was at rest now as he listened to the haunting strains of the music, but even so there was a latent power in the strong features and the somber eyes. His long, thin, forceful fingers beat a muted tattoo on the rough table top.

"Do you serve slaves in ye tavern along wi' white men?" Bard gave Cousins an insistent nudge.

"Koshi's no slave. He's a freeman now for nigh on twenty years. Ay, and he's a power here in the Island. Dinna let him hear ye speak so o' him."

"A power! The nigger! How?"

"He's said to be a high priest o' the Ashanti and the most powerful obeah man in Jamaica."

24

"Obeah? What the devil are ye talking about, Cousins? What be obeah?"

"Call it black magic if ye wish. Call it devil worship, or call it hocus-pocus—'tis all the same. Obeah is the religion of the blacks, and scoff at it all ye will, those o' us who have lived long in Jamaica have seen strange things. 'Tis said that Koshi can kill a man with his eyes or can put curses on him that will make his legs swell up until they burst with pus, or make a drooling idiot of a woman's unborn child, or cause burning sores to grow in the stomach of a man so that he howls with pain all the night long."

"Surely you do not believe in such folderol, Cousins."

"I neither believe nor disbelieve. But I've told ye, in the Islands we see peculiar things."

Bard rose drunkenly, "I'm going over and beard the old goat."

"Nay, Bard, dinna do it. A word o' caution—let me tell ye one thing: in the Ashanti tongue the word *obeah* means killing. And Koshi is the high priest of death."

"Go to the devil, Cousins. What Brandon says is true. No nigger has power over a white man. 'Tis not the law of God."

"That may be, but Koshi lives by the law of the devil, mon. Dinna trouble him."

But Bard had struggled up, and striking aside the innkeeper's restraining hand, he lurched toward the table where Kate was refilling MacFeathers' mug from a pitcher of tawny ale. The seaman's face was flushed and his speech slurred with drink as he swayed toward the white-haired Negro.

"Nigger, why be ye drinking in a white man's tavern? Get ye out or shall I toss ye out by the seat of ye breeches?"

Old Koshi sat completely motionless. His eyes continued to look down into the foaming ale and a faint smile was frozen on his lips.

"Speak, nigger," Bard bellowed, and his hand went to seize the Scotman's heavy mug. He raised the vessel high. "Did ye not hear me words?"

Bard swung the mug in a wide arc, bringing it down toward Koshi's head. Only the colored man's eyes shifted as he looked up into the seaman's red face. Bard's arm

25

came lower, increasing in speed, until the mug was within an inch of the old man's upturned eyes. Then suddenly the mug somehow spun from Bard's grip and at the same moment a torrent of tawny ale swept across the seaman's face.

The silence that had fallen in the dim room was broken with guffaws that grew into a roar of laughter. Bard stepped back, wiping off the liquor and digging at his smarting eyes. Standing directly before him was Kate Donley and she held the metal pitcher in her upraised hands. The pallor had left her face now and her green eyes reflected the light of the shimmering lantern hanging above the bar.

"Good gal," shouted a man at the bar. "Let the bloody swine have it."

"Do ye fight women, Bard?" another mocked. "Or only Negroes?"

There was a glittering rage in Bard's eyes and his lips curled back to show jagged yellow teeth. "A nigger and a bound gal," he snarled. "Two of a kind ye be. Ye need the feel o' my fists upon ye faces." He lurched toward Kate, but the girl stood her ground.

"Don't touch her." The words came softly from old Koshi. The seaman whirled swiftly at the sound and faced the aged colored man.

"Dare ye give me orders, nigger?"

"I tell you not to touch Kate."

"To hell with ye, ye black devil." Again Bard swung and his hand shot out and clasped the thin fabric of Kate's dress in the arch that it formed between her breasts.

But even as the sailor touched her, the blood drained from his face and the madness of his eyes changed to anguish. His free hand came up to his heart and he stumbled forward, his mouth open. The crash of the table and the splintering of glass drowned out his whimpering cry of pain. Kate stood over the fallen man. Her bodice had been ripped so that the rounded curve of her breasts was visible through the gaping cloth.

Bard groaned and raised himself on one arm, staring at Koshi. The old Negro's voice was still soft. "I warned you not to touch the girl, Bard."

26

The seaman's face was convulsed with pain. His hand clawed at his heart. "Oh, my God, my God. Stop."

"You cannot stand, but if you can reach the door, you will be all right," Koshi rose, and pushing the girl aside gently, stood with his legs straddling the stricken seaman. The man's choking whine was like that of a whipped dog. Desperately he began to crawl along the floor. His eyes did not leave those of Koshi, who loomed above him, and he stared as though hypnotized by the black man's face.

The uneven light threw grotesque shadows about the two men as they moved across the littered floor. Bard continued to whimper softly and one hand still clutched at his heart. His face was white, his mouth slack, his eyes staring. He did not turn over but lay on his back, using his elbows and his kicking legs to propel himself.

Koshi kept his position straddling the fallen man, walking slowly to keep pace with the other's tortured writhing. When they arrived at the door, Koshi leaned forward and opened it. A dank breeze swept into the room. Bard turned, got to one knee, gave a last frightened look at the colored man, then leapt up and fled into the darkness of the night.

The silent men in the tavern could hear the wild clatter of his heels on the rough cobblestones. Koshi pulled the door shut and walked calmly back to the table. He spoke to MacFeathers. "Play us the song of Galway Crossing, if you will, sir."

The pipes picked up the tune, playing quietly at first, then swinging into strident rhythm. The men began to drink again and called to Mannie Cousins to fill their glasses. Some of them speculated as to what Brandon would have done had he been present. But Kate Donley remained still, watching the old Negro. He looked at her, smiled and nodded.

"You will teach me," she whispered.

"Perhaps. We have much in common, have we not— a bound girl and a man who has known slavery?"

Mannie Cousins broke the spell. Her birdlike body shook with rage and her voice was waspish. "Who do ye think ye be, Kate—a queen? Ye've started a fight in the tavern and now ye stand there staring at the nigger. Pin up ye dress and git to the bar where ye're needed. Can ye not hear the men a-callin' for their grog? If I've me way, 'tis a taste of the whip ye'll be feeling tonight."

Again Koshi spoke in his slow drawling tones. "Leave Kate alone, Mannie. It's a bad time she's been having. Let her go to her room. You'll need her no more this night."

Mannie hesitated and Gabriel Cousins came up behind. "That's right," he stated. "Go to your room, Kate."

Kate did not answer but started for the wide stairway that ran along the far side of the tavern. She did not look at the men who cast sideways glances at her, but mounted the steps swiftly. At the turn of the stairway she stopped. Koshi sat in silence at the table, appearing to be absorbed in the music of the pipes. Mannie Cousins glared up at Kate, her face venomous.

The door through which Bard had passed opened again and a young man stepped into the tavern. His face was dark and burned with the sun and his tightly curled black hair grew into long sideburns.

Kate drew back into the shadows, but not before she had recognized the newcomer. He was Percy Morgan.

3

THE STREETS of Kingston were dark and the overhanging wooden balconies cast pitch-black shadows across the cobblestones. Kate was frightened and she pressed close to the sides of the houses. She was not sure of route for she had made only one trip through the city, trailing Gabe Cousins as he led her to the Laughing Donkey. Now she must find her way back to the warehouse where the *Liza Mae* had docked. Percy Morgan was to meet her there. That was the message he had slipped into her hand at the tavern.

Once a carriage rolled by and, in the passing glow of the lantern, she caught a glimpse of pink crinoline and heard the piercing laughter of a woman mix with the low-pitched voice of a man. She watched the carriage as it turned up the side street toward the Christian Steps. The drumming anger beat within her. There was life and laughter here in Jamaica, but she must scrub floors and serve ale to drunken sailors.

She stopped at the head of an alley, uncertain. She listened, but there was no sound save the soft slapping of water against rotting piling. She moved on swiftly, her fear tempered by the sudden sense of freedom at escaping Mannie Cousins' constant vigilance. The great, black hulk of the warehouse loomed before her.

Not until she came close did she see the open doorway at the side. An oblong patch of light fell upon a stunted tamarlod tree which grew at the water's edge. The black, stubby, swollen branches formed grotesque patterns in the pool of light. Kate circled in the darkness so that she could see within and still not be seen herself. Huge wooden hogsheads of rum, and burlap bags bulging with sugar, were piled in confusion about the warehouse floor. The sickening sweet smell of rotting sugar pervaded the air. A single lantern cast a flickering glow over the fantastic scene.

Kate stood silent for a full minute, seeing no sign of life. She wondered if Percy had given up his vigil because of the late hour. Then a slight movement caught her eye and she saw that a figure was sleeping on a crude pallet of burlap beside the wooden kegs.

"Percy," she called softly.

The figure stirred and rolled over sleepily.

"Percy," Kate called again. This time Morgan sat up and rubbed his eyes with the backs of his fists. Then he looked about and saw Kate, who had advanced as far as the doorway. He sprung up and went to her, both arms outstretched.

"Kate, I thought you were not coming. 'Twas so late." He tried to put his arms about her but she caught his hands in hers and held them instead.

"I couldn't get away sooner. I had to wait till the Donkey was closed and Mannie gone to bed." She was studying him as she spoke, wondering if he were strong enough to serve her purpose. She had seen him before only at a distance on the deck of the *Liza Mae*, or when he stood

29

beside her at the shadowed taffrail, or in the smoke-filled room of the tavern. Now she saw that he was younger than she had realized, nineteen or twenty at the most. He was handsome enough, reckless and wild, with some of her own defiance of the world. There was a stubborn line to his jaw and she wondered if she could handle him as easily as she had thought. No doubt he would want to prove himself a man in front of her. Suddenly she almost repented the danger in which she would place him. Then her mind hardened again; this was no time to go soft, and if Percy would play the game he would have his reward, and she would give it without stint. Her eyes rested on his youthful, eager face. Would it not have been better to have picked an older man? Again her thoughts went back to Mullen, of the steel behind his quiet manner, of the wild abandon that seized him in moments of exultation. Only Koshi among the Island men she knew had that calm assurance that flaunted fate. She thrust her doubts aside. She must gamble on Percy Morgan or seek some other plan where she needed no man to help her.

Percy was drawing her closer, pressing his body against her. His lips were feverish as they found hers. She felt her own breath coming in hot gasps. This would not do. This was not why she had come to him. She broke from his grasp and stood a few feet away, facing him.

Percy moved to take her in his arms again, but she held up her hand. "Wait, Percy. Wait. There's no time. I must get back to the Donkey before Mannie misses me."

"You needn't go back, Kate. Stay with me."

"You forget. I'm a bound girl and you're a deserter. How long would we stay free? A day, perhaps a week. That's no good, Percy."

"We could run away, up to the mountains. We could join the Maroons maybe. There's more than one white man among 'em."

"And live like hunted beasts for the rest of our lives? No, Percy."

"I could steal a sailing boat. We could get to Cuba. We'd be free there."

"The sea is rough and wide between here and Santiago. We'd need a man who knew his way. Besides, when we got to Cuba we'd have no money. Stealing a fishing smack would do us no good."

"I can't stay here long, Kate. I've bribed the watchman to let me sleep here, but they'll find me in a few days."

Kate thought out her words carefully. "Are you afraid to take that which does another no good, Percy?"

"It it stealing you're talking about?"

Kate shrugged. "Call it what you will. I know where there's money—lots of it. 'Twill be easy to get and with it we can hire a boat to take us to Cuba. We'll land with money enough of our own to get to Havana. Enough for the two of us to get a new start—together, Percy."

The boy's face was pale beneath its tan. "Ay, but stealing's a hanging crime in Jamaica, Kate. We may go no farther than the gallows."

"But we'll not fail."

"How can you be so sure, Kate?"

Kate laughed. "I did not pick you for a coward, Percy. I watched you snap the muscle of Captain Lunt's black cock so that Cousins would win me. I thought you a man then, not a boy. Was I mistaken?"

"Ay, I fouled the cock that I might be with you, Kate. But e'en if I were caught, 'twas only a flogging I'd get at Lunt's hands. But I've no wish to wear a noose about my neck, nor to see one about yours, Kate."

Kate whirled. "I've misjudged you, Percy. I'll be leaving you by yourself. 'Tis not ready you are for a woman." She moved off swiftly toward the open door. Percy let her go halfway, then raced after her. He seized her by the shoulders and twisted her about. "Lord, Kate, don't go. I'll do whatever you say. Only stay with me."

Kate broke away and stood looking at the youth. "You're not afraid to steal?"

"Not for you, Kate. I'd kill for you, if need be. Only do not leave me, not tonight."

"I'll stay. But first you must listen. We'll have the money and we'll not hang." She sat down on a bulging sack of sugar and slowly, carefully unrolled her plan. . . .

The gray light of dawn had come to Kingston when Kate made her way again along Harbour Street. Thin mist clung to the bay and gave to the water a hard, metallic sheen.

31

Kate did not press against the buildings now but walked in the middle of the roadway with her head held high, breathing in the cool air, thinking of the mists of far-off Ardrahan and how they swept down to Ballycas and hid the waters of the Shannon. She did not slow her step until she came to the side door of the Laughing Donkey, which she had left unlatched. She moved silently then, pushing the door gently that it should make no sound.

She crossed the length of the tavern hall to the wide stairs and swiftly began the ascent. She heard no sound, but when she reached the turning she saw there was a white-clad figure at the top. Mannie Cousins was waiting for her, a leather quirt in her hand.

Mannie's thin, birdlike face shone with malice and sadistic glee. "So ye've come 'ome, 'ave ye, Kate? And 'ow 'ave ye spent the night? Rolling in some cane field with a nigger, I'll be bound. I told Gabe that with all ye manners and all ye graces and ye sullen face and ye mighty ways, ye was nought but a she-cat, ready for the prowl. What 'ave ye to say for ye'self, Kate, ye slut?"

Kate peered up at the shaking woman in her white nightdress. Her lips twisted in a mocking smile. " 'Tis a long time since a man's looked at you, isn't it, Mannie? You've only the clink of gold to warm you at night, for not even Gabe Cousins will come to you." As she talked, Kate moved up the stairs until she was only a step or two below Mannie.

The older woman's face was contorted with rage. Her lips writhed but the ugly words she would speak issued as a strangled, inarticulate jumble of sound. She raised her skinny arm and brought the quirt whistling down.

Kate protected her face with her forearm. The stinging leather cut through the thin cotton of her sleeve and she felt the hot spurt of blood as the quirt bit into her flesh. Mannie raised her arm again but Kate was upon her, holding her by the wrist. She looked down at the twisted face. "Strike me again, Mannie," she said softly. "Strike me as often as you wish. 'Twill give me the greater joy to even my score with you. There'll be no guilt for me to feel."

She released Mannie's wrist and stepped down again,

facing the little woman. Mannie stared at her, eyes protruding, her gray face pale. "A she-devil, that's what ye are, Kate. A witch as should be burned. I'll make Gabe get rid o' ye. I'll no' stand for ye 'ere at the Donkey."

Kate's face was placid, expressionless. For a moment longer Mannie stared, then turned and ran swiftly to her room. Kate listened to the heavy bolt slide home.

That night there was trouble at the tavern. Picon started it. Picon was a little old Creole who had hung about the Kingston water front for years. No one knew how old he was, though his age was guessed to be anywhere from sixty to eighty; nor was it known from whence he came. Some said he was from Haiti; others that he came from Trinidad. Picon himself seldom spoke save to ask for liquor. Instead he sang songs, strange songs in broken English mixed with an archaic French patois. On Saturdays Picon hung about the market places, strumming his crude quartro which he had made himself. The instrument had only four strings, but Picon managed to get astonishing variations in his music. He knew all the digging tunes of the slaves and played them over and over again. The words he sang seemed spontaneous and he was never known to render an exact repetition of a song. Picon was a wispy little man, with pale face, unkempt long hair and broken shoes. He always stared down at his feet while he sang and when he was through "passed the bouquet," and sometimes even those slaves who had managed to secure a few coins dropped pennies into his bedraggled hat.

Picon made a round of the taverns each night singing for drinks or food or trying to pick up a game of dice. The habitués of the taverns knew Picon's nimble fingers and strongly suspected his dice were loaded, but occasionally Picon could inveigle a strange seaman into a game.

Picon offended Mannie Cousins' cockney sense of respectability and she would have ordered him out of the Laughing Donkey were it not for her cupidity. The men stayed on to listen to the little old derelict, and they bought him drinks and often ordered extra rounds for themselves. The tavern had been quiet during the early part of the night. MacFeathers had left his pipes at home and sat hunched over his ale in one of his morose and taciturn moods. Koshi sat at the table with him, looking from the Scot to Kate as she made her rounds. Mannie stood alone behind the bar, giving vent to her temper by slamming the glasses down hard. Gabe had gone to Port Morant to attend to a shipment of rum and would not be back until the following day.

Kate was watching Mannie covertly. She was sure that Mannie had no suspicion of what lay within her mind. Yet it had been unwise to pit herself so openly against the cockney woman. Mannie's sharp tongue had made her many enemies and no friends. Even so, if she were frightened enough she might ask someone to spend the night here and that would destroy Kate's plan. Kate served the men, walking flat-footed, keeping her face sullen, for no one must see a difference in her tonight. Yet she did not let Mannie out of her sight and whenever one of the men went to the bar she kept within earshot.

Mannie was becoming increasingly nervous, and when Picon came stumbling in she gave a start and let the rum pour over the glass's brim. She mumbled an oath and sucked her fingers. Picon tottered to the bar. His quartro was under his left arm and he rattled dice in his right fist.

"Who play Picon for de drinks?" he shrilled. "Who jambo de dice wi' Picon?" He slapped the dice on the scarred board and ran them the length of the bar. They jumped like living things, responding to his quick fingers.

Picon looked around and repeated his invitation. No one paid him the slightest attention. Picon's dreary eyes fastened on Mannie. "Gi' me a noggin o' rum to whet me whistle," he begged. "Den Picon will sing for de boys."

"Git out," Mannie snarled back at him, "we want none o' ye this night."

"Ah, Mannie," Picon pleaded.

"Git him his rum," called MacFeathers unexpectedly. "I'll pay to hear him play. I'm in need o' some cheer."

Reluctantly Mannie filled a glass and shoved it across to Picon. The Creole drank greedily and wiped his mouth with the back of a ragged sleeve.

Picon took a stance by the bar, feet outspread, hat pulled low over his face and his eyes cast downward. He

34

plucked the strings of the quartro, slowly at first, then more and more rapidly. The music took on a mounting rhythm strangely like the beating drums that sometimes sounded in the hills. Picon began to sing, improvising words, fitting them to the rhythm by slurring or skipping syllables. He sang with a rising inflection at the end of each line and distorted the words into matched endings where no real rhythm occurred.

Kate, with her Irish love of minstrelsy, was always fascinated by Picon. As she listened to him, the bitter hatred that had filled her days since she had left Galway receded and she found herself humming the provocative tunes. Picon sang in Creole:

> "Moi pas au zo la
> Pu feu zo la shuen par moi."

Then he switched to English dialect:

> "I am not in de dice
> To make it play as I like."

He repeated the chorus, then began to improvise, lampooning two of the seamen who were seated in the Laughing Donkey and who had quarreled over a dice game some nights before.

> "A quarrel arose dat night
> And de men began to fight
> De remark of Tom was not nice
> Dat Charl was playing de loaded dice."

Laughter filled the smoky room and the eyes of the men went from Tom to Charl, who sat at opposite sides of the bar. Tom joined in the laughter, but Charl's face was dark with anger.

The men, now familiar with the chorus, joined in. When the uproar had died down, Picon continued without looking up:

> "Here me I do say
> Whenever Charl do play

35

If de dice do be his
Dey must always to obey."

Again the seated men began to take up the chorus, but they were silenced by a roar from Charl, who came striding across the floor to stand before Picon with his arms akimbo.

"Be you insinuatin' I'm a cheat, ye little beast?" he cried.

Picon did not look at the big man. He kept his eyes on the floor and strummed the quartro. Charl was quivering with rage but the mocking cries of the men diverted his attention. He swung about, mouthing an oath. "Were ye the size of a mon, I'd break ye in two," he growled at Picon.

Mannie Cousins was watching the scene with frightened eyes. Brawls in the Laughing Donkey meant smashed chairs, tables and glasses and she was forced to draw from the hoard of coins beneath her bed to restore the broken articles.

As Charl turned away, Picon sang softly, "I am not in de dice."

Mannie swirled out from behind the bar. Her head was just level with the old man's. "Shaddap, you, Picon, and git out o' me house. Always you be up to making trouble. Git out, I say."

"Let me pass the bouquet."

"No." Mannie's hand whipped out and struck hard against the quartro. There was a sharp ping as two of the strings broke.

Picon looked at the instrument and then up at Mannie. The lines of his face seemed to blur and break. "Ye moshed it, 'ooman. Ye moshed me quartro." Without warning, sobs wracked the wispy body and Picon began to cry.

"Git out, I say! Git out!" Mannie screamed. She seized the old man by the shoulders, pushing him backward. Picon stumbled, clutching the quartro, then darted for the door. He turned his tear-streaked face to Mannie.

"I'll git ye for dis, Mannie Cousins. I'll put an obi on ye house."

There was silence when the old man had gone. The

men got up quietly and left singly or in groups, without saying good night to Mannie. In a few minutes only MacFeathers and Koshi were left. The Scot shrugged and rose to his feet. Koshi helped him to the door. Kate and Mannie were alone.

Mannie busied herself, shutting and barring the doors and windows. Kate watched her, not moving. Her thoughts were of Mullen, singing in a tavern in Galway. Mullen's voice had been strong, true and clear, not like the shaking voice of old Picon. Still the minstrels of the world were bound together by the thread of song. Kate's mind hardened. There would be a chance of striking a blow tonight —revenge for the broken strings of Picon's quartro, for the rope that encircled Mullen's neck.

Mannie was scooping up the coins from the tin box. She did not stop to count them tonight but dumped them swiftly into her apron. She scurried up the stairs and there was the sound of the key turning in the lock. She flung the coins on the bed and came back to the head of the stairs and called down to Kate, "Git to bed wi' ye. Gabe will be here in the morning. We'll see what happens to ye then."

An hour later Kate heard the stinging whisper of sand tossed against her shutters. She had been standing by the open window, but the sky was clouded and the night so black that she could see nothing in the alley below. "Percy?" she called softly.

"Yes, Kate. Let me in."

She slipped down the stairs softly in her bare feet. At the foot, she lit a candle so that she might not stumble over the litter of chairs and tables in the tavern hall. She unbarred the door and opened it a few inches. Percy Morgan squeezed his way in. Before she could replace the bar, he took her in his arms. "Kate, all day I've been sick with the wanting of you." He pressed his lips against hers. She responded to the warmth of his embrace, but only for a minute.

"There's no time for making love. We've work to do, Percy. Are you still afraid?"

"Scared?" he scoffed. "I'll never be scared with you. Where's the money? Let's do the job quick and get out. I've a man waiting with a skiff at Kerry's jetty.'

Kate raised the candle close to his face. Percy's eyes

gleamed in the flickering light. His smile was gay and reckless.

"Come with me, Percy." She led him back to the wood closet at the far end of the room. An ax lay there, its sharp edge catching the candle's dancing flame. Kate lifted it and handed it to Percy. "You must break down the door with a single blow. That will be the riskiest part of the whole affair. If you have to strike twice, or three times, Mannie may have a chance to unbar the window. She always keeps it closed at night, but if she can open it and scream for help we'll have no chance. The door is heavy. Can you do it, Percy?"

The young man nodded. "I'll have to."

Kate watched while he took off his boots, then again she led the way and they crept hand in hand up the stairway. A loose board creaked beneath Percy's weight and a few steps further another gave a loud groan. When they reached the landing, there was a crack of light beneath Mannie's door.

Kate saw that Percy's face was pale now. "She's awake," he whispered, "we must wait for another night."

"There'll be no other chance. Gabe comes back tomorrow."

They stood in silence before the door. Mannie's voice, shrill and plaintive, called out, "Kate, what are ye doing? 'Ave ye someone wi' ye? Kate, answer me."

Kate stood aside and motioned imperatively to Percy. He hesitated, then raised the ax high. He stood with the ax poised above his head, his eyes pleading.

Kate pointed. "For God's sake," she whispered, "strike before Mannie begins to scream."

The ax came smashing down. The wood splintered and formed thin shafts that scattered in the hall, but the lock did not give.

"Again! Again! Quick!"

Percy raised the ax and brought it down, this time on the lock. The door flew open as if blown by a heavy wind. Kate was in the room first. Mannie was working desperately at the window barriers, but her hands were shaking so that she could not release the bar. As Kate rushed to her, Mannie started to scream. Kate's fingers encircled the scrawny neck and choked off the cry. Mannie's arms shot out stiffly, then she clutched at the girl's wrists, raking the flesh with her nails.

Kate shook the woman roughly. Mannie's clawlike fingers left Kate's wrists and caught in the bodice of her dress. Kate looked down and the faces were only inches apart. Mannie's lips writhed in imprecation and foam trickled from the side of her mouth. The beady eyes glared up at Kate and they were filled with venom. Kate shivered and her hands seemed to lock upon the wrinkled neck.

Percy Morgan was watching wide-eyed. He took a step toward them. "Kate, Kate, let her go. You're killing her."

Kate thrust out with her hands, pushing the woman away. Mannie's thin body straightened and she fell backward. Kate watched her and the moment seemed to stretch out into eternity. Mannie's forehead struck against the jutting edge of the iron window fasteners. There was a dull thud and Mannie lay still.

Kate watched the trail of blood that oozed across the woman's cheek and for a while she could not move. Percy knelt beside Mannie. The rheumy eyes stared up sightlessly into his. His voice was unsteady. "My God, Kate, she's dead. You've murdered her."

Kate looked down at the dead woman in horrified fascination. She could still feel the loose flesh and the flabby skin on her hands. She had not meant to kill, yet in her heart, had she not hoped for Mannie's death? Percy's white face and twitching lips suddenly steadied her and she forced herself to think calmly. Without Mannie's evidence they could stay on the island. But could she trust Percy? After all, he was only a lad of eighteen and murder would lay heavy upon him. No, she decided quickly, she must walk this road alone. She must get the money and then be rid of him.

She forced harshness into her voice. She said, "It's not I who killed her but we—you and I. It's too late to change things, now. We must have the money!"

"Money! Money!" Percy repeated. Then his voice rose. "It's blood money now. How can you think of it? We've a skiff waiting. Let's get out quick."

"No, Percy. The money will save us. We've gone too far to quit. Here, help me push the bed aside."

"Lord, you're a cold one, Kate. We've killed her. Don't you understand?"

"Stop moaning. 'Twill do no good. We've work to do. I've seen my own father on the gallows and I'm bound it will not happen to me. They might not have followed us for robbery, but they will for murder. We must get the money and cover up as best we can. I'd no mind to kill her, but now it's done."

Kate was tugging at the heavy high-posted bed. Percy threw his weight against it too and the bed moved slowly to one side. Beneath it was the heavy teakwood strongbox, screwed securely to the floor. Percy raised the ax but Kate placed her hand on his arm. "Not that way, Percy. Mannie has the key. It's hanging 'bout her neck."

"I won't touch her. Let me break it open."

"No, you fool! Keep a clear head or you'll trap us both." She went to Mannie and drew the string with the key above her head, then knelt beside the strongbox and unlocked it. She raised the lid and the stacks of gold and silver coins came into view.

Kate got up and snatched Mannie's gray silk dress that was hung loosely over a chair. She took out the heaps of gold pieces and flung them upon the skirt. Then she rolled the dress up tight, tucking the arms inside to form a fastening for the cloth. She locked the box and went back to Mannie and hung the key about her head again.

Percy loomed over her. "Why didn't you take the silver? We'll need every penny. We've got to get away, far away."

"No, Percy. Flight won't do any good. The thing now is to conceal what we've done. No one but Mannie knows how much was in that box and she'll never tell now. No one can ever say that she's been robbed."

"What difference will that make? They'll see that Mannie's dead and they'll see the marks on her throat and the cut on her head."

"I've a plan, Percy. Here, help me get the bed back." Unwillingly Percy joined her in pushing the bed to its original position. Kate went to where Mannie had fallen. She raised the birdlike body in her strong arms and carried the dead woman to the bed. She folded back the coarse sheet and the thin blanket and laid the woman down. Then she turned abruptly and walked to the door. Percy was right behind.

"Stay here," she snapped.

"But we've got to get out of here. We must go quickly."

"There are things to be done. No one must know there's been a robbery."

"You're daft, Kate. There's a splintered door and a woman done to death. Oh, they will know who did this all right."

"No, they mustn't. Stay here, Percy." Kate's command was so sharp that Percy wavered. Then he stepped back and sank into a chair and covered his face with his hands.

Kate picked up the coins in their silken wrappings. She ran down the stairs and unbarred the door and walked swiftly to the jetty. She leaned over and thrust the package into the water. She did not hurry on her way back. She closed the door and lit a candle. Beneath the bar was a tin of oil, almost full. She carried it back up the stairs.

Percy was pacing up and down the floor nervously. The sight of his youthful weakness stilled the cold fear in Kate. She thrust from her mind the memory of the dead woman. She would not let herself be trapped as Mullen had been trapped. She would fight her way clear. Resolutely she lifted the can of oil and drenched the bed and the valances.

Percy came up behind her and seized her by the elbows. "You can't do this, Kate," he said, his voice taut. "Kingston's a city of wooden houses. Once a fire gets under way, there is no way of stopping it. You'll burn down the whole town. Thousands will be homeless. God alone knows how many may be burned to death."

He stepped back from her and she saw the horror and disbelief in his face. She twisted her lips into a hard smile. "Would it be better to hang, Percy? I thought you were afraid of the gallows."

"Yes, I'm afraid—not of the gallows, but of you. You're a devil, Kate. 'Tis not necessary to do this. Come, let us get away. If we're taken we'll have to pay the price, but I'd rather that than more people should die."

Anger swept away every other thought from the girl. "Ah, you need not be so noble, Percy Morgan. From what I've seen of Kingston, 'twould be as well if it burned to the ground. Besides, with Mannie's body destroyed there'll be

41

no trace of what we've done. The strongbox may last out the fire but it won't be empty, and who can say what should be in it? It's the only way. And now, Percy, 'tis time for you to go. You're needed here no longer and you've a skiff waiting you at Kerry's jetty."

"What do you mean, Kate? We're not going together?"

"No, Percy, I'm staying here."

"Then I'll stay too."

"No, Percy. You're too young. You've not the courage to face up to this—yet. If you stay and we're caught I'll say that I found you here, that you broke into Mannie's room and set fire to the place to cover your crime. It will be you who killed Mannie Cousins—that's the way it will stand."

Morgan swung her about and looked into her face. "Is that why you brought me here? So if there was danger you could place the blame on me? To save your own neck?"

"That was not the plan. But I've seen you go to pieces. I can't trust you. So now I'm through with you, Percy. You'd better go while there is time."

The youth's eyes were stricken. "I cannot believe it of you, Kate. Did you let me love you only to trap me? You must be the devil in person."

"If that be so, 'tis lucky you are to be free of me."

"Suppose I stay. 'Twill be only your word against mine. Who will believe a bound girl?"

"Or a deserter? You can do no more than hang us both. Go quickly, Percy. Go, while there's time."

"Where's the money?"

"Where you'll never find it."

"You planned from the first to cheat me of it, you slut. You've played me for a fool, Kate." He seized her wrists and pulled her arms behind her, but she kicked at him and twisted free. He lurched backward against the bed and his sprawling arm knocked the lamp from the table. It fell across the soaked blanket and a spurt of flame licked across Percy's wrist. He gave a gasp of pain and leapt to his feet and tried to seize the girl. She took up the ax and held it high, ready to strike. They stood still for a moment while the flames cackled about them. Hatred and love flared in his eyes, but he did not dare strike. The fire was spreading and a spark fell on his breeches and burned

42

through the cloth. He cried out hoarsely and then wheeled about and ran from the room. Kate heard the beat of his feet on the stairs and the slamming of the door below.

For a minute Kate stood in the glaring light, fighting the impulse to call him back or run after him. But there was little time to think and she realized that a mistake now might be fatal. She backed away from the flames slowly. Her eyes were smarting with the smoke but she was determined she would stay within the house as long as she could. An excited babble of voices already came from the alleyway. Mannie's bed was a flaming funeral pyre. Kate whirled and sped down the smoke-filled stairs, screaming, "Help, help—in God's name. Mannie Cousins is still in her bed."

She fell on the last step and sprawled on the tile floor. Rough hands helped her to the door. "Mannie," she cried, "I tried to save her. Reach her—quick—before she burns to death."

"We can't get up there," a harsh voice told her. "There's not a chance for a living thing up there. You're lucky, gal, to get out of that inferno alive."

That night the sky above Kingston glowed blood red and the harbor was bathed in a ruddy haze. Glowing sparks leapt from one wooden portico to another and soon tongues of flame licked at the sides of the buildings and turned the frame houses into fiery sheathes. The fire worked its way along the water front, streaking out along the rickety jetties and the rotting wharves. A stately fourmaster drawn up at Kerry's Pier caught fire. The flames raced across the decks, up into the mast. The ropes that bound the ship snapped and she drifted out into the bay and lighted the harbor from Dunroy Point to Port Royal. Other sailing vessels pulled up their anchors and sailed out into the bay away from the flaming port. Their furled sails caught the pink glow of the fire as their captains maneuvered their craft away from the doomed ship.

The streets of Kingston were in turmoil. Those who were made homeless carried what possessions they could save out into the open and then, as the encroaching flames came closer, they moved their goods again and again. The giant warehouse caught fire and men rolled out puncheons of rum. Some of these smashed on the wharf's sides and some were deliberately cracked open by seamen that they might dip their mouths into the rum and drink. Looters burst into the shops on King Street, stealing whatever they could lay their hands upon. Planters arrived with wagon-loads of slaves to fight the fire but they only added to the confusion in the city. At Dorcas Alley, a group of slaves revolted and threw their overseer into a burning building.

A light wind blew the flames along the harbor and bucket brigades retreated slowly before the oncoming fire. The only water came from the bay itself, and lines of workers passed the buckets from hand to hand for blocks so that the salt water could be dashed against the buildings in the path of the fire. Kate Donley worked in the line. Her eyes smarted, her hair was singed and her hands blistered. Doggedly she kept the buckets moving. Working beside her was a plump, red-haired woman in a purple taffeta dress. Her small, square, capable hands took the buckets from Kate.

At dawn a sudden blast of wind drove the flames against the lines. The workers screamed in fear and pain and scattered, running before the blaze. Gray clouds had gathered in the sky, unnoticed because of the smoke and leaping flames. The rain beat down, hissing against the red hot embers, sending up billows of black smoke. In a few minutes the fire was out, but eight city blocks along the water front lay in charred ruins. The skeleton of the four-master was keeled over on her side in the harbor. A dozen piers were broken black fingers pointing out into the bay.

Kate Donley had started to run when the lines had broken. Her eyes were stinging so that she could hardly see, and after a few steps she stumbled and fell to her knees. The woman in purple taffeta was beside her, help-ing her up. Again she ran and felt the woman's hand on hers. Then the rain came beating down on her, knocking her to the earth. She fell and felt the coolness of muddy water against her cheek.

A voice that seemed to come from a great distance said, "Open your eyes, dearie." She did as she was told and saw the plump face and the kindly eyes of the red-haired woman. She knew that the woman spoke, but she could not hear the words. She pressed her face against the woman's bosom and clung to her with both her hands.

4

KATE'S WAKING was slow and painful. Fear and a sense of guilt clouded her mind, but she had no memory of the sources from which they sprang. She gazed at her burned arms and blistered hands without understanding, then gradually she became aware of the soft bed, the clean sheets, the drawn jalousie that made the room cool and dim. The years seemed to roll backward until she was a child of seven again, living in a cottage in Galway. Panic engulfed her and she lived over again the scene in which she had first learned of betrayal and guilt—the necessity of being secretive to avoid the sting of her mother's whip.

A woman's footfall sounded in the corridor and Kate shrank back against the pillows. The door opened a crack and she caught sight of a woman in a dark dress. Her mother had always worn black. A long sob convulsed Kate and she turned over and buried her face in the crisp sheets.

Now the nightmare was upon her and she was unable to distinguish between the past and present. She tensed herself for the expected blows, feeling the hatred for her mother well up within her, wanting to call out her father's name. For it was Mullen who had told her of the little folk, and her mother who had claimed that they did not exist.

As a child, the little folks had been very near to her. She had even given them names—Paddy, Moira, Old Gus. She had played with them in the walled garden, even though her mother had told her she would grow up to be daft if she did not cease her imaginings.

Then once, as she was chasing Paddy, they had upset

45

the tea table and the dishes had fallen with a clatter to the earth. Her mother's fingers, hard and bony, had bitten into her shoulder and Kate had blurted out the whole story.

"Enough of lies," her mother had told her. "I'll have no more nonsense about dwarfs and fairies. There are no little folks."

"There are. There are," Kate had screamed.

Her mother had ordered her to her room and followed her, carrying a switch. Kate had borne the first few blows, screaming defiantly that the little folk were real. But in the end she could endure the pain no longer and she had denied the little folk, and in so doing had denied her father too, for she knew that the banshee's wail and the fairies' magic and the flickering lights of Moragh Dun were as real to him as they were to her.

Now as she cowered against the bed in Jamaica, she repeated tearfully, "Paddy is real. He is."

Not until the woman spoke to her did the insensate terror of childhood leave her. The woman's voice was rich, full and jolly. "Whatever ails you, child? Who's Paddy? Bless me, how you've chatted in your sleep."

The face above her was round and freckled, the lips full, the forehead broad but low, the mass of red hair done up loosely in a great bun. The gown which the woman wore was not black, Kate saw now, but a deep royal purple.

Kate sighed softly. Whatever the present held, the helplessness of childhood was past. "What place is this?" she asked.

The woman gave a deep-throated laugh. "I brought you to my house. Lord, you were done up, and there was no place else for you." As she talked, she went to the window and drew up the jalousie. Hot sunshine rolled into the room and the heavy scent of jasmine. Kate looked out and saw the harbor of Kingston and the black hulk of the four-master lying in the bay. A puff of wind brought the odor of charred wood to her and the events of the night before flooding into her memory.

"Then it was not a bad dream," she said softly. "It was real."

The woman turned smiling. "Many of us were asking

46

ourselves that this morning. It's no nightmare. The whole of the water front is burned to a crisp."

"Why did you bring me here?"

The woman shrugged irritably. "I told you there was no other place. If it's not good enough for you, you can go."

"I don't mean that. Why were you so kind?"

The woman looked at her shrewdly. "Who are you? What's your name?"

"Kate Donley."

"Donley? I don't think I know the name. Where do you live?"

"At the Laughing Donkey. I'm bound to Gabriel Cousins."

The woman opened her eyes wide. "A bound girl. You do not speak like one."

Kate answered sullenly, "I am in service for three years. She looked straight ahead. The woman laughed. "I was in service once myself, Kate. That's how I came to Jamaica. I thought you knew where you were and thought yourself too good for it."

Kate looked at her wonderingly. "Where am I?"

"This is the Christian Steps, dearie." There was a mixture of laughter and bitterness in the voice and it had suddenly lost its slightly stilted, artificial quality and become coarse. "As for me, I'm Laetitia Parsons, high priestess to the gents who prefer my brothel to St. Clement's Cathedral down the street." She turned and came back to Kate, "Now drink this eggnog I brought you, child, and we'll have a talk to see what's to be done."

Her eyes met Kate's and the girl saw the same defiance of fate in them that she had seen so often in Mullen's. Instinctively she reached out and took a chubby hand in hers and kissed it.

"Gaw, you shouldn't a done that," Lettie Parsons sputtered; "you make me all lushy, child."

Lettie Parsons came to Kate's bed on the third day after the fire. "Gabe Cousins has found out where you are, Kate. He's outside and wants to see you. Shall I let him in?"

"You might as well, Lettie. Will I have to go back?"

Lettie raised her plump shoulders. "I don't know. I could buy your papers if Gabe'll let me."

A few seconds later she came back with Gabe Cousins shuffling at her heels. Kate looked at the man's sallow, stricken face and a shudder went through her body. Again she felt the twisted skin of Mannie's neck beneath her fingers. "Oh, God," she cried to herself. "I did not mean to kill her." Momentarily the desire to confess was too great to be denied. She said, "I—I did," but with the words came the thought of Mannie's quirt and the bucket of filthy water Mannie had kicked across her face and she was silent.

Gabe sat down uncomfortably on the edge of a chair. He was silent until Lettie left the room. "I got some things to say to ye, Kate, and I'm not much o' a hand at such. I reckon as how ye've got a grudge against me and Mannie, gal, an' mebbe ye've got reason. Mannie was a hard un at times but she been wi' me a long time. She was purty once, more purty than ye'd believe, an' we had our good times together. That uz before our boy died; Mannie kind o' shriveled up like after that. She was mean to ye, gal, an' I'm not saying she was not. But that's not here nor there. I heard what ye done the last night."

Kate felt the cold sweat on her skin. What had happened? Had Percy Morgan been caught and had he confessed? Was she suspected of killing Mannie? She remembered the door that Percy had left open as he ran from the flaming building. Had there been questions about that?

Gabe was rambling on, taking no notice of her sudden panic. "Bard and Charl Loizeaur was first to reach the Donkey that night. They say ye was fighting to get to Mannie to save her. It was brave o' ye, gal, an' I'm a-thankin' ye for it. I been a-thinkin' what I could do for ye, Kate. I found me a new place down in Pickny Alley. 'Twill do for a while. I reckon I could force ye to come and jine wi' me. I been watchin' ye, Kate. Ye're a good gal. Mebbe when the time is decent you 'ud marry me. 'Tis lonely in Jamaica for a mon alone."

Kate fought the sudden impulse to laugh. She could scarcely believe the dour, silent man could speak so long, and the proposition of marriage was beyond credence. Her few days of comparative freedom at the Christian Steps and the warm kindliness of Lettie Parsons had given her a false sense of security. But she was still bound to Gabriel Cousins and he had the power to force her to his will.

She found herself speaking in the sullen voice of the inn. "Let me stay here a few days. I'm burned bad. Let me stay a while."

Gabe twisted the straw hat in his hands. " 'Tis no place here for a decent gal. A man 'ud not like to take his wife outen the Christian Steps."

Kate closed her eyes, hoping that Gabe would leave. He cleared his throat and walked to the window and spat down among the flowers. "They be a-sayin' in the town 'twas no accident as set fire to the Donkey. Charl Loizeaur says as how he seen a mon runnin' from the tavern just as he got there. Him and Bard found the door open, too. Charl claims he knows who it were. Bard ain't so certain. If he was, they'd be a lynchin' in Kingston long afore now."

Kate was trembling. Had they caught Percy? Would he be fool enough to confess? She did not dare open her eyes lest Cousins see the fear and tension in them. She asked tonelessly, "Who does Charl say he saw?"

" 'Twas the loony Creole—Picon. I al'ays thought him mad, but harmless. They say as how he was in the Donkey that night and threatened Mannie. Looks like he done what he said."

The sudden relief that came to Kate was supplanted by anger. "It's a lie," she flared. "Picon did not come back. Charl is making it all up because Picon lampooned him in a ballad. 'Twas a cruel thing to do to Picon."

"Could be," admitted Cousins. "But Bard seen the mon too. Bard had no grudge agin Picon. An' there's no denyin' as the loony made the threat."

" 'Twas not to burn the Donkey. Only to put an obi on the house."

"Obi is a strange thing, gal. Them as use it has sold themselves to the devil. I'm thinking 'tis a good thing if they be a-stringin' Picon up."

"Where's Picon now?"

"The gaol got burned down, so Croom the under-sheriff took Picon up to his place and has him locked up in a slave's hut there. Croom's place be a run-down cotton plantation a mile or so beyond the Cross Trees. A crowd be hangin' round and they say they'll git the old mon tonight. Croom got Bard to talk to 'em, to say the mon he saw was bigger than Picon and that he ran like a youngster. 'Tis not good. The mob believes Charl not Bard."

Kate turned her cheek to the pillow, hoping Cousins would leave. The innkeeper got up clumsily, still fingering his hat. He said, "I'll be gettin' along, Kate. When'll ye be fit to leave here?"

Lettie Parsons pushed her way into the room. "Run along, Gabe," she ordered. "The child's done in. I'll do the deciding when she's well enough to go." She took Gabe's arm and edged him out of the room.

When Lettie returned, Kate was standing at the window staring down at the blackened city.

"Land o' mercy," Lettie cried, "you should not be on your feet, child. 'Tis dangerous for you to move about so."

"Gabe told me they've arrested Picon. He had nothing to do with the fire."

"You can't be sure of that. Picon's weak in the head. There's no telling what the old fool will do."

"But he didn't. He didn't."

"How do you know?"

Kate felt the same desperate need as when she had pleaded with her mother to believe in the little people but, as then, she could not explain. "You've got to trust me, Lettie. Picon had nothing to do with this. I know. Don't ask me how. I just know."

Lettie smiled amiably. "I believe you, Kate. But what good does that do? I hear there's a crowd hanging about Croom's place. They've got a couple puncheons of rum and the talk is growing wilder and wilder. Charl Loizeaux is egging them on. Tonight they'll try to grab Picon for sure."

"Why don't they drive the mob away?"

"Governor Stallybrass is sick in bed with the gout. He cannot touch his foot on the floor. Jonathan Minor is standing guard with his deputies. But the police are Island men. I'm thinking they'll not shoot into the crowd. Picon

50

would be in the mob's hands hours ago were it not for Minor."

"Who's Minor?"

"The Governor's right-hand man and justice o' the court. A fine man he is too. Once he lived in the States, but he would not play with the Yankee upstarts and fled to Jamaica with a load of slaves when the Yankees rose up against His Majesty."

"I've got to save Picon. How can I get to Croom's place?"

"There's naught you can do, child. Go back to bed. If there's anyone can handle the mob, 'tis Minor. A soft voice he has and a gentle manner. But he's no man to cross. Once his temper is roused, I'd as lief face a tiger. Ay, Jonathan's quite a man."

Kate was scarcely listening. "No matter," she said, "I'm going to make a try to see Picon. Where's my dress?"

"Lord, child, 'twas nothing but a piece of blackened cloth, chucked out long ago. You can't go through the city in bare feet and a bit of rag. I'll get you a dress from one of the girls. One of Chloe's should fit you. It may be snug but I think 'twill do."

Lettie hustled out of the room and Kate stood by the mirror and brushed her hair. The sunlight caught its copper sheen and gave depth to the green eyes. Lettie returned with a gown across her arm. It was satin of a rusty green, flecked with threads of copper. There were slippers to match, shoes and a bonnet. Kate turned and caressed the garments with her finger tips.

" 'Tis long since I've worn such things. Won't Chloe be angry?"

"Leave Chloe to me," Lettie smiled. "I'm thinking it's a beauty you'll be when you're clothed proper."

Kate let the nightdress fall to the floor and stood naked before the mirror. She raised the rustling gown above her head and drew it down over her shoulders. The bodice was tight and she smoothed the crumpled fabric with her hands. The stiff cloth snugged the breasts and made them rise in firm molded curves. She lifted the skirt and thrust the slippers on her feet. The high heels gave a forward tilt to the full body and made the ankles show white and slim. She whirled about, laughing.

51

Lettie Parsons gave a cry of disbelief. "Lord, child, you must be a changeling. What's happened to that sullen face of yours, your stooped shoulders and your unkempt hair? You were a bedraggled slut when I brought you here. Now you're a blooming beauty. I canna believe my eyes. 'Tis any man on the Island you can have."

Kate's laughter tinkled. "Sailors, derelicts, barkeepers and stevedores—that's all there's been to see me. 'Tis safer to be ugly with such men." She laughed again. "What kind of man is your Jonathan Minor? Perhaps it will be well if I can please him."

Lettie chuckled. "You're setting your sights high. Next to Stallybrass, there's no richer man on the Island and no better one. But he's too old for you, Kate. There's a touch of white in his hair already and his visits to the Steps are not so frequent as they used to be. What you need's a buckra boy."

There was the grating of wheels on the gravel below. Kate ran to the window and looked out. A black carriage drawn by two spanking mares was outside. A footman in livery held the reins.

Lettie put her hand in Kate's. "We'll go to Croom's in style, though still I think you a fool. What matters the old Creole to you? Besides, Lord knows what tricks Charl Loizeaux and his likes are up to."

"There'll be danger, Lettie. 'Tis better if I go alone."

"And leave me out o' the fun? No, Kate, I'm going with you. We'll have no more talk about it."

The carriage rolled over the rutted back roads to Croom's. The distance was not far, but for Kate this was the first glimpse of the lush tropical countryside of the Island. Gigantic lignum vitae trees shaded the roadway, and the fringed fingers of the scada and the flamboyant whispered against the carriage's sides. Mangoes and plantains grew wild in the ditches and amid the lacy network of the stork and babies'-breath ferns emerged scarlet and flame-colored flowers. The mountain witches gave their haunting, almost human cry and the lizards slithered between the horses' hooves.

A clearing appeared and acres of level land spread out before them. Dried cotton plants, blanched by the sun, arose from the furrowed earth. Here and there a fuzzy gray ball clung to the shrubs, otherwise the fields had been plucked bare. Set square in the middle of the clearing was a solid, two-story wooden house, its white paint peeling and its steps slightly awry. Trailing behind the house was a jumble of slave huts, the walls of which were plastered with mud and dung and the roofs thatched with cane stalks and coconut husking. Genip trees cast flickers of shadow about the house and grounds, and a stone wall separated the house grounds from the open fields.

Men clustered in the roadway before the wooden gate or lolled in the shade of a scraggly tree. A rickety cart, with wheels askew, was drawn up by the roadside and an open puncheon of rum lay on its flooring. Men dipped broken coconut shells into the rum and drank deeply. A fire had been started and a big fellow with bloody arms worked over the mutilated carcass of a goat, preparatory to throwing it upon the flames. John Crows with scrawny necks and beady eyes wheeled above the scene or rested on the rough stones of the wall, attracted there by the scent of death.

More than a score of men lounged about the road, and on the other side of the fence six others, two of them in the red coats of the British regiment, stood guard, carbines in their hands. Lettie Parsons called to Straw the coachman to stop.

" 'Tis a nasty-looking bunch o' brutes there, Kate. Do you still wish to get through to Picon?"

Kate Donley raised her head defiantly, "Ay, that I do."

Lettie squeezed her hand. "You're a brave girl, Kate." Then to Straw, "Get as close to the gate as you can."

The men scrambled to their feet as the carriage drew up. For a few minutes Kate thought they would try to block the passage, but as Straw resolutely urged the mares forward the men fell aside and stared with bleary eyes at the carriage. Bard staggered forward. He had a matted growth of beard and his tan shirt and breeches were caked with mud. "Damme, if it ain't the Madame and Gabe's bound girl," he roared. "Be ye in Lettie's brothie now, Kate?"

A roar of laughter went up among the men and there was the interchange of coarse jokes. Lettie addressed a guard who had stepped forward. "We wish to speak to

Jonathan Minor. We have word of importance to communicate with him."

The guard stepped back and relayed the message to another, who started toward the house. The men milled about the carriage coming closer and closer. Charl Loizeaux had remained beside the rum, dipping his coconut shell into the half-empty puncheon and drinking greedily so that the brown liquor stained his beard and trickled down onto his shirt. He wiped his mouth with his bare forearm and strutted forward, his face belligerent. He put his hands on the carriage door and thrust his face close to Kate. "What tricks be ye up to, gal? What be ye doin' here and why the fine feathers?"

Kate fought down her sense of revulsion and spoke pleadingly. "Charl, 'twas not Picon you saw run from the Laughing Donkey. I was there all the time. Picon couldn't have come back."

Charl scowled and reached out and seized Kate's arm. "Be ye calling me a liar, gal? Why be ye so interested in the old mon? 'Twas him. I seen him with me own eyes."

"What of Bard? Does he not say the man looked bigger than Picon? 'Tis a grievance you have against the Creole. He meant no harm."

"Be it no harm to accuse a mon of cheating? Lud, 'tis hard enough to find a game of seven-eleven wi'out the old mon's nosy ways." He turned to Bard. "Come, mon, the bound gal's makin'' liars of o' us. What have ye to say? Was not this the gal who slewed you wi' the ale? Did she not have ye crawlin' on ye back out o' the Donkey? Now she would make ye out a liar. What have ye to say o' that, Bard?"

Bard's face was a mask of malevolence and Kate realized that her presence was the thing that would cause him to change his story and accuse Picon. He spat and put his hand on Charl's shoulder. "Ye be right, Charl. Both o' us seen the mon clear agin' the light o' the door. I'm a-thinkin' no mon could be there without Kate a'knowin'. I'm a'thinkin' too the gal had no love for Mannie Cousins and she knows too much o' obi from Koshi. No mon could a got in the Donkey without her help. Mebbe she was not a-tryin' to save Mannie. Mebbe she was a-lockin' the door. Mebbe she put Picon up to his trick of firin' the town."

He opened the door and pulled at Kate's skirt. "Where did ye get them fine clo'se, gal? Did ye buy 'em with money ye stole from Mannie?"

Kate shuddered as Bard's grimy hand flicked aside the skirt and seized her bare leg. Instinctively she kicked out and the sharp toe of her slipper struck the man's armpit. Bard uttered a grunt of pain and swore, then he leapt forward and seized the girl's arm and pulled her from the carriage. She fell against him heavily and both went rolling to the ground. As though the act were a signal, others attacked the carriage. The coachman was dragged from his perch and clubbed, and Lettie screamed as her arm was seized.

"Stay still, you ruffians, or I'll put a bullet in each of you." The voice that spoke was level and crisp; the men fell away from the carriage. Kate, shaken but unhurt, found herself supported by a strong, lithe arm. As she scrambled to her feet, she caught a glimpse of a flowered waistcoat and white stock. A moment later she was face to face with the man. She noticed first the slate gray eyes that were without humor, then the aquiline nose and the bloodless lips. The tan cheeks were heavily lined and the coarse black hair was streaked with gray. The face was hard but not unpleasing; it gave the impression of indomitable spirit, courage and intelligence. There was a self-assurance in his manner that bordered upon arrogance and his glance at the men about him was cold with disdain.

He kept the muzzle of his pistol pointed at Bard as he introduced himself to Kate. "I am Jonathan Minor. I believe you wished an audience, Miss——"

"Donley," Kate supplied.

"Ay yes, Miss Donley. Will you come with me?" He snapped an order at one of the uniformed guards and put his pistol in a holster at his waist. He offered his arm to Kate with the elaborate courtesy he might have used in the ballroom. Then, apparently seeing Lettie for the first time, he smiled at her and helped her from the carriage.

"It is good to see you again, Mrs. Parsons," he said stiffly.

A twinkle came into Lettie's eyes. " 'Tis true the Christian Steps has missed your presence of late, Mr. Minor."

Minor chuckled at the sally and signaled one of the

guards to act as Lettie's escort. The two couples walked stiffly up the path to the porch where Erb Croom and his wife were waiting.

The men left in the roadway growled among themselves and moved toward the puncheon of rum. Bard alone remained at the gate. "Ye bloody toff," he shouted, shaking his fist at Minor's back, "ye'll lie with the strumpets but ye'll na pay heed to decent men."

Minor ignored him. He whipped a lace handkerchief from his coat sleeve and wiped the grime from Kate's cheek. There was amusement in his voice when he spoke. "A dangerous mission you have chosen, Miss Donley. May I inquire why you have risked coming here?"

Kate answered breathlessly. "For Picon. He did not fire the Laughing Donkey. I was there."

"Have you any proof?" he asked gently.

"Proof enough to convince me. The fire started in Mannie Cousins' room. The door was securely locked from the inside when I got there. Indeed, I tried to break it down with an ax. Mannie must have tipped over her lamp—it would have been an easy thing to do. She kept her money under the bed and her lamp on a table by its side. When she got up, she could have knocked the lamp over. 'Twould be simple enough."

Minor's eyes looked into hers gravely, then he smiled. "I'm wondering, Miss Donley, if you do not know more than you are telling."

Kate felt a tug of fear at her heart. Minor was treating her with amused tolerance as though speaking to a child. Yet the man was clever. She must take care lest he get some inkling of the truth. She answered unflinchingly. "I know for certain Picon was not at the Donkey."

Minor took both her hands in his and spoke reassuringly. "That I do believe. We've the testimony of old Meg Houston who keeps a water-front gin house that Picon stumbled into her place dead drunk just before eleven. He was crying because his quartro was broken, and cursing Mannie Cousins. But he soon went to sleep in a corner and old Meg could not wake him when she closed. She let him stay there and he was still asleep when the fire reached her place. He had to be dragged out for he was too drunk to walk."

"Then why do you not release him?"

"I do not believe that Loizeaux and Bard made up their story out of whole cloth. They saw someone run from the Donkey. If it was not Picon, you should be able to tell us who it was."

Kate shook her head. "There was no one there."

"That will not do. If we could name another, Picon might be safe on the streets. But if we release him now, Loizeaux and his gang would surely murder him."

Lettie interrupted. "Why don't you drive the ruffians from the gate? A single shot would send them flying."

Minor looked down at the woman's round flushed face and flashed her a smile. "A bullet would be enough to seal Picon's fate. We've only eight able-bodied men here. If we killed or wounded one of the beggars, they would disperse for a while, but they would be back tonight with a hundred or more of the water-front loungers. They would certainly make a try for Picon and more than likely they would fire Croom's place. We've Croom and his wife and children to consider and furthermore, with a break of violence, the rioting and looting will begin again. The Governor has given word not to shoot except under the gravest provocation. It will be better to surrender Picon to the crowd than to provoke widespread terrorism."

Kate's eyes snapped and the color mounted to her cheeks, "You mean you'd deliver Picon into the hands of those beasts? It's inhuman."

Minor answered solemnly, "Which is better, that one old derelict should die or that many innocent women and children shall be killed in rioting?"

Kate tossed her head and her voice rang out. "What does death matter? To kill from hate or love or revenge, that I can understand. To kill cold-bloodedly in the name of justice, that is a crime more vicious than wholesale slaughter. If you hand over Picon to these men it is they who will kill him, but the real murderer will be yourself."

Minor looked at her mockingly and his voice was drawling as he answered, "A distorted idealism, Miss Donley, and highly impractical. What has Picon done to deserve life? I think it must be a burden for him."

"He has sung songs and he will sing others."

"Discordant ballads sung for blackmail."

"What of it? He has given happiness and caused little misery. Can you say as much for yourself, Mr. Minor?"

Minor looked at the girl in wonder. Her face was alive with some passion he could not understand. He had thought her a handsome piece when he first saw her, though a trifle heavy-featured. He had assumed that she had been drawn to Croom's by the excitement, but now he was uncertain. She was vibrant, her color high and her eyes sparkling. "Bravo," he said quietly. "I admire your spirit, though I disagree with your contention."

The Crooms had been listening at a distance. Mrs. Croom was a drab, heavy-set woman with a pale, mournful face. She came forward. "Canna ye get the old man off the place? I've me bairns to think about. 'Tis not safe they'll be while Picon's here."

"If we try to move the old man, it will be the signal for trouble. It's better to wait and try to spirit him away in the night."

" 'Twill be too late then, the mob will be upon us. At least get more soldiers to protect us."

Minor shook his head. "We've not enough men. There's only one regiment of redcoats stationed here, and with the city burned there's danger everywhere. We need men at the stores, about the harbor, in the Governor's house. The slaves are giving trouble all over Jamaica. They're ripe for revolt and every planter has a guard over his home. There's no more that we can do, Mrs. Croom."

Kate demanded suddenly, "Let me see Picon. At least there can be no harm in that."

Minor hesitated, then bowed. "At your service." Again he offered his arm.

As they rounded the house the stench of the manure used in making the walls and the rotting cane on the roof assailed their nostrils. They stepped around the puddle of muddy water and Kate caught a glimpse of slaves lying chained to posts sunk in the earthen floor. The third of the huts was used to imprison Picon. As Minor opened the door, the old man moaned. He was huddled on a pallet of coconut trash. His face and clothing were so covered with mud that he scarcely seemed human. He peered up at those who entered and inarticulate sounds issued from his lips. He lifted his hands toward Kate in pleading.

"Do you remember me?" Kate asked softly. "I'm the bound girl at the Laughing Donkey."

Picon nodded his head loosely. "Please do not let Picon die. Picon do nod'ding. Le' Picon go 'way." Kate saw that somehow the old man had kept the quartro with him. One of the strings was hopelessly broken but he had managed to knot the other together. The quartro alone of the few things in the hut was clean.

She spoke gently, and Minor watched her with interest. "If we got you out, where would you go, Picon? You would be in danger on the streets."

Picon's inflamed eyes rested on her face. "Take me to Koshi. Koshi me fren'. Koshi know 'ow to go to Accompong. He take me there. I be safe." His outstretched hands groped at Kate's skirts. Minor knocked the pleading hands aside with his boot.

Kate said angrily, "Leave him be." Minor shrugged slightly and his eyes rested on the girl's face. She thought a moment, then asked of him, "Is it true that Kosoi knows the way to Accompong? Will Picon be safe there?"

Minor answered slowly, "Rumor has it that Koshi is in touch with the Maroons and that he has taken more than one escaped slave to Accompong. Koshi is the only man in Kingston whom Buddhoe, the Accompong chief, trusts. Koshi has acted as mediator when Buddhoe has seized white men for ransom. He's done us many a service, so there are things we overlook. The Maroons might not welcome Picon to their midst. Still, they would not harm him, not if Koshi vouched for him."

Picon was jibbering, "Take me to Koshi, Missy. I plead you. Take me Koshi."

"Where does Koshi stay?"

Lettie Parsons, who had come in behind them, answered Kate's question. "He has a hovel beneath Pinchback Mountain, beyond Port Royal. I know the place well."

Kate turned back to Minor. "Will you let us take Picon out?"

Minor gazed at her incredulously. "That's impossible. You can't get him past the men at the gate. If you try to take him across the fields, he'll be spotted immediately. No, there's no way it can be done."

"There is. Let Picon lie in the carriage beneath our skirts. We'll go through the gates quickly. No one will know till we're safely away."

"It is too dangerous. The men would tear you apart if they caught you."

"Every course is dangerous. If Picon remains, Croom and his family may be attacked. If Picon is let loose, there may be rioting. If Picon is hanged, the mob may get out of control. This is the best way."

Minor looked at her reflectively. His slightly mocking manner had changed to open admiration. "By Jove, I believe you coud pull it off. What do you say, Lettie?"

Lettie Parson's grin was wide. "Gaw, 'twill be a lark."

Minor gave orders for Lettie's carriage to be brought to the back and five minutes later Picon was lying flat on his stomach on the boarding. Lettie climbed in and her voluminous purple skirt covered half of his body. Minor helped Kate to her place and Picon was fully covered. Kate held in her hand a piece of heavy link chain she had picked up from the earthen floor of the hut. Minor looked at the chain and his mouth crinkled. "Good luck to you, Kate Donley," he said. He touched her hand lightly. "I'm thinking it is your own luck you're making, though. When this day is over, I'll come to you."

The carriage circled to the front and Minor, pistol in hand, walked before it to the gate. The guards flung the gate open and Straw lashed the flanks of the mares with his rawhide whip. The men in the roadway scattered as the mares drove into their midst. But the horses swerved in fright and a hoarse cry went up as the coach wheel struck the old wagon on which the puncheon of rum was perched. The wagon collapsed and there was a sickening lurch as the puncheon struck against the back wheel of the coach. The mares slowed down and, without warning, a face appeared at the carriage window.

It was Bard, and as he clung to the carriage he shouted back, "Picon is in here. Cut across the field." Bard climbed up to the coachman's box. Straw turned and tried to strike him with the whip, but Bard was in back of him and had his arm about the Negro's throat. He pushed Straw from the seat and managed to rein the horses to a stop.

He leapt down and opened the carriage. "Out, ye bitches," he ordered, "and bring the murdering bastard with ye."

Kate started to obey. Her slipper rested on the footboard and she looked into the gloating face of Bard standing below her. Then as she stepped to the ground her hand lashed out and the heavy chain hissed with the whirring fury of a snake. The chain came within an inch of Bard's eyes. He gave a howl and scrambled backward, tripping in his haste to escape the swirling metal. The other men were nearly upon the carriage, but they hesitated when they heard Bard's cry. Kate took advantage of their surprise to leap to the coachman's box. The whip whistled in the air and the carriage bounded forward again. It was too late for them to pursue it.

Far down the road, where it left the cotton field and turned into the shaded wood. Kate slowed down. The men behind them straggled along the road and there was a cluster of them about the fallen figure of Bard. Jonathan Minor stood at the entrance of Croom's. Kate raised her hand in a salute and Minor waved back.

Within the carriage Picon was squatting, his fingers running across the strings of the quartro. Lettie Parsons hummed:

"I am not in de dice
    To make it play just as I like."

And Straw the coachman, who had managed to cling to the back of the carriage, came forward to take his place.

The sun was dipping down into the Caribbean as the carriage moved out of Kingston along the bay toward Port Royal. Great jagged lines of brilliant color, scarlet, orange and deep purple, spread across the sky and were reflected in the still waters of the bay. As the carriage rolled on, the sky changed to lavender, then to pearl gray. By the time they reached the narrow path that led to the foot of Pinchback Mountain, the stars were flickering feebly in the darkening night. The hardy eelgrass of the salt marshes clung to the spokes of the wheels and the road alternated between sharp rocks and oozing mud.

61

A hillock showed up ahead and at its rounded top was a gnarled wild orange tree. In the dim light a lonely figure could be seen and there was the muted beat of a drum. A voice called softly in the night, "Ai lai yeh, aylla woo."

Lettie Parsons leaned forward, clutching Kate's arm. "Stop," she called to Straw. "Swing the carriage around at the clearing."

Straw's answering voice was strangely gentle. "It's all right, Mis' Parsons. 'Taint nothing to worry 'bout. Old Koshi come to meet us. Them's the words of Amangbois to let us know who he is. Don' worry. Koshi's here."

The figure moved down the hillock, rapidly, yet without obvious movement. It seemed to glide rather than to walk or run. Almost before Straw had finished speaking Koshi was beside the carriage.

Straw drew up the horses on a rise of land and Kate alighted. Koshi stood before her, cap in hand, smiling slightly. The soft sheen of the moonlight deepened the lines of the old man's face and gave them a primitive dignity.

"I have come for Picon," Koshi stated. "He will be safe with me."

"But how did you know we were bringing him here?"

Koshi gazed at her and his voice was grave when he spoke. "Among the Ashanti, I was a priest. My people do not need words to speak to me. That which is seen by one among us, becomes mine. These are things the white man cannot understand. He scoffs at the power of belief and it is best that we should not tell him what he refuses to credit."

Kate put out her hand to touch the old man, but her fingers struck the minature drum of goatskin fastened about his waist. There was a note at once dull and resonant. She asked, "Do you believe that I have no faith? Will you not talk with me?"

Koshi turned so that his face was in shadow. "After I have taken Picon to Accompong, we shall talk of this." His voice grew deeper. "Today you have seen injustice and have tried to set it right. But remember that injustice is a part of the black man's fate and, because it springs not from himself but from the white, he is helpless to fight against it. There is a chance that you can act where I have failed."

Kate felt her mouth go dry. She recalled the words she had spoken to Jonathan Minor—the words she had learned from Mullen. She lifted her eyes proudly, but then a coldness seized her. She remembered her hands about Mannie Cousins' throat and the wild emotion that had filled her so that she had neither known nor cared what she was doing. She hesitated, thinking. Even now it is too late.

Picon had stumbled out of the carriage and he now stood beside Koshi. For the first time Kate saw him standing straight, his eyes not upon the ground but on Koshi's face.

Again Kate put out her hand, but Koshi withdrew from her, gliding back into the shadows. "We go," he said softly. Kate heard no sound as the two men left her, moving along the grassy pathway. She could discern no motion of arms or legs, and in the pale light neither man seemed to quite touch the ground. Within a matter of moments they were atop the hillock and there Koshi raised his hand, lifting it slowly, fingers pointed to the sky.

Lettie Parsons had remained in the carriage. Kate climbed in beside her. "Did you see—" she started to ask, but she could not find words for what she wished to say. Lettie took the girl's hand in hers. "There are strange things on the Island and sometimes it is wise to see as little as one can."

Kate looked at her but the darkness concealed the older woman's face. "How did Koshi know we were coming? No one knew but ourselves and Jonathan Minor."

"Drums, perhaps. The Negroes can convey almost any message by drumbeat."

Straw was closing the door. He said, almost in a whisper, "Old Koshi don' need no drums."

"What do you mean?" Kate asked. But Straw was mounting to his seat and he gave no sign of hearing.

The moonlight was bright now and the carriage rolled back along the road to Port Royal. At length they came to a place where the road dipped down to a beach of white sand. The water swept in softly, glistening black, laced with white foam. Kate leaned forward. "I want to get out, Lettie, and walk along the beach."

"Nay, child, 'tis too dangerous here in Jamaica."

"Just for a minute." Kate called for Straw to stop. She went down to the water's edge with Lettie, still protesting, following her. Softly through the night there came the tolling of a bell. The sound came from the depth of the water.

"What is that?" Kate asked breathlessly.

Lettie laughed a little shrilly. " 'Tis the church bell of old Port Royal. Did you not know the whole town has been buried under the sea for nigh on a hundred and fifty years? The church steeple is a full fathom below the water. The tides ring out the bell each night."

Kate turned to Lettie to ask another question, but as she did so, she saw behind them the outline of a high hill, and on a jagged plateau near its crest there was limned the silhouette of an ancient building. Rounded turret towers stood out in bold relief and a crenellated wall ran the length of the building.

Kate pointed. "What place is that?"

" 'Tis Rune Hall."

"I've seen it before," mused Kate. "But 'twas not here in Jamaica. I remember now, 'twas on a craggy isle off Connemara. I tell you, Lettie, 'twas exactly the same."

"Come, Kate," Lettie spoke peevishly, "come on now before we catch our deaths of cold." She swung about and started for the coach. Kate followed obediently, but she was lost in thought——thinking of an evening when she sat with Mullen beside a great rock and he had told her of Clare Island and the exploits of Grainne O'Maille.

"Lettie," she whispered, "the castle——to whom does it belong?"

"Rune Hall? Why, I thought you knew, child. 'Tis the estate of Jonathan Minor."

5

THE FLAMBEAU cast flickering shadows over the carriage as it rolled back along the deserted road to Kingston. The barren branches of the tamarind trees, like bloated, blackened fingers, beat tattoos on the sides and top. In accordance with custom, Straw ran ahead lighting the way, his flambeau held high. Lettie Parsons held the reins in her chubby hands. Kate pressed forward in the seat, half fascinated, half frightened by the strange tableau unfolding before her.

Out in the harbor a six-master rode primly on the gentle swells and her lanterns threw dull reflections on the scorched hulk of the upturned sailing vessel that had foundered off Kerry's jetty. A bonfire burned at the bay's edge and another mile or so beyond. The harsh cries of drunken men and the sharp yelping of dogs echoed across the water. And once there was the staccato crackle of pistol shots.

The wheels left the muddy tracks and grated against cobblestones. Houses slipped by, dark and silent, their windows tightly boarded up and barred against any intruder. Occasionally there were hushed whisperings within the framework shacks, or the frightened wail of a child. The night was heavy with the fear of those left homeless by the fire, the water-front marauders and the slaves who had escaped in the confusion of the burning city.

The beat of the horses' hoofs echoed eerily in the narrow streets and, now that they had turned away from the bay, all other sounds were muted. Not until they came to St. Clement's Cathedral was there any further sign of life. The stubby towers of the church were limned against the gray sky, and the thick tabby arches cast gloomy shadows about the entrance. But as the carriage drew abreast of the

Cathedral, Kate could see that the arched doorway was open. Spitting altar candles flickered over the bodies of women and children lying on crude pallets spread along the aisles. A priest walked softly among the sleepers, fingering his rosary.

A figure came to the door and peered out. Straw's flambeau lighted up the face of an old woman, gray and toothless, with eyes that were like coals. The dark shawl and shabby clothes were strangely like the vestments of a monk. The old woman raised her fist and screamed Lettie's name, and Kate heard the phrase "whore of Babylon."

Then the priest came up beside the woman and she fell silent. But there was something venomous in her squat, shapeless figure as she watched the carriage rattle by.

Lettie Parsons mumbled on the coach's seat but Kate could not hear the words. Incongruously, as they passed St. Clement's, Kate could hear the sound of a woman's shrill voice chanting a water-front ballad and the jingling, off-pitch notes of a piano. The sounds echoed against the side of the Cathedral and it took Kate a moment to realize that they came from halfway up the hill where the Christian Steps was glowing with bright light.

Lettie shouted for Straw to get out of the way and lashed the rumps of the mares with the full strength of her whip. The startled animals leapt forward and, despite the steep hill, broke into an awkward run. Lettie was standing in the coach's box and her whip came down again and again. The coach caromed into the wide circular driveway before the Christian Steps and jerked to a stop before the door.

Lettie leapt from the box, her plump, dowdy figure quivering with rage. A man and a girl were clasped in tight embrace in the lighted doorway. Lettie charged into them so that the man fell across the sill dragging the girl with them. They lay together, laughing and clutching at each other. As Kate stepped into the room behind Lettie, the man circled her ankle with his fingers. She kicked free and felt the heel of her shoe strike against his face. The man gave a sharp cry and, as though it were a signal, the noisy, smoke-filled room fell silent.

Lettie stood still in the middle of the room, her arms akimbo. Her face was aflame with anger and from her lips there spewed forth an almost unintelligible mumble of words. The whip rose from her hand at her waist and rested loosely across the disheveled red hair. The mumbling changed to a scream as she poured out all the words she had learned on the London docks and in the pit at Tyburn.

"Ye water-front scran, ye whores and doxies. I bring ye to me house and a decent house it is. I leave ye for a night and ye change it into a bawdy chive. Your caterwauling can be heard down to St. Clement's. And Father Maholan is there tonight. Tomorrow they'll be having me closed for the likes of you, carrying on."

Although Kate had been in the house for three days, she had not seen the reception room before. The velvet drapes, the lace curtains, the hand-carved mahogany furniture and the potted ferns all strove for respectability. But, like Lettie, they all had a dowdy character. A spindly-legged piano stood in one corner. Bard sprawled there and, at Lettie's words, he half-turned on the seat. One hand rested on the keyboard while the other held a glass nearly filled with rum. A girl stood beside him, one arm about his neck. She was a tall girl, big-breasted, with the pure cameo skin peculiar to the mulatto. The couple on the floor had not bothered to get up and a third couple was frozen in tight embrace on the wide divan.

The room was quiet after Lettie's harangue. Only Bard seemed to resent the vituperative words. His face was heavy with drink and his eyes blood-shot. He leaned back against the piano with an indolent gesture and the keys gave a crashing groan beneath his elbows.

"Be ye not gittin' too fine for ye'self, Lettie. A brothie's a brothie, no matter where ye find it. And a bawd's a bawd. Ain't she, Lettie?"

Lettie's voice was quiet now. "Get out, Bard. I want none of ye here."

"I come to be wi' Chloe and I pay me guinea like any other mon. Nay, I'm no goin', Lettie."

Bard got up and walked haltingly toward Lettie, his mouth open in a grimace. Chloe twisted her arm about his waist and came with him. She was flushed with drink and her steps were unsteady. The couple stood a foot from Lettie, swaying slightly. It was the girl who spoke. "I'm tired of taking orders from the likes of you, Lettie. If Bard goes, I go too."

"Get out." Lettie spoke hoarsely. "Get out before I kick ye out."

Chloe looked at Lettie, then her gaze shifted to Kate. Her eyes widened in surprise and anger as she saw the russet gown with its copper threads. " 'Tis my gown you're wearing. 'Tis mine I say. You thieved it from me, you slut."

Kate drew back, unable to speak. The girl followed her and sharp fingers prodded the bodice of the dress and pinched the flesh of her breast. Before Kate could move, Lettie struck down the hand and Chloe turned swiftly and raked the older woman's face with her long nails. Lettie's foot came out and tripped up the girl, who fell drunkenly to the floor. Lettie kicked the wide skirt upward until the bare thighs showed. Then the lash of her whip came sizzling down on the bare flesh. Chloe's piercing scream filled the room and drowned out the sound of the second blow.

Kate had shrunk back with horror. Next she was vaguely aware of the sound of a carriage in the drive and of footsteps on the stairs. As Lettie raised her whip for the third time, a man rushed across the room and seized her waist. Lettie struggled like a mad-woman, kicking, scratching, gouging.

"Easy, Lettie, easy." The man spoke softly.

Lettie suddenly slumped and the madness went out of her face. She looked up at the man who held her and said, "Gaw! If it ain't Jonathan Minor."

Minor smiled sardonically at her. "What ails you, Lettie? Do you want the city fathers to close up the Christian Steps?"

"Ah, 'twas just a spot of trouble."

Bard, who had stood by, too stupefied to interfere, roused himself. "Spot o' trouble, nothin'. She ordered me from her place and beat up the gal. 'Tis time Lettie Parsons was driven out of Kingston."

Lettie's hand was up again, but Minor twisted the whip free and tossed it to the floor. Bard lunged forward and got both hands on Lettie's shoulders. Minor chopped down with his fist on Bard's hairy wrist. The drunken man gave a howl of pain and released the woman. For a full minute he stood staring at Minor. His hands twitched but he dared not attack.

"You had better go, Bard," Minor said quietly.

Bard's eyes fell and he dropped down on his knees beside Chloe, who still lay sobbing on the floor.

Minor was holding Lettie securely by the wrist. She looked up at him and the anger left her face. She began to giggle and nestled close to him. "Gaw—ye're a strong man and a cushy one, Jonathan Minor. But it's not me ye came to the Christian Steps to softy up to. I allow you came to see Kate."

Minor's eyes twinkled and he looked from Lettie to Kate. "Did you get Picon safely to Koshi?" he asked beneath his breath.

Kate nodded. Minor dropped Lettie's hands and came closer to the girl. His dark face crinkled in a smile. "I've been worried about you, Kate Donley. You have been making too many enemies in Jamaica. And men like Bard and Charl Loizeaux do not forget—nor do they forgive. They'll be giving you a hard time if they get the chance."

Kate glanced from Minor to Bard. He had got the sobbing girl to her feet and was helping her to the doorway. But he glanced back and his small eyes were filled with hate. Kate shuddered and Minor put his hand on her arm reassuringly.

"The Christian Steps is no place for you, Kate. Is there nowhere else you can go?"

Lettie Parsons interrupted angrily. "She's safer here tonight than she'd be at St. Clement's. Be ye thinking I'm making a bawd of the gal, Jonathan Minor?"

Minor's eyes were like agates, despite the smile on his lips. "You know better than that, Lettie. And you know too how the town will talk if Kate stays here."

"And where else will she stay, with half the town burned out? Will you take her to Rune Hall with you?"

"Of course not."

"Then where is she to go? She's a room of her own here and white sheets on which to sleep. 'Tis better than the aisles of St. Clement's and my eyes are sharper than those of Father Maholan."

"I cannot say you did so well tonight."

Lettie flushed. "The gal's not been down here before.

69

I could not tell that Bard would come here drunk—or that Chloe would lead him on. Kate's a bar to her door and she can go to her room when she likes."

Minor bowed gravely to Kate. "May I escort you there?"

Kate took the proffered arm and they walked together across the floor that was strewn with broken glasses, and marched up the wide stairway as though leaving a ball-room. Those in the room below remained silent until they came to the bend in the stairs. Then there were guffaws of drunken laughter.

They stopped in Kate's doorway and Minor looked down gravely. "We must find another home for you."

Kate's lips quirked. "You forget I'm a bound girl with papers to Gabriel Cousins."

"That can be remedied. I'll buy the papers."

"So that I'll be bound to you instead of Cousins?' '

"No. You shall be free."

"And what does freedom mean in Jamaica—a chance to be one of Lettie Parson's girls?"

"You know I'll not leave it that way." He bent forward and with a gesture almost courtly, placed his lips on Kate's fingers. Then gently he put his arm about her and drew her to him.

Kate drew back for a moment, then let her face sink against his shoulder. He kissed her ear and said softly, "I shall be back for you tomorrow. We'll find a way."

Kate had the sense of being in Mullen's arms. The tears stung her eyes. She lifted her face and Minor's lips pressed down upon hers. The feeling of security left and she was trembling and excited. She broke away from Minor, stepped into her room, closed the door and placed the bar across it. She waited, listening, but she did not hear Minor's footsteps going away. Finally she turned and went to the window. There was only darkness outside and the sound of a whinnying horse. Without lighting the lamp, she slipped off Chloe's russet dress and kicked off the high-heeled slippers.

Naked, she slid in between the cool sheets. There was the soft rap of knuckles on the door and Lettie called her name. Kate started to answer but before the words came she fell asleep.

The haunting, almost human cry of the mountain witch awoke Kate. She got up and went to the window and looked out over the hills that were covered with a deep lavender mist. She stood at the arched window and forced the weariness away. The streets of Kingston were so quiet that she could hear the lap of the water down in the bay. The huge baring tona tree that grew outside the window stirred restlessly as a slight breeze soughed through its branches. A delicate blossom, like a gigantic snowflake tinted with pink and yellow, drifted downward and she caught it in her palm and pressed it against her face.

The russet gown with its copper threads was crumpled across the chair where she had thrown it the night before. The slippers, now slightly scuffed, lay on their sides by the bed. Kate dressed hurriedly, then listened at the door. There was no sound within the house and she unfastened the chain and stepped out into the hall. She avoided the main stairway and found a narrow flight of steps that took her to the back of the house. She stepped out onto the gravel path but then she thought of the chain she had used the day before. She had left it in the back of the coach.

The door of the carriage house was open. She walked swiftly across the damp grass of the lawn and peered into the carriage. The length of chain still lay on the floor. She drew it out and fastened it loosely to the belt at her waist. The folds of russet satin hid it from view. She started for the doorway again but stopped short. On a litter of straw, cast into deep shadow in the corner by the half-open door, a figure was sprawled.

Kate held her breath and came close, her fingers circling the chain that dangled at her waist. It was a boy she saw. A very thin boy whose skin had a slight purple sheen that made her think of a ripe damson. The boy was clad in ragged blue breeches and a jersey. He lay so still that Kate wondered if he were dead. She leaned forward and saw the scarcely perceptible movement of his chest. She could not remember having seen the boy before yet there was something familiar about him. She turned away with a slight sense of uneasiness and hurried along the gravel pathway to the street.

71

The door of St. Clement's was still open when she passed. The guttering altar candles gave a ruby glow to the stained glass window that depicted the Blessed Virgin. The old woman who had cursed Lettie Parsons the night before was sleeping in a crumpled heap in the doorway, her tangle of grayish-yellow hair touching the sill. Kate walked on swiftly, her heels clacking on the rough stone. At Harbour Street she came to the first of the buildings licked by the fire's flame. Soon she was in the midst of blackened debris. Already a few new shacks were being raised amidst the charred ruins of the old, and the white pine boards stood out like naked scars against the background of black and gray.

Kate picked her way between stones and burned timber to the alleyway at the foot of which the Laughing Donkey had once stood. Only the brick framework about the tavern's door remained and the big brass sign that announced its name. Begrimed tiles were scattered across the alley and a half dozen warped and blackened puncheons stood in a row before the charred ruins.

At the alley's end she saw that the tiny jetty had, almost miraculously, escaped the fury of the flames. The wind must have swept the fire away, for the gray boards stretched out twenty feet into the limpid water. Kate turned and stared back at Kingston. Neither sound nor movement came from the sleeping city, though now a tiny rim of the sun shone blood-red in the valley between the high hills. Kate had not passed a single person on the street, although once or twice she had glimpsed men sleeping in makeshift shelters.

She made her way along the frail jetty and got down on her hands and knees at the third stanchion. She peered down through the gray-blue water at the piles of stones that supported the staples. For a full minute she could not find what she was seeking and fear twisted through her body. Then the movement of the water flicked the sodden cloth of the gray dress in which Mannie Cousins' sovereigns and guineas were wrapped. Kate gave a sigh of relief and again stood up and searched the blackened water front for signs of life. She saw nothing. She slipped the dress over her head and felt the damp wind bite into her flesh. She crouched at the jetty's edge and then let herself into the water as noiselessly as she could. The shock of its coldness numbed her and the first time she went down she did not touch bottom. She dove again and the surge of the water thrust her against the piled rocks. It was not until the fourth try that she grasped and brought up the bundled gray dress.

She flung the bundle on the boarding and climbed up on the jetty. For a moment she stood there, naked in the morning sun; then she raised the russet gown above her head and pulled it down over her wet body. As she looked up she saw that a man stood at the water's edge, blocking the foot of the jetty. He wore a broad-rimmed hat that shaded his face and she could not be sure who he was. But she thought she recognized the hulking figure and the stance, at once slovenly and arrogant.

She reached down and picked up the dripping gray dress and felt the dampness of it and the sharp edges of the coins against her breast. She fitted her feet into the slippers without taking her eyes from the man. Then she walked toward him step by step, one arm holding the precious bundle, the other at her side, the fingers tight against the length of chain that hung there.

The man shifted his weight as she approached, and took off the wide-brimmed hat. She stared into the dark, sallow face of Charl Loizeaux. His eyes were blood-shot and his broad nostrils were quivering. The loose lips parted in a grin to show the brown stumps of his teeth.

"I thought ye'd be a-comin' back 'ere, Kate. I been a waitin' for ye. Gawd, but ye're a bleedin' beauty without no clo'se, gal. 'Tis lucky the lads what takes ye to they bed." His grin broadened.

"Let me be, Charl. Keep away from me."

"Not so high and mighty, gal. Don't ye think Charl knows what ye be up to? Ai, 'twas good to put the thumb on Picon for the fire, but there's a lot that only you and Charl knows. Eh, gal?"

"Get away, I tell you."

"Don't be hard on Charl, gal. He's no wishin' you a harm. I been thinkin', gal—thinkin' lots. Mebbe us two can git together. Charl ain't so bad. I been a-thinkin' about Mannie Cousins' money and 'oo could a got it. I'm a-thinkin' I know now. But I'm not a-takin' all, gal. You

73

and me'll go halfers on it. That is, if you'll be good to Charl."

Kate said coldly, "I told you to leave me be." She raised her arm and the chain leapt out and whistled within a finger's span of Charl's chest.

The big man stepped back and anger brought the blood to his face. Kate's chain whirred round and round, but made no noise. Step by step she forced the man back. Once he put out his hand to snatch the chain but the metal links sliced the flesh of his palm and started a trickle of blood down his wrist. He gave a grunt of pain and stepped back quickly.

Charl's eyes watched the chain as he retreated. Kate knew that once it struck against his shoulder or chest, he would be upon her like a wild animal. There was only one chance—to strike for his face in the hope of blinding him until she could get away, at least. Slowly she drove him back, away from the jetty toward the stone wall that bordered the alley. Charl weaved from side to side, waiting for his chance to spring, but he could not get past the whirling chain.

Kate's arm was getting tired and she knew that she must strike soon if she was to break away. She lunged forward and the chain hissed softly. Then there was a sickening thud and Kate saw that she had failed. Charl had got his arm up in time and the chain only bit deep into the forearm. Blood spewed from his arm and soaked the shirt, but the speed of the chain was lost and he lurched toward her.

Kate turned and ran. Charl's hand touched her dress but the wet fabric slipped through his fingers. She ran on, fear giving her speed. She heard his crashing footbeats behind her and the sound of his cursing. He fell on a loose tile and went crashing into one of the empty puncheons. But he was up again in an instant. As she reached the entrance of the alleyway, she felt his hand on her shoulder. He spun her around, and as she tried again to get the chain into play, he ripped it from her hand. His hands were on her throat and his face was close to hers. She smelt the sour rum on his breath and saw the madness in his eyes. His thick hands clutched tighter. She

74

tried to scream but no sound came. Her throat and chest ached with the squeezing pressure.

He shook her like a rat as he mumbled obscene names. His eyes were reddened with fury and his loose lips were twitching.

Then, without warning, the eyes went blank and the hands on her throat were slack. He slumped forward and fell, thrusting her beneath him with the weight of his body. She lay still, fighting for breath. Then she struggled to free herself from Charl's inert figure. She got to her feet before she realized that there was a third person there.

The boy whom she had seen asleep in the carriage house stood grinning at her. His eyes sparkled and his white teeth shone. He had a piece of metal pipe about three feet long in his hand.

"What happened?" Kate gasped.

The boy laughed aloud. "I mooshed him, Missy."

Kate glanced down at Charl. Blood stained the cobblestones beneath his arm, where the whirling chain had slit the flesh almost to the bone, but the blow of the pipe had not cut the skin. Charl moaned softly and his breathing came stertorously.

The boy reached down to pick up the begrimed and sodden bundle, but Kate thrust him aside.

"I'll carry it for you, Missy."

"No. I'll carry it myself." She looked curiously at the boy, wondering who he was and where he had come from. Again there was the tantalizing sense of familiarity that she could not place.

"We better go now," the boy said. Kate nodded. They moved quickly through the rubble, Kate watching the boy covertly lest he attack her and steal her precious burden. Not until they reached the cleared section of Harbour Street did she speak to him.

"What's your name, boy?"

"Mario."

"I saw you in the carriage house this morning. You were pretending to be asleep."

Mario grinned. "Yes, Missy."

"But you followed me. Why did you do it?"

"To take care of you, Missy."

"But why?"

"I had orders to see no harm came to you."

"Orders? From whom? Do you belong to Lettie Parsons?"

The boy raised his head proudly. "I belong to no one. Sometimes I work as groom for Mr. Minor, but only when I want to. I am free."

"Was it Mr. Minor who set you to spy on me?" Kate's voice was sharp.

"No, and I was not spying. I was taking care of you. If the man had not troubled you, you never would have known that I was following. Anyway, Mr. Minor did not give me any orders. It was my grandfather."

"Your grandfather?"

"Yes," the boy said proudly. "His name is Koshi."

Kate looked at Mario and realized now why he had seemed familiar. The oval face, with the high forehead, the jutting cheekbones, the thin line of the nose and the firm, narrow lips, was almost a replica of Koshi's. Only the boy's skin, which was fine and smooth, differed from the parchment-like skin of the old man.

"Why is Koshi watching me?"

The boy looked up at her. "He is not watching. He is taking care of you. He says you are not like the others. That you see the things that are hidden from the eye and hear the voices that do not speak." Mario's voice was surprisingly rich and strong and he spoke with the same flowing precision as Koshi.

"Will you tell him what you have seen?"

"Only if you wish it. It does not matter."

"Why do you say that?"

"With the Ashanti, it is not necessary to tell the high priest in words. Koshi knows what lies within the minds of his people."

Kate felt an odd sense of safety in the boy's presence. Then the thought of Charl Loizeaux lying inert in the alley sent prickles of fear through her. She wondered what story he would tell when he was picked up and how much he knew of what happened the last night in the Laughing Donkey.

As though in response to her thoughts, Mario said softly, "Do not be afraid of Charl. My grandfather does not like what he did to Picon. I think he will make no more trouble."

Now they had come to St. Clement's. The sleepers were rising from their pallets and the hum of their voices drifted out into the street. Father Maholan stood in the doorway and beside him was the old woman of the night before. The woman raised her gnarled hand but the priest touched her and she made no sound.

Kate was aware of her straggling hair and her drenched clothing. But Father Maholan only looked at her gently, without expression, and his hand formed the all-embracing gesture of the cross.

6

HOURS LATER Kate awoke calling Mullen's name. Bright sunlight was falling across her face, nearly blinding her. The suffocating heat of Jamaica at noon parched her throat and covered her skin with beads of moisture. The terror of a nightmare was still with her as she pulled the jalousie and bathed in luke-warm water from the basin near the door.

She threw herself back on the bed and buried her face in the pillow. Her throat ached where Charl Loizeaux had choked her and she raised her hands to caress the great purple bruise. But the touch of her hands frightened her. She turned over on her back and held them before her eyes. They were reddened with the washing of mugs and the scrubbing of floors at the Laughing Donkey and there were great welts on one palm where she had held the chain. She remembered when the hands were white and soft, when Mullen had gazed at the slender, supple fingers and whispered to her. "Ah, these are the hands to play the harp of Ireland, my Kathleen. It's shapely and lithe

77

and strong they are, to tear music from a harp's strings, or to tear a man's heart with the love of thee."

But these were the hands that had held Mannie Cousins' scrawny neck so tightly and pushed her away so that she fell to her death. Kate began to sob. "I wanted her dead, Mullen, but I did not intend to kill her." Then the dream from which she had awakened came back to her with such vividness that Mullen seemed to be standing before her, his face kindly, but a little stern. "Tell me the truth, Kathleen," he had commanded.

"I don't know. I don't know. I wanted vengeance upon her. Vengeance for you and for me. Vengeance for injustice. I could feel my fingers on her neck and I pressed down and down to squeeze the evil out of her body, not the life. Was that so wrong?" Then in the dream, it was not Mullen whom she saw but Father Maholan. His face had been set and resolute and his voice unrelenting. " 'Tis black sin upon your soul, Catherine. And the stain of it will grow and grow until nothing is left but the rotten core of you." "Is there no escape?" she had cried. But the priest only shook his head.

The recollection of the dream was more real than the life about her so that it was a long time before she heard the pounding on her door or Lettie Parsons' frightened call. "Kate, Kate, open up. What in the devil is wrong with ye, child?"

Finally she went to the door, unbarred it and took off the chain. Lettie came in with dresses and petticoats across her arm. Just behind her was Agnese, the serving-maid, with a tray laden with tea, scones and tropical fruit.

"What ails ye?" Lettie sputtered. " 'Tis past noon and I could not wake ye." Then she saw the great bruise on Kate's neck. "Lord of Mercy! What ha' happened, child?"

Kate turned away without answering. Lettie looked from her to the chair where the sodden russet gown was spread and then to the water-soaked shoes. She grasped Kate by the shoulder and spun her around. "Tell me what is wrong, child. Where have you been?"

But Kate's face was sullen. "I can't tell you, Lettie. I can't tell anyone. Don't ask me. Please don't."

Lettie flushed with anger. "You use me house, and

Lord knows what tricks you are up to. Am I not to ask what goes on beneath me own roof?"

"I'm sorry, Lettie. But I can't tell you."

Lettie looked at the girl and her manner was grim. Then suddenly she laughed. "So be it, Kate. I'll ask ye no more. I've brought clothing for ye. These things were Chloe's, but she'll not be needing them. She'll not be showing her face about here again."

Agnese had placed the tray by the bed and now stood at the doorway waiting for her mistress. Lettie surveyed Kate from the open door. "Eat well and put on some pretty clothes, dearie. There's a friend of yours a-waiting to see you when you've done."

The scalding, bitter tea brought relief to Kate's bruised throat. She broke open a soursop and sucked the thick white juice. She had no doubt that it was Jonathan Minor waiting for her below and, as she brushed her hair, she began to hum a little tune. She spread the dresses that Lettie had brought her out on the bed. She selected a pale blue crinoline, with a high neckband and flounces at the hip. Agnese came back with shoes, stockings and gloves and helped Kate to hook the dress. The colored woman gazed admiringly at the girl and her round face creased in a wide smile. "You be a beauty true, true, Miss. How it happen you be bound? You could make plenty guineas with Miss Lettie."

Kate tossed her head in annoyance and thrust her way past the woman. She ran lightly to the head of the broad stairway, but there she slackened her pace. She walked slowly down the stairs, holding her head erect, unwilling that Jonathan Minor should see her eagerness.

The odor of green rum and raw tobacco still clung to the parlor. The glare of light showed the too-bright coloring of the drapes and the tawdriness of the glass chandelier. There was a figure in the big armchair by the piano. The man came toward her and spoke, and disappointment filled her. It was not Jonathan Minor but the Scot, MacFeathers.

The little Scot came to her, his round puckered face suffused with pleasure. "Ay, lassie. 'Tis a grand lady you are today. I'm a-thinkin' there's no greater beauty come out o' Galway for many a moon."

Kate laughed and held out both her hands to the little man. Now that the first disappointment had passed, a glow of warmth filled her at the presence of the lawyer. She laughed gaily. "And I'm a-thinking 'tis no Scot ye be but a man o' Cork who's heard the bells of Shandon and kissed the Blarney Stone."

"Right ye are, Kate," he answered, laughing, "and many a night have I been chased by all the divils of Cobh. But come where nane can hear us, lassie—for I've a message for you. A message from Koshi."

"From Koshi? Is he not on his way to Accompong?"

MacFeathers shrugged. "He may well be. 'Tis a six-day journey, lassie. But the ways of the Ashanti are strange. Some nights the dondo will beat so soft you can scarce hear it and other times the merrymaking will whistle like a bird's call. The white man says 'tis but the heathen ways of the Negro, but Buddhoe up in Accompong knows every move o' the English in Kingston, and the Negroes in the slave huts share his secrets."

As he talked, MacFeathers led the way through a narrow portico onto a tiled veranda that overlooked a garden. Now he lowered his voice. "Captain Gwynn is in Kingston harbor with a French prize he took off Santo Domingue. He's a need for men to take her safe to Liverpool."

Kate crinkled her brow in perplexity. "I don't understand."

MacFeathers laughed. "There's none as knows the name o' Captain Gwynn will sail wi' him. His gang o' crimps is on the water front and the few redcoats there be are looking the other way. No mon is safe on Harbour Street this day."

"But why do you tell me this?"

"'Tis Koshi's notion you should know. For one o' the men they crimped was Charl Loizeaux. Found him in an alley near the Laughing Donkey, they did, and fair drunk they say he was. Wi' the tide he'll be on his way to Liverpool and, knowing Charl, I'd say 'tis many a lash will be on his back afore he reaches England. I dinna ken why Koshi wishes me to tell you this, lassie, and I dinna care. But I'm a-thinkin' 'tis good riddance that the island has o' Charl."

Kate took rapid stock of the situation. With Charl out of the way there was none among the whites who knew of the gray dress and its precious burden, locked in the chest upstairs. Of Koshi and Mario she had no fear. Like herself, they lived outside of the barriers of society. That was but one of the links that held them close together. But what of MacFeathers? How much did he know and how much could he be trusted?

She put her fingers on the back of his wrinkled hand. She said slowly, "You know I'm still bound to Gabriel Cousins."

"Ay, lassie. And 'tis said he wants you back."

"I've the money to buy my bond."

MacFeathers' brows raised questioningly, but he merely said, "Cousins is under nae obligation to let you do so."

"I'll pay twice over if need be."

"I dinna think Cousins will let you go."

"You're a lawyer, MacFeathers. Can you not arrange it?"

"Maybe, Kate. But I must know from whence the money comes. Is it from Lettie Parsons or Jonathan Minor?"

"What difference does it make?"

"A lot, lassie. If Minor's putting up the money, Gabe will think twice afore he comes up against him. Jonathan's a power on the island and Gabe's a wee mon. Minor could break him like he could a stick across his knee. But Lettie's a horse of another color. This bagnio o' hers is outside the law. Gabe need not give in to her."

Kate said quickly. "The money comes from Jonathan Minor."

MacFeathers' brown eyes twinkled. "In that case, I'm a-thinkin' Gabe will come to terms, lassie. You need na worry."

From the reception room they heard the chatter of Lettie's voice and the booming tones of Jonathan Minor.

"Speak of the devil—" said MacFeathers. "I'll be leaving you now, lassie. But take care ye do not burn y' fingers wi' Jonathan Minor. 'Tis an arrogant mon he is and used to having his way." He stepped down from the raised veranda to the garden walk. Kate watched his figure bobbing along the path before she turned to find Minor gazing at her fom the dooway.

Barraca Cove lay sheltered by great ledges of rock that rose almost perpendicularly from the sea. Outside, the giant swells lashed themselves into frenzied whiteness against the pointed fingers of stone that showed glistening gray as the waves rolled backward. Within the cove itself there was peace. The strip of beach was almost pure white and the waves that rolled in were so filled with the white sand that they resembled old lace. Coconut palms grew close to the beach and the side of the hill was spattered with the rich flame of the flamboyant trees.

From the cove one could look upward to the ivy-covered walls and the massive turrets of Rune Hall and to the sugar fields and the mahogany forest that lay beyond. Jonathan Minor's carriage was in the shade of the spreading genip tree at the cliff's top. Mario lolled on the grass, joking with Curtius the coachman.

Down below, Jonathan Minor had spread blankets on the sand. He and Kate Donley rested upon them. Jonathan had brought the girl here first nearly a month ago, but he had never taken her through the wrought-iron gates that guarded the entrance of Rune Hall. Kate had remained at the Christian Steps, despite Minor's protest; there was no other place to go. Each day Minor's coach rolled up before the ornate doorway of the Christian Steps and Jonathan stepped out, his stock immaculate, his hair pomaded, his fingers glittering with gold and rubies. He bowed to Lettie Parsons, kissed her lightly on the cheek and pressed small gifts upon her. For Kate he brought perfumes or bonbons brought in by the sailing vessels that filled Kingston harbor.

Kate accepted the gifts smilingly, though deep within her a hot fire of resentment smoldered. Kingston was gay this season. The fire that had swept the docks, the waterfront bars and the homes of the poor had not touched the big sugar and pimento estates. The vast houses were lighted until the early hours of the morning and tales of almost incredible orgies were bruited through the town. The gaiety was tinged with fear, too, for Buddhoe and his men had twice descended on Kingston. The single regiment of redcoats was quartered at the homes of government officials and on the plantations near Montego Bay. Many of the private estates boasted small armies of armed retainers, and their roofs were mounted with swivel guns.

The theater too flourished in Jamaica. Rival companies of French and American actors vied with one another to attract the parties of the rich planters and merchants while the crowd, drunk and noisy, assembled nightly on the Parade to toss jests at the dandified young clerks and their richly accoutered concubines. The revelry was interspersed with violence. Occasionally there was swordplay among the gentlemen. But more often the fighting was done with fists or the jagged edges of broken bottles. Coachmen cleared pathways to the theater door with their whips, but once their white masters were safely within, the mob was likely to turn on the servants, flog them, and even hang them from the limbs of the high trees in the center of the Parade.

Amidst this colorful, rowdy night life of Jamaica, Jonathan Minor walked with certainty. In the absence of Governor Stallybrass, who was in England, none among the island men held so much authority. Minor held aloof from the planters, and though they resented this, his coolness, courage and physical prowess won awe and a certain respect.

Whatever popularity Minor lacked among the men was more than made up for by the ladies of Kingston and Montego Bay. Many a feminine leg was bent low in curtsy as Minor passed through the lobby of the Kingston theater or entered the great reception room of Hibbert Hall. Wives looked coyly over their spread fans and the concubines of the clerks stared brazen invitations at the tall man with his calm face and the touches of gray hair at his temples.

All these things Kate Donley knew by rumor or from the gossip of Lettie Parsons. Jonathan Minor had never taken her with him to the theaters or to the balls—not even to the grounds of Rune Hall. In the early afternoon Minor's carriage would roll up before the Christian Steps. There were drives in the country with the carriage well guarded by Minor's men. There were elaborate meals, served on the terrace at the beach. Wild game, tree oysters, succulent turtle steaks and gammon were accompanied with the finest wines seized from the French ships captured on their way to Port-au-Prince. Sometimes too there was a swift embrace and the touch of Jonathan's lips on hers. Always the gesture was gentle at first. Then came a moment of hot passion, followed by unexpected withdrawal and the casual word.

Each evening at dusk Jonathan brought her back to the Christian Steps. He kissed her lightly as he left her and usually stopped to chat with Lettie. Kate was perplexed and vexed. Kingston with all its gaiety engulfed him during the hours of the night and only the sunlit hours were hers. Sometimes she heard carriages passing by, and the sounds of light laughter and singing voices filled her with envy and resentment. Her life at the Christian Steps was more imprisoning even that that of the Laughing Donkey. There at least she had mingled with people but here she spent much of her time alone. Jonathan Minor had given Lettie Parsons strict orders that Kate should never be seen in the downstairs rooms and accompanied his commands with a threat to close the Christian Steps if he was disobeyed.

Several times Kate came close to open rebellion but each time judgment tempered her actions. She was uncertain whether Jonathan was ashamed of his dallying with a bound girl or if he was motivated by a solicitude for what he believed to be her innocence. Surely, no matter how oblivious to gossip Jonathan might be, he must realize that the daily presence of his carriage before the Christian Steps would set the tongues of Jamacia rattling. Then could it be that Jonathan had plans for her, plans that would make her mistress of Rune Hall? This would be worth the weary nights of waiting.

Kate bridled her tongue, concealed her temper and choked back her complaints. But her nights were spent in secret yearning. The gossip of the theaters which Lettie told her brought forth poignant memories of her childhood when she had wandered through Ireland with her actor father. The glow of the lamps in the footlights, the sound of applause and the hurried excitement of dressing rooms —the whole world of make-believe spread out before her, with Mullen's voice, rich and vibrant, at its center.

How changed her life now, with only the chaste, evasive kisses of Jonathan Minor to look forward to.

Suddenly she would feel again the arms of Percy Morgan about her. There had been a warmth and youth and eagerness in him that was matched in her. His lawless passion suited her better than the disciplined control of Jonathan Minor. She had branded Percy a coward, but who would not have blanched at murder? She shrugged. Perhaps she should have had the courage to take her life in her hands and run away with him. Was not that what Mullen would have urged her to do? If once she and Percy had escaped, they would have been truly free. Life would have been fresh, not old and stale as it was here in Jamaica, waiting in the Christian Steps for Jonathan Minor. She turned her thoughts aside heavily for they always ended in Mannie Cousins' death. When one has killed, one has forfeited youth, she thought, and in its place there can remain only gnawing ambition and the sense of completion that comes in pitting oneself against the world, breaking its laws and escaping the penalties of the violations.

The stigma of her bondage still lay heavy upon her, even now that she was free. MacFeathers had brought her the release proudly. Cousins had not wanted to sell, but the Scot had used the name of Minor to intimidate him. Kate had told Lettie that Minor had paid the bond money but did not wish it known, and she had then exacted a promise from Lettie that, in case of questions, she herself would claim to have put up the money. To Minor, Kate told the story that Lettie had loaned her the money, and that she was ashamed of this and so, in turn, asked him to cover up for her. Thus with two people each admitting to putting up a sum which neither had paid, Kate was secure in the belief that there would be no discovery of the true source of the guineas which had purchased her freedom from Gabriel Cousins. After the purchase was made there was surprisingly little of the money left. But Kate realized that even these few guineas would arouse suspicion should they be found. She dared trust none among the whites with her secret so at length she had given the remaining coins to Mario to deliver to Koshi for safe-keeping.

Still Kate was never sure how much she had concealed the truth from Minor. Now as they lay in Barraca Cove, side by side, she wondered if he did not see through her subterfuges. She turned and examined his lean face and he smiled at her. He asked softly, "Are you happy, Kate?"

She shook her head. "How can I be? What lies ahead for me?"

"What would you like, Kate?"

Without answering, Kate raised her eyes to the gaunt turrets of Rune Hall. A colored sentry in one of the towers shifted the swivel gun so that it covered the roadway. Jonathan Minor's eyes followed those of the girl. He touched her outspread palm. "The Hall fascinates you, doesn't it, Kate?"

She nodded. "Why have you never taken me there?"

"It would not do." His tones were soft but the words carried a finality that Kate dared not question. Tears stung her eyes and she looked away.

"Why does Rune Hall mean so much to you?"

"It is as though I had seen it before. It is a link with the past. With Mullen—my father . . . and with Ireland. Once I saw a castle just like it on a desolate little island off the coast of Connemara. It was once the stronghold of Grainne O'Maille, the woman pirate. Mullen told me she was an ancestress of mine. He was proud of the blood of the O'Malleys."

"O'Malley," Jonathan repeated. "Why, Rune Hall was built by a man named Piaras O'Malley nearly a hundred and fifty years ago. He was a pirate of sorts too, though he never flew the skull and crossbones. He was a friend of Sir Henry Morgan, Esquemeling, Blackbeard, and half the pirates that sailed the Spanish Main. Scarce a privateer went out of Old Port Royal but what was paid for and provisioned by Piaras O'Malley. And when the buccaneers came back to Jamaica—half the loot was his and half divided among the pirate crew! A rich man was Piraras; there was none richer on the island. Rune Hall in those days was the center of Jamaican life and a lusty place it was. Anne Bonney, the greatest of the women pirates, lived there with Piaras for a while. And finally when Henry Morgan turned respectable and was made governor of Jamaica with orders to stamp out the buccaneers, it was at Rune Hall that the pirates took their last stand. Morgan's men laid seige to the grounds, but O'Malley held them off for more than a month. O'Malley surrendered under a flag of truce but Morgan and his men paid no heed to it. They clubbed him to death and hanged his body over his own wrought-iron gates.

Kate's eyes glistened with excitement. "It can be no coincidence that Rune Hall is built in the image of Carrigahowly Castle and both were the strongholds of O'Malleys."

"Carrigahowly Castle—once Rune Hall was called something like that but 'twas too hard on the tongue and it was changed." He looked at the girl's sparkling eyes and some of her excitement passed to him. "Tell me of Grainne O'Maille, Kate. I should like to hear."

Kate sat upright, her hands about her knees, remembering the day that she had shared with Mullen sitting in the ruins of an old abbey, looking far out across Clew Bay. Slowly the story Mullen had told came back to her and she repeated it to Jonathan Minor, trying to use the words, the very inflections of Mullen's voice.

"Grace O'Malley they call her in English history, but to the Irish she will always be Grainne O'Maille, the greatest she-pirate that ever lived. A huge woman she was, with black, flashing eyes, a hawklike nose and skin the color of an oak tree's bark. As for the voice she had, you could hear it across the length of Galway Sound. And she was strong as any man in all of Aran. Daughter she was of Owen O'Malley, the Black Oak, whose power was unchallenged from Ardrahan to Mallargany. Even as a child she went with him in the horsehide coracles that preyed off the English ships that came to Galway, and when she was nineteen and her father dead, she became chief of the clan, fighting her brother with a knife to win her place.

"Grainne added wooden ships to her fleet of coracles and became the scourge of the Irish coast. Many a proud Spanish galleon, with its cargo of wine, fell into her hands, but like a true Gael, it was the sailing ships of England that were her chief prey. She built Carrigahowly Castle right by the edge of the cliff that overlooked the harbor of Clare Island. And 'tis said that each night when her fleet came in she bound her ships together with a great rope and passed that rope through a hole in the castle wall and tied it to her arm while she slept that no ship might leave the isle without her knowledge."

As she talked, Kate's voice became richer and more and more filled with the haunting quality of the Irish bards. She told of Grainne O'Maille's marriage to O'Donnell O'Flaherty and how when they quarreled she had challenged him to a fair fight; of Grainne's defiance of haughty Queen Elizabeth; of her seizure of a Turkish corsair on the very day she gave birth to her first child; and finally of her death beneath the storm-ridden waves of Clew Bay.

Dusk had fallen in the cove when Kate had finished her story. Clusters of stars cast a reddish sheen over the gray sky. Kate rose and went to the water's edge. Jonathan Minor followed her and took both of her hands in his. "Kate, I have never seen you so beautiful. You speak as though Grainne O'Maille were a part of you."

She tilted her head back proudly. "It is true, I've the blood of the O'Malley in me."

He put his arms about her and tried to draw her to him, but she struggled against his embrace.

"Kate," he whispered. "You frighten me tonight. There is something wild about you, something cruel, something I can't understand."

She laughed mockingly and taunted him. "Once I thought you a man, Jonathan Minor. But now you say you are frightened. Are you in truth naught but a milksop and a lollyboy?"

The arms that held her tightened until her breasts were crushed against his chest. Again his lips tried to find hers, but she threw her head back and his lips brushed her throat.

"Kate, Kate. I must have you tonight. I would have you even though I died tomorrow."

"You will not die tomorrow, Jonathan," she mocked. "But you will take me to Rune Hall."

"Anything, Kate. Rune Hall will be yours—all my possessions. Kate, my beloved."

The cloth of her bodice ripped beneath his fingers but she no longer struggled against him. The tale had brought up all the ancient passions that had slept within her. The waves tingled across her ankles. She slipped sideways to the damp sand and Jonathan Minor stood above her. His dark face was no longer serene and he was shaking as with ague.

7

THE HIGH WALLS that surrounded Rune Hall were a mass of color. Bougainvillaea and flame vine cascaded over the rough stones, almost concealing them from sight. The massive, arched gateway was of intricate Italian workmanship, for it had been stolen more than a century and a half earlier by English buccaneers who looted the splendid Cathedral of St. Rocco in Cienfueges and brought their spoils back to Port Royal and the hands of Piaras O'Malley. The passing years and the salt wind had given to the wrought iron a pale green patina. An armed mulatto sentry, clad in a blue and white uniform with froggings of gold, pushed back the heavy gates as Jonathan Minor's carriage appeared on the roadway below.

The winding driveway was shaded by almond trees whose thick upturned leaves were stained with carmine. A gardener raked up the fallen leaves, and an occasional lizard—a wood slave—darted across the lawn and disappeared in the crevices of the wall. Jonathan squeezed Kate's hand. "Welcome to Rune Hall," he said. "Is it still like Carrigahowly Castle?"

Kate turned shining eyes upon him. "More than ever," she breathed.

Curtius reined in the bays and Jonathan jumped lightly from the carriage and held out his hand to help Kate. She clasped his arm lightly as she stepped to the flagged pathway. He led her up the stone stairs to the massive front door of hand-carved mahogany, set with huge breast-shaped ornaments of iron. As they mounted the steps, the ponderous door swung open slowly and a footman, garbed in the same blue and white uniform as the sentry, bowed to them and smiled a welcome.

Kate turned in the doorway and lifted her face to be kissed. But Minor averted his eyes. Surprise and anger brought color to her face but she said nothing and stepped into the high hallway. The great hall was to her right and she pushed aside the dark red portieres and stepped into the room. The floor was laid in mahogany, polished and waxed until it formed a darkly tinted mirror that reflected the carved panelings of the wall, the glistening crystal chandeliers and the silver sconces. The tall, narrow windows ran from floor to ceiling. The glass was deeply colored in an elaborate design of royal blue and blood red. Kate placed her hand on the silver knob of the one nearest.

"Can we see Barraca Cove from here?" she asked.

"No, but the ledges are visible from the mistress' bedchamber upstairs. You can see the village of Baraçong too and a part of the fortress which is all that remains of Port Royal."

Kate laughed and ran to the massive stairs that came down through the center of the hall. Like the floor and ceiling, the stairs were of burnished mahogany. The handcarved balusters were of African design, wrought by Piaras O'Malley's own cabinetmakers.

The front room of the upper floor was nearly as large as the great hall itself. A huge four-poster was raised on a triple dais. The towering headboard was carved with the setting sun surrounded by rays. Kate flung the glass doorway open and stepped onto a narrow balcony paved with gaily colored mosaics. She stood with her hands in back of her, the fingers twisting about the slender wrought-iron railing, and waited for Jonathan to come to her.

Jonathan was not smiling. His gray eyes seemed unusually pale and cold against the brownness of his face. His voice was formal as he pointed out the line of churning water that marked the submerged shoals of Barraca and told her about the tiny fishing village formed there by the freedmen of Jamaica.

She tugged at his arm but he stared out moodily at the shimmering, cobalt water.

"You're angry with me," she said. "You did not want to bring me here."

"Ah, but I did. But it was madness to bring you so soon."

"What do you mean, Jonathan?"

"When I brought you here the first time, it should have been to stay. This is dangerous."

"I do not understand."

"Stallybrass will hear of it."

"The Governor! What has he to do with you and me?"

"A great deal, Kate."

"I still don't understand. You say you want me to come to Rune Hall for good. What is to stop it, if that is what you wish?"

"Stallybrass." Jonathan spoke dourly. "It is all very well as long as you are a bound girl on whom I've taken pity. But once the Governor suspects what lies between us—" He shrugged and turned away.

"Can it make so much difference that I was bound?"

"Listen to me, my dear. You have been in Jamaica too short a time to understand how strict are the rules of conduct here. It is unimportant when young clerks have their concubines and planters their second homes. Life may seem riotous and gay, but there are certain appearances that a man like myself must observe. I cannot flaunt Stallybrass—especially not where marriage is concerned."

"But, Jonathan, if you want me—"

"Perhaps I should have told you sooner, Kate, but I have been waiting, working out a plan for you to come here to Rune Hall. Two years ago I went to London as Stallybrass' courier. There I met his daughter Rose. She was just a child then. Fifteen, and in school. But she was lovely in her childlike way and when I came back I asked Stallybrass for her hand in marriage. Not, of course, until she should be old enough. Everything was arranged by letter. Stallybrass has gone back to England to bring Rose to Jamaica. As soon as he returns, the betrothal will be announced."

The blood had drained from Kate's face, and her hands had tightened against the railing until her knuckles were white. "You mean you intend to marry this girl?" she asked unbelievingly.

"I must, Kate. That is why we must take such care. If you are to come here—"

"I? Come to Rune Hall?"

"Rose is young. She will need a companion. Rune Hall will need a housekeeper."

Kate's high-pitched laughter interrupted him. "So I am to come as a servant."

"Not only that, Kate."

"As your bawd too, I imagine."

"Kate, be reasonable. Last night was madness."

She drew herself up. "Yes, it was madness, Jonathan Minor. It was insane for a bound girl to think she could be mistress of Rune Hall. Truly I was mad to believe you."

He stretched out his hands to her. "Kate, I love you. But I have given my word."

"Your word to Stallybrass and your word to me. There can be no doubt which word a gentleman will keep."

Minor dropped his arms to his sides. "Let me explain this thing to you, Kate. Last night was something which I did not plan. I was carried away by wanting you. It was weakness in me, I admit. But the whole fabric of one's life cannot be changed in a moment. I only wish that I could undo what is done."

Kate's eyes blazed. " 'Tis cheaper than the water-front scran you are, Jonathan Minor. You think yourself such a noble fellow that you cannot deny your word to an English baronet and would like to forget your dallying with a servant girl. 'Tis not honor but cowardice. I've been soiled by the very touch of you."

Minor's face turned white beneath its tan and his eyes were hard as slate. "You have said enough. I've tried to tell you kindly. But surely you cannot think the Christian Steps a fit training ground for the mistress of Rune Hall?"

Her hand lashed against his face. He dropped back a step and looked at her expressionlessly. Suddenly she turned and ran, down the wide mahogany staircase, through the great hall, into the yard. The carriage was still there. She jumped into the coachman's box and plied the horses with the whip. The frightened animals broke into a run. The carriage swayed crazily as it swirled down the winding driveway, through the open gates into the road.

Kate never once looked back. She stood in the box, beating the animals into a frenzied panic.

The echoes of Father Maholan's knuckles beating against the thin door had a somber sound. Kate and the priest waited in silence until they heard the light scraping of feet on the rough floor.

"Do not be frightened, Catherine," Father Maholan said; "this is a place of refuge."

The door opened with a faint squeal of protest and a bent figure, clad in the dull brown garb of a lay sister, peered out at them. The pallor of her skin, her rheumy eyes, her colorless lips and blue-veined, clawlike hands all made Kate think of Mannie Cousins. The girl sucked in her breath sharply and Father Maholan, hearing the sound, murmured a word of comfort. To the nun he said, "This is the girl about whom I sent a message to Sister Madelava. She is in need of your kindness." Then as he turned to leave, he spoke again to Kate. "There will be no luxury here, my child, but there is safety and time for contemplation."

After he had gone, Kate and the lay sister looked at each other in silence. "I am Sister Mathilda," the woman said in a scratchy voice. Then she stooped to pick up Kate's small parcel of clothing.

Kate protested, "No, let me." But the woman snatched up the package almost greedily. "It is my duty to be of service," she said. Kate was unable to tell whether the tones were those of true humility or of self-pity.

They entered the bare hall of the Convent together. The scent of religious places came to Kate's nostrils—a mixture of bare scrubbed floors, musty rugs, the lingering odor of incense and tallow.

The lay sister scurried into an anteroom and came back a moment later with a piece of stiff paper filled with spiderlike writing. "You will read this list of rules," she said severely; "then you will sign your name in the visitor's book."

Kate's eyes skimmed over the handwriting, but she paid little heed to the words. When she thought the sister was satisfied, she let herself be led to the book that lay open on the table. She dipped the quill pen into the ink and signed her name.

The sister smiled. "Now I will show you to your cell."

Kate followed the shuffling footsteps of Sister Mathilda down the bare, silent hall and up a flight of wooden stairs. On the first landing the woman opened a door and motioned Kate to enter.

The room was truly a cell, dark and narrow, with only a small window. The bed was a wooden couch raised about two feet from the ground. Over it was thrown a mattress of straw, a blanket and a straw pillow. The crude washstand and the wardrobe were made of unpolished wood, and the walls were naked save for a rusty crucifix. A battered faldstool stood beneath it.

Sister Mathilda untied the rope that bound Kate's parcel and, without a word, unpacked and laid out the few things which Kate had brought to the Convent. She looked sideways at the girl as her fingers slid over the red silk dress that had once belonged to Chloe, but she said nothing. She went out of the room and returned a few minutes later. A shapeless gown of coarse brown cotton hung across her arm. She laid it across the cot and turned to Kate.

"There will be an hour of rest," she said. "Spend it well—in contemplation of your soul. Examine what sin may be within you and cast it out." This time when Sister Mathilda left she closed the door with finality.

Kate stood still until the whisper of the nun's sandals could no longer be heard. Then she went to the window and looked out into the sultry garden on which dusk had descended. The window was of Gothic design but the panes pushed outward, giving her a limited view of a stone wall, a lawn, and almond trees. A grotto broke the even contours of the wall, and the figure of the Virgin gleamed white in the pale evening glow.

There was movement in the garden and Kate saw that a woman walked along the path. Despite the shapeless brown kirtle, Kate could see that the body was young, lissom and strong. A second woman came into her range of vision. This nun was tall and she walked with a monotonous habitual stride. As she came closer, her white face and moving lips were visible. Fingers, skeletal in the pale light, caressed the beads of a rosary.

The two nuns passed close to each other but there was no sign of recognition. Only the younger one shrank back a little as though fearful of interrupting the other's meditation. The tall nun knelt before the grotto and the mumbled words of her prayer drifted up to the open window. She rose and the bright moonlight fell upon her face. Her eyes were dull, lifeless. Kate shivered and drew back from the window.

The narrow cell seemed suffocating and Kate felt the swift desire to beat upon the walls. In a panic, she crossed to the door and opened it, but the long corridor was barren of life. She threw herself on the cot and wished that tears would come, but they did not. Instead there were memories—the days she had spent in the debtors' prison in Galway, where walls like these had hemmed her in; the cubicle on the *Liza Mae*, which she could only leave to experience the brutality of Captain Lunt; the bare room above the Laughing Donkey; the gaiety and laughter of the Christian Steps from which she had been barred by the orders of Jonathan Minor—and now this tiny cell in the Convent of the Immaculate Conception. Was there no release from prison? Her hands tore at the thin blanket until it shredded beneath her fingers and her body arched in a tension of anger and frustration.

Her hatred became a living thing, stretching into every part of her body. And the symbol of her hate was Jonathan Minor. She thought of his lean face, his pale gray eyes and his debonair manner. Where was he tonight? In a box at the theater? At Hibbert Hall, as guest of honor at some gay party? What did it matter? Someday he must know loneliness and suffering and the slow movement of endless hours. That would be her gift to him.

When Kate had driven Minor's coach up to the Christian Steps, Lettie Parsons had thought the quarrel was a mere jest. Within an hour, Jonathan Minor had ridden up and called to Lettie. The two were closeted together for half an hour and then Jonathan had gone raging out of the house.

Lettie came to Kate's room and stood just inside the door. She did not look at the girl, and when she spoke her voice was harsh. "You got to get out o' here fast, girl. Take the things I've given ye and leave."

"Lettie," Kate protested, "I've no other place to go."

"Ye've stayed here long enough, I'm a-thinking. Out with ye now within the hour."

"But where?"

"That's no affair o' mine." Then as the girl did not answer, she added: "It's you or me, Kate. Minor says I'm to throw you out or he'll be back with his deputies and close the Steps. There's nothing else that I can do, girl." She went out and shut the door and the Christian Steps became strangely quiet.

Kate gathered up the dresses, an extra pair of slippers and the undergarments that had once belonged to Chloe. Koshi still had her small supply of money and she had no idea where she could find him now. She thrust the package beneath her arm and went down the stairs and out through the front door. She did not see Lettie, or Agnese, or any of the girls.

When she reached the street, she did not know which way to turn. She went down the hill until she came to the door of St. Clement's. Loneliness and fear were deep within her and she remembered the comfort that prayer and the confession had once brought before the tragedy of Mullen's death. She climbed the steps slowly, genuflected and crossed herself. She knelt before the shrine of Saint Veronica. And when she rose she saw that Father Maholan was at her side. She had told him her story, and Father Maholan had taken pity on her and brought her here to the Convent.

She rolled over on her back and looked up at the blank brown ceiling. Slowly, very slowly the boards seemed to descend and the walls began to close in on her. She shrank back in horror—and then the voices began to speak. There was Mannie Cousins' nasal twang: "Ye killed me, Kate. Ye soul will rot in hell for this." Charl Loizeaux's brutal chuckle: "A bleedin' beauty ye are without no clo'se on." Jonathan Minor's clipped, austere tones: "Do you think a bound girl can become mistress of Rune Hall?" There were other voices—those of Lettie Parsons, Chloe, Bard, Captain Lunt—all run together until they became a mad jibbering. Then they stopped and she thought she heard

Father Maholan in the dream saying. "There be black sin on you, Catherine, and it will spread until there be naught but the hardness and evil within you." She uttered a strangled scream and Mullen was there beside her, pacing up and down, as he had that last time she had talked to him. "There are times, Kathleen, when a man must be harsh and ruthless. Neither the laws of man nor God can guide him. He must fight his enemies as best he can, showing no mercy and expecting none. It is better to wreak vengeance against the tyrant than to live meekly."

As swiftly as the horror had come, it passed away. She felt calm and relaxed. She knew now what she must do; it only remained to find the first step toward its doing. The path to power and security would be slow and tortuous and the effort could leave no room for kindness. But she would find the way. Resolutely she closed her eyes. When Sister Mathilda returned at the end of the hour she found the girl asleep. She woke her and whispered, "Come with me."

Kate followed the sister along the corridor where the scent of incense told her they were going to the Chapel for compline. She sat apart from the sisters on a backless bench reserved for visitors. When compline was over, she listened as the nuns sang the Salve Regina. But the words so filled with longing, faith and the aching desire for eternity held a different meaning for her. Far up in the hills she thought she heard the rhythmic beat of jungle drums. The softly intoned words of self-abnegation blended strangely with the urgent, insistent demand of the warrior gods of the Ashanti. She lowered her head, not with humility, but for fear lest the anger, the passion and the determination that had come to her should show in her eyes. As the nuns filed out, Sister Madeleva sprinkled each of them with holy water from an aspergillum. The sisters moved wraithlike down the dim corridors and disappeared into their cells. But Kate walked proudly, her head high, and as she moved she flicked the beads of holy water from her skirt.

When she had regained the sanctuary of her cell, she threw off the coarse brown dress and tossed it into a corner. Naked, she went to the window and listened. But if the beat of the drums was real, it had ceased now. She lit a candle and took out the red silk dress. She drew her fingers across the cloth caressingly and then she slipped it on. She snugged the soft fabric across her hips. She put on stockings and Chloe's high-heeled slippers and brushed her hair with long, rhythmic strokes.

When she had finished, she went again to the window. The statue of the Blessed Virgin still showed startlingly white against the gray stone walls. But in the hills beyond, there were moving lights like giant fireflies. Out of the hot night came the soft, slow muffled beat of the giant gumby drums. The rhythm grew faster and the goombah took up the off beat. The music became a part of the night and the whole city seemed to vibrate. The drums rose to a pitch of defiant frenzy, then slackened off slowly, slowly.

Kate waited until the night was quiet again. Then, still dressed in her red gown, she dropped down on the crude convent cot and fell asleep.

8

FOR THREE DAYS Kate had not left the grounds of the Convent of the Immaculate Conception. The days had been spent in contemplation, but Father Maholan might well have been shocked had he known the nature of the girl's thoughts. True, she fought down the passions of intemperance, lust and envy and the weaknesses of indecision and self-pity. She was shaping her emotions into a hard mold that would serve her surging ambition and her overpowering desire for revenge.

She ate the simple food of the Convent and wore the ugly brown garb of the sisters. Her eyes followed the celebrants as they moved smoothly through the intricate ritual before the chapel altar. Her face was remote, her eyes veiled. She no longer shuffled as she walked, nor looked down at her feet. She held her head upright and the last traces of awkward adolescence left her. Sister Madeleva noted the change in her and believed that the look of brittle calm sprang from some deep spiritual peace. She was mistaken. Kate's mind was in a turmoil, but slowly she forced down every passion that would not serve her ends, until only one was left—the overweening lust for power.

Kingston slept at noon. The wide expanse of King Street was empty and the Parade shimmered in the blistering heat. Even the birds fell silent and the rustlings of lizards and wood slaves in the parched grass were the only signs of life. This was the time that Kate chose to leave the Convent. She selected the simplest of Chloe's dresses—a loose, flowered cotton print with high neckband, flowing sleeves, flounced skirt and wide belt—and the more practical pair of slippers. She walked softly along the dingy corridor, down the stairs and out through the squealing door.

Across the street a boy squatted on his haunches, his body only partially shaded by the thin line of a palm tree. Kate knew instantly that he was Mario, but she gave no sign until he had followed her to Harbour Street. Then she turned and waited for him.

Mario approached shyly until he stood close to her, his eyes downcast.

"Where is Koshi?" she asked.

The boy's white teeth flashed. "He's up to Brandon's plantation putting an obi on the banana trees."

"An obi? Whatever for?"

"So no one steals any. Brandon wouldn't like that."

Kate nodded, thinking of Sydney Brandon as he stood at the bar of the Laughing Donkey, spewing out words of hate against the blacks. She remembered stories about him. It was said that he had become rich through the ruthless driving of his slaves, and that now he harbored political ambitions and wished to unseat the Governor and Minor in order to seize power in the name of the planters. The mention of his name sent a chill of premonition through her. She thrust aside her thoughts and asked, "How far is it to the field?"

"About a mile and a half."

"Take me there."

Mario looked at her thin slippers and shook his head. "It's a long way to walk."

"That doesn't matter."

The boy started on ahead and Kate followed. Mario whistled tunelessly and looked back over his shoulder from time to time to see if his pace was too rapid.

Kate walked erect, and though perspiration soon beaded her forehead and soaked the back and arms of her dress, she felt the exhilaration of freedom.

Mario led her along the water for some distance, then he turned sharply up a rutted donkey-cart path. A lane led along the border of a sugar cane field and ended in a clearing where banana trees, their heavy burdens of green fruit swaying slightly in the warm breeze, grew in uneven lines. In the distance she saw a cluster of Negroes, the men in breeches, naked to the waist, the women in brightly colored cotton dresses and bandanas. Koshi stood among them speaking, and when he finished, there was a murmur of voices.

Koshi came across the uneven earth toward Kate. A long, thin, three-pronged pole rose upright from his waist and he walked in a ceremonial pattern that was at once stiff and filled with rhythmic grace. His left leg swung forward in a stride and he planked the left foot firmly on the ground. Then he drew the right foot even with a slight mincing gesture, which permitted only the toe to touch. He moved rapidly until he came to the tree closest to the point where Kate and Mario stood. Once Koshi's eyes flicked to Kate's face but he gave no sign of recognition.

The Negroes formed a little circle about Koshi and he spoke a few words to them in Ashanti. Then he brought forth from his pockets a bottle of lavender-colored water, a triangular board to which was nailed a triangle of black cloth, a bag supposedly made of human skin, an egg, some nails, three dried beans and an assortment of colored ribbons. He unfastened from his waist the three-pronged pole, to which wisps of dried plantain were attached. He nailed the triangular board to the tree, then planted the pole firmly in the ground. He stretched the skin bag across the prongs, dropped the beans into it and filled the sac with the lavender water. Then he knelt before the tree and

100

raised the egg in his left hand. He talked earnestly to the egg, starting in Ashanti but lapsing into the broad island dialect, which Kate could not follow.

"What is he saying?" Kate whispered to Mario.

"He is telling the egg who may and who may not enter the field," the boy replied solemnly.

Koshi placed the egg in the sac of colored water, then turned and addressed his following, still speaking in patois. He warned them: "Any mon wha' he name I no speak come into this field, snake fly after him and bite. Y' hear me?"

The men and women nodded.

"You go tell um evumbody—Koramantyn, Yaruba, Ashanti—he steal one fig outa this field, he gwan get awful bellyache. Don't he call on me. I ain gwan cure he—he gwanna die sure sure."

The Negroes stood silent and then one by one walked away from the group, leaving only Koshi and Mario with Kate. Koshi, without speaking, went to the edge of the sugar field and took a seat in the shade of the high cane.

Kate looked at Mario with questioning eyes. The boy grinned. "In three days the egg will have a black ring around its center. In six, it will change to a snake that will attack anyone who steals the figs."

"Figs?"

"That is what the people here call bananas."

"Do you believe this?"

Again the boy's teeth flashed. "I believe that none among our people will steal bananas from this place."

"Why did Koshi speak in patois, not in Ashanti?"

"Many of the slaves do not understand the Ashanti tongue. They come from tribes all over Africa and some were born here in the island. Patois is the only language all can understand."

"Do they all believe in the power of the Ashanti priest?"

The boy answered quietly. "They have reason to do so."

"Does not Koshi weaken his influence with his people by tending to such trifling matters as the theft of bananas?"

"No. Food is not trifling. It is the source of life. Our religion is not a thing apart. The high priest of the Ashanti is the tribal leader, granting rewards, wreaking punishment. His power depends on his ability to work daily miracles—to cure sickness, to provide means of vengeance, to give food and to help men endure the shackles of slavery."

Kate looked at the boy in wonder. "How do you know these things, Mario?"

"Koshi has taught them to me. When he is gone I shall be the high priest of the Ashanti."

Koshi had not moved while the boy spoke; his eyes were closed as though in slumber. Now he stretched out his hand bidding Kate come to him. She took a place on the raised earth beside him and was again aware of the latent power in the placid face and the suppressed fire in the somber eyes.

He said, "You have seen the homely miracle of the field and it has made you question the power of obeah. You are white; therefore you wish your miracles to be both spectacular and meaningless. But we whose skins are black know that every act of life is a miracle. The woman who bears a child has committed an act of magic; so has the sick person who recovers or the one who dies. You think that I have wasted my time by casting a spell over these bananas. But my people reason: What good is a miracle if it cannot be put to practical ends? Can your religion protect a field from theft? You know it cannot. The Ashanti pays no heed to a promise of a hell or heaven to come, but he is tolerably afraid of a bellyache."

Kate was again struck by the man's perfectly modulated voice and his precise English. She asked, "If obeah has such power, why do you not use it to free the slaves or to make them masters of Jamaica?"

A smile lighted the old man's features. "As always you want things done on a large scale and that is not the way of the Ashanti. Your god is all-powerful, capable of sweeping a nation into the sea, or of shattering the earth with a blow of his hand. Our gods are fallible, full of mischief and even malice. They like to get drunk, to dance, to make love. Papa Legba is old, lame and dirty. Erzulie is loud, lusty, boisterous. They are vindictive and greedy. They can be offended easily and bribed cheaply."

Kate's disappointment showed in her face. "Then obeah is naught but charlatanry. I came to you for help because

102

I believed you possessed power. I do not want to give a man indigestion or raise warts on his hand. I want power in my hands, Koshi; the power of wealth; the power of vengeance; the power to kill."

Koshi looked at her soberly. "Do you know what obeah means in Ashanti? It means killing. I have not said obeah is a jest; it is far from that. But one does not learn the magic powers of obeah overnight. In obeah, you do not pray for favors; you make demands. Then through knowledge and skill, through the power of the will and the mind, you attain mastery over the forces that control your destiny. But the person who uses obeah must be stronger than the power he invokes." He paused. "I am growing old and I have been too weak a vessel for my people. Even with his knowledge of magic, the black man is often helpless. The unity of our tribal customs has been lost in the struggle between the priests of the Ashanti, the Yaruba, the Koramantyn. But you do not spring from among us and therefore you could belong to all. With your youth and your dreams, what is there that you could not do? You could bring back to life the forgotten aspirations of Africa, infuse in our people the pride that has been beaten out of them."

"You will teach me?"

"I can teach you words, rituals, forms, the mixing of herbs, the mystic signs—but these are not enough. The power must grow within you."

"There is no time. I am alone and I am with child. What shall I do?"

Koshi's eyes rested on her for a long time, weighing, measuring her. Then he spoke slowly. "There is a man in Kingston who will marry you. Go to him. He will give you a home, security. It is the first step that may lead to power and to freedom—for you—perhaps for my people."

"No," Kate cried, "no."

Koshi spread his hands over his knees and his eyes closed. Kate called his name several times but there was no answer. She stood up and Mario came to her side. They started back down the rutted lane, this time walking side by side.

The flimsy shanties and bars of the water front had

103

sprung up again, as closely bunched together as before the fire. In the late afternoon the harbor was in a tumult. A Yankee trader and a blackbirder hugged the new wharf at Kerry's jetty. Men rolled hogsheads through the cobbled streets, stood about in clusters arguing the price of slaves, or drank in the dingy bars.

The presence of a white woman amid the hurly-burly of the docks was enough to turn the eyes of the men or cause them to stop in the middle of an oath. But the sight of Kate Donley, walking serene and level-eyed through the turmoil of Musty Lane, changed the brawling and the hubhub to tense silence. She pushed her way among the half-naked Negro stevedores, the snarling foremen and the drunken sailors without giving them a glance. The rays of the sun sent red gleams through the upswept mass of her hair. Color was in her cheeks and her eyes were bright. If she heard the comments that followed her, she gave no sign.

"Gawd, she's a beauty. Who is she?"

"Like as not she's o' the Christian Steps."

"Leave her be, mon. She's some captain's bawd."

The Salamander Tavern stood at the head of Pickny Alley, not far from where the Laughing Donkey once had been. The Salamander was made partly of charred boards from the buildings which had not completely burned, partly from the dark lumber of the island. Even from a distance the sound of raucous laughter was clear and above it was the mournful strain of the bagpipes.

Kate gave a twisted little smile. She was glad that MacFeathers would be at the Salamander. It would not be so hard to face Gabe Cousins. She forced herself to remember the words of the tune the Scot was playing. Mullen had taught them to her long ago.

> The fair was just the same as then
> Five years ago today,
> When first you left the thimble men
> And came with me away;
> For here again are thimble men
> And card-trick men and maggie-men
> Of all sorts and degrees.

Yes, there would be card-trick men and maggie-men aplenty at the Salamander, she thought wryly. And there would be the sour face and crabbed voice of Gabriel Cousins. The stench of stale beer, the leers, the rough hands, the coarse speech of sailors. She shuddered, stopped and half turned. The wild instinct to run was upon her, but her face remained calm. The fear went and nausea took its place. She grasped the dusty spoke of an empty wagon to steady herself. She spread her begrimed palm in front of her and looked at it, but what she saw was the barren cell of the Convent and the mahogany staircase at Rune Hall. Then there was Mullen, back erect, walking up the thirteen steps to death. She straightened and her eyes sparkled with anger. Unhurriedly and surely, she crossed the roadway and entered the open door of the Salamander Tavern.

A seaman at the bar turned and saw her. "Gaw help me," he cried, " 'tis a vision!"

Silence came over the dingy tavern at the other drinkers stared at the girl. Gabriel Cousins, his shirt rolled, his arms elbow-deep in a pail of murky water, glanced up. His tight mouth fell open to show the yellow stubs of his teeth. No one moved until MacFeathers began to play a lilting tune. The men resumed their talk, but their eyes kept flicking back to the girl.

Gabe Cousins wiped his arms slowly on the black apron that dangled at his waist. Kate came to the bar, so that she faced him.

"What be ye wantin' o' me?" he growled. "Ye've bought y' freedom. Now I've naught what ye want."

"You're wrong about that. Let me talk to you—some place where no one will hear."

Cousins scrowled, but he tossed aside the apron and led the way through a door beside the bar. The tiny room was bare save for a cot, a crate, an empty hogshead and a few scattered clothes.

" 'Tis hard times I've been havin' since the Donkey burned," Cousins grumbled. "And all o' Mannie's savin's disappeared." His eyes swept Kate's face and she thought there was suspicion in them. " 'Tis fine clo'se ye be wearin'," he continued, "for one as was a bound girl six weeks gone by. Jonathan Minor it is what pays for 'em, I'll be bound."

Kate flushed but she kept her voice even. "You're mistaken, Gabe."

Cousins spat on the littered floor. "So Gabe it is now. A fine one ye be and a bold one, Kate, comin' here to flaunt in me face that ye choose to be the tart o' the likes o' Jonathan Minor rather than the wife o' the likes o' me."

"That's not true."

"He bought ye from me, did he not? Am I to believe that Jonathan Minor's a mon of charity? Do ye think me daft, Kate? Ye've sold ye'self to be his whore."

"No." The word came shaply and Kate's eyes blazed.

Cousins' gaze dropped to the floor and his voice changed to a mumble. " 'Tis a cruel lass ye are, Kate. In the nights I been a-thinkin' o' ye and a-wantin' ye bad. And once I had ye for me ain and I could have had me way wi' ye. Now ye come back and flaunt ye'self before me. Ay, what's a mon to do?"

Slowly, painfully, Kate spoke the words she had come to say, "You asked me once to marry you, Gabe. Do you still wish it?"

Cousins looked up startled. "Be this some jest? Ye've gone far since ye left the Donkey."

" 'Tis no jest. If you want me I'll come to you."

Cousins' face suddenly turned livid, "Ye'll come to me stained wi' the Christian Steps. Ye'll come to me fobbed off by Jonathan Minor." He jumped up and paced the room. " 'Tis not for love of me ye'll come. Be ye wi' child o' Jonathan?"

Kate looked down at her swelling breasts. "No, you do Minor wrong. But I am with child. It happened before I knew Minor, before you won my papers."

"Lunt," roared Cousins. "Am I to give name to his bastard?"

"Not Lunt either."

"Then who?"

"I do not even know his name." She hesitated as she told the lie and Percy Morgan's handsome, youthful face was vivid in her memory. "He was a seaman on the *Liza Mae*. By God, you cannot blame a bound girl for what happens by force."

Cousins sat down on the bed. His face worked with passion. He clasped and unclasped the fingers of his hands and rubbed them over his knuckles. Then, without further warning, the tears started down his face and spasms shook his frail body. "Kate, I been a-wantin' and a-wantin' ye. All through the day. All through the day. And now ye come to me like this. A-scornin' me, I know. Takin' me 'cause there's none other. Well, I'll take ye, Kate. I'll take ye any way ye will. I'll take ye. But tell me one thing. Tell me ye dinna hate me."

"I do not hate you, Gabe. Why should I?"

"Can ye say ye love me, gal?"

"I've said I'll marry you."

"But ye dinna say you love me."

Slowly, coldly, Kate forced herself to speak the three words.

Gabriel Cousins came to her and fell on his knees before her. He buried his head in her lap. Kate shuddered and lifted her hands to push him away. But the hands stopped in mid-air. Slowly they dropped to her side. Her body was cold, even here in the stifling room. She did not look down at Gabe Cousins but straight ahead. "This is the first step," she told herself, "the first step."

She pulled herself free from his embrace and went swiftly to the bar. When Gabe followed her to the door she was behind the counter, her hands deep in the bucket of murky water in which he had been washing the pewter tankards.

He went to her and placed his hand on her arm, but she turned to him for only a moment. "There are men that need serving, Gabe," she said. "Do not keep them waiting."

BOOK TWO

1799

9

THE SALAMANDER TAVERN at the edge of the Parade bore little resemblance to the patched up water-front shack which had borne the name five years before. A wide veranda circled the lower floor. Within, there was a great hall, kept moderately cool by the high ceiling which stretched all the way to the roof of the building. Two tiers of balconies, with wrought-iron balustrades, broke the severity of the design. Square pillars of mahoe wood supported the balconies, and the potted palms which stood before each pillar gave an air of shabby gentility to the hall. The Salamander was neither large nor ornate but it represented the best that Jamaica had to offer in the way of inns in 1799.

Kate Cousins looked out through the jalousie over the Parade. The years had dealt kindly with Kate. The sullenness had left her face and was replaced by a look of calm pride that verged upon arrogance. None of her movements was awkward now, and though she held herself erect and haughty, there was an almost feline grace to her full body. Her eyes took in the familiar scene. Red-coated soldiers promenaded in solemn dignity before their low barracks to the east, and the new Theatre Royal, with its red brick front and white balustrades, could be glimpsed on the far side of the open square. A few horsemen, with frock coats and high hats, cantered across the Parade. The rich, lazy voices of nursemaids and the cries of their charges floated into the room. Kate tapped an impatient foot and moved to the doorway, searching for Mullen.

She saw the boy now. He was squatting at the corner of the house. Kneeling beside him was Gabriel Cousins. In

111

Gabe's hand was the young red cock which was his pride and joy. He flicked a twig before the bird's eyes. The cock's flat head darted out venomously and he gave a sharp crow. Mullen laughed and threw back his head and imitated the cock. Gabe's dour face twisted into a crooked grin.

The blood mounted to Kate's cheeks. She took an angry step forward, then checked herself. She did not want Mullen to sense her anger. She wondered how long it would be before the boy heard the story of how Gabe's cock had won her from the Captain of the *Liza Mae*. Mullen's face was turned toward her now and he was still laughing. His hair was blond like her father's but his thin, bronzed face, brown eyes and sensitive lips were strikingly like those of Percy Morgan. Kate's throat tightened as she looked at him, but he turned away almost instantly, fascinated by the cock which was crouching and leaping under Gabe Cousins' skillful guidance.

Gabe did not see his wife until she towered over him. He looked up and licked his gray lips guiltily. His eyes flickered. He cupped the cock in the crook of his arm and got up.

Kate kept her voice cold. "I've told you not to teach the boy your rough ways."

"Ah, 'tis a mollycoddle ye'll make of him."

Kate's eyes sparkled dangerously, and she seemed about to exchange sharp words with her husband. But at this moment from the Parade came the sound of a conch shell being blown and the uneven beat of goatskin drums. A man, mounted on a bay, rode from King Street onto the Parade. He was dressed in a high hat with a wide yellow band, a coat of black and yellow stripes, and yellow breeches. Flanking him on either side were two Negroes in red and yellow uniforms, straddling mules. Just behind was another liveried Negro on foot, staggering under the weight of a gigantic flag of England which hung limply from its white pole.

The leader raised his conch and let out a long blast. The two behind him beat the drums. Out onto the Parade stumbled a mass of nearly naked Negroes, shackled and bound together in groups of four. Six guards with blunderbusses and lashes watched over them. From time to time there was a sharp swish of a lash and an agonized cry.

As the procession came closer Kate could see the terror in the faces of the slaves. Their eyes rolled, their lips drew back from their teeth and some were shaking so that they could scarcely walk. The last two lines were women. Bands of Russian duck circled their waists loosely but their breasts were bare and their kinky hair awry. The belly of one was round, swollen high with child. She gave a cry that changed to a moan, and lunged forward. The heavy chain jerked her back and she fell to the ground carrying another woman with her. To Kate's horror, a guard stepped close and his lash cracked. A scream rent the air as the long strap curled about the woman's waist.

The lead man stopped his horse and raised his conch to his lips again. "Hear ye! Hear ye!" 'he cried. "Ye good people of Kingston. Tomorrow at nine o'clock, at Kerry's jetty, will be sold the slaves brought to Jamaica on the brigantine *Crescent Moon*, sailing out of Lourenço Marques. Thirty-two men and sixteen women will be placed on the block at Kerry's jetty at nine o'clock tomorrow. Hear ye! Hear ye!"

The ragged procession straggled on. Mullen pulled loose from his mother's hand and ran to join the children and the loungers who attached themselves to the parade. Kate called to him but he did not return.

Gabe Cousins grumbled, "Leave him be, Kate. 'Tis a mon he must learn to be."

" 'Tis a gentleman and a power on the island Mullen will become, not a ruffian nor a sniveling drunk."

"Ah, be not so hard on me, Kate—nor on ye'self or the lad."

" 'Tis little you can say. Taking him with you midst the water-front scran. Teaching him the ways of the cock-fighting bullies. 'Tis a fine one you'll make of him, fit for a cell in Kykorn gaol."

Cousins spat and his voice was sour. "Gaw, 'tis no fine blood I have in me veins, but none o' me kin e'er trod the air of Galway Crossin'."

Kate's face turned scarlet and her eyes were ablaze. "Keep away from Mullen. I warn you, Gabe Cousins."

"You're a harsh un, lass. 'Tis good enough I am to give

113

ye bastard a name but not good enough to have a hand in his raisin'."

Kate stemmed the angry words that sprang to her lips. She said softly, "A black gal I'll be getting tomorrow. He'll have no further need of you."

"Ay, a black nanny and a velvet coat to make o' Mullen a cockalorum. Were he mine, it wouldna' be, so help me, Kate."

Next day, a stiff breeze whipped the huge black and yellow flag of the slave market so that it snapped and crackled. The *Crescent Moon*, still reeking with the foul stench of its burden, lay off the jetty, while within the dark warehouse nearly six hundred slaves were packed. Their long, slow, dolorous chanting rose and fell. The men were firmly shackled to long strands of heavy wire that ran the length of the warehouse. Most of the women and children ran free within the enclosure.

Already the square at the head of Kerry's jetty had taken on the look of a fair. Factors in gayly colored breeches and white stocks argued with shabby lawyers. A few carriages were drawn up by the wharf and the planters called to one another while their ladies cooled themselves with bright Chinese fans. Liveried servants lolled on their boxes and bare-footed Negroes, free for the day, champed sugar cane as they lounged in the sun.

Fat, ebony-colored women dressed in bandanas and linsey-woolsey petticoats of pink, red and blue sold the island fruit from grass braskets or form improvised stands. Mangoes, genips, soursops and tamarinds gleamed brightly in the hot sun. Beneath the raised stand that bore the giant block of mahogany wood a group of musicians beat out an excited African rhythm. The instruments were crude, made on the island. There was a kitty-katty, a thin board beaten with incredible speed until it howled like fighting cats; a cassand grater rubbed with spoons to make a cracking noise; a jenkoving, two jars with ordinary-size mouths over which the player brought down his palms, making sucking sounds; a calabash filled with Indian shot. The musicians laughed and called to one another as they played, so that the moans of the shackled captives in the warehouse could scarcely be heard.

MacFeathers was there, his bagpipes slung across his arm. He sat chatting with Bard, who had just returned to Jamaica after two years at sea and who was now commissioned by the master of the *Crescent Moon* to see that no slave went too cheaply. Jonathan Minor's coach, with Mario on the box, was close to the slave block. Jonathan stood with his hand resting on the bay's flank. A little group of men had gathered about him to ask questions. He answered softly, nodding his head from time to time. Jonathan's face had grown leaner and more sallow. The gray at his temples had spread until now there was little color left in his hair. He stooped a little, but he was still commanding in appearance and still dressed fastidiously.

Kate Cousins' kittereen pushed its way into the crowded square just as Isaac Gomes, the auctioneer, took his place on the raised platform. Eyes turned away from the platform toward Kate. A space had cleared around the kittereen, and as she stepped to the ground, the bright sun caught the gleam of her hair and flashed on the flame-colored satin of her gown. She stood tall, erect, smiling a little but nodding to none. Even Gomes stopped after the first few words of his harangue to look at her.

The Negro women with the fruit baskets crossed themselves, for already the word that Kate possessed the power of obeah had spread among the slaves and the freedmen. The ladies in the carriages looked with envy from behind their shielding fans at Kate's clear skin and firm breasts. The youthful bookkeepers, just out from England, shifted their positions to see her better, and the petty officers on guard at the warehouse door winked at each other. But only MacFeathers approached her.

Kate smiled down into the Scot's wrinkled face and tapped his hand with her fan. "Was there sickness on the *Crescent Moon?*" she whispered. "Surely she did not come from Lourenço Marques with only forty-eight slaves between her decks."

The Scot grunted. "Indeed she didna. There's more than six hundred in Kerry warehouse. But 'tis always the same. They're marked for St. Joseph or Charleston, while Kingston gets the culls. Ay, 'tis a pity. The weak and the sick have no the backs for the cane. Here we are the center o' the trade but we get naught but the worst o' the pickings.

115

They'll put a few strong men up as a sop; the rest will go to the Yankees."

As MacFeathers talked, the slaves who were to be sold were led out on the platform. Shackles bound their ankles so that they walked with a shuffling gait. One by one they mounted the steps with difficulty, were paraded across the length of the platform and then pushed to the back. The crowd gathered close, peering at the nearly naked blacks. Coarse jests and laughter made it almost impossible to hear Gomes' words.

The first slave placed on the block was the color of coal. He was thin to the point of emaciation and his head hung to one side as though it were too heavy to raise. The factors ran their hands across his arms and Gomes forced open his mouth.

"He's sick, mon," a factor cried. "What good's a pulin' nigger? He'll go first to the pen."

Gomes' lash struck the slave's bare buttocks and the Negro gave a bleating cry.

"Up with ye head, nigger. Let 'em see what a pocky boy ye be."

The slave cringed and whimpered. Gomes' lash came down again. The slave hid his head in his arms. Gomes' face turned dark with anger. "Lift ye head, I tell ye. God Almighty!" His arm raised a third time. From the fruit stalls there came a woman's call, clear and piercing, and then a tumble of words in Eboe dialect.

The Negro raised his head and looked dully at his tormentors. The bidding started but it was slow. After a few minutes the sick man was knocked down to Brandon's factor for fifteen guineas.

The next slave was brought to the block. He was a huge man, with great shoulders. The muscles bunched in his arms and thighs. Besides the shackles on his ankles, his wrists were securely tied together. Even so, as he was led forth he lunged forward and his teeth sank deep into the arm of a guard. Gomes struck him brutally with the butt of his whip and the Negro fell down face forward. Instantly Gomes was on him and twisting a length of rope in his mouth. The Negro stood up, his eyes wild, the muscles of his face and throat straining, his hands pressing against

116

the bonds until blood covered the chain. Crimson welts crisscrossed his back and shoulders.

"Here's a strong un for ye," Gomes cried. "A nigger who'll make ye a fine field hand. Look at the chest, the arms—"

"Gaw, I couldna sleep with the likes o' he about," a factor complained.

"Ach! A few drops o' the ebony and ye'll na know a meeker slave."

"Send 'im to Saint Jo. Once he's loose, he'll jine o' Buddhoe's men."

Sharply, peremptorily, Jonathan Minor's voice broke through. "Ten guineas."

"Ah, Mr. Minor, 'tis an insult ye offer, not a price."

Bard's surly voice raised the bid at a signal from the Captain of the *Crescent Moon*.

"Don't close the bids. Don't close the bids." The call was shrill and fluttery. Guffaws came from the crowd. " 'Tis Connie Abbott, I'll be blowed. . . . Hah, Connie."

An angular woman with carmined cheeks, painted mouth and tight, yellow curls sidled her way toward the block. Her step was mincing and her multicolored parasol bobbed up and down as she walked. Her wide-rimmed, floppy hat was decorated with bows of ribbons and artificial flowers. Her pastel gown was somewhat stained. The yellow skin of her hands and arms was nearly concealed by masses of rings and bracelets. She was Constantia Abbott, who had come to Kingston two years before and opened the most luxurious of the island's bawdy-houses. Queen's Court had nearly put the Christian Steps out of business and Connie Abbott and Lettie Parsons had become the most bitter of rivals.

Connie Abbott stepped up to the platform. "Coo, he's a handsome beast," she fluted.

"Be not the lads o' Kingston strong enow for ye, Connie?" someone called.

Connie glanced up at the speaker. "They tell me it's no man of iron you are, Job, my friend."

While laughter rocked the crowd, Connie's clawlike hand stroked the arm of the huge Negro. She gave little cries of pleasure as she rubbed the man's flank and slapped the buttock. The Negro's mouth worked until the gag cut deep into the sides and the blood trickled across his jaws. His eyes were frantic with fear and anger.

MacFeathers had edged his way close to the woman. "Be not such a fool, Connie. The mon's killing mad. He'll break ye in two once his bonds are loosed. Let him be. Dinna play such a game, 'tis too dangerous."

"Ah, pay your garnish, MacFeathers. Next time you visit the Queen's Court, I'll have him in a jacket o' green, serving confect cakes." She raised her narrow brows archly. "A handsome boy he'll make. More than fit to serve the jack-boots o' Jamaica." She turned to Gomes. "I bid thirty guineas."

"Thirty-five." Bard raised the price.

"Forty, 'tis my last bid." Connie looked at Bard defiantly. Bard's eyes swung to the Captain, who made no sign.

Gomes said gruffly, "We'll deliver him to ye in chains, me lass, and we'll not be there when they're taken off." The crowd was growing rowdy and Gomes signaled nervously for the next slave to be brought to the block.

Few of the slaves looked fit for heavy work and the bidding was slow. The factors resented the fact that the cream of the crop was being shipped on to the States and they called out insults to Gomes. From time to time the swarthy auctioneer ordered one of the black women to the dock. After all, the women were the main reason for the gathering of the crowd. The factors and bookkeepers fingered the merchandise lasciviously. They pulled breasts, slapped buttocks and examined tribal marks, to the accompaniment of jests and laughter.

Kate had taken no part in the proceedings. She stood aloof, her face expressionless. She had seen the slave whom she intended to purchase and she waited patiently until the girl should be brought to the block. She could not be more than fourteen, small-boned and thin. Her skin was deep-black, tinged with blue. He face was sensitive, the forehead high, the lips thick but finely formed, the eyes set deep.

Kate moved forward only when she saw that the girl had been ordered to the block. Kate's movements were swift and sure. The men fell away at the sight of her and the mockery and lascivious laughter ceased. Gomes looked at Kate curiously as he motioned the girl to take her place. The girl's breasts were newly formed, firm and pointed, and the slender body was still that of a child.

Gomes did not call for bids but spoke directly to Kate, asking her for a price. Kate bid thirty guineas—a more than fair price for the frail girl. Gomes nodded as though to close the deal but a second bid came in. Jonathan Minor raised the price by a single guinea. He had come close to the block and his gray eyes searched Kate's face with mocking arrogance.

Kate's eyes rested on him for a moment, but she gave no sign of recognition. Since the day five years before when she had slapped his face at Rune Hall the two had never spoken. Calmly Kate raised the bid still another guinea.

The crowd was quiet, sensing the conflict between the two without understanding it. Slowly guinea by guinea, the price rose until it was more than twice the original bid. Sixty guineas for the girl was incredible and when the bid rose to seventy-five it was fantastic. Gomes looked uncomfortably from one to the other of the contestants and the crowd moved restlessly.

Jonathan Minor gave way at last. With a shrug of his shoulders and a half-bow to Kate he signified the close of his bid and, without further word, he turned and strode away.

Kate was angry with herself, with Minor. True, the Salamander brought in a fair revenue but not sufficient to pour out money on an act of willful pride. She knew that Minor had intended to humiliate her, that in some subtle way, he wished to re-establish the relationship of the powerful government official taking pity on a bound girl. She half suspected the truth—that if she had closed the bid, Minor would have offered her the girl as a gift.

Kate's eyes stung with vexation as she looked at the girl and a flood of hatred enveloped her. The girl moved quietly from the block and came to stand beside her new mistress. Kate had the desire to strike her but fought it down. The girl's eyes had remained cast down at her feet, but now she looked up quickly, hopefully. Then Mario stepped between them.

Mario was no longer a boy. He was well over six feet, and though he was still thin and his shoulders narrow, yet there was lithe strength in his movements. Mario spoke swiftly in Ashanti dialect to the girl. She nodded and again looked at Kate.

Mario turned. "She is one of us, an Ashanti," he said. "I have told her to obey you in all things. I have told her that you will be good to her—that you will see no harm comes to her."

When Kate did not answer, Mario added softly, "I hope that what I have spoken is true."

But Kate's face remained expressionless as with a peremptory gesture she signaled to the girl to come with her.

10

FEAR WAS NEVER ABSENT in Kingston. Despite the gay balls, the house parties, the flourishing theaters and the horse races, men seldom walked the streets of the city unarmed. Danger came from many sources. There was the tropical hurricanes against which there were no weapons. There was an occasional marauding ship which dared the cannons of the harbor. There was the constant danger of fire which could not be checked. There were crimp gangs which had even been known to set upon a gentleman in satin breeches and stock if he were found in a lonely spot. There were bands of thugs that roamed the water front, ready to waylay and rob any chance passer-by.

But the most pressing danger sprang from the very source which had brought prosperity to the island. The slave trade had made Jamaica rich but it was also the cause of constant alarm. Far up in the Cockpit country more than three thousand blacks had formed a colony of their own called Accompong. It dated back to 1665 when a ragamuffin British army, under the command of Penn and Venables, had landed on the island and slaughtered the Spanish garrison. The slaves had revolted during the fighting and, led by a pitch-black Ashanti priest named Cudjoe, had made their way to the hills. No English expeditionary force had ever been able to route them from their fastnesses among the cockpits nor to stop their depredations of the countryside. Contemptuously, the remaining Spanish planters had given the name Marroñas, meaning pigs, to the Negro band. The English, with equal contempt, had changed the word to Maroons.

The name had stuck, even when the contempt had disappeared. Cudjoe and his band had proved themselves masters at bushfighting. One English regiment sent to Accompong had disappeared completely. At length the British, in despair, made a treaty with Cudjoe. They promised not only freedom from further attacks, but semi-annual supplies of food to the Maroons. In return the Maroon chief Cudjoe agreed to stop his raids and to return run-away slaves.

Neither side kept their promises well. A new governor seized the Maroon emissaries and tortured them to death and the reprisals started again. When food was scarce, the Maroons descended on the sugar estates and plundered them. Few slaves were ever returned.

The Maroon chiefs were known alternately as Cudjoe and Buddhoe. For almost a century and a half the lineal descent of the chiefs had been kept intact. The present Buddhoe was a squat, ill-formed man, ugly of face and feature, but a capable warrior. When Governor Stallybrass first came to Jamaica, Buddhoe had presented himself at the Governor's palace. He wore a tricorn hat over his frizzy head, a red jacket, white silk breeches and no shoes. The jacket had been taken from a British soldier killed two decades before. Gold buttons and yellow braid had been sewn upon it in profusion. The silk breeches were stained and they bagged at the knees. Buddhoe's feet were large and caked with mud. His toes were splayed. Stallybrass looked the Maroon chief over with ill-disguised amusement. An aide whispered a word of warning in the Governor's ear and Stallybrass proceeded with the conference with dignity. But Buddhoe was not deceived. He never forgot the first look of mockery and disdain on Stallybrass' face and he never felt bound to honor his pledge to the rotund governor.

Buddhoe's raids were not frequent but they were always daring and spectacular. He invariably appeared on the scene himself. Once resistance had been quelled, he rarely used violence. The ladies were treated with elaborate courtesy. The men were bound but seldom hurt, save in those instances where one had dared to hurl an insult at the Maroon chief. In such cases Buddhoe could act with merciless savagery. Once he had ordered a white planter stripped and flogged before the women of his household. Again when dealing with a brutal and foul-mouthed overseer, Buddhoe himself had cut out the man's tongue and sliced off his ears and the tip of his nose.

The big estates had been made over into arsenals, with swivel guns on their roofs and armed sentries at the entrances. Almost mockingly, Buddhoe had offered a detachment of Maroon soldiers to guard the Parade and the Governor's mansion. Stallybrass accepted and the red-coated Maroons formed the bulwark of Kingston's garrison. They had proven themselves capable soldiers but their constant presence in the center of the city did not soothe the uneasiness of the white Jamaicans.

Buddhoe had pledged the return of runaway slaves, but he seldom admitted that one had arrived in Accompong. Under the legal code of Jamaica, the most drastic punishments could be exacted upon the runaways. Either for the sake of appearance, or because a Negro had given trouble in Accompong an occasional slave was returned. However, in these cases an agreement was always reached, through one of Buddhoe's emissaries, concerning the punishment of the runaway. Koshi was frequently called upon in such transactions for he was trusted by both the English and the Maroons.

The passes that led to the Cockpit country were kept under vigil day and night, and the guards mercilessly beat and tortured any Negro whom they caught trying to slip through. Nevertheless, the freedom offered at Accompong served as a constant lure for the slaves.

Few men and no women cared to travel outside of Kingston except under heavy guard. Kate Cousins alone among the island women ignored the taboos and defied the dangers of the open places. Her kittereen, drawn by her white stallion, was often seen passing through the freedmen's settlement of Baraçong or dashing along the beach road that led to Port Royal. The strip of white sand that overlooked the old sunken city had a particular fascination for her. Rumors spread through the island. Some said that she talked aloud as she walked along the beach, calling up the power of the damned souls of those who had died when a tidal wave had plunged the wild pirate stronghold of Port Royal to the bottom of the sea on a sweltering June morning in 1692. The Negroes swore that they saw ghostly forms walk with her and that whenever her kittereen appeared on the roadway, the church bell which lay in its tower twenty feet beneath the surface of the water began to toll softly.

Only one human was ever seen to join her on the beach. This was Koshi. Slowly, carefully, he taught her of the power and the menace that lay in simple things. An ordinary lime, cut in half, could suck up evil. If the two halves were placed at either side of the doorsill of a house, trouble would enter to afflict those within. Kate had laughed but the old man's face was grave. "The lime is the fruit of death," he warned.

"Then murder must be easy."

"No. The lime is the symbol of malevolence. The power springs from the mind, the will and the spirit of him who uses this symbol. Obeah is not to be trifled with, my child. The weak one who traffics in obeah courts insanity. Obeah is the evil that fights evil—the power that resists power. It is the word of death, the source of life."

"You speak in riddles, Koshi." She stopped and looked up at the high turret of Rune Hall, rising above the almond trees of the hill. "Can obeah make me mistress of Rune Hall?"

Koshi smiled sadly. "You want too small a thing. Do not let petty ambition shrivel your soul."

Kate glanced at him and her eyes were angry. "Is Rune Hall less important than the theft of a banana, or the making of a love philter?"

"Stealing and loving are a part of life. One is the same before and after either act. There is no dissipation of the spirit."

"I have done with the kneeling for prayers and the burning of candles. Mario told me once that obeah is practical.

It can cure the sick or kill the healthy. It can bring wealth, power, revenge. Such is the religion I want."

Koshi shook his grizzled head. "How impatient you are, my child. When you are angry you forget all that I have told you. Obeah is not a religion like Voodoo. Voodoo keeps alive the tribal ceremonies and old religious rites of the Ashanti. In Voodoo, a priest and a priestess must meet together in the presence of the sacred fetish, but this is not true of obeah. The adept works alone. He uses his knowledge of the ways of nature, the effects of drugs, the fears and ignorance of mankind, to free himself from the molestations of life."

Kate was not listening. Her eyes were still on the turret of Rune Hall. When she turned the old man had disappeared. The sky was flooded with the brilliant colors of the tropical sunset. She walked back across the beach to where the stallion pawed the sand. Discontent showed clearly in her face. Her affairs were moving too slowly. She was twenty-three and saddled with a dreary old man whom she despised. The rich and varied life of Kingston was not for her. The Governor's ballroom, the spacious courts of Hibbert Hall, the luxuries of Montego Bay were denied to the wife of a mere tavernkeeper as completely as though she were still a bound girl.

At the thought of Gabriel Cousins her face hardened. She remembered his clumsy embraces on their wedding night, the foulness of his breath as his lips touched hers, her shock and horror at the moment of coition. The humbleness had gone out of him then. "Ay, ye be mine now, gal," he had gloated, "ye be me own true wifie." He had fallen asleep beside her and numbly she had endured the touch of his head against her breast, the pressure of his thigh on her cold skin. She had neither slept nor moved during the night. But when the gray light of early morning had filtered into the room, she freed herself from Gabe's slack embrace and stood up. She looked down at the ugly, sallow face, at the balding head. His mouth was open and the teeth showed like blunted fangs. His breathing was hoarse, labored. A stubble of gray beard stained the yellow skin.

She had been sick with loathing. She went swiftly to the doorway and flung it open. She fell on all fours amid the weeds of the garden, rested her face on the damp earth until the nausea passed. When she came back, Gabe was awake. He had tried to pull her down beside him, murmuring endearing words. She pulled herself free and he sat up on the bed and grasped her firmly about the waist. She pushed his face backward with the heel of her hand.

"Leave me alone," she had shouted. "Never touch me again."

Gabe's mouth fell open in unbelief. "Ye be me wife, lass. Do ye not know the duties o' a woman?"

"If you ever do that to me again I'll kill you."

"Ye canna treat me this a-way. I'm your 'osband. Dinna ye understand?" He leapt from the bed, his short nightshirt ludicrously tight across his knobby knees. His arms encircled her breasts and his fetid breath was on her face.

She raised her knee with all the weight of her young body behind it. She felt the sickening impact as the bone struck the groin. Gabe's scream broke off almost as soon as it had started. His eyes glazed over. She pushed him back on the bed and stood over him as he lay writhing in pain. There was no pity in her face, only repugnance and cold anger. "Never try that again. Never—never—never."

She had walked away from him and gone to the little kitchen. She had built a charcoal fire, found salt pork and rice and cooked it for him. This she would do—prepare his meals, clean his house, tend his bar. But never again would she go to his bed.

Now, as she strode across the sands of Port Royal, she was so engrossed in her angry memories that she did not see the figure that waited, squatting by her kittereen.

The man arose and his hand was on her wrist before she realized that he was there. She sucked in her breath sharply as she recognized Bard. The seaman had been away from the island for several years, but when she had seen him at the slave auction, she had feared he might make further trouble for her. Bard chuckled. "Ye need na be afeard o' me, Kate. 'Tis only an old friend come to see ye."

Dusk had fallen and a pale gray mist was beginning to blow in from the bay. The man's wide-rimmed hat cast a shadow over his eyes and his round face was a pale brown blob.

Kate kept her voice level. She said, "You're right, Bard. The likes of you could never frighten me."

Bard's chuckle turned to laughter. "What a high and mighty wench ye be, Kate. Have ye no kind word for Bard?"

"Not now or ever. Why are you traipsing after me? Did you not get a bellyful at the Laughing Donkey?"

"How harsh ye speak, Kate. But 'twas not for love I came to see ye. Though 'twould not make me unhappy to spend a night with ye."

"That will never happen. What do you want?"

Bard's tones assumed a whining quality. "Always it's the bad luck as comes me way, lass. Up to Salem I been in a four-master. An' a thievin' captain I drew, who ne'er a penny would gie us when back to Kingston we come. A-liftin' prices for the master o' the *Crescent Moon*— that's been me lay sin' I been back. A stingy mon is Master Creighton and the guineas he gie me have went for food now two days gone."

" 'Tis grog, not food, that picks your pockets, Bard. Grog and dice, I think."

"Maybe it is you're right, gal. But I seen ye biddin' in the black wench for seventy-five guineas—a fortune! 'Twas a pretty sight to see ye take her off o' Jonathan Minor. When the gal is older, she'd a-give Jonathan many a merry night."

"What's all this to do with me?"

"It could be ye could spare a few bits for a man as needs it bad. Eh, gal?"

Kate looked about. The mist was blowing in thick, carrying a thin spray with it. Bard's hand was still heavy on her wrist, the fingers bruising the flesh. She saw that he had taken the whip from its socket and thrown it on the sand. She said slowly, "I've only a few coins in my purse. You know 'tis dangerous to carry much in Kingston."

" 'Twill do, lass. 'Twill do for the present."

Kate let him take the purse from her and dump the coins into his palm. He jingled them a few times. " 'Twill buy me a noggin. Ye're a good lass, Kate. 'Tis soon I'll be seein' ye again." He released her wrist and mockingly offered her his arm as she stepped into the kittereen.

Kate felt a chill of fear sweep over her, sensing the threat in his words without understanding their meaning. She reached for the reins but Bard's hand clasped them close.

"I want no more of you, Bard," she said. "You've what coin I have, now let me go. I'll say nought of this, but next time 'twill be different."

Bard guffawed. "It's not murder ye're thinkin' o', be it, Kate?"

"Murder?" Kate's heart beat fast at the word. "No, 'tis Kykorn Gaol, where you'll land."

"Not me, Kate, not me."

"What do you mean?" Kate could not keep the shrillness from her voice.

"In Salem town I met an old friend o' yourn. Name o' Percy Morgan. Ah, Percy's doin' all right by himself, you'll be glad to know. A bonnie boy is Percy and tight-lipped enough most o' the time. But I put enough drinks in 'im to loosen his tongue a bit. With a mite o' proddin' 'twas a strange tale I got from the lad. A tale o' Mannie Cousins' gold and Mannie's broken head. Yes, Percy's a good lad, Kate. Ye should have kept 'im with ye; 'tis a better mon he is than that Gabe o' yourn."

Kate sat still on the seat of the carriage. Her hands were trembling and she dared not speak. She was surprised at the sudden rush of emotion which had swept over her at the mention of Percy Morgan's name. She had thrust the memory of him back into the hidden places of her mind, yet sometimes in the night when she was sickened by the breathing of Gabe and her anger at Jonathan Minor, her pulse would quicken with the thought of Percy. She doubted that he had told the full story to Bard, but in some way he had confirmed the sailor's suspicions. She struggled to keep her face expressionless, to give no hint of the turmoil within her.

Bard turned and took a few steps from her. He picked up the whip that lay on the sand, then returned and handed it to Kate. He said softly, " 'Twould not be wise to make me angry, gal. Because I'll be seein' a lot o' ye. For Percy's sake. Percy would like us to be friends."

11

THE SERVANTS of the Salamander were gathered about the stairs that descended from the balconies to the main hall of the inn. Their high-pitched voices rose to an excited din. "Ge' i-way. Don' ge'ee near me," an excited fuzzy-haired black woman said. "In this house bad bad," another woman stated solemnly. Servant girls from the Parade crowded into the doors and loungers peered in through the jalousies. Squeals and groans added to the confusion.

Kate Cousins owned but two slaves. The other servants of the Salamander were freedwomen, working for a daily pittance. The slave was a chattel owned outright by his master, but for this very reason he often fared better than the freedman. The slave was clothed, fed and provided with some medical care. He was usually given two half holidays a week, permitted to grow a small garden, and he was bred with the same care that the planters gave to their horses. Inasmuch as he was a salable object his value was not permitted to deteriorate. The freedman could not be compelled to work and, theoretically at least, he could not be beaten. He had certain rights in a court of law though the word of a black, according to colonial decree, must be considered void if contradicted by a single white person.

Kate paid a quattie a day for the services of the freed-women and used them when she wished. The arrangement was cheaper than the purchase of slaves, but when the women were slack in their work she had little power over them. It was common knowledge that she herself had once been a bound girl and she often suspected that the words she heard muttered in various African dialects were pointed jibes at her former position. Her tongue was sharp as she moved among the women, seeing that the floors were scrubbed, the beds made, the food properly cooked. The faces of the women turned sullen at her approach. They mumbled to themselves and kept their eyes averted.

Sister Sweetie Gourd was the largest of the women. She had skin that was jet black and smooth as velvet. Her eyes were huge. Her broad, flat nose ended in flaring nostrils. Her lips were thick and pink, her large teeth glistening white. Her hair was always bound in a bandana and great loops of gold hung from her ears. She liked bright colors, especially pink. Her laughter was rich and strong and it shook her whole massive body. Her appearance of good humor, however, was deceptive. Kate soon learned that the other women feared Sweetie Gourd, not only because of her quick temper and great strength, but also because she was rumored to have "pow'ful obi."

The special butt of Sweetie Gourd's ill-humor was the young slave girl whom Kate had bought in Kerry Square. The girl was so shy that she would scarcely speak. When anyone came near her she drew away as though in fear and lowered her eyes. When touched, even in kindness, she squirmed and tears trickled down her cheeks. The name of Shamey Lady had been given her, for this was the local term for the sensitive plant which recoils and withers at the slightest touch. Only two people had been able to make friends with her. One was Mario, who came to see her nearly every day. He was teaching her English and already she spoke better than many of the slaves who had spent years on the island. The other was Mullen, who adored her. Kate felt a pang of jealousy sometimes when she saw the child clinging to the girl's skirt, or heard him repeating stories to her in his high fluting voice.

Kate had long noted the cruelty of the older woman to Shamey Lady but she had given it little care. The price which she had paid for the slave girl still rankled in Kate's mind. Moreover the meekness of the girl, her shy manners and Mullen's obvious devotion to her, all served as irritants.

The matter had come to a head the afternoon before. Sweetie Gourd had been washing the great hall's floor of tiled wood when Shamey Lady came in with the boy. Mullen was flushed and excited after a walk through the

Parade. Kate had told him to sit still on the divan with Shamey Lady and she had gone to the cook house to draw a glass of milk for him. While she was still there she had heard Sweetie Gourd's voice raised partly in mockery and partly in anger.

When Kate returned, Sweetie Gourd was on her knees a few feet away from the frightened girl and the excited boy. "Why ye no speak? An'her me, ye Ashanti bitch," the big woman was shouting. Shamey Lady hid her face in her hands and her slender body shook.

In a sudden rage, Sweetie Gourd hurled the cloth, dripping with filthy water, at the girl. The cloth missed, spread out and struck Mullen full across the face. The boy howled in terror, and flung it to the floor. He rubbed the dirty water from his face, still screaming.

Then he saw Sweetie Gourd still on all fours, her face loose with fear at what she had done. Mullen ran at her. His foot kicked her in the stomach and his tiny hands clawed her face. Sweetie Gourd scrambled to her feet, and as she did so, the boy fell on the slippery tiles. He lay on his face, kicking and screaming.

The blood mounted to Kate's face and neck as she moved toward the big Nigress.

"I didn' mean nuffin. I didn'—"

Kate still held the glass and she hurled the milk in the woman's face. "Get out," Kate commanded. "Get out."

Sweetie Gourd's fists clenched and for a moment Kate thought she might strike. Kate almost hoped that she would. In Jamaica there was a law that a white who struck a free Negro might be fined two shillings. But a Negro who struck a white or threatened him with violence could be pinched with a red-hot iron or hanged, at the pleasure of the victim.

Sweetie Gourd backed away. Her lips mumbled but there were no intelligible words. Her eyes were bright with malevolence.

Now, on the following morning, the servants were gathered together at the foot of the stairs. Kate heard excited cries and came to the balcony and looked down. At the sight of her, the servants fell silent. Kate looked over the group, Sweetie Gourd was not among them, but she was visible, seated just outside the door. Her bright pink dress made her seem enormous. Her hands were folded in her lap and she stared sightlessly ahead of her.

Shamey Lady saw Kate and slipped away from the group and up the back stairs. She moved toward Kate, her eyes pleading. "Missy no go down stairs. Sister Sweetie Gourd put obi on house. Is bad."

Kate was frightened but she managed a smile. "Don't be silly, Shamey Lady. Sweetie Gourd has no obeah power."

"Oh yes. She have pow'ful obi."

"Nonesense. Let me see the charm." Kate had spoken loudly so that those below could hear.

"No, Missy—"

"Obey me, Shamey Lady. Go to my rooms and bring me my gloves—the white ones."

Shamey Lady darted away and Kate walked slowly to the head of the stairway. She came down the stairs step by step, her eyes on those below her. When she was half-way down, Shamey Lady brought her the gloves. Kate stopped and put them on. Then she started down again very slowly.

As she neared the bottom, the women began to back away. At each of Kate's steps, they retreated almost as though they were engaged in some ritualistic dance.

Kate did not see the charm at first. It lay half hidden beneath the potted palm. It was a small bag of lavender silk, loosely sewed together at the top.

The servants were wide-eyed with terror and several were weeping. "Don't touch ee, Missy," they cried, "don't touch ee. 'E be obi."

Kate looked at them, keeping her face calm, despite her trepidation. This was the test, she knew. If she showed fear of the charm, the servants would leave her and no others would ever stay in the house. If she ignored it, the servants would wait until some slight accident occurred in the house, and then would attribute it to obeah and leave. Only by turning the tables on Sweetie Gourd could she strengthen her position.

Kate's voice carried out to where Sweetie Gourd sat. "Whoever puts an obi on my house is a fool, for I have more powerful obeah than she."

Kate leaned over and picked up the bag. There was a

gasp from the women and the soft sound of wailing. Kate was glad that she had thought to send Shamey Lady for the gloves. Sometimes the charms were rubbed with a local weed which the Jamaicans called cow-itch. This had the power to sting and even to raise blisters on the bare flesh. Kate turned the bag over in her palm but saw no sign of the sharp nettles nor of powder. She felt a sense of relief; the charm was carelessly made. She ripped the silk open and scattered the contents of the bag in her gloved palm.

There was the crisp crackle of thin paper. Some of the strips were red and some black. They were fastened together by hairs which Kate presumed to be her own. She folded back the paper and at the center of the wad found a crudely shaped heart, hacked out of soft pine wood. Glued to the heart was the paring from a fingernail. Kate laughed aloud and looked around at the staring women.

"Come, follow me," she said. She balled the charm loosely in her hand. The sense of foreboding had gone from her, and was replaced by a feeling of power. She walked out onto the Parade where a huge tamarind tree, with bloated limbs and ugly, fore-shortened branches, spread a network of shadows over the parched earth.

She ordered Shamey Lady to go to the kitchen and bring her a live coal. Then, while the Negro women watched in silence, she built a little pile of dried grass and twigs and drew a circle about it with a branch from the tamarind tree. When Shamey Lady returned, Kate placed the coal on the pile and watched until the flames licked upward. She remembered vaguely some of the cabalistic signs that Koshi had taught her and drew these on the ground, adding nonsense symbols of her own. Then she tossed the paper, the crude heart, the hairs and the fingernail on the flames.

The women drew back in terror. Kate looked about for Sweetie Gourd but could not find her. She walked leisurely away leaving the fire burning. The servants did not come back to the Salamander that morning and Shamey Lady lay whimpering and quivering on her pallet in the slave's shed behind the tavern.

At noon, news was brought to Kate of Sweetie Gourd. The big Negress had run from the Parade in fright. At

Harbour Street she had fallen down exhausted. She had screamed of "fire burnin' me heart" and clawed her chest, ripping the cloth of her dress. Her sharp nails lacerated the breasts until blood dripped from them. Her hoarse screams and wild gesticulations drove away those who would have helped her.

She rose again and began running desperately, screaming, swaying, circling. "Obi got me. Obi burn me." The terror blinded her. At Pickny Alley, Brandon's coach with its six horses galloped into Harbour Street. Sweetie Gourd plunged beneath the horses' hoofs. Brandon's coachman had been unable to stop until the huge wheels had passed over the woman's body. Sweetie Gourd's skull was crushed. She died almost instantly.

Kate appeared to be unmoved by the story. She sent for the serving-women. They were frightened and did not want to return. But throughout the afternoon they came back one by one, their faces sheepish. They worked silently for the most part but from time to time Kate heard the whispered words, "double obi." At dusk Koshi came. His face was solemn and stern. He said, "You killed her, my child."

Kate answered softly, "No, her death was of her own making. She died of the fear she herself created."

"That may be. But you knew the power of fire and the ritualistic sign."

"What else could I do? At least the others will not bother me further with obeah."

"That is so. They are afraid. But they will not forgive. They will not use obeah unless they are sure they can destroy you with it. You have taken a step from which there is no return."

"Then I must learn all that I can of your black magic."

"I am not sure that I should teach you more. It was not thus that I had planned that you should use the power. I had hoped that you would be a friend of my people."

Kate thought of Bard and his threats. She felt her skin turn cold. She spoke swiftly to Koshi: "You have said there is no return and you are right. Then let me learn more quickly. There is danger here for me and I must be able to protect myself. Take me to the Ashanti ceremonies. Provide me with a weapon that—"

Koshi broke off the words. "No," he said softly. "You are not ready."

She held out her hand pleadingly but Koshi took no notice. His eyes were veiled as he turned and looked out over the Parade where Mario sat with Shamey Lady. Mullen squatted before them, his piping voice raised in shrill excitement.

Bard had taken to lounging about the Salamander. He and Gabe sat together in the bar drinking, their heads close together. Kate watched them with loathing. For her the two men had become symbols of fear and frustration. Bard's hulking figure and round, brutal face haunted her nights and days. How much had Percy Morgan told him? What proof had he offered? These were things which she could not know and which she dared not put to the test. She doubted that Bard's unsupported word would be taken against hers, but she had other enemies. How much could she trust Lettie Parsons? Jonathan Minor? Mario? Even Gabe Cousins? Without Koshi's friendship she felt defenseless. Bard had approached her only once since the day on the beach and that time he had been satisfied with a pound. But Bard's eyes were constantly on her and she knew he was watching, waiting until he had her in a state of panic before he struck.

Gabe Cousins was drinking steadily. His first act in the morning was to reach out for the jar of rum he kept by his bedside. By noon he had usually reached a state of semistupor. His sallow face was lugubrious; his sunken eyes sometimes reproachful, sometimes filled with venom. There were times when he sat bolt upright staring down at his mug while tears trickled down his cheeks. At other times he wept loudly and openly, pillowing his head in his outstretched arms and sobbing out obscenities.

Only when he fought his cocks did he remain comparatively sober. He spent most of these days at the pits and did not return until evening. Kate had learned to dread these days more than the others. If his cocks had been successful, he came back flushed with victory. He would throw his arms about her in elation and, if there were others about, she would submit to the embrace. He had never given up the hope that their marital relations would

134

be renewed. There were alternate scenes of pleading and threatening. And always, at the end, the same question asked over and over again: Who was Mullen's father?

Kate hated his wheedling more than his abuse. The full task of keeping the Salamander had fallen upon her almost from the beginning. To this she did not object. She had a good mind for business and the tavern was successful. Now that she could afford servants and slaves, much of her time was free. But the hours and the days were empty.

One day when she had walked the beach at Port Royal in vain hopes of seeing Koshi, she came back to the inn weary and dejected. She saw that Gabe and Bard were in the bar, and for once, Gabe was laughing. As she watched them, the hatred grew within her. Bard threatened her security, perhaps her life. As for Gabe, as long as he lived she was tied to him and to the Salamander. These two men stood in her way. She thought of Sweetie Gourd, maddened with fear, plunging to death beneath the hoofs of Brandon's horses. She repeated to herself Koshi's words—obeah means killing.

She jumped when someone touched her arm, and whirled around to face Mario.

"I'm sorry if I frightened you, Miss Kate. I didn't mean to." Mario turned his hat in his fingers. He spoke with a humbleness that was strange to him.

"What is it, Mario?" Kate asked sharply.

"I want to speak to you, Miss Kate. I want to ask you something."

Kate remained silent, waiting.

"It's about Shamey Lady."

"Yes. What about her?"

"Well, Miss Kate. She and I get along fine together. We were thinking, maybe there'd be a way we could get married."

"She's only a child. Not more than fourteen."

"I know she's young but I've been afraid, Miss Kate, that maybe you'd sell her. Then maybe she'd have to go away. If I could marry her, I'd come here and work for you."

Kate looked at the young man who was usually proud

135

to the point of arrogance and saw the pleading in his face. "She's too young to marry," she repeated.

"Later, in a year or two, could I marry her?"

"She's a slave, Mario, and you are free. Moreover, you will succeed Koshi as high priest of the Ashanti. What you suggest is not wise, even if it were possible."

"I want Shamey Lady. I don't care about the rest."

Kate was thinking rapidly—thinking of the two men she loathed; of Koshi who had deserted her; of Rune Hall, high up on Pinchback Hill. She said slowly, "I paid a good price for Shamey Lady."

"I know."

"What would you do in return for her?"

"Almost anything, Miss Kate."

"I've asked Koshi to take me to the Ashanti pallays. He has refused."

Mario's eyes were frightened but he said nothing.

"Will you take me?"

"Koshi wouldn't like it."

"Koshi doesn't have to know."

"He would. I couldn't conceal it from him."

"Very well." Kate turned and walked away. She heard Mario take a step after her. "Miss Kate," he called softly. She did not answer. She went to the door where Shamey Lady was waiting and ordered her sharply to her quarters. She turned and saw the look of misery and indecision on Mario's face. She smiled a little to herself, knowing that she would have her way soon.

12

BONFIRES FLARED all over the city and even far up in the hills. Men moved in little groups along the harbor, across the Parade, down King Street, over sugar cane fields. Their hoarse shouts filled the night.

The water front was in turmoil. Men scoured the dark alleys, searched warehouses, went aboard the ships anchored in the bay. The passes that led to the wild Cockpit country were under double guard. Jamaica's biggest man hunt was under way.

Bard and Gabe Cousins stood outside the Salamander, their faces red in the glow of the bonfire on the Parade. Both men carried muskets and both were drunk. There was the tattoo of hoofs and the whining of wheels on gravel.

Upstairs young Mullen leaned out over the window ledge. His face was aglow with excitement. His bare legs kicked out from beneath his nightgown. He shouted down to Gabe Cousins but his voice was drowned out by the coach. Then a sound within the room startled him and he turned to see his mother in the doorway. He looked from her and called again to Gabe.

Kate came to the boy and put her hand on his spare shoulder. He shook her hand off. "Hey Gabe! Gabe!" he cried.

The coach had stopped below. Sydney Brandon lumbered down from the seat. The coachman's hands were trembling and the whites of his eyes showed enormous in the flickering light.

"Got any word of the damned nigger, Syd?" Bard asked.

Brandon grunted. "They say they got him cornered up by Baraçong near Johnson's place. He's hiding out in the cane. They'll get him, all right."

"Be they sure it's Connie's boy?" Gabe asked.

"They're sure enough it's Nigel to hang him. Mike Beddoes seen him run from the pimento brush across the road into the field. There's forty men up there beating the cane right now."

Gabe spat. "Take us along, Syd. We won't be a-missin' the sight o' Nigel swingin'."

Brandon nodded. "Come on, they should have got him by now." He pulled back into the coach followed by Bard. Gabe Cousins stumbled over the footrest and sprawled across Brandon's lap.

Mullen called, "Gabe, Gabe! Take me."

Cousins peered out of the coach and cocked his hand

137

at the boy. The snap of the whip sounded and the coach was off.

Mullen turned around, disappointed and nearly in tears. "Why wouldn't Gabe wait for me?" he asked.

"You're too little to see such things." Kate regretted her answer the moment after she had made it. There was withdrawal in the boy's face and he jerked away from her. She floundered about for some phrase that would bring him back. "Besides you've got to stay here to protect me."

Mullen looked up, interested. "What's happening to Gabe? Where's he going?"

"Up to Johnson's." Then she added almost to herself, "There'll be violence, I'm afraid."

Kate took him in her arms and deposited him on the bed. She sat beside him and held his hands, but the boy squirmed free. "Why can't I ever go anywhere with Gabe?" he asked. Then before she could form an answer, he cried, "Where's Shamey Lady? I want Shamey Lady."

"She's asleep, Mullen."

"She'd wake up if she knew I wanted her."

Kate sat grim-lipped, watching the boy long after he had dropped off to sleep. The shadows made his face seem pale and the closed eyes hollow. How much alike they were—Mullen, her father and Mullen, her son. And she was losing one as surely as she had lost the other. Losing the boy to Gabe, to Shamey Lady, to the roisterous life about the tavern and the Parade. Her eyes were hot, but no tears would come. For a moment she thought of dropping on her knees beside the bed to pray, but she stopped herself angrily. Prayers had not saved the one Mullen from the gallows; they could not bring the other back to her. "No prayers," she said aloud, "no candles for you, my lad. There'll be Rune Hall instead. There'll be wealth and power so that no man's hand will ever dare to touch you."

She kissed him on the forehead and he stirred restlessly. She went to the open window and stared out over the Parade. Its details were clearly defined in the red light of the fires. People thronged about the barracks and the theater, and every few minutes a horseman or a carriage would come galloping across the cleared space and hoarse voices would ring out in greeting or there would be the sound of ribald laughter.

She wondered if Nigel had got away. She hoped so, though she found it hard to care. It was five years since she had saved Picon from a mob much like this. Tonight if they killed Nigel in her presence she would not raise a hand to prevent it. Or would she? The memory of Sydney Brandon's coarse voice and the brutal glee in his announcement that Nigel was cornered filled her with a swift hatred. How often had she watched Brandon swaggering across the Parade and thought of the contemptuous English officers patrolling the streets of Galway. There was a time when her father was hunted and she had seen him force back the fear from his face that she might not witness it.

Kate's body tensed now as she thought of the big black man fleeing in terror through the night. She became one with him and felt herself in flight, running zigzag across cotton fields, seeking the protection of the mahogany trees on Pinchback Hill, running close to the surf that the lapping waves might wash away the footprints. There was stark fear that acted like an intoxicant. The lights of the flambeau behind men with guns, knives and ropes in the narrow pathways.

Nigel was the giant black whom Constantia Abbott had bought in Kerry Square the day that Kate had purchased Shamey Lady. He was a Koramantyn and, in Africa, he had been a fierce warrior without fear and without mercy. Connie Abbott did not know these things nor would she have cared. She had made good her boast, putting him in a green velvet jacket with gold frogging and having him serve confect cakes to the gentlemen who visited the Queen's Court.

Connie taught the towering Koramantyn all the ways of the pimp—the whining voice, the elaborately obscene gesture, the cringing manner. Dutifully, he repeated after her the simpering phrases of the bagnio. "You like nice flippy-floppy? My sister gives nice flippy-floppy." Nigel soon became the jest of Kingston. In the privacy of the club or the smoking room, Kingston's elect recounted with gusto the tales of Connie Abbott's pander. At the balls and banquets the stories were told more discreetly and in

139

hushed voices. Behind the protecting fans of the ladies the exploits of Nigel were whispered with renewed relish even if with less pungency. The Queen's Court flourished, for no sporting gentleman of the island felt that he could miss the entertainment of the big Negro's debasement, nor, while he was there, fail to sample the other delicacies provided by Constantia Abbott. Even Stallybrass was rumored to have been privately amused by Nigel's performance and it was said that, after a long evening at the Queen's Court, he patted his hostess' cheek, chucked her beneath her angular chin and vowed that no woman in Jamaica had such an exquisite sense of humor.

So Nigel bowed low over his tray of confect cakes and whispered the phrases he had been taught. The spasms of laughter that greeted him were part of a new world which he had no way of understanding. The frogged jacket, the satin breeches tinted pink, the white stockings and shining pumps must have seemed strange clothes indeed, but he had no others. They were better than the whip, the chains and the dark closet where Constantia had first imprisoned him and apparently broken his spirit. In Jamaica life was strange indeed, filled with brightly clothed girls, music, white men who laughed constantly and a simpering old woman who had the power to whip him.

How much Nigel understood of his own perversion no one could tell. Constantia kept him well away from the other slaves and the only English he understood was the obscene jargon she had taught him and a few simple commands. On occasion, she took him out on the streets of Kingston, leading him as she might an animal. The freed Negroes and the slaves on their half holidays joined the whites in their mockery. But there were some among them who looked with anguished faces at the huge Negro warrior who had been turned into a pimp. Perhaps Nigel caught the words of derision or pity spoken by his tribesmen in singsong Koramantyn dialect, or maybe he understood the messages of the drums that beat in the hills. If he did he gave no sign. He kept his features impassive and maintained his wide-mouthed grin.

Only MacFeathers had caught the warning behind the Negro's vacant eyes. The little Scot had gone to Connie Abbott and pleaded with her. "Leave him be, Connie.

Give him his freedom or sell him for a field slave. But dinna keep him here. 'Tis a powerful mon he is and I've no doubt a brave one. Ye canna dress a Koramantyn warrior in the fiddlin's o' a puddle boy. Ye've little enow brains within ye head, Connie, but this be pure madness."

Connie giggled and patted the Scot's wrinkled cheek with a blue-veined hand. "You're a sweet boy, Alex, and I'm glad you're looking after me. But Nigel's good for my trade and you're wrong about him being brave. He's a coward. Why, he winces at the very sight of the whip."

"Dammit, Connie, 'tis not ye'self I care aboot. Ye're laying in a pack o' trouble, I tell ye. Let the mon go."

"A pretty price I paid for him. Would I be wasting it?"

"Forget the money. If I had the guineas I'd pay ye me'self. For wha's money up against a mon's life. I'm telling ye one fine day it's waking up Nigel will be. And then hae a care. 'Twill be ye own neck broken in his hands, and maybe many another before it's through."

"Ah, you're a quaint one, Alex. There's nothing will happen here at the Queen's Court. Even Stallybrass comes here."

MacFeathers shook his head and went away. His prediction of Nigel's revolt had come true even sooner than he had expected. That night Connie had a new uniform for the Negro—a jacket of purple brocade, a turban with a high feather. Before the crowd came in from the theater she handed the clothing to him.

"Here, Nigel, go put this on. You'll look pretty tonight." The Koramantyn grunted but did not obey.

Connie Abbott's voice rose shrilly. "Do as I tell you, Nigel. Or I shall send a girl for the whip!"

Nigel looked down at the turban and seized it. His strong fingers stretched it until it was a mass of ribbons. Connie glared at him and words of vituperation spat from her lips.

Isaac Gomes was the only customer in the Queen's Court at the moment. He was chatting with two of the girls. He was the first to sense the danger. "Easy, Connie," he warned softly. "The fellow's dangerous."

Nigel lifted his hands slowly toward the woman's neck. She stared at his fingers, fascinated by their purposeful movement. Not until he touched her did she scream and then the sound was broken off almost as soon as it started.

Gomes seized a chair and crashed it with all his might against the black man's body. Nigel let the woman drop to the floor and turned on his new tormentor. Gomes saw the pent-up rage and the murderous madness in the Negro's eyes. For a moment he was paralyzed with fear, then he turned to run. Nigel was upon him with a single lunge, and with one blow on the back, he knocked the dandified auctioneer to the floor. The Negro reached down and clutched the thrashing ankles. He whirled, lifting the other upward in a flying arc. Half a dozen times he swung the white man about in faster and faster circles. Gomes let out a long piercing scream. Nigel shifted his balance and, with almost incredible force, smashed the auctioneer's head against the heavy mahogany balustrade. There was the splintering sound of shattered bone and the sickening sweet scent of blood. Nigel stared down at the man he had killed and then at the two girls crouching in fear in the corner. From there his eyes went to Connie Abbott. The woman still lay on the floor, gasping for breath. The rouge formed splotches of red against her white cheeks and she writhed in the agony of anticipated death.

Nigel moved silently toward her until he stood above her. He looked at her and his eyes became vacant once again. She hid her face in her hands. Contemptuously he pulled her hair until her face was tilted up toward his. His lips moved and his voice took on the sycophant's whine she had taught him. "Nice flippy-floppy," he said. "Gen'le-man like nice flippy-floppy?" Then he released her and started for the door. As soon as he was on the street he began to run and, as he did so, he ripped off the frogged jacket and the pink breeches. He hesitated when he came to the first intersection, then turned blindly toward the hills where he had heard the drums beating the night before.

Within an hour the town was in a turmoil. The big fire lighted in the Parade gave warning to the planters in the distant indigo and cotton estates that there was trouble. Men came on horseback, singly or in groups, listened to the tale of the berserk Negro, and joined in the hunt. Their first move was to cut off the known passes that led to Accompong. Then systematically they blocked the roads while all possible hiding places in the town were scoured. It was known that Nigel had never been free in the city and it was thought that in his desperate bid for freedom he would move without direction, merely seeking a place to hide. In the clamor and confusion, the low guiding tap of the dondo drum went unnoticed.

The men who stood watch over the bonfire in the Parade had tales to tell of Nigel, but now he was no longer the butt of their lascivious jests. Instead he had become the incarnation of evil. His perversions were willful acts of degeneracy, attributable to his race, rather than to the coercion of Constantia Abbott. Men told with gasps of horror the same stories which had choked them with ribald laughter the week before. Connie sat among them, her thin legs crossed, her cheeks freshly rouged, egging the men on to make extravagant and profane promises as to the obscenties they would commit on Nigel's person once he was caught. Connie displayed with pride the bruised spots on her neck and recounted with swiftly growing details the depravities of the slave.

It was past midnight when huzzas, whoops, drunken cries and the blowing of horns at the foot of Tom Tom Hill announced that the searchers were returning from Johnson's place. A few minutes later Brandon's coach bumped onto the Parade. A huge black man, naked and begrimed, was chained to the bar that joined the rear wheels. As the coach jerked over the rough ground the man was pulled forward and fell. He was dragged about a dozen feet before the coach slowed to let him stand. As he stumbled to his feet, boots lashed out savagely at him. Men ran across the Parade from every direction toward the coach and the captured black. The shouts fused into a murderous roar. A few men threw fresh wood on the fire and its flames danced high above the barracks in which the Maroon soldiers had been locked.

Three figures strode across the Parade. Something in their determined manner must have attracted Syd Brandon, who held the reins of his coach. He shouted and pointed his whip in their direction. The man in the center was tall and lean, with broad shoulders. To his left was a slender man whose priestly garb gave him the appear-

143

ance of a woman. The third was small and round but there was a jaunty swing to his walk.

One by one, the crowd identified them and called their names. "Father Maholan—The Scottie, MacFeathers—Jonathan Minor."

The crowd drew away from the battered Negro and formed a rough crescent, awaiting the oncoming men. The shouts died out and there was near silence over the Square. Syd Brandon tossed the reins to a man beside him and jumped from the coach. He stood between the Negro and the three men. Only two men took their places with him, Bard and Gabriel Cousins.

Brandon had a pistol in his hand. When Minor was six feet away, Brandon raised the weapon. "Stop where ye be, Jonathan Minor, or it's a bullet I'll be putting in ye belly."

Minor stopped. Neither his face nor his voice showed the slightest emotion. "Give me Nigel, Brandon. We'll take care of him by the ways of the law."

"Stow ye gaff, Minor. We got the bloody nigger and we keep 'im. 'Tis a noose around his neck and a roastin' o' his filthy black body over the flames."

"There'll be a noose around his neck never fear, but by the process of law. There'll be no bacchanal this night."

Brandon asked mockingly, "Will ye be takin' 'im from us, Minor?" Behind him the mob rumbled threateningly and Brandon smiled.

"Put your pistol down, Brandon," Minor ordered. "'Tis His Majesty's law I'm representing. Put it down, I say, or tomorrow you'll be finding yourself in the dock."

Brandon spread his feet wider and spat. "Be you a friend to a murderin' nigger? Let him go, and in the week the niggers'll be in revolt. Come and get him if ye dare, but I'll put lead in ye and not a planter in Jamaica but what'll back me up."

Save for mutterings and mumblings the crowd had been silent, but there was no doubt where their sympathies lay. The naked Negro shivered and tried to speak, but the words turned into a meaningless wail.

Father Maholan touched Minor's arm. When he spoke, he addressed himself to the crowd. "There be many a good

144

Catholic among you. Come and take your place beside your priest."

A little man took a step forward, but someone pulled him back. As the eyes of the others turned at the disturbance, MacFeathers stepped close to Cousins and for the first time caught a view of the shivering Negro.

"Holy Mother o' God," he cried. "'Tis not Nigel ye have. Why, 'tis old Buck Blubo from Baraçong. Ye blithering idiots, where'd ye catch him?"

The bright flames of the fire lighted the Negro's face but he was so battered, bruised, bloody and begrimed as to be scarcely recognizable.

"'Tis a trick," Bard cried. "Do not be taken in by the Scottie."

"There be no trick," a man from the crowd shouted. "It be Blubo right enough."

"Where'd ye find him?" demanded MacFeathers.

"He was sneakin' down the road when we spotted him. Took a header for Johnson's cane."

Brandon strode to the Negro and cupped the man's face roughly in his own palm. The resemblance between Blubo and Nigel was strong. Both were Koramantyns, sprung from a tribe where generations of interbreeding had given a tribal identity to its people.

The Negro gibbered. "I Blubo, Massa. I try tell you. I do no wrong. I Blubo. I Blubo."

"What were you doing out at night? Why were you at Johnson's place? Whose nigger be ye?'"

The Negro looked at his tormentor blankly. His teeth were chattering. "I Blubo," he repeated over and over again.

A voice from the crowd shouted, "I know Blubo all right. He's a freedman. Every night he goes down to Johnson's to stud old Nanny."

Laughter ran through the crowd. Jonathan Minor took advantage of it to thrust Brandon away from Blubo. He shouted loudly, "Now you've got the wrong man, let him go."

Bard shook his fist in Minor's face. "Not so fast. A nigger killed a white man tonight and a nigger's got to die for it. There be a fire and a rope a-waitin' for him. 'Tis not good to waste 'em."

145

The crowd was uncertain, hating to let the night's sport end so mildly. Brandon jumped to the box of the coach. "Three uprisin's there's been in the last six months. Let the nigger go and we'll have more. Are ye men who'll fight for ye rights or do ye cower to a braggard like Jonathan Minor? Isaac Gomes was killed tonight. Do we forget a nigger killed him?"

The crowd shouted its approval of what Brandon said, with only a few dissenting cries.

Father Maholan and Minor flanked the Negro now. The priest raised his arm. "Hear what I have to say," he pleaded, but the clamor of the mob drowned out his words. Yet the crowd held back, none among them wishing to be the first to lay hands upon a priest.

Then someone gave a shout of surprise and pointed. The eyes of the mob were deflected from the Negro and the priest. A woman moved across the Parade toward them, a woman dressed in a white gown. Later some said that she did not walk, but that she floated. But then many of them were drunk and anyway the long, loose gown concealed any movement of her feet.

As she drew close, the crowd mumbled the name of Kate Cousins, and Brandon spat out an obscenity. Kate approached the men slowly until she stood beside Father Maholan. Her face was filled with contempt as she looked from Brandon to Gabe Cousins. Gabe stepped back, muttering unintelligibly.

Kate's voice rang out across the Parade, crisp and clear. "Is this your idea of sport—a hundred men to torture one who is helpless?" Her eyes caught those of Brandon and held them. "Ah, but you're a brave one. Will you attack a woman next?"

Brandon's face darkened. " 'Tis no woman's affair, why be ye interferin' here?"

Kate turned her back on him and spoke to Father Maholan. "You need have no fear, Father. I will take charge of this man."

The moment of silence that followed was broken by a pistol shot. No one knew whence the shot had come, for all were looking at the tableau of Kate, Father Maholan and the Negro. Blubo threw up his arms and screamed. Then his hands clasped over his stomach. A gush of blood

146

spurted out through his fingers and stained his hands. He fell over slowly and Kate Cousins caught him and lowered him softly to the ground. The blood spurted over her dress and made a splash of carmine on her cheek.

The men crowded close but Kate kept her position beside the Negro, looking up at them defiantly. The red glare of the fire was reflected in her eyes. None touched or spoke to her. At the far end of the Parade there was the harsh beat of a drum and an officer's hoarse shout calling to the soldiers in the barracks. The men grumbled and someone cried out, "Where's Brandon?" But the planter had slipped away in the darkness and left the mob without a leader. The men muttered to one another. Then, fearful of the arrival of Stallybrass' soldiers and of the charges that might be brought against them, the mob began to break up. One by one, each man went his own way until only Father Maholan, MacFeathers and Minor remained with Kate.

"Help me get him to the Salamander," she said.

Father Maholan bent above her. "He's dead, my child."

She nodded. "I know, but we must get him away from here."

By the time they had carried the giant Negro's body into the patio of the Salamander, a morning light was creeping through the latticework. MacFeathers made a hasty departure and Kate was left alone with the priest and Minor.

She stared down into the dead man's face and her thoughts were tumultuous. Instinctively she had allied herself with the hunted as she had done in the case of Picon. But was not this wrong? Had she not taken a vow to become one of the strong? Compassion was a weakness that could destroy ambition.

Father Maholan's voice startled her. "I'll send Brother Charles to watch over the body until it can be removed." He rose to go and Kate went with him to the door. The old man's eyes rested on her face and he spoke softly, but she refused to understand the words. She started back into the patio, but stopped as Jonathan Minor took a step toward her. She waited until he came close, then she wheeled and ran up the stairs.

She heard her name called but she did not turn until

she reached the landing. Then she looked back and saw the pleading in Minor's face. She felt no compassion, only a swift sense of elation in the knowledge of the power she held. Even that turned to bitterness as she remembered the scene at Rune Hall when he had rejected her. She had promised herself that she would even the score and that Rune Hall should be hers. She would keep that promise. She must not give way to a yearning for the tenderness or the safety she had once felt in his arms. He must be a means of attaining her ambition—that and nothing more. She must play the game skillfully, waiting until the time should be ripe. She looked down at him coldly, her face showing only anger and disdain.

13

THE MURDER of Isaac Gomes kindled the fire of fear and resentment that had long been smoldering in the island. Nigel had escaped and there was no trace of him, but it was generally believed that he had got safely to Accompong. Nevertheless, the hunt for the giant Negro did not die down. Groups of armed men patrolled the road and stopped any black whom they met for questioning. The shacks of Baraçong were searched for weapons, and any free Negro who raised his voice in protest was severely beaten.

The blacks were without defense, but their eyes grew sullen and wary. Each night drums beat intricate patterns in the hills and from somewhere beyond Baraçong there was a muffled reply, fingered lightly on the stretched goatskin of the gumby. The soft, penetrating, rhythmic beat of the Ashanti drums sent shivers up and down the spines of the planters' ladies. They whispered to one another stories of the slave uprising thirteen years before when more than a hundred whites had met their deaths at the hands of a mob of desperate slaves. At that time Kingston had been a shambles for more than a week. Homes and shops were burned and looted.

Governor Stallybrass was worried. He hastily dispatched messages to London, asking for another regiment of redcoats, and the Maroon soldiers were disarmed and confined to their barracks. The possession of a drum by a freedman was made an offense punishable by death but, despite floggings and hangings, each night the rhythmic tattoo came down through the hills and the rumors of widespread revolt became more and more insistent.

Scores of conflicting stories circulated about Jamaica concerning what had happened the night that Blubo had been shot on the Parade. There were some among the planters who still insisted that the captured black was Nigel and that MacFeathers had played a trick upon the crowd. Most of the Jamaicans were violently partisan in the quarrel that had sprung up between Sydney Brandon and Jonathan Minor. The planters, their factors and bookkeepers, as a whole, sided with Brandon. Brandon himself kept the flames of the dispute alive. Almost nightly he took a pitch on the Parade and harangued the roistering crowds. "We had a murdering nigger bastard in our hands and who defended him? 'Twas Jonathan Minor. Minor'll sell out his own people for a mess o' porridge and let the heathen blacks rape our women. 'Tis Jamaica for the Englishman, the Irish and the Scot—the mon as works the soil, not the fop as sits in Government House and puts on his airs and graces over his sherry."

The officials and merchants backed Minor. But calm words had little effect against the rantings of Brandon. The planters wanted the freedmen back in shackles. They resented the fact that more and more of them were obtaining land and that their rum presses worked in competition with those of the whites. Too many slaves had escaped to Accompong. The planters, forgetful of the fiascos which had marked every attempt to destroy the Maroons, put pressure on the Governor to attack Buddhoe.

"No mon is safe to walk the streets o' Kingston while free niggers be about," Brandon bellowed. "Let us petition his Majesty to get rid o' Stallybrass and send us a mon what's got the good o' the planters in his heart."

149

Stallybrass was not a man of action or decision and he depended heavily on Minor. He was alarmed by his growing unpopularity and besought Minor to put matters to rights. As he rambled on in his cracked, irritable voice, a young man stood beside him. This was his nephew Sir William Elgin, who had recently come to Jamaica. Minor looked from the Governor's purple-veined face to the impassive one of Elgin. The young man's lips parted in a little smile and his face was blandly friendly, but Minor knew that Elgin had talked with Brandon earlier that day, and he suspected the tenor of their conversation. Beneath the young man's calm demeanor Minor sensed some urgent driving force that he could not understand. Elgin was, of course, a cousin of Minor's wife and an occasional guest at Rune Hall. The Governor's nephew always addressed the older man with punctilious courtesy, but there was a withdrawn quality about him. The calm face masked passions that Minor could not fathom. Of only one thing he felt certain: Elgin was an enemy with whom to reckon, and sooner or later there would be open conflict between them.

As Jonathan Minor's coach left Government House and rolled by the Salamander Tavern, he saw that Lettie Parsons' coach was drawn up before the door. Momentarily, he had the desire to turn his own horses into the driveway, but he fought back the urge. He thought of Kate's eyes, cold with disdain, as she had looked at him across the body of Buck Blubo. Well, he deserved her scorn, he admitted to himself. The anger that had driven him to the Christian Steps that afternoon five years ago with orders to Lettie that she should send Kate away had lasted for only a few hours. That night he had got drunk and in the morning he was ill.

When he had gone back to the Christian Steps, Lettie had no idea of where the girl had gone. Jonathan had picked up the trail through Father Maholan and learned that Kate was in the Convent of the Immaculate Conception.

" 'Tis the best place for her," the priest had warned mildly.

Minor was forced to agree. Once he had walked to the

Convent and looked in through the grilled gate. Kate was inside and he would have liked to have gone to her, crushed her against him, forced her to love him again. At the thought, flame shot through his body and his hands had trembled. But in the end, he had turned away. The thing which he wanted was madness, he told himself. There was Rose to think of—Rose who was his betrothed.

His marriage had been happy enough. Happy as he had a right to expect. He was aware of Rose's delicate beauty, the lovely symmetry of her face, her fragile body, her gentle manners, the bell-like quality of her voice. She was obedient, pliant to his every wish, constant in her attention to his needs. Yet how many times as they lay side by side in the darkness had he felt that there was no one there, that he was alone. He would run his hand across the cool, thin body, touch the tiny rosebud breasts. She would sigh softly and turn toward him. Sometimes he would turn away. But there were other times when he would take her in his arms and make wild love to her. He would pretend that the limbs were full-fleshed and soft, the breasts swelling and the body beneath him pulsing with the rich breath of passion. When he had exhausted himself, he would feel the tears wet and cold on her cheek and her faint, sighing breath. Anger would rise within him and a desire to crush and destroy the birdlike body beneath him.

He was glad when he knew there was to be a child and hoped it would be a boy. Rune Hall would be passed on to a son and there would be added purpose in his life. But Rose had given him a daughter and as the child grew, he had seen there was little of himself within her. She had the auburn hair, the heart-shaped face, the fragile body of her mother. From the first, Ishbel was quiet, obedient, undemonstrative in her affections. Later there was a son but he died within an hour of his birth. Jonathan turned bitterly away from his wife's sickbed that she might not see his hurt.

Ishbel was not more than eight months younger than Kate's son. When he had first seen Mullen, Jonathan wondered if the boy could be his. He did not know the exact date of the boy's birth for Kate had kept her secret well, and in this, Gabe had aided her. Jonathan saw there was nothing of Cousins' coarseness in the child. Mullen was well-formed, with fine bone structure. He had Kate's coloring, but not the boldness of her features. No, certainly the boy was not Gabe's, Jonathan assured himself. Then was Mullen his own son? And if not, whose?

Jonathan called to Curtius, his coachman, to turn back across the Parade so that his coach would repass the Salamander. He had hoped that he might catch a glimpse of Kate but instead he saw Shamey Lady and Mario sitting beneath a wild orange tree. Mullen squatted before them. Jonathan stopped the carriage and got out. He spoke a few words to Mario, but his eyes were on the boy, studying his features.

Mullen came towards him, holding in each hand dried pods of the acacia in which the seeds rattled, and which were used as musical instruments by the natives, who called them shak-shaks.

"Look, I can play them." Mullen shook the pods vigorously.

Jonathan knelt beside him and reached in his pocket for a coin, but as he did so, a shadow fell across the child and a harsh voice said, "The lad has no use for ye money, Jonathan Minor. Enough grief ye've caused this household. Leave us be; that's all we ask o' ye." Gabe Cousins put his hand on the boy's shoulder. "Come, Mullen, me lad. I'll show ye me red cock whether ye mother likes it or no."

"The cock? Can I really, Gabe?"

"Ay, lad. Come along wi' ye."

Jonathan watched as the gnarled, uncouth man shambled across the road, holding the boy by the hand. He was more certain now than ever that he had been correct in his surmise concerning Mullen.

Minor's thoughts were interrupted by a gushing voice. "Gracious be! If 'tisn't Jonathan Minor. 'Tis long since I've seen you. Have you quite forsaken me for the Queen's Court?"

Minor smiled wanly. The years had not been kind to Lettie. What had once been mere plumpness was now ungainly fat. She was pasty-faced, so that the freckles stood out like the marks of the pox. Her red hair was streaked with gray and she huffed and puffed at the slightest exertion.

Lettie waited for no answer. "I've been to see Kate.

152

Is it not terrible the things they be saying about the poor child? 'Tis a witch they're calling her—all because she went to save poor Blubo. Not that I'm agreeing with you, Jonathan. Had you and his Excellency taken strong measures, the blacks would not be breathing on our necks each night and beating their awful drums. Why, the sound of them makes my knees all water-wembley."

Jonathan was scarcely listening. "How is Kate?" he asked. "Are Brandon's men giving her trouble?"

"She's haughty and proud as ever. Lud, but the gal's got a way with her. Sometimes it's the creeps she fair gives me. And I, who took her in when she was a bound girl. As for Brandon, he's keeping well away from her. They say if Kate gave the word, the blacks would rise tomorrow. 'Tis a tall tale, but there are some that believe it."

Jonathan shrugged and signaled to Curtius to bring his carriage close. He knew as well as Lettie the rumors that were bruited about concerning Kate Cousins.

The Negroes had already given her the name of the White Witch. It had started the night in the Parade when she had dared to defy the mob that held Blubo captive. The coachman and flunkies who had been with their masters said that she had floated across the Parade, her feet never quite touching the ground. It was recalled how she had put an obeah on Sweetie Gourd that had ridden the Negress to her death. Of late, it was said that the spirit of Blubo walked with her to protect her from harm. In Baraçong many claimed to have seen a green emanation in her wake.

Constantia Abbott, knowing Kate had sought to defend Nigel, spread gossip openly. She claimed that Kate practiced black magic and attended the tribal rites of the Ashanti and Koramantyns. People laughed at Connie, but still they repeated her malicious words. The loud voices of the Negroes turned soft as Kate moved about the market, and some of them crossed themselves surreptitiously. The whites were caught between ridicule and apprehension. The arrogant tilt of Kate's head and her tight-lipped smile did not invite confidence. The men of the island stopped to stare at her full figure, her clear skin, the sway of her supple body. The women declared that she should never enter their houses and disguised their envy by clothing her with a nameless wickedness.

Jonathan Minor cursed softly to himself, for his thoughts of Kate were always filled with longing and remorse. The horses ambled along the beach road and he looked up to see the turret of Rune Hall rising above the almond trees. He was going back to Rose, he reflected bitterly. His wife had been sickly ever since the death of the second child. Her body seemed to have shriveled and there was a constant look of patiently endured pain in her eyes. Damn it! He would not go back to her, not yet. He thought of returning to Government House and of having dinner with Stallybrass. But Sir William would be there and the picture of the young man's bland features and dulcet voice filled him with a sour rage. Did Elgin believe him so stupid that he did not know what went on in the island? Minor banged his open palm on his knee, and Curtius looked around inquiringly.

"Take me to Barraca Cove," Jonathan ordered tersely.

Curtius nodded. "Long time since we been there, Master Jonathan."

Yes, it had been a long time, Jonathan reflected—five years since Kate had told him the story of Grainne O'Maille—five years since he had held her in his arms.

14

KATE SAT BEFORE HER MIRROR, daubing her cheeks carefully with the crushed red powder from the tiny jar. Tonight she had promised Mullen that she would take him to the theater for the first time. This would be the first time for her too, since the night she had gone through the narrow black door that was the stage entrance of the Mourne Theatre in Galway. Mullen, her father, had held her hand tightly and she had felt happy, gay and secure. She had watched him from the wings as he played his part. She had felt no premonition of the disaster that was to come, not even when she had gone back to Mullen's dressing room and found the two men there.

Their harsh whimperings had only aroused her. For at first she had believed they were actors rehearsing the scene in a new play.

"You've got to help us, Donley. The place is surrounded and if they find us here we'll be treading air before the week is up."

"Ah, Padraic," Mullen had answered softly, "'tis a noose around me own neck you're tying."

"Lock us in. They'll na search here. Is it an Irishman ye call yourself, yet willing to see us hang for the killing of a murderous red swine of an English bailiff?"

Mullen had sighed. "Let me get the lass away. I'll come back and help ye when I can."

He had led Kate to the door and whispered to her. Only then did she realize the threat to their safety. "Get ye home, Kathleen," he had commanded softly, "and ask no questions. The less ye know, the better it is for all of us."

He had kissed her again and she had slipped out into the shadows and had not even dared to look back to see if he was watching her.

Now she forced the memory away from her and looked down at the crushed handbill that Mullen, her son, had brought to her that afternoon. It was crudely lettered, and as Kate read it she smiled.

By Permission of His Excellency the Governor
Sir George Stallybrass
The Incomparable Young Hollander
Will exhibit this evening, various surprising
Deceptions
with cups, cards, snuffboxes, watches, money, hand-kerchiefs, etc., he will take any gentleman's snuffbox and convey it into a small tin box, under three locks and keys, without touching anything.

Also many other feats never before performed on this island.

Ticket 6s. 8d.
To Begin Precisely at Eight O'clock.

155

Kate folded the handbill and stuffed it in her purse. This was not the entertainment she would have chosen for Mullen but she knew that the planters, the factors and the bookkeepers dearly loved such acts. The theater would be crowded. She had sent Shamey Lady and Mario ahead more than an hour earlier to hold their places, for the Royal Theatre had not yet adopted a system of reserved seats.

She surveyed herself with satisfaction in the mirror, wiped her fingers on a soft pad of paper and went to Mullen's room. The boy stood on tiptoes at the window peering across the Parade. His whole body wriggled with excitement. Kate went to him and put her hand on his. The boy's eyes were so glued to the panorama that stretched before him that he scarcely glanced up at her.

The Parade was filled with laughter, rolling voices, rich colors. The jostling crowd was gay. Two dandified young bookkeepers strolled by, arms linked with those of over-dressed mulatto girls. Negroes in a multitude of diverse liveries hurried toward the theater door. A batman from the barracks, his face the color of chocolate, sported his officer's discarded finery. There were erect young Negresses with velvet skins and fresh, gaily colored bandanas; fat, laughing nanas with shining bangles dangling from their ears; a houseboy from Government House, looking haughty and proud in elaborate livery, although his bare feet kicked up the dust as he walked.

Mullen tugged at Kate's hand, eager to start.

"It's early yet," she warned.

But Mullen was insistent and so, although there was a half hour to spare, she led him out onto the noisy Parade. The Negroes milled about the theater doors but they fell away at her approach. Already the theater was crammed and the servants were pushing and jostling one another to secure the front seats in the boxes for their masters.

The theater was still in shadowy gloom, for the management wasted no candles upon the servants. The figures swaying in the semidarkness, the cacophony of the many voices and the jostling of the crowd all frightened Mullen and he clung close to Kate's skirts. An usher soon appeared at Kate's side, a lighted candle in his hand. He

156

bowed obsequiously and led Kate and Mullen to a front box where Mario and Shamey Lady sat. Mario got up quickly and took the candle from the usher's hand and fitted it into the boxholder.

But Mario did not leave immediately. Instead he bowed low over Kate's chair and whispered a few words in her ear. Mullen heard only three of the words: "It is arranged."

"When?" Kate asked.

"Tomorrow night, perhaps the next. I will let you know."

Mullen noticed the strange lights in his mother's eyes. Maybe they came from the candle, he thought. But soon he was too much engrossed in the scene before him to think of Kate or Mario.

The audience was beginning to assemble and the ushers went from box to box lighting the candles. And as the boxes filled with the guests of the night, the servants who had held their places slowly sidled away. The newcomers were scarcely less noisy than those who departed. Youthful officers, arrogant in their red jackets embroidered with gold lace, swaggered down the aisles gallantly escorting their pretty ladies. Coarse planters with their dowdy wives looked askance at the Creole ladies whose olive skins, bright brocaded silks and shimmering satins added to the gaiety of sparkling eyes, scarlet lips and daintily powdered hair.

Down in the pit were the less well-to-do of the town. Here were assembled the overseers, bookkeepers, factors, and sailors from the harbor. But even so there were gay colors, for many a slant-eyed Quasheba from the Queen's Court or the Christian Steps twined a bare arm about a bookkeeper and exhibited silver lace, jangling bracelets, flashing glass jewels and bright brocade. At the far back of the pit, still in darkness, were the Negro house slaves, crowded together, their eyes glistening in the light of the many candles.

There was a sudden clamor of high-pitched voices and a whisper filled the theater. "The Governor is coming." The manager himself lighted the Governor to his box. Stallybrass looked old and a little tipsy. He shuffled his feet as he walked and stumbled as he took the step to the

157

box. Sir William Elgin, his handsome face impassive as ever, his back stiff, his clothes immaculate, supported the old man. Behind them loomed Jonathan Minor, and beside him was his wife Rose.

Even in the shadowy light, Kate could see the gray pallor of the girl's skin and the glitter of her dark eyes. The hand that rested on Jonathan's arm was clawlike in its thinness and the rings that caught the gleam of the candles fitted loosely over the bony fingers. Rose Minor wore dark green satin and her auburn hair was coifed in a high heap which seemed too heavy a burden for her child's head and thin, arched neck.

Kate glanced toward the Governor's box. Jonathan Minor bowed slightly and Sir William followed the direction of the older man's glance. His eyes rested on Kate speculatively and as he turned back to Minor there was a quizzical smile on his lips. Kate flushed. The antagonism between the two men was all too evident and she sensed that Elgin had already divined some intimacy between herself and Minor. The man was a fop and a dandy, she thought, but he might be dangerous too. And already she was beset by too many dangers. She knew that Elgin was watching her covertly and she turned haughtily, her eyes sweeping the pit. The ushers touched tapers to the footlight lamps and the rustling and chatter of the audience ceased. The violins of the orchestra squeaked sharply and the curtains went up. The box candles were extinguished. The Hollander, in full evening regalia, leaped to the front of the stage.

Mullen cried out with excitement and clutched the rail of the box. But Kate was suddenly trembling. As the last candle in the pit was blown out, she had seen Bard standing close to it; his eyes, lifted to her box, were filled with venom. As the Hollander scattered cards over the stage, Bard's words of the afternoon kept coming back to her.

"I'll be needing a heap o' money soon, Kate."

"Wait a while. I'll give you a few pounds to see you over."

"It ain't enough, Kate. I'm a-tellin' ye—there ain't much time. No, gal, there ain't hardly no time at all."

158

15

A CANDLE MOVED in the darkness of the room but there was no noise. Not until the candle came close could Kate see the glistening eyes of the one who carried it. She sat up, startled, and a little cry sprang to her lips.

"Be not afraid," a low voice said. " 'Tis only Shamey Lady."

The girl was leaning over her now and Kate saw that she was covered with a robe of black.

"What is it?" Kate asked quickly. "What do you want?"

"The young moon is high, Missy, and Mario has persuaded Koshi that you shall have your desire."

Kate threw the light covering from her, but before she could arise Shamey Lady touched her hand. "First drink this." The Negress thrust out a cup of mahogany wood. Kate's fingers circled the cup and she felt the cabalistic signs carved crudely about it—the triangle, the cock, the snake, others with which she was not familiar.

The fluid within the cup was opaque. Kate touched her lips to it and found it almost sickeningly sweet with the flavor of the soursop predominant.

"Drink quickly," Shamey Lady commanded.

Kate gulped the whitish liquid and handed the cup back to the girl. "Now take these. Put one in each cheek." Shamey Lady held out her palm, and though Kate could not see what lay there, she reached out her hand and touched the rough texture of the two parts of an obi nut. The obi, about the size of a chestnut, splits in two in a ragged line and has the texture and coloring of the Brazil nut. Kate obediently put a half in each cheek.

"Now stand."

Kate got to her feet. The drink was still sweet in her mouth but already it had sent a tingling force through her body. She felt both strong and unusually calm. There was a glow of pleasure and almost erotic excitement, but also a sense of detachment. Her body seemed to have neither weight nor form, yet to be possessed of a driving power.

Shamey Lady draped a black robe about her, tossed a black shawl over her hair and thrust black slippers on her feet. "Come," Shamey Lady said, "the moon will soon be at its height."

Kate knew that they traveled far, but she had little memory of the journey. The buoyancy remained with her. There was the soft darkness of the Parade and the touch of the moist grass on her ankles. Then there was the measured rhythm of waves; lines of sugar cane, tall and slender, sharply etched against the starlit sky. There were stones beneath her feet and a wild tangle of weeds. Then the forest with high mahogany trees, and finally an open space and the sound of drums that seemed to vibrate from within her body. She could remember the touch of grass and stone, but not any movement of her own. Her breathing was soft and gentle; only her heart throbbed in a swift spasmodic rhythm.

She saw the pallay, an enclosed place about twenty feet square, made of bamboo poles and covered with coconut branches. At the entrance, two knives lay on the earth, their long jagged blades crossed. Their handles were carved with the same symbols as the cup from which she had drunk—the interlocked triangles, the twining serpent, the cock.

At the far end of the enclosure was an altar, lighted by a single candle. On it were three calabashes. The first was piled high with thunderstones, arrow-shaped rocks which the Ashanti claimed were the spent weapons of the gods. The second was filled with the gray ashes of a sacrificed animal. The third contained food for the gods—the raw, ground liver, kidney and heart of a white goat. The skin of the goat, still bloody, lay on the packed ground before the altar.

Many Negroes squatted in a semicircle within the enclosure. They were moaning a slow, monotonous chant, without beginning or end. The chant grew louder as Kate stepped forward. Shamey Lady placed a bottle in her hand and Kate, remembering what Mario had told her, went to the altar and placed the wine before the candle. She saw then the tiny bowl of white powder already there and she poured the powder into her palm and made a small cross with it on the hard black earth, then stepped back and took her place in the semicircle.

The same monotonous humming came from her lips as from those of the Ashanti who crowded about her in the near darkness.

A figure arose from near the entrance and, as he stood outlined in the door, Kate recognized Mario. He stooped and picked up one of the knives, then brought it forward, carrying it carefully on the palms of both hands. He dropped to one knee and plunged the blade into the center of the goatskin.

His voice penetrated the humming. "Yeh irrawa, yeh irrawa, kuja dini sheray dilogoowah."

The humming ceased and the drums outside grew silent. The semicircle answered in a chorus. "Babawah! Babawah!"

In the semicircle opposite Kate, a second candle was lighted. In its arc of light, Koshi's features could be seen and his long, slender hands. He placed a shallow pan before him. Then he lifted a branch of dried leaves and brought it down so that candle's flame touched the hanging leaves. There was the snap and crackle of fire and the charred leaves fell one by one into the pan. Koshi ground them into a black powder with his fingers. Mario rose and went to Kate. With a small knife he clipped off a lock of her hair and carried it across the pallay to Koshi. The old man held the hair over the flames until it caught fire and then dropped it into the black powder of the burned leaves.

Next Koshi went to the altar, uncorked the bottle of wine and raised it to his lips. He turned and sprayed the wine over the goatskin from which the knife still protruded. He knelt slowly, raised the knife and rubbed its blade with the black powder. He stood before the semicircle, his arms outstretched. The crouching Ashanti called in unison.

"Babawah! Babawah!"

Mario inserted three candles into the earth so as to form a triangle in front of the old man. The flames glistened on the dark skin of Koshi's face and made darker shadows in the hollow cheeks. The face was stern and cruel and the eyes which sought out Kate were commanding. Kate rose, her body swaying, and went to him.

Koshi held out his left hand, palm upward and Kate extended hers. The point of Koshi's knife rested in the center of the palm.

Again the cry came from the crouching Ashanti. "Babawah! Babawah!" Kate knew the meaning of the word now. "We sacrifice! We sacrifice!"

The knife cut the skin until blood stained her palm but she felt no pain. Koshi drew it swiftly along the line that circled out and about the mound of her thumb. Shamey Lady squatted beneath the outstretched hand and caught a few drops of the blood in an earthen vessel. She ran to the altar and poured the blood upon the calabash which contained food for the gods.

Koshi's eyes did not leave Kate. But now he took some of the ashes and rubbed them in the open wound. Then he twisted a piece of red ribbon about her hand .

Kate waited. The old man raised the knife high again and then laid it gently across Kate's palm, the point directed at her heart.

The drums outside broke into a frenzied rhythm and the Ashanti chant took on a quickened tempo. Koshi spoke, his soft voice penetrating the din within the enclosure.

"This knife I give to you, my child. It will reach the heart of the man who most threatens your happiness. Yet I present it to you with misgivings and only because it is Mario's desire. Obeah is a weapon against injustice, to be used for vengeance, but not for personal gain. Use wrongly the power that the gods have given and they will turn upon you and destroy you."

Kate was awakened in the morning by Shamey Lady, who was arranging a breakfast tray at her bedside. Kate pushed the pillows beneath her and sat up, her eyes on the girl's face. Shamey Lady looked away.

"Is there anything else you wish, Miss?"

162

Kate asked softly. "Where did you take me last night, Shamey Lady?"

"Take you?" The girl's hands twisted in embarrassment and her eyes looked puzzled. "I don't know what you mean, Miss."

"Where did we go to meet Koshi?"

"Koshi? You must have been dreaming, Miss Kate. I haven't seen Koshi for weeks. Mario says he's in Accompong."

Kate reached for the tray and placed it on her lap. She was uncertain now whether the Ashanti ceremony had been a dream or reality. She could not remember coming back to the Salamander and the details of the scene in the tent were hazy.

She waited until Shamey Lady left the room, then she looked about and saw no sign of the black cape or shawl she had worn; but her black slippers, scuffed and damp, lay at the foot of her bed. Then she spread out her left palm in front of her. There was a thin red line like a scratch running from the center of the palm to the mound of the thumb.

She sipped her strong tea thoughtfully. If this was not a dream, the knife must be here.

She got up hastily and searched the room but did not find the knife. Then she saw the glitter of metal beneath her bed. She knelt and picked up the knife. Its edge was jagged and its handle carved with cabalistic signs as she had remembered. But the knife should be stained with black powder, with earth and her own blood. It was not. The blade was razor sharp and shone as though it had been recently scoured and the mahogany haft was polished and gleaming.

16

GABE COUSINS crouched before the cockpit. His hands lay on the back of his favorite red cock, but his eyes kept flicking up to his wife's window. His sallow face was filled with venom and his tongue came out from time to time to moisten his dry lips. Wife indeed! He damned the day he had climbed aboard the *Liza Mae* to match his Blonde against the captain's Brassy-bones. He could curse all he wanted, yet the aching need for Kate would never leave him. It might not have been so bad, had it not been for their wedding night. Even now, the memory of it ripped at his groins, and his eyes became beady with desire.

Kate was a smart one all right and she had trapped him good. She had changed him from a man into an empty shell and she was up to the same game with the boy. She would have Mullen a mollycoddle and a mother's darling. The thought of Mullen heightened Gabe's anger. She had played another slick trick on him there. He had always thought the boy's father was Jonathan Minor and his resentment had been mixed with a secret pride that Jonathan's son should bear the Cousins name. But he knew better now. He could see what was going on right in front of him. Kate thought she was pulling the wool over his eyes; so did Bard. But they had another guess coming. Gabe smiled bitterly as he saw Kate come to her window. She was a beauty right enough. Was there any way he could play the game to possess her again? The mere thought of it almost choked him with passion. And to think that Bard had been her lover all the time! Gabe wiped a sleeve across his face. How many times had he been cuckolded? Well, let that pass. If he could prove himself a man now, things might be different. And tonight would be the test.

Bard had been hanging about the Salamander ever since he had come back from Salem. Real matey he had been too, offering to stand for drinks as often as not. But Gabe had an eye in his head, even when he had a load on. He had seen the play, right enough——Bard hanging around Kate whenever the bar was empty and her slipping him a bill or some coins. He had been told too about how Bard met her on the beach at Port Royal. The grapevine always brought things back to the tavern.

Then there was all this business about Kate and obeah. He didn't like that. Kate was getting a bad name for herself. Mixing up with Koshi and Mario. Obeah was all right for the blacks; maybe it had something in it. He had to admit he had seen some strange things. But he wanted no part of obeah, not for himself nor Kate. After tonight maybe things would be different; maybe he would be master in his own home again. He spat in his hand and rubbed the saliva into the newly cut comb of the cock.

Kate had been giving Bard money for weeks now and God knew how long she had been doing it before that. The last week or so she had not even seemed to care if he knew about it. Bold as brass she had been, passing a note across the bar. And Bard with that grin on his face. Gabe had wanted to mosh him right then and there, but it would have been no good. Bard was bigger than he, stronger and younger. Gabe couldn't hope to stand up to him in a fair fight. But there were ways of whittling a man down to your own size.

Today was pit day and they were reckoning on him spending the day fighting his cocks and coming home drunk, late at night. He had heard the two of them talking. Kate hadn't even seemed to care that he heard. She must have known he was just the other side of the door and she hadn't bothered to keep her voice down.

"Wait 'til tomorrow night," she said. "Gabe won't be around then. You don't want him to find out about this, do you?"

"What do I care what the lily-livered little bastard knows. Let the world know, far as I care." His words were slurred with drink. "Gabe Cousins'll be the laughingstock of Kingston. But what do we care about Gabe? C'mon, Kate, gi' me a kiss."

"Not here, Bard. Wait 'til tomorrow."

"I been doing too much waitin'. I'm gittin' tired of it."

Kate had come out into the kitchen and seen Gabe standing by the door, but she didn't even blink an eye. Well, no drinks for him today. Maybe just one or two to buck him up. He'd never killed a man yet, but tonight he was going to do it—with the help of God and a piece of iron pipe. Kingston would see he was no man to cuckold.

The rain had started early in the evening, a steady relentless downpour that turned the Parade into a field of mud and the cobbled streets into shallow rapids. The wind came later, in great gusts that battered the sides of the tavern and uprooted the rotting tamarind tree that stood before it. One of the limbs had come hurtling onto the veranda where it broke the spokes of the railing and lodged itself securely between the splintered spokes and the heavy balustrade. The wind ripped at the branches so that they slapped against the balcony with the sound of whips.

The Salamander was nearly deserted but still it was alive with sounds. Kate had dismissed the servants and she stood behind the bar herself. Somewhere above a board creaked sharply. Kate's lips tightened. Gabe was somewhere in the house. She had heard him slipping in just before the rain started. He had always come directly to the bar before, for he could never stand to be alone. Kate was sure now that he had heard the words between herself and Bard, that he was lurking somewhere in the shadows above, waiting.

Only three men were in the public rooms—Mac-Feathers, Brandon and Bard. The little Scot had his bagpipes with him, but the skirling mingled eerily with the wind and heightened the melancholy of the stormy night.

Brandon turned angrily to the Scot. "Put ye bloody pipes away, Alex. They fair gi' me the creeps, like as though the ruddy wind were risin' out o' the table."

MacFeathers shrugged and raised his mug of ale to his lips. " 'Tis no soul ye have for music, Syd."

Brandon growled an answer and moved toward the shuttered window, trying to peer out.

Bard struggled to his feet. He was already drunk and he walked with an unsteady step. He came to the bar and Kate lowered her hand to where the jagged knife lay hidden beneath the mopping rags.

" 'Tis time I talked wi' ye, Kate. Have ye got the money ready?"

Kate spoke softly. "Wait. Wait 'til the others have gone."

" 'Tis always waitin' ye're asking o' me. I've waited long enough. If ye think to be trickin' me, Kate, ye've got the wrong mon. I'm no spineless lochy like that Gabe o' yourn, nor no—"

He broke off sharply at the sound of carriage wheels and a loud halloo. Kate slipped past him to the barred door and flung it open. The wind whistled into the close room and blew a chair over near the doorway. A moment later, two figures came stamping into the tavern.

Kate forced the door shut, dropped the bar, then turned to look at her guests. It was a man with a small, fragile woman on his arm. He helped her to a chair, then doffed his hat and threw back his cape. His eyes met Kate's squarely. There was something disconcerting in the level gaze and the composed face that gave no clue to the man's thoughts. He was tall, strikingly handsome, blue-eyed, fair-skinned, with hair that was almost yellow. When he spoke his voice was melodious, though a trifle high-pitched. "A big tree's blown across the road leading to Government House. The carriage cannot pass it and my cousin's in no shape to walk. We turned back, thinking maybe you could give us shelter and a little brandy and let us wait out the gale."

Kate recognized him with a start. This was the man whom she had seen supporting the dissolute old Governor to his box in the theater—Sir William Elgin. Even before she turned she knew who his companion must be. She shifted her gaze and looked into the pale, heart-shaped face of Rose Minor.

Rose plucked at Sir William's sleeve. "We should not have turned back. If papa is so ill, he needs me. We must get through somehow."

Sir William smiled down at her, but his eyes kept turning back to Kate. "You worry too much about your father,

Rose. It is only gout and his choleric temper that ails him —and that he ate too much turtle and too many tree oysters. I should have refused to fetch you from Rune Hall. Every time Sir George has a pang of indigestion he cries he's dying."

Rose looked about nervously. "I know you're right. Still, I can't help worrying." She shivered a little and swished her damp skirts. Her gaze met Kate's. "Some brandy might take the chill out, if you could spare us some."

Kate nodded. She was glad for the respite, yet uneasy, for the presence of Elgin made her plans hazardous. She passed Bard on her way to the back room to fetch a special brandy from the wine closet. Bard lolled insolently at the bar, one arm spread across the stained mahogany. His eyes watched her speculatively; then he turned his attention to the newcomers.

Kate slipped the bolt of the door through which she had passed in place. She leaned against the wall for a minute listening to the sounds of the storm. The showdown must come tonight, she thought, no matter who was present. She had been disconcerted by Brandon's appearance for she hated and distrusted him. And now Elgin was here too. No matter, she must go through with her plan. Bard's demands were too urgent to brook delay and in his drunken state he might blurt out anything. She smiled to herself. Perhaps it was better to have Elgin here in the Salamander after all. It was obvious that he was attracted to her. If her plans went well, he would vouch for her. And if something went amiss, she suspected it would be easy to win the young man to her side. She sensed the ruthlessness within him and judged that he had little use for abstract justice. He would try to turn events to his own ends. Well, two could play that game and she had no doubt but what she could outwit him if need be.

She uncorked the brandy and brought out fresh glasses so that she would not need go behind the bar until she so wished. When she returned to the public room, she saw that Rose and Elgin had taken the table beside that of Brandon and the Scot. Sir William was speaking so low that she could not hear, but MacFeathers was protesting his words. Bard still sprawled half across the bar, his appearance of complete drunkenness belied by his watchful eyes.

Kate took the single lamp from the bar and placed it on Elgin's table. She put down the glasses and filled them slowly.

MacFeathers was talking. " 'Tis a mad idea ye have, Sir William. If Buddhoe has Nigel, no threat will make him gi' him up to ye. Buddhoe's a code of honor, though it be different from a white mon's."

"Code of honor!" sputtered Elgin. "The man's broken every treaty he's made with the English."

"Ay, he's not alone i' that. We've no right to be proud of our record."

"There's only one thing to do with Buddhoe and his cutthroats—wipe out every last man of them."

"Ye could not do it, not in years. Send up your red-coats, marchin' in formation through the pit country. What will happen? Buddhoe's men will pick them off from the trees, from behind stones, from the depth of the sillow brush. With their red coats and their solid formation, they'll be like sitting ducks. 'Tis madness, I tell ye, and well Jonathan Minor knows it. Why does Stallybrass not heed his words?"

Kate listened no further, for she saw that Elgin was paying no real attention to the Scot's words but was watching her. Quickly she turned back to the bar. The whole side of the room was in deep shadow, so that Bard's body seemed misshapen in the semidarkness. She went directly to him and faced him across the mahogany counter.

"Have ye the money, Kate?"

"I have it. But I'll not give it to you, tonight or any other night."

"So ye've changed your mind?"

"Yes."

"But ye've the money?"

"Yes."

"Where is it?"

"I'll not tell."

Bard reached behind the bar and seized Kate by the wrist. The fingers dug into her flesh, but she did not draw

169

back. Out of the corner of her eye she had seen Gabe Cousins on the stairway. She leaned forward and whispered to Bard, " 'was a joke, Bard, I'll fetch it for you. 'Tis upstairs."

Gabe Cousins was only a few feet away now and his arm was upraised, a length of solid piping in his clenched hand. There was a scream of warning from Rose Minor. Bard whirled and the pipe grazed his chest. Bard staggered backward, but before Cousins could raise the pipe again the big man was on him, pinning his arm behind him. Gabe Cousins gave a roar of rage and frustration and with surprising strength drove his fist into the big man's stomach. Bard grunted and fell forward, carrying Cousins with him. The two men rolled on the floor, side by side at the end of the bar.

Kate held the knife concealed by the folds of her skirt. She bent over the fighting men. A hand came up, palm open, and Kate thrust the mahogany handle into the clutching fingers. The blade made a short arc and buried itself in flesh.

Gabe Cousins gave a soft moan and lay still. Bard got to one knee, the knife still in his hand. His eyes were wild and his face drained of color. He looked down at Cousins, then up at Kate. He staggered to his feet. He drew his arm back, the bloodstained knife held in a threatening gesture. He looked dazedly from Kate to the group across the room. His mouth twisted and inarticulate sounds came from his lips.

Only Elgin moved. He walked slowly toward Bard. "Drop that knife and surrender to me," he ordered.

Bard swayed drunkenly toward Elgin. "Get out o' me path."

Elgin reached for his pistol but, as he did so, Rose Minor ran to his side. "He's dangerous, William! Leave him alone."

Bard gave a baffled roar and started for the door, but Rose was in his way. His knife lashed out again and Rose screamed. Bard got to the door and fumbled with the bar. As the wind slammed open the door, there was the crash of Elgin's pistol, but the shot missed and splintered the woodwork. A third crash followed as the swirling wind toppled over a lamp.

While Brandon and MacFeathers beat out the licking flames, Sir William rushed to the veranda, but Bard had already disappeared in the engulfing blackness of the storm.

Kate and Rose knelt beside Cousins.

"Is he dead?" Rose whispered.

Kate nodded, then she reached out and took the girl's hand in hers. The knife had raked the side of the hand. The wound was not serious, but it was bleeding freely.

Kate said softly, "You are hurt. I must take care of you."

"But this man—he is your husband."

"He is dead. There is nothing we can do for him."

Kate stood up and drew Rose close to her as the three men came to stare down at Gabe Cousins' body. She looked at their faces to see if there were any signs of suspicion. Brandon and the old Scot showed only the horror that comes with unexpected, violent death. Elgin's face was inscrutable. The pale eyes met hers calmly, giving no slightest clue to his thoughts. Then a sound attracted her attention and she glanced quickly to the top of the stairs. Mullen stood there in his nightshirt, his eyes wide with fright. He saw his mother's eyes upon him and whirled about. She heard the soft swift padding of his bare feet as he ran back to his room.

17

A FRESH CONTINGENT of soldiers—five hundred strong—had arrived in Kingston. They swaggered about the Parade, thronged the shops of King Street, idled in front of the Royal Theatre or drank in the Salamander Tavern. A holiday spirit filled the island as the old century neared its end. The streets were noisier than ever, the banquets more colorful. Strolling singers entertained the soldiers. Duels were fought over trivialities. Hundreds of pounds changed hands daily in the cockpits.

Yet there were some who viewed the presence of the soldiers with misgiving and were aware of new tensions beneath the gaudy display of prosperity. The planters were beginning to feel the squeeze as the market price of sugar dropped and as more and more of their ships were being seized by the French. Back in England there were debates in parliament on abandoning the slave trade, and even talk of abolition. The planters cursed the meddling reformers, talked of revolt against the Crown and entertained more freely than ever.

Close at home there was more cause for worry. The Maroon soldiers were deserting and finding their way back to Accompong, taking their guns with them. Sydney Brandon was becoming a political power on the island and his demagoguery threatened to touch off the spark that would bring open warfare between the English and Buddhoe's men. It was known now that Nigel was with Buddhoe in Accompong and that he was whipping up virulent hatred against the whites. Picon the old minstrel had wandered back into Kingston after five years among the Maroons. He had been timorous at first, fearful that his life might still be in danger, but with Bard in hiding and Charl Loizeaux out of the island, no one molested him. Kate let him come to the Salamander to sing his ballads and one of his most ribald ditties dealt with Nigel and Connie Abbott. Nigel's giant body, his fierceness and the fact that he had killed a white man with his bare hands, all served to give him a prestige which placed him second only to Buddhoe at Accompong.

Governor Stallybrass had sent a curtly worded command to the Maroon chief to hand Nigel over to the British authorities. Buddhoe had openly flaunted the Governor's power by a direct refusal. Stallybrass had nearly choked with rage on receiving the answer. Only Jonathan Minor's intervention had prevented him from immediately sending a punitive expedition to the Cockpit country. And now Minor's power was waning and the choleric old Governor was depending more and more on Sir William Elgin.

Mullen was enchanted with the resplendent uniforms of the soldiers. The officers who frequented the Salamander made a favorite of him, offering him sweets and coins and sometimes a surreptitious sip from their mugs. Kate's eyes sparkled with anger but there was little she could do. The boy stood sullenfaced before her when she scolded him. When she tried to caress him, he slipped through her hands and ran to find Shamey Lady. In the months that followed Gabriel Cousins' death, the tavern prospered as it never had before, but Kate was unhappy. Kate's release from Cousins had cost her the love of her son and now the need for Mullen became a burning thing, so that she could scarcely let him out of her sight. She would have prayed for him but she was held back by superstitious fear. Had she not made the sign of the cross backward and practiced the magic rites of obeah? Surely the prayer would turn to a curse if it came from her lips. It was better to think how she might secure for him the things he needed. Her fingers bit deep into her palm and opened the tiny wound that still remained tender.

On the second day of November the troops were mustered on the Parade, and Stallybrass himself with Sir William Elgin at his side came to speak to them. They must take Buddhoe, he admonished them, and destroy Accompong. The threat of the Maroons must be wiped out forever, so that Jamaica could be free of this perpetual menace. The throng cheered at the Governor's words and the soldiers in their red coats and white breeches stood erect and proud. But there were some who listened with foreboding. MacFeathers cursed beneath his breath. Jonathan Minor, exhausted by hours of useless pleading, looked away from the troops. His eyes touched those of Kate Cousins, and for the first time since she had struck him in Rune Hall, she met his gaze directly. While the words of the Governor still rang across the Parade, the dondo drums beat softly, relaying the message of the forthcoming attack to Buddhoe's men, waiting in the hills.

By the end of the month a few of the redcoats stumbled back into Kingston. Their uniforms were in tatters and caked with mud. They were wild-eyed and some could only gibber of ghosts and of drums that killed. Those who could talk coherently told how every minute of the night and day arrows, stones and spears had fallen among them, seemingly thrown by invisible hands. The beat of the drums surrounded them, rising, falling, but never ceasing entirely. Shots came from the darkness though one could neither see nor hear the sound of a man. Disembodied hands reached out from the sillow brush and plunged knives into their bodies. Soldiers dropped and died, though no wounds showed upon them. The rivers were poisoned and sometimes when the leaves of a tree brushed a man's face, a great welt appeared and he felt burning pain that spread to torment the whole body until the man turned raving mad. The English guns were useless against Maroons, who never showed themselves. At night the soldiers were afraid to light fires, for those who came anywhere near the flames were picked off one by one. They huddled together in the darkness waiting for a warning sound, but they could hear nothing save the constant throbbing of the drums. They shot at moving shadows and killed one another in a frenzy of fear.

Not more than fifty men came back in all. The planters drew a long breath and cursed Stallybrass and Buddhoe impartially. If they feared reprisals, they showed it only in the quickened tempo with which they prepared to celebrate the turn of the century.

The Christmas season was a slack time for the plantation workers and it was a custom of the island to give all house servants and the trusted field hands a three-day holiday. For the special occasion of the coming year of 1800, the days of grace were extended. The strong clan feeling of the Negroes still existed. Koramantyns, Ashanti, Yarubas, Eboes, Papaws, Whidahs and scores of other tribes banded together and sought to outdo one another in adding to the merriment and wild excitement of the holidays. Slaves and freedmen joined in little bands, dressed in gaudy costumes and put on hideous masks. They paraded, gamboled, danced and played on their goombahs, merry-wangs, benders and banjils.

The Parade seethed with movement. Sometimes the parading bands met in mock warfare. At other times a leader would challenge another to a "stick battle," a mock duel fought with the stripped limbs of the cannon ball tree and with all the punctilio of the genuine duel. The swishing limbs had the hardness, the suppleness and the cutting edge of fine steel. The sticks could slice through the flesh to the bone, or crack a man's rib, and there were times when the duels became deadly and only one man emerged from the ring alive.

All night long there was drinking and feasting about the bonfires. The rich planters rolled out puncheons of rum from which all were free to partake. Negro women boiled huge kettles of pepper pot, containing fish, shrimp and vegetables stewed together with rich island spices. Wild pigs were roasted over the open flames and turtles baked on the living coals. Slave and master ate and drank side by side and all the misery of the cane fields, the flogging sheds and gnawing hunger were forgotten.

The Salamander Tavern was crowded night and day. Cavorting dancers whooped through the halls and the verandas were filled with revelers who peered in through the windows. Some of the celebrators never paid for the ale or rum they drank; others threw down handfuls of coins and bills. Kate Cousins watched the frantic scenes played in the public rooms and on the Parade. She was half amused, half angry, and a little frightened. But as a whole she kept her temper, stowed away all that was breakable and watched the mounting heap of coins that passed over her counter.

On the last night of the bacchanal, Kate stood watching the revelry in the tavern. MacFeathers disentangled himself from the throng and joined her. His face was flushed with drink and he carried a joint of a wild pig in his hand.

"Ay, lass," he greeted her, " 'tis no place for the pipes tonight. 'Tis the goombah and the merry-wang as sets the tune."

Kate looked down into the Scot's merry face. "I've been thinking 'twould be a fine time for Buddhoe to strike at Kingston."

MacFeathers chuckled. "Nay, lassie. Should Buddhoe's men come here tonight, who would gie them heed? Stick a pistol in a man's pot and he will laugh at you. 'Tis more safe tonight than ever in the island. I'll warrant there's many a one o' Buddhoe's men a-frolickin' in the Parade. And would Buddhoe be a-spoilin' the fun for the slaves? Nay, nay, he's the need o' the help o' the blacks o' Kingston."

He bit into the meat and tore a chunk loose with his teeth. "Lassie, this thing is hard to believe, but when St. Clement strikes midnight tomorrow the blacks'll be back in their compounds and the fun'll be over for another year. The redcoats'll take over the streets and the blacks'll be shot on sight. And when it's all over there'll be the big ball in Government House and the planters' ladies will dance and drink their punch. The bookkeepers'll bend their knees and old Stallybrass'll pass among the ladies, has he not manured his belly so he canna walk."

The Scot's eyes twinkled as he looked up at Kate. "Be ye going to the Governor's ball, lassie?"

"I've not been asked."

"Ah, 'tis once that Government House is open to all. Besides 'tis a mask ye'll be wearing, though none could doubt the carriage of ye, lassie. There's not another so proud in Jamaica."

As MacFeathers spoke, there was a footfall behind them. Kate looked up to find Sir William Elgin joining them. He bowed over Kate's hand. MacFeathers growled with distaste and turned away.

Elgin paid no attention to the little Scot, but smilingly he scanned Kate's face. "My cousin Rose and I have talked about you many times. She is grateful to you for binding her hand. She requests that you come to see her."

Kate gazed levelly back into Elgin's pale eyes. She was unable to tell whether mockery or genuine kindness lay behind his courtesy. But the foppery, the blandness of speech she recognized as a pose. This man had steeled himself to cast aside all else save his ambition, even as she had done. For a moment she felt drawn to him—but this she knew was dangerous. She responded stiffly without answering the implied question. "Mistress Minor's hand, I hope it is better?"

"Yes, thanks to you. But Rose is not well. You touched her deeply with your kindness. She has few friends here; will you not come to Rune Hall to see her?"

"Can she not come here?"

"It is not seemly——" Elgin saw the flame of anger in Kate's eyes. "She is not well enough," he added lamely.

Kate breathed deeply and her face flushed. "I understand, Sir William. The mistress of Rune Hall can scarce

meet openly with the mistress of the Salamander Tavern."
She walked swiftly by him. Elgin's hand touched her
sleeve, but she shook it off.

"Mrs. Cousins, I beg of you——" Elgin's voice trailed
off as the beating of shak-shaks and the cries of a band
of mummers flooded the public rooms.

Kate walked on through the throng and up the wide
stairs. Her cheeks were still hot with anger. She clutched
the railing with her fingers. So Rose was too fine a lady
to visit her here at the Salamander! Well, the tables would
be turned in time, not only on Rose and Jonathan Minor
but on this young popin-jay too. She drew her breath
in sharply. The others would be easy, but Elgin might
prove an enemy worthy of her steel. For a moment, hot
excitement ran through her at the thought of humbling
him and the sweet sensation of it made her knees weak.
With Elgin it would be a real victory, for only he would
understand the stakes for which they played. If she lost
she would become a pawn in his hands. This must never
be, or her dreams of power and vengeance would fade
away. And then what would be left for her?

At the top of the stairs she hesitated, then moved toward Mullen's room. She placed her hand on the knob
and then stood silent. Mullen would turn from her as he
had every night since Gabe Cousins' death. The thought of
the child's face, stubborn and defiant, was too much for
her to endure. How much had he seen that night? He alone
could have watched her hand as it fitted the knife into
Bard's, for the bar blocked off the vision of the others.
If he would tell her what he knew, she might make him
understand why she had done it. But could she succeed in
this with a boy of four? Better to say nothing, perhaps. In
the years to come, he might believe himself mistaken. He
might even forget.

She realized she was indulging in self-pity and roused
herself angrily. In a few minutes the new century would
roll in. She must listen to every stroke of the bell of St.
Clement and harden herself to the tasks that lay ahead.

18

THE FIRST DAY of the new century had come and Kingston, exhausted by its ten-day orgy, lay motionless and silent, blanketed by a thin mist that hung like steam above the sweltering earth. The festivities were over for the blacks and they had returned to the shacks of Baraçong, the bare barracks, or the slave quarters of dobe and wattle. Only the remnants of the gaiety remained in the Parade and on the streets—beads, tinsel, bright paper and bits of broken mirrors, trodden into the earth or resting between cobblestones. An occasional Negro, too drunk to return to the safety of his quarters, slept in an alleyway. A single mummer, still dressed in tattered finery, sprawled in the Parade. At noon a redcoat prodded him with a pointed shoe and the bleary-eyed Negro looked up in confusion, then frightened by the face looming above him, scuttled off as fast as his legs could carry him.

For the whites, however, the main event of the holiday season lay ahead. The masked ball at Government House was open to every man and woman with white skin in Jamaica. The planters' wives, who had stayed behind barred doors during the riotous street celebrations, were looking forward eagerly to the more decorous entertainment provided by the Governor. "God Save the King" would be sung lustily and frequently; and the dance music would be played not with goombahs and dondos, but with violins and the booming note of the bass viol. There would be a steaming roast of beef on the table, Yorkshire pudding, roasted pigeons, ham and capons served on silver trenchers. Sometime during the evening the servants would march in with a huge silver tray which, when uncovered, would disclose a gigantic plum pudding. The Governor would call for a toast and the ladies would fill their cups from the cut-glass punch bowl and drink to the King. For a while they would forget the eternal heat, the incessant fears of Jamaica, and would be back in that England from which many of them had fled to avoid punishment for debt or crime, but which they now remembered as a land of comfort, ease and luxurious living.

To Kate Cousins of Galway, the name of England was the name of tyranny. Yet she felt a little breathless as she prepared her dress for the Governor's ball. Since she had been in Jamaica, she had been ostracized by the planters' ladies and even the wives of the government clerks. When chance had brought them to the tavern, they had eyed Kate's full-blown beauty with haughty disapproval, or whispered sly remarks behind their spread fans. Today was the beginning of a new century, Kate thought, and tonight she would stand proudly among the women of Jamaica. Let them whisper the name of the White Witch that had been given to her and let them tell the story of how she had been won in a cockfight on the deck of the *Liza Mae*. It did not matter. She would draw the eyes of the men at least and many of them would think with self-pity of the dreary women with whom they must spend the long, hot Jamaica nights.

Kate turned the dress over in her hands. It was of white crepe, embroidered with silver spangles, cut much like a child's frock with a round skirt and not much train. The gown was sleeveless with broad silver-spangled shoulder straps. On her head, she would wear a turban of spangled crepe looped with imitation pearls and a paradise feather. The white crepe domino was to be worn until midnight, but as MacFeathers had said, there would be none at Government House who would fail to recognize her.

She arrived at Government House late. The street was already lined with many carriages. The liveried footmen, waiting for their masters, talked softly to one another. Even from the outside she could hear the high-pitched violins playing a polka. She gave her cloak to an attendant and passed through a hall overhung with the branches of lime, pomegranate and mango trees. Beyond was the ballroom, but as she stepped forward she felt a touch on her arm.

179

The man bowed and raised her hand to his lips. He wore a domino, but as in Kate's own case, it was the merest pretense of disguise. He said mockingly, "You have come too late to hear the Governor's speech."

"A pity."

"Is it not? But there is still punch left in the bowl and the Governor's supply of champagne is not exhausted. Perhaps you would care to dance."

Kate's lips twisted into a smile. "The fiddlers are not skilled at the polka."

"No. Perhaps we can persuade them to try an Irish tune."

Kate's laughter tinkled a trifle apprehensively as she took the proffered arm. The music was drawing to a close as they entered the ballroom. The dancing couples, still chatting, turned to leave the floor and caught sight of Kate and her escort. Their voices turned to whispers. The booming talk of the men who surrounded the food-laden tables stopped as, one by one, they turned to look at Kate. Almost in silence, the pair walked toward the orchestra.

The voices rose again, whispering sharp, high-pitched. " 'Tis Kate Cousins . . . the bound girl . . . the one the Negroes call the Witch." "Lord of Mercy, who'd have thought she'd make such a catch . . . why, 'tis Sir William Elgin with her." "He must have taken leave of his wits— Sir William, my God!" "What will Stallybrass say to this?"

If Elgin heard the whispers he gave no sign. A few minutes later, when the orchestra started to play, he led Kate out onto the floor. At first no one joined them and they danced alone, Kate to some inward pattern of rhythm. Elgin moved close to her and she felt his quickened breath against her cheek. As she drew away from him she said mockingly, "Sir William, you do your reputation no good."

But there was no humor in his reply. "Damn them. Damn them all. It's many a fine tale they have to tell of you, Kate Cousins. But there's not one with your beauty nor your spirit on this accursed island."

Kate tapped him with her fan. "As for you, Sir William, 'tis said you have no blood in your veins, that you're cold as steel, that you think only of politics and personal ambitions."

"They were right once, Kate, but that was before I met

you and saw the fire in you. My God, I never thought I'd want to take a woman in my arms over the body of her husband—"

"Say no more now. There is much time—and you know little of me."

"I know the richness of your voice, the litheness of your body, that there is beauty in every line of your face."

"Be quiet, Sir William. 'Tis too public a place in which to seduce a bound girl, the widow of an innkeeper."

"Seduce?"

"Sh-sh, whatever you wish of me, you must tell me later."

He was silent for a moment. When he spoke his voice was brittle, strained. "You're right. You're right. It's madness."

"Madness," Kate taunted, "sheer madness, Sir William."

When the dance was ended, Elgin led Kate out through the latticed doorway into the sweeping floral gardens. The air was fragrant with the scent of the flowers which lay hidden in the shadows. Elgin was silent until they came to a bench over which a lime tree cast a pattern of black lace.

"Come, Kate. Let us sit down."

"No, Sir William. The night is pleasant. Let us walk a bit further."

"Kate, have I been wrong to dream of you?"

"I do not know the nature of your dreams. But you are not a boy. I have been told that you are haughty, arrogant, bold."

"Do not mock me. You seem to have the calmness and assurance of a goddess. What lies underneath? Some passion, I know. What is it? Anger? Fear? Hate? Love?"

"You are imagining things, Sir William. Has it ever occurred to you that your face too gives little hint to what thoughts lie within your mind? Yet I doubt if you deceive me.'

Elgin's arm encircled her waist and he leaned forward to kiss her. Kate broke away, laughing, and held him at arm's length. "No, Sir William, I do not come so cheaply."

"Cheaply! What do you think I wish of you?"

"I cannot know unless you tell me."

"Kate, I saw you first in the Royal Theatre with your

face lit up by the candles' glare. It caught the flames in your hair but it left your face as though carved in alabaster. I though you beautiful, but I was unmoved. Then that night at the Salamander, when you tended the cut on Rose's hand, I had to admire your coolness and your courage. Something happened. You looked upstairs and your son was standing there. Your face became soft, filled with love and despair. You were off guard for a moment only, but I saw the way your face would look to one whom you loved. Oh, I am speaking awkwardly."

"Perhaps you speak too well. You think that I might love you?"

"Is it too much to hope?"

"I think you play the game of love well, Sir William. I have no doubt you've been a great success with many a scullery maid."

Elgin's eyes were burning. He stepped toward her but she moved away. "Kate, I swear by all——"

A firm step sounded on the gravel path. Kate ignored Elgin's outstretched hand and turned swiftly away. Elgin hurried after her but before he could speak again, they came face to face with Jonathan Minor. Minor wore no mask and, in the sudden rift of the clouds, his face showed white and set. He bowed slightly and addressed himself to Elgin. "His Excellency has sent me to find you. He wishes to retire, but he requires a word with you first. I think that he is fearful lest Buddhoe may strike tonight and he desires to place authority in your hands. Captain MacIntosh is with him now." Minor's voice was calm but he could not conceal completely the surging anger which filled him.

Elgin glanced from Minor to Kate. There was mingled frustration and victory in his face. Until now Jonathan Minor had stood second in power to Stallybrass and all orders not signed by the Governor himself had passed through Minor. It was obvious that this was no longer true. Elgin was superseding Minor—the Governor had chosen the first day of the new century to make this clear.

The two men faced each other in silence—Minor stiff, unbending—Elgin smiling and debonair. The tension between them was unbroken by words, but each understood the mortal hatred of the other. Elgin bowed to Kate and excused himself hurriedly. Kate and Jonathan listened to his quick footfalls as he returned to Government House.

Jonathan's voice grated when he finally spoke for he could canceal his anger no longer. "The young whipper-snapper! He came here without a farthing to his name to suck upon his uncle's blood. He cares nothing for the lives of the soldiers that he's thrown away. He would make of Jamaica a charnel house, did it serve his ends. Buddhoe will stay in Accompong if he's left alone. He knows things are better as they are. But if the soldiers reach Accompong and burn it Buddhoe will lose control of his men if he does not start a revolt. I've warned Stallybrass it will mean endless fighting. The old man thinks only of his gout and lets his rascally nephew twist him about his finger. Elgin has the Governor betwitched, and he uses his power only to bring bloodshed to Jamaica."

Kate was silent, waiting for Minor to speak further; but he stared moodily at the lighted doorway through which Elgin had passed. Finally she asked, "What does he want, Jonathan?"

"What does he want?" Minor repeated the question harshly. "The man wants to be the next governor of Jamaica. Stir up trouble—then crush it down. That's his formula for success. God knows, it may work out that way. Syd Brandon and the planters are howling for the blood of Stallybrass. Brandon's in the pay of Elgin, but that is something the Governor will never believe of his own nephew. Should I try to tell him, 'twould be the end for me."

"Perhaps you are mistaken."

Minor turned upon her, his eyes angry. "There is no mistake." He looked at her silently for a moment, then asked grimly, "Why do you defend him, Kate?"

"I am neither defending nor condeming him."

"Has he been making love to you?"

Kate smiled and looked up at Minor. "He does so most persuasively."

"I've no doubt of that. Don't be a fool, Kate. The man is hard and selfish. He offers you only pain and suffering. When you're of no use to him, he'll turn on you like a panther cub."

"And you, Jonathan, were you so different? Did you

have more to offer? Maybe your warning springs from the knowledge of yourself, not Elgin."

Minor turned to her and placed both hands on her arms. She felt the trembling of his body as he peered down at her through the darkness. "Kate, you are right. I must not condemn another. I have been cruel, and a fool. I was caught between two loyalties and perhaps I chose the wrong one. I've tried to hate you, Kate, and I've tried to love Rose—and I can never do either. You've haunted my bed and my home. Every day when I go to Rose's room, you are standing at the balcony, your hands clasped about the railing. I hear your voice, your laughter. I kiss Rose's lips and they are thin and cool and I turn away that she may not see the longing in my eyes. You have possessed Rune Hall, Kate. I see you at the table where you never sat. I see you in the garden where you never walked. I have gone to Barraca Cove many times to see you again on the sands. I call to you and you are gone."

Kate felt his fingers bruising the flesh of her arms and she tried to pull away but he would not let her free. "I've been wrong, Kate, and I cannot blame you for hating me. If it were to be done again, I would marry you and take you to Rune Hall, and to the devil with Stallybrass and Rose and all the rest. Take pity on me, Kate, for I acknowledge the wrong and 'tis so deep it has no bottom."

Kate asked coolly, "What would you have me do?"

Minor's hands fell at his side. "I do not know. I truly do not know. It has been worse of late, for Rose is sick nigh unto death. She lies, her eyes open, but seeing nothing. She will not eat, she will not look at me, sometimes I think she will refuse to breathe. But she remembers you, Kate, and how you bound up her hand at the Salamander. She has had no mother. No one in her life has loved her. Maybe Stallybrass, somewhere in that cantankerous old heart of his, has affection for her, but if he has, he's shown it only in making demands upon her. Rose came to me for love and I could not give it. And then when she was hurt, you took care of her. You must have been gentle with her. Sometimes I think you must have rubbed some magic lotion in her cut. Anyway, she asks for you, begs me to bring you to her. What can I say?

Can I ask the woman I betrayed to come to Rune Hall to comfort my wife?"

Kate spoke slowly. "Do you want me at Rune Hall, Jonathan?"

"Rose wants you."

"That is not what I asked."

Minor looked up, his face haggard. "My God, yes. More than anything in the world."

"Then I'll come."

"You mean——"

"I'll come if you'll take me to Rune Hall tonight."

His arms stretched out to hold her. "No," she cried sharply. "Now I'll go to Rose. Where is your coach?"

"In front of Government House."

"We can go out through the gardens. We need not pass through the house."

She walked ahead of him, almost running. But in the dark arbor, she turned. Through the lighted window she caught a glimpse of Elgin as he stood before Stallybrass. She could go back now, she thought, and leave this aging man here. She could go back and give herself to Sir William, who was young. His ardor might give her a passing happiness. But it would not last. Jonathan was right when he said that Elgin would only use her for pleasure and then discard her. She dared take no such risk. Almost frantically, she threw her arms about Jonathan. Their lips touched and they clung together. Again and again she heard him repeat her name, until finally she pulled herself free. She was trembling, but she knew she must go with Jonathan tonight. If Elgin should speak of love again, she would listen and then all her plans would come tumbling at her feet. She would become hollow, a mere actor in another's play. Her longing changed to hate. Why could not Elgin have left her alone? Why must he make her ambition have such a bitter taste?

"We must go," she whispered savagely.

"Yes, my love—to Rune Hall."

"Later, Jonathan," she said. Then deliberately, knowing that she was cutting off her last retreat, she added, "There is another place where we must go first—to Barraca Cove."

BOOK THREE

1805

19

MULLEN hated Rune Hall. He lay in the shadow of a wild orange tree and looked up at the gray turrets and wished that he could live again amidst the constant movement of the Salamander Tavern and the Parade. The glistening mahogany floors of Rune Hall, the high ceilings with the enormous rafters, the wide sweep of the stairway, even his mother's bed raised on its triple dais, all served to emphasize his own smallness and his sense of insecurity. The grounds were not much better. The lawns were close-cropped, the hedges flawless in their symmetry, the sentries on guard at the gate too austere to play with a small boy. In back of the house, sugar cane fields stretched almost as far as the eye could see and beyond that mahogany trees made the hills dark with their heavy foliage.

There was fun to be had in the slave quarters if only his mother would let him go there. Sister Anna or old Job liked to tell him Anansi stories remembered from their own childhood in Africa. Mullen had listened in wide-eyed wonder to tales of the miraculous spider 'Nansi, of his half brother Brar Dead, and of the cowardly buffoon, Brar Rabbit. But Kate had found him one day lying at Sister Anna's feet and she had sent him back to the house and threatened to use an ebony branch on Sister Anna if she caught her filling Mullen's head with such nonsense again. After that Sister Anna always gave him a sideways look and then pretended that he wasn't around. Mullen felt he had betrayed her in some way and his face flushed with shame. So he stopped going to the slave quarters altogether.

Sometimes he hated his mother. She wanted him to call her Mama, but he always called her Kate in his own mind. When she came into his room at night to kiss him, he would pretend he was asleep. There were times when she would stand by his bed for a long time. He would have liked to have jumped up and twined his arms about her the way he used to long ago. But he couldn't because he was frightened of her although he didn't know exactly why. She never hit him or even scolded him much, but all the things that seemed such fun to him met with her cold disapproval.

Sometimes he loved her too, with all the desperation of his loneliness. He wanted to go to her and tell her, but then the awful picture would come to his mind. Maybe he would have thought it was something he had dreamed if it wasn't that Gabe had been dead the next morning. He had stood up at the top of the stairs and seen Gabe killed. He had watched Kate take the knife out of the folds of her skirt and put it in Bard's hand. Maybe Kate had meant to give the knife to Gabe. That was what he would like to think, but the picture was too clear. Bard's great fist was twice the size of Gabe's. Besides, Kate had not grieved over Gabe—not a bit. She almost seemed glad that Bard had got away. Mullen had wanted to see Bard hanged like the men about the Salamander said he should be. He had dreams at times of killing Bard himself to avenge Gabe. After all, Gabe was his father, wasn't he?

And that was something funny too. Kate had never wanted him to be with Gabe—never let him go to the cockfights, or down to the harbor—never minded that he called him Gabe. But now she wanted him to call Mr. Minor "Father," Mullen always gagged over the word. Usually he said "Yes, sir" or "No, sir." No one could say that wasn't polite. Not that Mr. Minor didn't treat him well enough, but the man was so big and tall and gray-haired and old, and his voice was so deep and his manners so formal, Mullen would rather have Gabe for a father any day. Gabe never talked down to you. He showed you his cocks, or ate genips with you or took you to gather tree oysters if you could slip away from Kate.

A wood slave rustled among the dry leaves at Mullen's

feet. The little gray lizard somehow made him think of Rose Minor. She had gone away a long time ago and had taken Ishbel with her. Neither of them ever came back and he knew that Rose had died at sea, on her way back to England to see the doctors. No one ever spoke about Rose now, but sometimes when a ship came in there was a letter to Mr. Minor from Ishbel. The girl was in school in England. Mullen shivered at the thought of England. Kate had told him it was cold there and that there was snow on the ground for months at a time. Mullen wouldn't like that. Maybe it would be fun though to go to a real school instead of having a tutor like Mr. Forbes.

The wood slave came close, peering out of its beady eyes at the boy. Mullen reached out a tentative hand, but the creature scuttled away, frightened. Rose had been afraid too. Mullen had only seen her a few times, lying straight and still on her great bed—the bed that Kate slept in now. Rose's hands had been almost as delicate as the lizard's tiny claws. Her eyes in her sunken face had seemed enormous and her voice was so faint that he could scarcely hear her words. Ishbel was very much like her. The heart-shaped face, the brown eyes and the pale skin were the same. Mullen had felt sorry for Ishbel but he had not been able to think of anything to say to her. Once he showed her his collection of thunderstones. She examined them carefully, picking up each one and laying it back in the box as though it were something quite precious. Mullen had wanted to say something to make her smile but could think of nothing. Besides he felt a trifle ashamed of accepting a girl as a playmate.

Her separation from Shamey Lady was the worst blow of all though. Kate had pretended that she didn't want Shamey Lady to go, but Mullen knew better. He had seen the look of victory in Kate's face as she told Shamey Lady, "Now you're marrying Mario, it will be better for you to live in Baraçong."

"Mullen needs me, ma'am," Shamey Lady had protested.

"He's too old to need a nursemaid any longer. Mr. Forbes will start giving him lessons as soon as the cane is in."

Shamey Lady had begun to cry and Mullen tried to rush to her, but Kate held him back.

"You should be happy," Kate chided the girl. "Not many slaves are given their freedom so soon."

Shamey Lady had turned away, still sobbing. Kate took Mullen's hand but he broke from her. He ran into the high cane and threw himself on the ground and wept bitterly.

Shamey Lady still came back to the grounds of Rune Hall each morning to take care of the cabins where the bookkeepers lived, but Mullen seldom saw her. He suspected that, as in the case of Sister Anna, Kate had threatened Shamey Lady with the ebony. Mullen had peered into the slave shed once when Hodge the overseer was thrashing fat old Dowsie, the cook. He had only caught a glimpse of her body, spread-eagled across the bare earth, writhing under the first blow of the ebony, but her screams had followed him as he ran blindly up the hill toward Rune Hall. He had been sick when he got to his room, but when Kate came in to comfort him, he ran away again and he did not come back until dusk had fallen.

Now as Mullen lay in the grass, a longing for Shamey Lady came over him. If he went back into Rune Hall and out onto his mother's balcony he could see Baraçong far below at the water's edge. It couldn't be so awfully far. A new idea filled him with sudden excitement. Why couldn't he climb down the hill and back again, before dinnertime? True, Kate had forbidden him to leave the grounds, but if he crawled over the wall where it was covered with heavy bougainvillaea no one would know that he had disobeyed.

He caught a glimpse of his mother's white dress as she came out on the balcony. She called his name. He did not answer. His breath quickened. As soon as she was gone, he would climb the wall.

Jonathan Minor stepped back so that the low branches of the silk-cotton tree concealed him from Mullen's sight. He watched the boy scale the wall and waited until he heard the soft plop which let him know that Mullen had landed safely on the other side. Perhaps he should have stopped the boy, he reflected. Jamaica was not a safe place for a lad of ten to be wandering about in—not with runaway slaves and the waterfront scran that were loose about the place. Yet, in a way, he was pleased that Mullen had gone. Kate kept the boy too close to her, watching him constantly, yet never able to cut through Mullen's reserve. Jonathan wondered again if the boy was his. He would like to think of him as his son. Once he had suggested to Kate that Mullen should use the Minor name. Kate had turned on him angrily.

" 'Twas well satisfied you were once that he should bear the name of Cousins. 'Tis good enough for him now."

Jonathan had shrugged and let the matter drop. It was true enough that the boy showed little affection for him, but perhaps that was his own fault. He had no knack with children; he had never been able to come close to Ishbel. The notes she sent him from time to time were written with childish formality, filled with the little polite phrases she had picked up from teachers. But Ishbel never expressed a yearning to see him, nor to come back to Rune Hall. The child was only nine and she had left when she was five; he could scarcely expect her to have much memory of him. Ah well, it was better that she should stay in England. Jamaica offered little enough for Mullen; it was no place for Ishbel. Certainly not with Kate and himself at loggerheads. If they could quarrel and have it out it might not be so bad. But it was as though Kate scarcely knew he existed. Yes, he had played her false once, but he had remedied that as best he could. Blast the woman! Perhaps he should beat her, but he couldn't imagine himself doing it. And now there was this new trouble. How would she take that? He'd find out soon enough. He couldn't conceal it from her much longer. Unless there was good news, Elgin would take over Rune Hall within the next six months.

At the thought of the debonair young man, Minor stirred angrily. Elgin had outwitted him at every turn, drawing closer and closer to Stallybrass and cutting Jonathan out. Minor had had nothing but bad luck since Elgin had come to the island. His ships had been wrecked or captured by privateers; his crops had spoiled; everything had gone awry. He had borrowed heavily from Stallybrass, thinking the old man would give him ample time to pay. But with Rose's death, his father-in-law had turned against him. And then Stallybrass too had died and all of the estate had gone to Elgin or to Ishbel in trust—with Elgin as the executor.

So now Elgin held his notes and how the young popinjay enjoyed putting on the squeeze. Jonathan winced, for Elgin had won every play of the game. It was the young man, not Minor, who had succeeded Stallybrass, first as provisional Governor and later as Governor. And now Elgin would take Rune Hall too. There was only one chance left of saving it. Jonathan had thrown aside his scruples and dipped into the slave trade. He had gambled heavily on a Yankee clipper and financed the *Melanie*, a blackbirder. An ugly business—but there was no other hope.

Minor had one other thing left that Elgin wanted. That was Kate. A vague suspicion stung him—Kate might leave him if he lost Rune Hall and go to Elgin. He had seen the way Elgin watched her. But it did no good to dwell on his hatred for the new Governor. He must place his faith in the *Melanie* and the belief that she would repair his fortune.

Minor rounded the corner of the walk and drew up sharply. Kate was on her balcony overlooking the bay. He drew in his breath. God, could he never get used to the look of her? He remembered the story Kate had told him of Grainne O'Maille. Grainne must have looked like this, proud and defiant, as she watched her fleet at anchor in Clew Bay. Jonathan felt the blood rushing through his body. He wanted to run to her, take her in his arms, possess her as he had that first night in Barraca Cove—as he had again five years ago while Rose lay close to death in the high daised bed which was now Kate's.

Rose and Kate. Kate and Rose. He had betrayed first one and then the other. He had spurned Kate to keep his promise to Rose; then had slept with Kate while Rose lay choking for breath in the room beside them. He had married Rose, and on their wedding night he had imagined that her lips were Kate's. And on his second wedding night he had slept alone. Kate had turned from him at her bedroom door. "You've had your fill of me already, Jonathan. Let me have this night alone."

He had stood dazed while the door shut, but the sound of the bolt had wakened him to fury. He had called her name a hundred times but there had been no answer. He had gone beneath her window and called softly. He had thought of trying to scale the wall, but he heard the chatter of the house servants and he feared their ridicule. On the morrow, it would be all through Kingston that Jonathan Minor had mounted the balcony to climb like a thief into his own bridal chamber.

He had gone to his own room instead and poured himself a stiff drink. Kate was not altogether wrong. They had shared many a night together and there were many more to come. Perhaps in the denial of this one night, Kate sought to be shriven for what she deemed a sin. Jonathan poured himself another drink. By dawn he was in a drunken stupor and he woke with a start as the sun struck his eyes. Rose and Kate. Kate and Rose. He kept repeating the names.

Kate was not always cold. There were times when her ardor was so fierce that it almost frightened him. But these times grew less and less frequent. One by one, the things which had belonged to Rose disappeared from Rune Hall—the gaily colored religious triptych that Rose had hung in his room—the portrait of Ishbel—the china that bore the crest of Rose's family. Jonathan had watched Kate deliberately smash the fine china and had seen the passion in her face.

"Why do you do it, Kate? Why? You never hated her."

Kate had turned on him, her breath coming hard, but she had not answered. It was then that Jonathan remembered a scene when Rose had been ill. Kate was preparing her medicine for her. Jonathan had looked at the bottle, then turned to Kate in surprise.

"That's not what Dr. Gibbon ordered for her."

Kate smiled. "No—Gibbon hasn't done her much good, has he?"

"Perhaps not, but he's the best doctor we have."

Kate shrugged. "I doubt it."

"What do you mean?"

195

"Koshi knows more of drugs than Gibbon will ever know."

Jonathan stared at her, horrified. "You don't mean you've been getting medicine from that old black fool?"

Kate returned his look calmly. "He's cured the slaves where Gibbon has failed time and again."

"Leave the blacks to their superstitions, Kate. Koshi's a charlatan."

Kate answered him fiercely. "You've no right to say that. Oh, I know some of the black witch doctors are frauds—making themselves up by painting one eyelid red and one white, wearing stuffed snakes around their foreheads, frightening quatties out of the slaves—but there are others like Koshi who have spent years learning the powers of herbs. The drugs that he carries in his gourd are well tested."

Jonathan had gone to Rose's side. For the first time in a month there was a spot of color in her cheeks and her eyes were not glazed with pain.

"Jonathan," Rose whispered, "please don't stop her. I begged Kate not to let you know. I'm getting better, really I am and the pain's going. I can't stand the pain any longer. Please, Jonathan, let Kate take care of me."

But Rose had not got better. She had died on the way to England, where Jonathan and Stallybrass had insisted she be sent. What of the drugs that Kate had given her? Suspicion flared up in Jonathan's mind. When the news had been brought to him, he had paced his room for an hour before telling Kate of Rose's death.

He had intended to upbraid her but the words choked in his mouth. Kate took him in her arms that night and her wild passion changed to a comforting tenderness. He fell asleep with his head cradled against the softness of her breast and all the angry words, the ugly suspicions, were left unspoken. In the morning his thoughts were of Kate, not of Rose, and the week that followed was the happiest in his life.

It was easy to forget Rose. It was as though she had been a frail phantom that had never truly lived. But Kate he could never forget for a moment. And the more he needed her, the more she drew away from him. Then

196

when the dam of his anger was about to break, she was unexpectedly soft and gentle again.

Kate was his wife, yet he knew her less than any other person. He thought angrily of the stories that were told about her in the island. The servants at the other plantations spread tales of her occult powers. They said that she came to the palley of the Yarubas and that she lit the candles before the altars with her bare fingers. She was the White Witch, more powerful than any native African wizard.

Jonathan had laughed at the stories and mocked those who brought them to him. Still they worried him and he remembered the nights when he had gone to Kate's door and found it locked. And that one night when the door was open but Kate was not there. He had searched the house, but not found her. He had waited all night on her balcony, listening to the faint, distant beat of the dondo drums. At dawn he had fallen asleep, and when he woke, Kate was lying on the high bed breathing softly. He went to her and thrust the netting aside. She opened her eyes and stretched her arms out to him and pressed her mouth hard against his so that all the questions that were on his lips were never asked.

20

THE WILD ORANGE TREE was in bloom and its spicy fragrance hovered tantalizingly over the lawn of Rune Hall. Kate waited in the shadows near the gate. Her breath was coming sharply and the blood tingled in her cheeks. Far below, she had heard coach wheels grating in the roadway and she knew that Sir William Elgin's carriage would soon pass through the gates.

As the horses stopped by the sentry tower she stepped out into the bright moonlight. A moment later, the carriage passed by her, and while it was still moving, Elgin leapt lightly to the lawn. He came to her quickly. His hands circled her wrists and forced them behind her. He stooped and kissed her hard upon the lips.

She wrenched herself free and her eyes blazed with anger. Yet she could not stop the trembling within her, nor the swift tingling desire that coursed through her body. Her weakness added to her fury, but she kept her voice cold. "Is this your accustomed way of greeting your hostess, Sir William?"

In the pale light she could see the arrogant smile on his handsome, almost boyish face. He asked, "Were you not waiting for me, Kate?"

"Yes, but surely you are not so conceited as to believe that I would hurry from the house in order to snatch an embrace from you? It is information that I want. I have heard that the *Melanie* has been seized by the French and her cargo taken to Santo Domingue. Is it true?"

"True enough. This is the end for Jonathan Minor. He's getting to be an old man and he's lost his grip. It is only a matter of a few months and Rune Hall will slip out of his hands. He's over twenty thousand pounds in debt and scarce a farthing to his name. Why do you stick with him, Kate? You are young and he is old. You should not be living as a recluse. You need a man who can stir your blood and set you on fire."

Kate retorted mockingly. "How well you know me, Sir William."

"Better than you think." Again he put his arm about her and strained her to him. For a moment she struggled to free herself. Then she tilted up her face and let his lips press hers.

"Come with me," he said hotly. "Come with me to-night."

"No," she answered fiercely. "I'll not leave Rune Hall."

"It will soon be mine. Share it with me."

"There is no sharing with you. You must possess all that your hands touch."

"Ah, you do me wrong, Kate. Can you not see that we are bound together by a common ambition—perhaps by a common evil that dwells within us both? Kate, leave this old man; leave your dreams of power before they destroy you. I have harbored such dreams as yours—the desire for revenge, hatred fostered by injustice, but I would discard every other dream for that of being with you."

"No," Kate answered harshly. "It is not true. You would break down the hard core within me and then when I was weak you would want me no more."

"I swear that I shall want you forever."

"You lie. It is a game you play. You would make me a bound girl again, bound with love so that I can be the victim of your whims. No, Sir William, you will not succeed. Nor will Rune Hall ever be yours—that I promise."

The paneled door of Rune Hall opened and the lawn was suddenly flooded with light. "Go," Kate said quiely. "Go to Jonathan Minor. He is waiting for you. Boast if you wish of taking Rune Hall from him. But your boasts will be idle. Rune Hall will be neither yours nor his. It will be mine."

Kate watched as Elgin mounted the steps and passed through the lighted doorway. Mullen, her father, had mounted more steps than Elgin, she thought bitterly—thirteen of them that led to the gallows. Suddenly she was shaking with hate. Elgin the Englishman thought he had honored her in asking her to be his mistress—in offering Rune Hall as the reward for her compliance. Her nails bit into her palms and opened up the tiny scar which had always remained tender despite the passing of the years since Koshi's ceremonial knife had slit the skin.

She looked up into the mountains, wishing to hear the sound of the drums. But there was only stillness. She walked slowly to the slave quarters. An old Ashanti slept before one of the huts. She wakened him. "Find Koshi," she told him. "Tell him that I have need of him. He must come to me tomorrow."

Then she returned to the house. She stopped in the doorway of the great hall. Elgin sat opposite Jonathan Minor. Minor's face was gray and haggard in the dim light; Elgin's was bland, self-confident. As she stepped forward both men rose. She went to her husband and stood by his side but she addressed herself to Elgin. "Jonathan is not well and it is growing late."

Elgin bowed and a slight, mocking smile came to his lips. But Kate scarcely noticed. From outside, there came the soft, muffled beat of drums. Her message was being relayed to Koshi.

Here in the great hall Koshi looked small, withered and old. He had doffed his hat and the fringe of white hair emphasized the darkness of his skin. His bare feet were stained with brown loam and his breeches were ragged. His sunken face was impassive save for the eyes that glittered as he darted glances about the huge room. A thin, veined hand clutched the gray sack in which he carried the paraphernalia of his calling.

Kate Minor, watching him, wondered that this could be the same man she had seen in the pallays of the Ashanti. Then he had taken on height, dignity and a great strength. The flames of the altar candles had cast immense swaying shadows behind him and he had seemed to grow until he became a part of the shadows filling them with throbbing life. The voice with which he spoke to his people was rich and vibrant and his body moved with the litheness of some jungle animal. But it was in his eyes that his main strength lay. His eyes drew those of the Ashanti to him and held them in some strange communion. At Koshi's command the assembly swayed to the movement of his hands, obeying without questions the orders which he issued, repeating, now soft, now loud, the words he spoke. Kate had seen inexplicable things happen in the pallays. A man could hold his hand over the candle flame and there would not be even a blister on the skin. Women and children walked through living embers without pain or injury. Nails could be driven into the flesh without a quiver while, at a single word from Koshi, the whole body could be wracked with tearing pain.

Kate knew that within her too there existed this same power though she was unaware of its source. In Accompong and Nanny Town, the Ashanti carefully cultivated the leaves, roots and pods of many African plants. Kate learned painstakingly which among them gave surcease from pain, which caused illness, which excited and which dulled the senses. The concoctions brewed by the witch doctors contained many other ingredients—hair, fingernails, the entrails of animals, blood, dust from the graves of the dead. Kate had learned the words of incantation, the cabalistic signs, the power that came with the incessant rhythmic beat of the drum. She knew obeah's potency in the matters of sickness, pain or death, but she still fumbled blindly to find the way in which it could be used to secure social position, wealth and prestige. To her questions Koshi always answered, "That is not the way of obeah. The power springs from within and joins itself to external symbols. The knife does not kill; the herb does not cure; the fetish does not fertilize. They are the tools of obeah, but they must be guided by the gods that live within the body and the mind."

Now as Kate watched Koshi there was faint mockery in her smile. She had learned not only from the Ashanti priests but from the Koramantyns, the Eboes, the Yarubas and the other tribes. None of the witch doctors dared to refuse her their secrets lest she use her knowledge of black magic to harm them. The practices, which they so jealously guarded from one another, all fell into her hands. The legends of her prowess grew and spread through the island. It was said that she could shed her skin and take the form of a wild dog or a vampire bat or that her detached spirit could rove the island at will discernible only as a pale circle of green light. The Negroes avoided her when they could, but they were careful not to risk her enmity. They groveled in her presence and made the sign of the cross when she had passed.

Only Koshi dared to stand against her. He looked at her calmly now. "What you ask is dangerous," he told her. "No white woman has even been in Accompong."

"Then I shall be the first."

"No. I see danger if this is done. You are using the secrets you learn unwisely."

"Not this time. There is profit for Buddhoe and for me in the plan which I shall suggest to him. For you too, Koshi."

"You will bring the wrath of the English down upon us."

"Does Buddhoe fear the white man?"

"You know that he does not."

"Yet he has let Elgin's attack on Accompong go unpunished."

"You know why. I pleaded with him and so did Jonathan Minor. Vengeance means bloodshed and it the blood of our people that will flow."

Kate was silent for a minute, then she asked, "Why do you cringe from danger? Buhhdoe needs the money and I can guarantee his success."

"The dolos bones have warned me."

"The dolos do not always tell the same tale twice. Let us see what they will say in my presence."

Slowly Koshi knelt and undid the gray sack at his feet. He lifted the dried, whitened bones in his hands and shook them like dice, then rolled them across the polished mahogany. The bones bounced and slid and came to a stop. Koshi got down on his hands and knees to examine them.

"Look," he said, pointing to the small bone that lay nearest Kate. "It is the last joint of the second finger of the right hand. It is the sign of malediction and it points to you. It warns of sickness, injury or death within this house unless you give up your plan."

Kate swept up the dolos. Her face flushed. "Let us see what will happen if you do not grant my wish." She scattered the white bones across the floor. They took the shape of a crude circle and in their center lay the collar bone of a cat.

Kate spoke softly. "You know the meaning?"

"Yes. But I have no fear of death."

"The death sign is not for you."

"Then who?"

"Mario."

Koshi raised his eyes and they sparkled with sudden anger. "The bones do not make the threat. It is you."

"Perhaps. But does it matter? All that I wish is that you take me to Buddhoe. After that, the decision will be his."

Koshi's nod was scarcely perceptible. "I will do as you command."

"You will be rewarded, Koshi."

"I want no part of this thing." He turned slowly, then looked back. His voice was suddenly filled with pleading.

"Once you saw beauty where others could not see it. You felt pity when others could not. Your eyes beheld a country greener and fairer than that in which we lived. Your anger was for the strong who trespassed against the weak. There was hatred in you, but there was also compassion. You have let the good dry up within you and the evil take possession of you. You mastered the mysteries of obeah but the power of the magic is greater than you understand. It will destroy you unless you use it well. When I knew you first, you revered a man who was gentle and kind—"

"And who was hanged on a gallows at Galway Crossing."

"But now there is a son whom you love. Do not do anything that may destroy him."

Kate's face was set. "Obeah shall secure Rune Hall for him."

"What if he does not want it?"

"He is too young to know."

"There are more important things."

"That may be, but he shall have Rune Hall."

The mean little donkeys trod gingerly along the narrow stony path that led through the Cockpit country. On one side a hill rose almost perpendicularly; on the other there was a sheer drop into the cockpit. The deep green vegetation grew so thickly along the earthy sides of the glen that it was almost impossible to gauge the pit's depth. Huge flat-leaved trees, tangled brush and heavy dark-green vines cast impenetrable shadows over the pit's bottom, despite the glare of the noonday sun. A thin stream of water, like white lace, foamed down the hillside and flowed sluggishly across the pathway, turning the copper to mud.

Mario, not Koshi, was leading Kate to Accompong. This was the sixth day they had traversed the mountain passes and Mario had said they would reach Accompong before nightfall. Only once had a bare-footed, half-naked Maroon come in to join them at the campfire and to share their supplies of salt meat and yams; other than that, they had not seen a soul. Nevertheless, Kate was aware that ever since they had first entered the almost hidden pass the Maroons had known their exact position at every moment.

Sometimes there was movement in the thick shrubbery or a stone rolled lazily down the slope of the mountains. The eerie note of the abeng and the slow beat of the goombah echoed along the cockpits so that it was impossible to judge from which direction the sounds came. Mario too had an abeng slung across his shoulder on a cowhide strap. Each evening he raised it to his lips and its shrill notes filled the night with sibilant whispers. At Kate's request, Mario had slipped the leather cord from his shoulder and permitted her to examine the instrument, but he had cautioned her not to place it to her lips. This horn, Kate realized, provided the explanation of a phenomenon that perplexed the whites of Jamaica—how, without visible means of communication, the island Negroes know almost instantly of events that happened at far-distant points.

The abeng was the small horn of a cow, the tip of which had been bored off so as to form a hole about the size of a pea. On the concave side, about an inch from the tip, a narrow oblong slit was scraped out and against this the player pressed his lips, while blocking the end hole with a finger. The messages which were sent by means of the abeng required no code, for the words were actually pronounced and, although they were distorted into a discordant, high-pitched whine, the trained ears of the Negro could easily pick them up, even at a distance of twenty-five miles.

Now, as Kate and Mario stopped to drink from the frothing stream, the first of the high coconut palms of Accompong could be seen through the pass. Mario's teeth flashed in a grin as he pointed it out.

Kate gazed up at the slender outline of the palm, etched against the depthless blue of the sky and, for the first time since she had begun the journey, she felt the swift stir of excitement. No white woman had ever trod these paths before and not more than a handful of white men.

"Will Buddhoe be glad to see me?"

"He will welcome you," Mario answered. "If it were not so, he would have stopped you long before now."

204

The sun lay red against the far mountains when they finally reached the clearing. Mario stopped and tethered the beasts to a breadfruit tree, and as he did so, the goombah drums beat close at hand. Some forty huts, hung with thatched banana leaves, dotted the sides of a narrow, twisted road. At the far end, was a single wooden frame house, supported by posts of mellow blackwood which shone with a high patina.

A man, dressed in a tricorn hat of red with a parrot's feather fastened to it, a tattered scarlet jacket with tarnished gold lace and white silken breeches, came toward them. As he drew near, Kate could see the gnarled black face and the sunken, glistening eyes and she knew that he was Buddhoe. A step behind the Maroon chief came Nigel, his almost naked body shining like highly polished mahogany. Men, women and children flocked out of the huts as Buddhoe passed and they formed a ragged, silent procession behind him.

Kate stood still, her hands at her side, her head held high, awaiting them. Buddhoe came close to her without speaking. He stopped and the goombahs which were being played somewhere in the jungle growth fell silent. Buddhoe doffed his hat and bowed low. When he spoke his words had almost the same clipped precision as those of Koshi and Mario.

"You are welcome," he assured her. "Tonight we have prepared a special feast for you. But you cannot wait till then to ease your hunger. A light meal is waiting for you now."

Kate curtsied solemnly. She took from Mario the gift which she had brought. This was a bolt of rich red silk. She laid it in Buddhoe's hands.

The Maroon chief laughed and the silence and the solemnity of the occasion were broken. The Maroons called to one another in loud, high-pitched voices. The women stared at Kate in open wonder and the children came close to peer up at her.

Side by side, Kate and Buddhoe walked back to the frame house. There a table was set with a huge calabash, from which steam rose, in its center. Buddhoe, Mario, Nigel and Kate sat while a woman served them. The other

205

Maroons crowded about the door or peered in through the window frame.

The highly spiced stew was made of chicken, pimento, peppers and yams brewed in a sweet rich broth of coconut oil. Small gourds of opaque rum were passed around. Kate forced herself to eat the hot sweet stew and wash it down with the fiery rum. Buddhoe scarcely spoke but his eyes never left her face. Only when they had finished and risen from the table did he speak further of the plans for the night. There was to be feasting and dancing. His people had been told that the goddess Erzulie would appear in the form of a white woman. He, Buddhoe, was honored by the visitation.

Kate's lips shaped a thin smile. She realized that the old Maroon was using her to glorify himself in the eyes of his people. It did not matter, she thought; it might well serve her purpose. In silence, she followed the serving-woman to a back room. Here a banana-trash mattress was thrown over a marosh of river reeds which, in turn, rested on the hard parched earth.

Despite the arduous journey, Kate was not tired. However, she judged that Buddhoe wished her to appear among his people only on ceremonial occasions. She threw herself down on the banana trash and closed her eyes. Outside she could hear the eerie sound of the abeng and she knew that a message was being sent to the Maroons in the surrounding hills. The dried leaves rustled beneath her as she moved and a rat scampered across the packed earth.

In the darkness she began to think of Sir William Elgin and smiled to herself. Unless her plans went awry, she would make good her promise that he would never own Rune Hall. The thought of his humiliation sent a sensuous pleasure through her and, at the same time, a vague longing that she could not control.

21

BEADS OF FAT dripped from the spitted iguana and sizzled in the leaping flames. A row of agouti, the wild guinea pigs of Jamaica, glowed like copper as the Maroon women turned them above the fire. Corn, breadfruits and yams were thrust among the red embers to roast. Puncheons of oily rum with sliced green limes floating on top were placed by the palm-covered chairs that were in the center of the clearing. Loaves of bread, heaps of mangoes, bananas and pineapples were spread on the cedar table. Two huge iron kettles bubbled and boiled on a separate fire and filled the night with the odor of cooking goat meat, curry, coconut oil and a variety of pungent spices.

Already many of the Maroons had dipped into the puncheons. Their laughter and loud shouts echoed across the cockpits. But there was silence as Buddhoe led Kate toward the chairs with their leafy coverings. A dondo drum beat out a steady tattoo and the Maroons fell to one side as their leader passed. Buddhoe's face was unsmiling as he bowed to Kate and indicated that she should be seated. The iguana, crusted brown, was served to them on long green banana leaves. Buddhoe sliced off a chunk of the sweet-smelling flesh and handed it to Kate. She took it in her hands and bit into the soft meat. Buddhoe raised his hand, and at the signal, the clearing was again filled with laughter and the rich voices of the Negroes.

The Maroons gorged themselves, sticking their hands into the blackened kettles and pulling out the goat bones, sinking their teeth into the meat, then sucking the oil from their fingers. The calabashes flashed in the flames as they dipped again and again into the rum kegs.

Kate remained silent, eating and drinking what was placed before her. She could not understand much of what was said around her. The Maroons spoke in a dialect that was even broader than that used by the Negroes of Kingston. They came from many tribes and they spoke a patois of English mixed with French and Spanish and interspersed with words from the Ashanti, Koramantyn and a dozen other tribal tongues.

After a time, Mario and Nigel had disappeared among the throng and Kate sat alone with Buddhoe. The old Negro ate sparingly. He sat bolt upright, his eyes half closed, but occasionally he looked at Kate. She wondered what his thoughts were and how much he knew of her purpose in coming to Accompong. She presumed that the abeng had relayed its message from Koshi to Buddhoe; yet the plan must be kept secret. She waited patiently. She had tasted the unmistakable musty flavor of the obi seed mixed with the rum and now she felt the sense of spreading power, of lassitude that could shift to the swift desire for violent action, the confusion of time and space that made one omniscient and filled the body with swelling pleasure that pressed out pain or grief.

The Maroons had begun to dance. They danced form-lessly, without partners, without unison. Their bodies jerked and swayed in the shadowy light. They called out words the meanings of which they had long forgotten. Each was lost in some tribal memory, seeking again the patterns of Africa from which he had been torn.

Buddhoe leaned toward Kate. His gnarled face was solemn. "You see Accompong. You see a people irre-trievably lost, blinded by passions they cannot understand, suspended between life and death, released from slavery into nothingness. Tonight they live in the vast plains of Africa; they are about their tribal fires; they call out to those who speak their tongue."

Kate nodded. She too had forgotten the dark clearing and the frantic beating of the drums. She had walked with her father Mullen down a cool, clear lane in Galway and held his hand as she listened to the surf breaking against the rocks of Claddagh.

Buddhoe raised a conch shell to his lips and as the piercing blast echoed among the hills, silence crept over Accompong. The old Maroon rose and went to the fire. He spoke in the broad patois of his people and when he finished there was laughter. He motioned Kate to come to him, and the chairs were brought to the fire's edge. Slowly men and women crept from the shadows of the trees and formed a great circle about them. The drums beat softly, scarcely touched by the fingers of the players. A low, wailing chant came from the lips of the women.

A girl broke away from the circle and staggered into the center. She fell upon her knees, crying out in anguish. She dropped to the ground, her body writhing, then she lay rigid—the eyes fixed in a sightless stare, the taut breasts pointing upward, the legs sprawled as though in the agony of death.

Into the circle a man crept slowly. He brought with him the gray sack of the obeah man. He advanced and retreated, circled about the motionless girl. The wailing of the women rose and fell according to his movements. He reached the girl and crouched before her; he opened his sack, brought out a powder and threw it across her naked breasts.

The girl moaned and sat up. The man moved to embrace her, his arms wide, his fingers spread open, the hands twitching with eagerness. She backed from him, frightened. They stared at each other. He stepped forward, but she darted away, leaping across the circle, her face hard, taunting, her body swaying. The man came after her, his hands interlacing, his face menacing. She waited until he was close, then reached toward him. Now he fled from her but she pursued. They came face to face in the center of the circle, their bodies trembling, their elbows bent, their hands outstretched, their fingers palpitating with the rhythm. Slowly they crouched, approached each other, moving an inch at a time, their bodies sinuous, their eyes glowing in the near darkness.

The watchers were quiet now. The wailing had ceased and there was only the stertorous breathing of the Maroons. Kate felt her own breath come in great choking sobs. The dance was the symbol of life's beginning—its consummation the omen of success in any venture that was to come.

The man and woman in the circle moved nearer and nearer, their arms locked together in tight embrace. Kate's skin tingled with revulsion that was mixed with desire.

209

For a moment Elgin's face seemed suspended close to hers, his features distorted in an ugly grimace. She tried to shut her eyes but could not.

The Maroons closed in tight upon the crouching couple, hemming them in, concealing the final stages of the dance from Kate's sight. Their bodies were tense, every nerve strained. Then there was a soft sigh and the drums beat quickly, lightly.

Buddhoe touched Kate's arm. "It is well," he said simply. He rose and led the way back along the dark path to the frame house. Behind them they heard a sudden cry and a burst of laughter but they did not turn.

The drums beat throughout the night, but Kate paid little attention. She was watching the face of the old Maroon slowly, carefully as she unrolled the plan for which she had come to Accompong. Buddhoe sat unblinking and for a long time gave her no answer. Then he began to ask questions—times, numbers, all the minute details. His face remained blank, his eyes unchanging. But finally, when the details had arranged themselves into a clear-cut course of action, he began to chuckle. "Sir William Elgin," he said, "Sir William Elgin—his ransom will make us both rich." He broke into laughter.

Kate knew how Buddhoe hated Elgin. It was the young man who had urged Stallybrass to the futile attempt to wipe out the Maroons. Elgin, as chief magistrate, had ordered that two of Buddhoe's men, captured in the outskirts of Spanish Town, should be hacked to pieces and their bloody limbs thrown to the dogs. After Stallybrass' death, when Sir William had become Governor, he had consistently refused to honor the English treaty with the Maroons and had had Buddhoe's emissaries publicly flogged. Buddhoe had stayed his hand, for Elgin had threatened a mass revenge against the island blacks if the Maroons struck at Kingston. But the hate was strong within the old man and he knew that his prestige had waned because of the young governor's contemptuous treatment of him.

He struck his knee with his doubled fist. "Elgin," he roared. "By God, Elgin himself. 'Tis a master plan and who would think of betrayal within the household of Jonathan Minor?"

"You will do what I ask?" Kate spoke softly.

The old man's face clouded with suspicion. "It may be a trick of the English to capture me. Elgin himself may have sent you."

"No. You cannot believe that."

Buddhoe rose and stared down at her. Kate lifted her eyes unflinchingly.

"Let us see first how the portents read," he said.

Kate waited in the dark, bare room where a single candle gave the only light. Through the dried leaves that hung over the paneless window frame she could see the new moon, the sky filled with countless stars and the slanting shadows of the palms. The sweet odor of cooling cane syrup mingled with the clinging aroma of the gardenias growing in profusion behind the house. The voices of the Maroons, rich and mellow, drifted in to her along with the bleating of goats and the plaintive bray of a donkey. All day she had waited for Buddhoe, sensing that the next move must come from him.

At noon a woman had brought her a basket of fruit and a kettle of steaming herb tea in which the distinctive scent of the obi was dominant. The drink had soothed her nerves and blurred the passage of time. From her window she could watch the women grinding juice from the sugar cane in their crude presses. They slit the ripe stalks with machetes and forced them between the wooden rollers. The juice trickled into a trough and was drained off with calabashes and emptied into huge iron pots. All afternoon the pots bubbled merrily over a fire, and when dusk came, the syrup was poured into square bins, covered with cane leaves and left to dry.

Kate lay down on the banana trash and the languor induced by the obi took hold of her. Outside the voices grew dim and muted and there was only an occasional sharp cry. The scent of the sugar and the gardenias seemed that of incense and she was a child again, kneeling before the altar of St. Veronica with Mullen beside her. She stirred restlessly. The horror and violence of the years since Mullen's death were woven into an intricate pattern that was spread before her. She felt Captain Lunt's whip across her back, the touch of her own hands on Mannie

211

Cousins' wattled throat, the trembling passion when Jonathan Minor's lips first touched hers, the loathing of her wedding night with Gabriel Cousins, the prick of Koshi's knife as it cut across her palm, the confused excitement of the fight between Gabe and Bard, the hurt look in Rose Minor's eyes, the anger combined with an uncontrolled excitement which had taken possession of her when Sir William Elgin had made love to her. She moaned softly, seeking to avoid the one memory she could not endure—Mullen her son, turning from her, shivering at her touch.

The door opened soundlessly. A man in a long robe stood in the doorway, a candle in his hand. Kate was startled and she crouched on the rustling trash, her eyes wide with fear. Momentarily the figure seemed that of Father Maholan, and the overwhelming need for confession made her cry out to him.

Buddhoe stood above her. The candlelight formed deep lines in the gnarled face and made the eyes unusually bright. "Come," he said, "it is time."

A question sprang to her lips but she fought it back. She got up and without a word followed the old Maroon into the night. He led her along pathways black with the shade of breadfruit trees. She stumbled on loose stones but he neither turned nor spoke. They passed through a clearing and the pale moon shone down upon them. The little man, bent and old, his triangular hat perched upon his head, a cloak wrapped loosely about his body, his bare legs bandy and mud-crusted, had an unearthly dignity.

He walked rapidly and Kate had difficulty following him. At the foot of a valley, he turned sharply and started a deep ascent. Kate knew now where they were going. Mario had pointed out the graveyard on the opposite slope. As they stepped among the graves, Buddhoe took a gray sack from beneath his cloak and scattered grains of corn before him as he walked. He moved to the far end of the cemetery where a mass of stones held a strangely formed cross of mahogany on which the name of Cudjoe, the first of the Maroon chiefs, was crudely carved.

Buddhoe knelt and removed the rocks, murmuring

Ashanti words as he cupped each one in his hands. He smoothed the disturbed earth and then raised a bottle of rum to his lips. He filled his mouth with the liquid, then sprayed it across the grave. With a piece of sharp bone, he drew the rough outline of a man on the damp earth. A deep hole formed the mouth and into this he poured more rum. He began to chant softly, then more and more distinctly. Kate did not know all the words, but she caught the name of Cudjoe and knew that the old man was invoking the spirit of the dead warrior.

He finished and turned to Kate, but his eyes passed on beyond her. Kate whirled about. Behind her stood the girl who had danced the night before. In one hand she held sprays of the jonka weed upon which the obi grew. In the other was a blackened kettle of steaming rum.

The girl and Kate stood facing each other until Buddhoe's footsteps died away. Then the girl came to Kate and loosened the white dress so that it fell to her feet. She undressed her skillfully, until Kate stood naked in the moonlight. The girl took the thick, oily leaves of the jonka weed and smeared them on the full breasts, the throat, the arms, the thighs. The oil burned and seared the skin until Kate cried out in agony. The girl dipped her hands into the hot rum and rubbed the smarting skin. Kate's whole body was suffused with warmth. The dondo drums began to beat and Kate's blood throbbed to the music. She had the sense of growing enormous, of towering up over the mountains, of soaring flight.

Dimly she was aware that the girl led her to the grave and thrust her face downward on the warm, moist earth. She writhed in sudden ecstasy and heard her voice repeating the words that Buddhoe had spoken. "Cudjoe, bahni-wah, hi, eekeeto." The night was shot with colors she had never seen before, sounds that were new. Her body arched upward, higher and higher. She opened her mouth to scream, but there was only silence.

The girl was beside Kate when she woke. Kate's memory of the night was vague and she was not certain where the dream had ended and reality begun. She was stretched out on the banana trash and she saw that her body was coated with brown earth. Her throat and breasts

213

throbbed with pain. The girl pressed a gourd to her lips and Kate gratefully gulped the contents. There was again the taste of rum and the musty flavor of the obi, and Kate sighed softly.

The girl had dragged a great flat wooden bowl into the room. The wood was worn satin smooth by many years of use. The girl filled it with sweet-smelling water into which she crushed the waxy petals of gardenias. She helped Kate bathe and dress, and when the toilet was complete all the soreness had left Kate's body and she felt strangely rested.

The girl spoke for the first time. "Buddhoe has told me to tell you that Cudjoe has accepted you and that the portents are favorable to the Maroons."

Kate remembered Koshi's dolos bones and the warning they had given. "What of me?" she asked. "What of Rune Hall?"

The girl shook her head. "I cannot say."

Slowly the girl led Kate down the twisted road that led through the village. There was not a sound, not a sign of life in Accompong. At the far end of the clearing the donkeys were tethered to the same tree where Mario had tied them. Mario came forward a few steps to join them. The girl moved away and left Mario and Kate facing each other.

"What has happened?" Kate whispered. "Why is there no sound?"

Mario answered, "They are waiting for us to go."

Kate looked back in bewilderment at the lifeless shacks. She said, "I am not sure. Maybe I was wrong."

"Buddhoe has agreed to what you ask. He will send his message through me."

Kate trembled. "I am frightened."

"Let us go quickly."

At noon they reached the foaming stream that cut the mountain pass. Mario looked up at the tall coconut palms that cleft the sky. Kate followed his gaze and saw that a man was perched among the high foliage. A shrill, wailing sound broke the silence. Mario listened, his head tilted to one side, his lips repeating the message of the abeng.

22

JONATHAN MINOR peered down the carved mahogany balustrade and his face flushed with displeasure. A Negro orchestra plucked at the strings of their violins and arranged their chairs in a corner of the great hall. The huge mahogany table was set with silver and linen napery. The odor of roast beef drifted in from the cookhouse. Damn it all, had Kate taken leave of her mind? Here he was down to his last few hundred pounds and suddenly Kate must give a banquet. Didn't she know she was opening herself to insult and ridicule? The wives of the British officials would never accept Kate as a hostess. He had warned her of that, begged her to give up the whole fantastic plan, but she would not listen.

Kate had met all of his protests with bland unconcern. "The women came to Rune Hall when Rose was mistress. Why should they not come now?"

There was no answer that he could give without hurting her. He could not tell her that Jamaica would never forget that she had been a bound girl, that she had taken refuge in the Christian Steps, that she had been the wife of a tavernkeeper. He could not tell her that the tongues of the island clacked with gossip about her meanderings in the realm of black magic. Nor that a hundred rumors went the rounds about her strange disappearance of two weeks. He wondered about that himself. Kate had told him she was going to Montego Bay, but she had never arrived there. Certainly she knew that he would learn of her deceit. But he would not question her. It would only add to the coldness between them. Jonathan looked at his hands on the railing. He was growing thin and old, he thought bitterly, and life was escaping him. Soon even Rune Hall would be lost. With the *Melanie* seized, his last chance was gone. Elgin held him in the palm of his hand, and he would show no mercy.

Soon Elgin would be here. So would Sydney Brandon, young Cockeray, the whole lot were in power now. He despised their indifference to the welfare of the Creoles, their injustice to the freedmen, the savagery with which they treated the slaves. He thought of the years he had spent in America, in Salem in his youth. In 1776 he had thought the Yankees turncoats and rabble. He had joined the fight against them and was glad of the chance to escape to Jamaica when the war was lost. He was not so sure he had been right now. What if he had thrown in his lot with the new country? He might not be on the edge of bankruptcy now—nor would he have Kate.

She came into the hall and stopped to chat with the musicians. There was color in her cheeks and a touch of excitement in her voice. Jonathan felt his palms grow moist. She was in for disappointment tonight. The women would not come. Already a few of them had sent messages that they were ill or called out of Kingston. The other women had not deigned to answer, but they would not arrive. He had told her as gently as he could. She had given him a brittle smile. "Anyway the men will come —Elgin, Brandon, Cockeray—those who are important."

Yes, the men would come all right. They would come to sneer and mock. "Poor old Minor," they would say. "Look how the mighty are fallen. You can hardly believe it now, but once it looked as though the old boy would be Governor of Jamaica. Might have been too, if it wasn't for these newfangled ideas he's got about the blacks, and his infatuation for the Irish girl. He courted her in the Christian Steps, they tell me, before she married Gabe Cousins." He'd heard the words many times, in the club, at the courthouse, at the theater.

He descended the stairs slowly. Kate was waiting for him at the bottom. He went to her, put his arms about her and kissed her. He was surprised at her warm response. She put her cheek against his and clung to him.

For a moment he was moved. He said, "I love you, Kate. All through the years I've loved you."

Jonathan was still holding her when Sir William Elgin strode into the room. He did not release her immediately, but stared over his shoulder at the young man's handsome, cynical face. I'd like to kill you, he thought; I'd really like to kill you—and was surprised at the violence of his own emotions. He forced himself to smile and went to Elgin with his hand extended. Elgin took his hand, but the Governor's lips moved in a fleeting smile. Kate stepped between them and the eyes of both men went to her face. Kate's manner was gracious, her voice warm as she greeted Elgin. Minor felt his pulse beating rapidly. By God, Elgin would not have Kate! Minor would see him dead first, no matter what the price. He forced himself to be calm but he was glad when there was a stir in the hall and Mullen's tutor, young Forbes, already a little drunk, came in. The orchestra began to play a lively tune and there was the sound of carriage wheels outside. Loud voices drifted in through the doorway and the servants busied themselves serving drinks to the guests.

Dinner was stiff and formal at first with Kate the only woman at the table. Jonathan was proud of her. If she was hurt she gave no slightest sign. She flirted with Parker who was past eighty and joked with MacFeathers so that the little Scot's laughter was as loud as his bagpipes.

The meal could not have been better, Jonathan thought wryly, nor more English. Game, fish and fowl and rare roast beef—even an English plum pudding. The wines must have nearly exhausted the cellar, but he had saved the best to the end. But what would happen after dinner? There was an orchestra but there could be no dancing and several of the men were drinking heavily. Sydney Brandon was talking loudly and his manner was quarrelsome. Forbes had taken exception to Brandon's remarks and the older man was taunting him.

Jonathan was grateful to Michael Scott, the tall sandy-haired freckled-faced ship designer whose sketches of sailing vessels appeared at intervals in the *Jamaico Advertiser*. Scott had recently returned from the States and he introduced a subject in which all present, with the exception of Jonathan himself, were in agreement—the perfidy, the uncouthness, the obstinacy and general worthlessness of the Yankees. Already there were rumors that America would declare war on England and side with the French. The Jamaicans scoffed at the infant nation and

217

boasted that with the help of a dozen British frigates they could overrun the American coast from Falmouth to Charleston.

Scott's voice boomed out above the others. "Not so fast, my lads," he shouted. "I don't like Americans. I never did and never shall like them. I've seldom met an American gentleman in the large and common sense of the term. I have no wish to eat or drink or consort with them in any way, but let me tell the whole truth—nor would I fight with them, were it not for the laurels to be acquired by the overcoming of an enemy so brave, determined and alert, in every way so worthy of one's steel."

"Pah," snorted Brandon, "their ships couldna last a week again' the British fleet."

Scott looked the planter over coldly. "Mon, you do not know the Yankees. They've sailing vessels beautiful beyond anything known in naval construction. No British builder could build them and no British captain sail them. They're too lightly built; too heavily sparred—neither comfortable nor safe, but with more speed than any ship that's ever left the dock at Liverpool."

Brandon's retort was drowned by the grating of carriage wheels outside, shrill laughter and the sounds of women's voices. Jonathan, startled, glanced at Kate. He saw the shock of surprise on her face, then her features became masklike. There was the clatter of high heels on the stone steps, mumbled words of protest from the lackey at the door, then the chatter of feminine voices in the hall.

The men sat back in their chairs, their faces blank. Lettie Parsons stumbled in first, her hat askew and her bright red hair straying over one cheek. She had grown enormously fat, so that her lavender silk dress was on the point of bursting at the seams. She was obviously drunk and, as she waddled toward Kate, the tears flowed down her raddled cheeks.

Kate rose as the brothelkeeper flung her arms about her. " 'Tis a bleedin' shame what the women have done to ye. Too fine they are to come to Rune Hall. The bleedin' snobs! But we won't let 'em spile ye party. I've come and I've brought me gals with me."

Jonathan was proud of Kate. She moved forward easily and showed no sign of embarrassment. Just behind Lettie was Constania Abbott. Connie's state of intoxication was not so obvious. She stood straight as a ramrod, her narrow horselike face frozen in a simpering smile. She raised the lorgnette which she bore on a long black handle and peered about at the assembly. She giggled and swayed a little. "We heard you boys were up here all alone without any women. 'What fun can that be?' I said to Lettie. 'No fun at all,' she answers me. So we got the girls together——" she spread her arms in an all-embracing gesture——"and here we are."

Crowding into the great hall were the mulatto girls from the Queen's Court and the Christian Steps. They were dressed in the low-cut, brightly colored gowns of their profession. Already they were scampering about, helping themselves at the punch bowl, flinging themselves into the laps of the men. Chloe, who had long ago made peace with Lettie, chose old Mr. Parker. She cupped his face in her hands and pressed her lips to his. He tilted back in his chair and nearly upturned. He straightened himself and pulled her down upon his knee.

Syd Brandon's chortle changed to boisterous laughter. The girls moved from man to man, twisting, cavorting, pulling their skirts up over shapely brown legs. The great hall rang with the din of their merriment. The orchestra played a Spanish dance tune and the girls whirled their partners onto the clear floor. Jonathan was watching Kate. She still stood with her arm about Lettie Parsons. She was smiling now but he sensed the lurking anger in her eyes. He shifted his gaze to Elgin. The young man's face was as bland as ever as he bowed with exaggerated courtesy over the hand of one of Lettie's girls.

Jonathan swore beneath his breath. His fists clenched at his side. He strode over to Kate and pushed Lettie aside. He put his arm about her and held her tight and kissed her. There was a moment of silence and he said loudly so that all could hear, "Kate, you're the loveliest woman in Jamaica and I'd not trade you for all the wealth of England."

The din closed in about them. Kate broke away and went to the punch bowl. "It's empty," she cried and clapped her hands for the servants. "Fill it up," she ordered, "keep it full."

The party went on endlessly, or so it seemed to Jonathan, although he knew that, in reality, it was less than an hour since the girls had come. Everyone was drunk except himself and Kate and possibly Michael Scott, who viewed the scene with twinkling, tolerant eyes. Even the servants were tippling, and Kate had sent drinks to the sentries and to the men in charge of the swivel guns in the turret. Jonathan had thought to stop her, but this was scarcely the time to make a protest. He saw Mac-Feathers with a bottle held high against his lips. He went to the little Scot, took the bottle from him and drained what was left of the liquor in a single draught. He felt the sting of the whiskey in his throat and choked and gasped as the heat of it struck his stomach.

In the center of the hall two of the girls were staging an imitation cockfight. They hopped about in a circle, crowing, bobbing, weaving, hitching their skirts high, mimicking the cocks. The orchestra caught the spirit of the dance and the violins played a squealing staccato rhythm. The girls switched their middles, tore at each others' clothes, grimaced and stuck their necks out and crowed challengingly. The men and their partners watched tensely, then broke out in hysterical laughter. One girl lifted her foot high and hopped about in a circle. The other followed, jumping up and down and flapping her skirts as though in victory. The first girl gave a feeble squawk, rolled over on the floor, her legs treading the air. The other strutted about her, crowing, flapping the winglike skirts, jumping up and down on her toes.

Jonathan turned away in disgust. He walked into the garden and sat down beneath the silk-cotton tree. The air was cool and refreshing. After a while he crossed the lawn and went down the path to the sentry box. He called softly to the guard but there was no answer. He heard a low moan and saw a figure huddled on the ground beside the box. He hurried forward and bent down. The smell of rum was heavy on the Negro's breath and Jonathan thought that he was only drunk. He lifted the man's head and saw the trickle of blood across the forehead. He called him by name but the head hung limply and there was no response. Jonathan raced to the next sentry box; the guard lay on the grass a few feet away in the same state.

Jonathan sprinted across the lawn, shouting, "Elgin— Scott—Cockeray."

The sounds of merriment within the house had stopped, but he scarcely noticed. He flung open the door and rushed into the great hall. He drew up sharply. The women were huddled to one side of the room. Standing guard over them was a motley array of half-naked Negroes. Some had old-fashioned pistols, others rifles; a few displayed long, curved knives or stilletos. The men were on the far side of the hall and the Maroons were busy tying their hands and feet. Elgin, Brandon and Cockeray were already trussed up like fowls and lay doubled up on the floor.

Facing Jonathan, twenty feet from him, was Buddhoe. Jonathan had dealt with him often and knew him well. As always, the Maroon chief was dressed in his cocked hat, red coat and white breeches. But now he wore a long cloak of bright red silk. Buddhoe came toward Jonathan slowly, his pistol pointed directly at Jonathan's heart.

Buddhoe spoke softly. "I wish you no harm, Jonathan Minor. You have always dealt fairly with our people. Do not force me to use violence, please."

Jonathan felt the sweat pouring down his face. For a moment he thought of making a desperate leap and of trying to seize the revolver. It was madness, he knew. Resistance could only lead to tragedy, and Lord knew there was little enough in the house worth the stealing. He turned his eyes to Kate. She was standing calmly among the women and he caught the gleam of triumph in her eyes. She nodded a warning for him to be quiet. Suddenly he realized that this fantastic scene was partly of her making. It was madness, he thought. Yet he would not give her away.

He shrugged and managed a smile. He turned back to Buddhoe. "Rune Hall is yours. Take what you will. Only do not harm the ladies."

Buddhoe bowed slightly and showed yellowed teeth in an answering smile, but his pistol did not waver. "None of the women shall be injured. But it is wise to take

221

precautions. Your hands must be tied, Mr. Minor." The old Maroon gave a signal with his left hand. Nigel came forward with a piece of rope. Jonathan did not recognize him at first, for this huge Negro with his fierce face and gleaming body bore little resemblance to the whining sycophant who had once worn Connie Abbott's gold-braided livery and served her guests with confect cakes. Jonathan sighed and made no struggle while the Koramantyn bound his hands tightly.

"There is nothing worth your while here, Buddhoe," he said calmly.

"We shall see." He turned to Nigel and spoke in the Maroon dialect, ordering him to take charge of the captives. Two of the Maroons were at the head of the wide stairway. Buddhoe called to them, asking them about the guards in the tower. Jonathan could not understand their answers. Buddhoe crossed the hall and clumped up the stairway. He spoke a few words to his men and the three of them disappeared along the corridor. A few moments later, their footfalls could be heard on the turret stairs.

The great hall was silent save for Elgin, who tossed about on the floor trying to free himself from his bonds. Nigel strode to him and tightened the ropes. Elgin swore fiercely and Nigel struck him across the face. He turned about and went to the foot of the stairs and listened. Far above, the sound of Buddhoe's voice could be heard calling to the guards who surrounded the hall.

Nigel whirled about and he looked directly at Constantia Abbott. His heavy lips parted and his eyes blazed. Softly as a cat he moved toward her, his bare feet silent on the mahogany floor.

The room watched as though hypnotized as the big Negro stepped across the floor to where the woman who had once been his mistress stood. Connie Abbott's eyes popped, her throat contracted and her mouth opened as though to scream, but no sound came.

Nigel seized her by the waist and held her high. Her legs kicked feebly and she began to gibber with fear. He swung her up on the mahogany table and his great hands tore and ripped her clothing so that she was naked to the waist. The scrawny neck, the loose breasts, the

222

wrinkled flesh gave her the appearance of some grotesque caricature of a woman.

Nigel turned and the blazing anger left his face. It was replaced by the whining sycophancy that Connie had formerly demanded of him. He parroted the words she had taught him. "Any gem'mem like nice flippy-floppy?" He bowed low, his features wreathed in a stupid grin. Then he whirled quickly and there was a quirt in his hand such as Connie had beaten him with.

Jonathan Minor gave a roar of anger. Despite his bound hands, he flung himself forward. He rushed at Nigel with his head down, hoping to catch the Negro in the stomach. Nigel's quirt hit him on the side of the neck, and as he fell, he saw the black man's foot come up in an arc. The foot was bare, almost as hard as stone. Minor felt the crack of his ribs as he went down. Then the foot struck again with paralyzing force.

Through the haze of pain, he heard a bellow of rage and looked to the head of the stairs. Buddhoe was shouting wildly at Nigel. Jonathan watched the old Maroon as he descended the stairway, strode to Nigel, took the quirt from his hand and slashed it across the huge Negro's face.

Nigel screamed and whirled upon the old man. Buddhoe's eyes were masklike, his body tense. Slowly Nigel dropped his hands to his sides. Buddhoe went to Jonathan and crouched on one knee beside him. Jonathan saw the old man's gnarled face filled with concern. He tried to speak but the pain was like a flame that filled his body. The room whirled about him and then there was only blackness.

BOOK FOUR

1812

23

AT SIXTEEN, Mullen was slender and wiry. The bone structure of his face was delicate, but well formed. His crest of long hair was almost golden and his deep-set eyes were turquoise. With animation, the face was attractive, but often he was sullen and had a look of stubborn defiance.

His loathing for Rune Hall had grown with the years, even though now it was his. The deed to Rune Hall had been his mother's gift to him on his fifteenth birthday. He had looked at the deed uncomprehendingly, his eyes skimming over the legal language. At first, he had thought of tearing it up or of throwing it at Kate's feet and shouting that he did not want it. But Kate's eyes were aglow and her face filled with a warm tenderness that he had almost forgotten. So instead, he tucked the paper in his belt and went to Kate and kissed her. He was surprised and taken aback as her arms circled him and pressed him close to her. He felt moisture on his cheeks and realized that Kate was crying. He couldn't remember ever having seen her cry before and had no idea of the reason for it now. There was something obscene in her tears, he thought, as though Mr. Minor were crying—or like the time Mr. Forbes got drunk and wept and threw bottles about in a tantrum shouting that he couldn't stand the bloody cesspool of an island any longer.

He had got free of his mother's embrace at last. He stood watching her for a minute. She was beautiful, he thought, with her full, firm breasts, the copper glint in her hair and her skin as smooth as a baby's. She made the other island women look like slatterns; maybe that was why they hated her so. He wished that he could comfort her, but he couldn't imagine comforting Kate. She was too confident, too self-reliant, too proud. Besides, some of the stories they told about her were true. A couple of times he had got into fights down on the Parade because someone had called his mother "The Witch" and had said that she was an obeah woman. You had to stand up for your own mother, he guessed, no matter what she did.

But once he had found a Shango pallay up in the mountains and had gone back late at night to watch the drazzon. He had hidden high up in a flamboyant tree. It had been fun watching the dancers while they howled and shrieked and imagined themselves "mounted" by the spirits. But suddenly there was a hush and someone cried, "She's coming."

Kate, dressed all in white, had entered the pallay. The dancing and laughter stopped and the ceremony became solemn. Mullen had watched until the white goat was brought into the center of the ring. He saw Kate approach the frightened animal and there was a shining cutlass in her hand. He had not waited any longer. He had shinnied down the tree fast, careless of what might happen to him if he got caught.

All the way home he had had visions of Kate severing the animal's head—of the blood spurting across her hands. He remembered tales of the "goat without horns" —the sacrifice of a child. And then, though he tried to force the picture from his mind, he could see Kate holding out the knife to Bard, the glint of metal as the blade plunged into Gabe Cousin's chest. He shivered and felt ashamed and soiled—yet there was an edge of pride on his thinking too. His mother was no soft island woman, frightened of her shadow. He remembered the stories she had told him of the fierce pirate, Grainne O'Maille, who had been his ancestress. And of his grandfather after whom he was named: how proudly the old Mullen had trod the thirteen steps that led to the gallows. Hanging was no disgrace when one died for Ireland. The memory of his grandfather's death was something hallowed, something that shone like new gold.

Mullen hadn't spent his fifteenth birthday at Rune Hall

228

even though his mother had planned a party for him. He knew there would be trouble afterward, but he couldn't bring himself to spend his birthday in a place he hated. Anyway what fun was a party in those great gloomy rooms, with only Kate and sick old Mr. Minor, his tutor and maybe the overseer? There were far more exciting things than that in Jamaica. Way up in the hills he had trapped a mongoose the week before and he was slated to fight his animal against a bushmaster that one of Brandon's bookkeepers had captured. Mullen had scraped together every shilling he could lay his hands on for the bets. The bookkeeper was a ninny, he thought. Didn't he know that the mongoose always won?

The fierce little rodent had made short shrift of the snake and Mullen had walked away from the pits with his pockets jingling with coins. After that he had gone down to the docks and eaten bully beef and crackers with the seamen off a Yankee sailing vessel. He had filled his belly with ale too and he had felt good strutting up King's Street and along the Parade. The theater had always been his love, and even though he had money in his pockets, he preferred to take his place in the pit. He liked the jostle of the crowds. He champed sugar cane and loudly applauded the exploits of Three-Fingered Jack, the bandit.

Mullen always grinned when he thought of that fifteenth birthday. Oh, he had proved himself a man, right enough. After the theater he had gone down to the Christian Steps and walked in bold as brass. Lettie Parsons gasped at the sight of him and then began to titter.

"Why, Mullen, what are you wanting here, lad?"

Mullen felt his face go red, but he tried to carry it off well. He pitched his voice low. "The same as any other man, Lettie. Do I have to tell you your business?"

The girls had gathered around, giggling. One of them put out her hand and carassed Mullen's cheek.

Lettie slapped the hand away. She tried to be severe, but couldn't keep the giggle down. "Why, Mullen, you're a mere lad. I should take your breeks down and spank ye. Out ye go, lad, afore they close me house down for serving the likes o' ye."

At first, Mullen had tried to bully, then to plead. Lettie

laughed until the tears rolled down her cheeks but she was adamant. Back on the Parade Mullen had nearly wept with frustration. Someone touched his arm lightly. He looked up into Chloe's face and he knew that she had followed him. She had led him down a back alley and into a dark shack. She had lit a candle and poured rum into a grimy glass and handed it to him. He had kissed her, felt the warmth of her breasts, and then he was suddenly sick and frightened. He went to the door and fiddled with the latch. Chloe watched him, her face amused. He flung the door open and ran outside. He kept on running until his chest hurt so that he had to stop. When he got home, he had climbed in through the window and bolted his door to delay Kate's scolding until the next day.

Now at sixteen, Mullen could look back at the boy of fifteen and laugh. But he still didn't like Rune Hall. There was a curse on the place and Kate had put it there. Kate had sent him away to Montego Bay the night before Buddhoe and his men had raided Rune Hall and seized Elgin, Brandon and Cockeray—the three richest men in the island. Their ransom was said to have been fifty thousand pounds. It took four months to raise the sum, and when the men were returned to Kingston they were gaunt and haggard. Cockeray had gone mad later and shot himself.

There were rumors throughout the island that Kate had planned the whole affair, drugged the guards and signaled Buddhoe when the time was ripe for attack. Mullen didn't know whether to believe this or not. All he knew was that Kate had had a lot of money shortly after the raid. She had claimed to have come into an inheritance from Ireland, but she would have needed some such story to cover up her sudden wealth if she had shared the ransom with Buddhoe.

Mullen always shivered when he thought of the night he had crawled along the balcony and peered into Jonathan Minor's room. Minor was propped up in bed. There were thick bandages where his ribs had been broken by Nigel's savage kicks. His face was thin and filled with pain. Kate and Elgin were in the room too. Kate's cheeks were flushed with victory as she handed a stack of bills to the Governor. But strangely enough it was not Elgin who had the appearance of being beaten, but Minor. The young Governor's face was mocking, cynical, but Minor's was bitter with defeat.

Elgin slipped a paper into Kate's hand which Mullen presumed to be the deed of Rune Hall. When the young man spoke his voice was low but so clear that it carried to the listening boy. "I do not blame you overmuch, Kate. Indeed I must admit a certain admiration. 'Tis the sort of thing I might have planned out myself. Have I not said that we were bound together by the common evil that dwells within us?"

Kate's eyes met his levelly. "Methinks you have too much imagination, Sir William. Be that as it may. You have your money and now you are no longer welcome at Rune Hall."

Elgin bowed and started to leave the room, but Minor had stretched out a hand. "Stay," he called. Elgin ignored him and walked out into the corridor, and Mullen, fearful of discovery, had hurried back to his bed.

Jonathan Minor had never been the same since. He never fully recovered from Nigel's brutal blows. The ribs did not set properly and he was in constant pain. Most of his days were spent in bed, though sometimes he hobbled out onto the wide balcony. His voice became thin and cracked, his skin gray, his eyes sunken and his face lined as though with deep scars. He could not endure Kate out of his sight and cried out for her pitifully.

Rune Hall had grown gloomier than ever. The few friends who had come to visit Jonathan came no longer. The freedmen avoided the place and even some of the slaves had run away. No outward change took place in Kate. At thirty-five she was more striking than she had been as a girl. The men still stopped to stare at her as she passed through the streets of Kingston in her white kittereen. But none among them stopped for an idle word or to jest with her save MacFeathers, Michael Scott or, strangely enough, Sir William Elgin. Of the women, none but Lettie Parsons ever called on Kate. She sometimes spent full afternoons at the Hall, chatting amiably and following Kate from room to room.

Mullen's only companion had been Forbes, his tutor. Forbes had taught him to read, write and do simple

231

arithmetic, but not much more. Mullen was no student. He scorned books and he refused to learn to play the violin. Forbes proved to be an easy taskmaster. His drinking usually started early in the day and by midafternoon he was ready for a doze. Then Mullen climbed the wall and was on his way to Kingston.

The theater drew him like a magnet. He slipped in through the stage door to watch rehearsals. He breathed in the oily scent of the make-up, the perfume, the powder, the stale air of the dressing room—and he was happy. Most of the traveling companies were Americans. He spent hours listening to the yarns of the actors. John Street in New York, Cedar Street in Philadelphia, Queen Street in Charleston seemed as familiar to him as the Parade. Now and then he got a walk-on part. His fee was a shilling or so at the best, but he would gladly have paid for the privilege.

Forbes had left suddenly for England and even the slight restraint of his studies was gone. Now Mullen left Rune Hall by noon and often did not come back until midnight. Kate scolded him at first. He listened patiently to all she had to say, but the next day he was gone again. He had an easy, friendly way with the sailors and they often stood him to a meal in the taverns. Moreover, he had a magic hand with fighting cocks. The owners paid him to handle their favorites. Sometimes his winnings were as much as five guineas in a day, but usually he lost it all by evening playing games of chance with the Magi men who hung about the theater entrances.

But now there was an unexpected threat to his freedom. Kate had told him about it that morning. A new tutor was coming out from England. A former Oxford student named Rodney Penney. Kate wanted to make a gentleman out of Mullen.

He listened in silence, but his lips twisted in amusement. Mr. Penney would have a job on his hands.

Rodney Penney was hot, tired and angry. His shirt was stuck to his back with sweat and his boots, polished this morning, were already coated with dust. He stood just within the far gates of the grounds of Rune Hall, watching the lines of slaves as they passed by carrying loads of sugar cane from the fields to the presses. They were bowed beneath the weight of the cane and their skins, in the glow of the sunlight, had the quality of black parchment.

Penney swore softly to himself. Already he hated the place with its dreary streets, burned with the sun in the daytime, black as pitch at night. Well, he had only himself to blame. He had been sent down from Oxford and it served him bloody well right. It was funny though how a man could smash up his whole life in a single night. He had liked Oxford and looked forward to a scholarly life—eventually he might be a don. Then there had been a party in Oliver's rooms, with a few drinks—then they had moved on to the Sixpence Tavern. More drinks, a lot of singing. When the beadle came the rest of them had run. But when Penney had tried to escape he fell. When he got up the beadle was over him. The liquor, the fall, the sense of being deserted by his companions churned up a red hot anger inside of him. He lashed out wildly. The man went down, struck his head on the cobbles and lay still. It was sheer luck that the beadle had pulled through; otherwise Penney might have had to face a murder charge. Anyway, it was the end of Oxford for Rodney Penney, the end of his dream of a life in cloistered halls. He had been sent down in disgrace. He thought of his father, shaking his fist in apoplectic rage, his mother's soft weeping. Rodney had been glad enough to get away when there was a chance, even if it was to Jamaica to share the duties of bookkeeper and tutor. He was numbered among the black sheep now. He might as well face it and crush out his self-pity.

The *Walrus*, on which he had sailed, had not put in to Kingston but to Montego Bay. He had caught a coach and landed in the city the night before. He had not slept much; he had walked the dark streets and the water front. He had taken a drink or two and finally throw himself down on his crude bed at the tavern and lain sleepless, waiting for the morning.

He made the journey to Rune Hall on foot and now he was waiting for Hodge the overseer to come down and show him to his quarters. On the way from Montego Bay he had learned what he could about the Minors. The

233

information was far from comforting. Jonathan Minor was a hopeless cripple; his wife was not of good repute. She was supposed to dabble in necromancy and once she had been an indentured servant. The boy ran wild and cared for little but cockfights. There were sly innuendoes about Mrs. Minor that he couldn't understand. It was hinted that she worked in league with the Maroons, had been responsible for the kidnapping of the Governor. She was called the White Witch of Rune Hall—probably a harmless old harridan, Rodney imagined. Maybe she was touched by the Jamaica sun—and little wonder.

He saw Hodge coming toward him—a burly man, with a red, brutal, pockmarked face and a leather quirt in his hand. Hodge looked him over insolently from top to toe. He spat on the ground, and when he spoke his voice was a snarl.

"So ye be the brat's new tutor, eh?"

Rodney held back his anger. "Yes, sir."

"Ye'll be no worse than Forbes, that be sartin. Nor much better, I suspect. The boy's a handful right enow." Hodge broke off to curse a laggard black. Then called to Penney over his shoulder, "Come along, I'll take ye to the Hall."

They were passing beneath the shade of the huge silk-cotton tree when the boy rounded the corner of the house and ran full tilt into Hodge. He fell, but sprang up quickly. He was trembling a little and his eyes sparkled with fire.

"What be the hurry, me lad?" Hodge's voice grated. "The cocks'll wait and so'll the Yankee scran at Kerry's jetty."

Mullen's hands clenched at his side but he said nothing. He turned from the overseer to Rodney Penney.

Penney looked at the boy's sensitive face and the wild eyes. Mullen's movements were swift, graceful, almost like those of an animal. Penney felt a quick sympathy and a pang of pity too. This was not the spoiled and pampered youngster he had expected. The boy was frightened, angry and hurt. Rodney stepped forward and stretched out his hand.

"I'm Rodney Penney," he said.

The boy looked at him doubtfully. "My new tutor?"

"Yes, Mullen."

The boy hesitated, then grinned. He reached out and took the proffered hand.

24

KATE STOOD BY HER WINDOW thinking of Mullen and Rodney as she had seen them hours earlier, walking down the hill away from Rune Hall together, laughing and chatting together. A thin blade of jealousy, sharp as a knife, sliced through her. Mullen had changed in the three months that the new tutor had been here. The world of books which he had scorned now fascinated him. He lay for hours beneath the wild orange tree on the lawn, reading and discussing his new knowledge with the tutor. He learned great sections of Shakespeare and Marlowe by rote and recited them dramatically while Penney cued him. He was studying music and carefully scoring the African tunes that were played on the merrywang and the bangil. The two of them often went to the offices of the *Jamaica Advertiser* to see Michael Scott. Mullen brought back sketches of the frigates that Scott drew. Sometimes he copied them or made improvisations of his own. He and Penney argued hotly over the relative merits of the British and American sailing vessels.

Much of the wildness had gone out of the boy; in its place was a reserved calm that was much like that of Kate's father. He did not avoid Kate any longer, nor tear away from her grasp. He was studiously polite and even went upstairs each day to pay his respects to Jonathan Minor. But Kate knew that he was farther away from her than ever. She had understood, in part, the wild passions that raked him, the longing, the desire for freedom. But now she knew him not at all.

Kate had wanted Rune Hall, first for herself, then for

Mullen. How proudly she had given him the deed! Yet it had meant nothing to him. She had found the paper, crumpled and dirty, on the floor at his bedside the next morning.

Perhaps Mullen was right and Rune Hall was not worth the price in suffering which she had paid for it. She felt unutterably lonely. She moved away from the window to the room where Jonathon Minor lay sleeping. The gray skin was pulled tight across the high forehead, the peaked cheekbones. The face was like a death mask, she thought, and she wondered how this man could ever have raised her to either the passion of love or hate.

At thirty-five she was alone in the great house that she had bought with ransom money. She thought hungrily of the Cathedral of St. Clement—the shadowed nave, the altar candles, the sweet scent of incense, the clear touch of holy water on her fingers, the cleansing power of the confession. The monotonous chant of Father Maholan's voice seemed to echo along Rune Hall's wide corridors and it filled her with a yearning that was sensual and sweet.

She started swiftly down the stairs, but when she reached the bottom she stopped. A dondo drum beat in the hills. She had made her choice and there was no withdrawal. The pallay of the Ashanti, the sacrifice of the white goat, the voice that spoke the words of Erzulie or Mamma Oshunai, the magic rites of obeah—these were her religion now. They had brought her wealth, Rune Hall, all the material things she wanted. Obeah could bring her love, too. But whose love? Certainly not the turbulent emotions set up in her by Sir William Elgin.

She thought of Rodney Penney and wondered if he had returned. She went out to the veranda and saw him. Rodney had an easel set up before the slaves' quarters. Shamey Lady was posed in the doorway and he was sketching her. As Kate walked toward them, she noted that his face was alive, eager and youthful. He jumped up when she stopped by his side to admire his sketch.

"You should be a portrait painter," she said. "Why do you waste your time on the blacks?"

"Shamey Lady's features are distinguished. Look at

the sweeping line of forehead and cheek, the firmness of the lips, the long oval of the jaw, the distance between the lobe of the ear and the hollow of the neck. Have you seen such perfection in any white person on the island?"

It is a pity that you feel that way. I should like you to have painted me." Kate's sharp retort betrayed her instinctive jealousy.

Penney's face reddened. "I did not mean," he stuttered. "I did not think——"

She laughed lightly. "You take things too seriously, Rodney Penney, including your duties as a tutor. Mullen does not need all your time. You must find other pleasures or soon each of you will be bored with the other's company. My husband and I see too little of you. Rune Hall is lonely at times and I am sure my husband would welcome a game of chess."

She walked away, but not before she had seen the eagerness in his eyes. This man could be wrapped about her finger too easily, she thought, yet he had a certain youthful charm. He was having too much influence over Mullen. Well, she would put a stop to that—and have pleasure in the doing. Yet she wished that he were stronger. Or did she? Had she wanted a man of real mettle, why had she not pitted herself against Elgin? At the thought of the Governor, she felt his strong fingers about her wrists and the burning of his lips as they touched her mouth. Why had she run away from him? Was it because she sensed in him a ruthless power that surpassed her own strength? Ah, what did it matter? Penney might be a weakling, but he was young and attractive and he could make no demands upon her.

As her foot touched the lowest step of the stairs, she heard laughter and turned. Shamey Lady had moved from the doorway and stood beside Penney. The girl's rich voice carried across the cane field and the broad lawn. Though Kate could not catch the words, she sensed mockery in the girl's tones. Penney laughed again and glanced quickly toward the house.

An unreasoning fury seized Kate. Was the girl regaling him with stories of Kate's obeah practices? Was she warning him away? Kate remembered Mullen's affection for Shamey Lady and how he had followed her about as a child. Now Penney was falling under the girl's spell. Kate should have ordered her from the grounds long ago. Kate took a step forward in anger, then checked herself. It would not do for Rodney to witness her jealousy. She would tend to the girl later. She smiled slightly. Her game with Rodney Penney might be worth the candle after all.

As she started again up the stairs that led to the wide paneled door, a carriage rolled through the gates. Lettie Parsons, dressed as ever in purple, called a shrill greeting. Kate forced the anger from herself as she took Lettie in her arms. She looked with misgiving into the round, seemingly guileless face. In a moment of weakness, Kate had once tried to put into words the wildly conflicting emotions which the thought of Elgin always raised in her. Kate comforted herself that Lettie had not understood, yet she could not be sure.

Lettie dug into the folds of her voluminous skirt and brought out a package. Kate tore away the paper wrappings and lifted out a box. She pressed back the lid and held a flask of French perfume in her hands.

"He asked me to bring it to you—to pretend it was my own gift."

Kate had no need to ask whom Lettie meant. She knew the gift was from Elgin. This was the same perfume she had worn when they had danced together at Government House long ago.

She only half heard Lettie's voice. "Why do ye not let him come to ye, Kate? I'm thinking 'tis each o' ye has need o' the other."

"No," Kate answered fiercely. "No." She raised the flask and dashed it onto the stones of the walk. The perfume spattered her gown and soaked into her shoes, but she did not move.

"Why do ye fear him so?" Lettie asked. "He's grown more kindly with the years."

"Fear!" Kate repeated. "That is a strange word indeed! It is simply that I know the ambition within the man. He would possess me, possess Rune Hall. He would make me weak with the wish to give myself to him and he would grow stronger and mock me."

"You do him wrong, Kate. You read in him your own madness."

"That may be. I dare not risk it." The scent of the perfume, sickeningly strong, whirled about her. She looked down at the broken glass and her spattered skirt. The perfume was gone and that was well. She would take no gift from Sir William Elgin. But she would not change the gown nor the shoes—not today.

In the office of the *Jamaica Advertiser*, Michael Scott sat facing Penney and Mullen. "War with the States is only a matter of time," he stated confidently. "When Madison takes the oath of office he is committed to naval warfare with England."

Mullen looked at him puzzled. "But why? Certainly the Americans will not fight merely because a few of their seamen have been impressed."

Scott shrugged. "It's growing pains, my lad. A nation must grow up the same as a boy and both have got to test their strength by having a good fight."

"England is in the wrong. Why does she not make restitution? With the Yankees on our side we could sweep the waters clean of the French."

Scott laughed and clapped the boy on the shoulder. "Do not say such things aloud. Even though you be but a lad, they'll have you up for treason."

Mullen's face flamed. "To hell with dunderheads! Why should Jamaica be under England's thumb? Why did we not fight for our freedom like the Yankees did?"

"Careful, lad," Scott cautioned. He turned to Penney. "How did the boy come to such notions? 'Tis dangerous."

The tutor shrugged even though he knew the answer. Mullen spent many hours with the troupe of American comedians who were booked at the Royal Theatre, many more with the seamen off the Yankee sailing vessels. Besides the boy was a rebel at heart and, with his Irish blood, had little enough love for the English.

The Yankees were in disfavor in Jamaica already. A week ago the comedians had been driven from the stage by hurrled bottles, fruit and sticks. Brawls had broken out on the water front between English and American seamen and one American, accused of accosting an Eng-

239

lishwoman, had been strung up with rope in Kerry Square.

But Kingston was still in the center of trade for the blackbirders and Jamaica waxed fat with the profits of the slave exchange. The big buyers were the Americans, and the Jamaicans were in two minds about their Yankee neighbors. Fear, jealousy and a certain contempt for the harsh-voiced New Englanders and the uncouth Georgians who flooded the slave mart were balanced by greed for the Yankee dollars.

Penney knew that Scott's warning was valid. Mullen was saying aloud what many a Jamaican whispered in private. The boy would make an easy target for zealots like Brandon and there were those who would not hesitate to use him to even their scores with Kate. Penney determined that he must caution Mullen more soundly, even at the expense of losing the boy's regard.

He got up a bit stiffly and put his hand on Mullen's shoulder. "You're taking me to the cockpits today, my lad."

Mullen looked up and grinned. "I've a half crown to put on a cock called Cocoa. Lay your bets beside mine and you'll not go wrong."

Penney linked his arm with Mullen's and, side by side, they strolled down Harbour Street in the direction of the dried mud huts beyond the docks where many of the cockfights were held. Mullen felt a growing sense of pride in his role of guide as he kept pace with the tutor's long strides. But when they reached the beach, instead of excited voices and the crowing of the cocks, they saw a group of men standing about in tense silence.

A dead cock was sprawled at the edge of the circle and two young bookkeepers were staring balefully across the ring at each other. Their voices were pitched low but there was deadly anger in their eyes. One had called the other "Yankee," the one epithet that was unforgivable in Jamaica.

Suddenly the maligned man strode across the ring, his face white and set. His hand lashed out and struck his adversary across the face. The second bookkeeper drew back and crouched as though about to spring. But before further violence could be done, Rodney was between them. Both men were demanding the satisfaction of a duel.

Good-naturedly Rodney took charge, receiving the cards, appointing seconds, and arranging the time and place for combat. Not until the two men had gone off, each surrounded by his friends, did Rodney look at Mullen and break into laughter.

Mullen's excitement was tinged with uneasiness. By morning both men would be shaking with fear at the situation which their hot tempers had brought about. Yet neither would withdraw lest he be charged with cowardice.

Rodney saw the misgiving in the boy's face and clapped him on the shoulder. "Don't take it to heart, lad," he warned, smiling broadly. "I've a trick or two up my sleeve that I learned at Oxford. I'll warrant neither man will be hurt. By tomorrow they'll be drinking grog together and boasting what brave fellows they are. Now listen to this—"

He bent over and whispered in the boy's ear. Mullen's face cleared and he joined in the tutor's laughter.

As they made their way back to Harbour Street, Mullen's eyes kept flicking to the tutor's face. Never before had he felt such closeness to another person. He tried to find words to express his emotions, but none would come. Instead he noted how Rodney wore his hat cocked to one side and he raised his fingers to his own brim and poked it sideways. And when he spoke again, he pitched his voice low to make it more like Rodney's.

25

MULLEN, astride his bay gelding, cast an almost idolatrous look at Rodney Penney. As the tutor had promised, the duel that had taken place in the gray light of dawn had turned into a riotous fiasco. At Rodney's instigation, the seconds had loaded the long pistols with dried peas. The duelists, white, shaking and bolstered by far too many drops of rum, had stared in consternation as the peas dribbled out onto the dried grass. But after their first indignant protests, they too had joined in the merriment. In the end, the whole party had withdrawn to the Pickny Tavern and toasted each other over oft-repeated mugs of ale.

As Mullen and Rodney had taken their departure the two bookkeepers were warmly embracing each other and vowing eternal friendship. Now, as Mullen rode up the hill toward Rune Hall, he was still shaking with laughter. But as he passed through the wide gateway with Rodney at his side, he saw that Kate was watching from her balcony. By the time they reached the driveway, Kate had come to the door.

Mullen expected to be scolded, for the clinging odor of the tavern could scarcely fail to attract his mother's attention. And, of course, he had not taken a single lick at his studies all day. As Kate appeared, her face was severe but Mullen was surprised to see that her eyes were twinkling. Rodney launched into the story of the duel before Kate had a chance to speak. Rodney told it well, imitating first one bookkeeper, then the other. Kate held her sides, shaking with laughter. It was years since she had laughed like this, Mullen thought, and on a sudden impulse he threw his arms around her.

He felt her hands soft and caressing. She kissed his ear, stroked his hair and the back of his neck. He turned from her to Penney and the glow of warmth, the sense of well-being, was almost unbearable. He looked up at the towers of Rune Hall and, for the first time, they did not seem cold and forbidding. He whirled and buried his head in his mother's breasts. Her arms tightened and grew rigid but he could not see that she did not look down at him—that her eyes met those of Rodney Penney and held them challengingly.

Through the open window of Jonathan Minor's room, a plaintive voice floated down to them.

"Kate—Kate, where are you? Kate, I need you."

Kate said quickly to Penney, "I must go. But do have

242

dinner with us at the Hall tonight. Jonathan needs cheering up. You've scarcely got to know him, Mr. Penney."

Rodney had dinner with them that evening and almost every evening that followed. For Mullen the days were not long enough. He was learning to paint, to score music, even to write poetry. His sketches of ships were almost as skillful as Michael Scott's. In the afternoons, the role of tutor and student vanished. Mullen took Rodney to cockfights, led him through the back doors of the theaters, showed him how to trap the mongoose, took him to see the pallays of the Ashanti and introduced him to the freedmen of Baraçong.

After dinner, Rodney often played chess with Jonathan Minor. Sometimes the games lasted for hours and Mullen soon tired of watching. There were times when he would go to his room, fling himself on his bed and go to sleep. But there were others when he would hear the drums in the hills and the soft whine of the abeng. Then he would get up and follow the narrow paths that led to the pallays. If the drazzon was a social one, he might stay outside and watch, tapping his feet to the age-old rhythm of the African tunes. The blacks had come to know, trust and accept him. Even so they would not let him enter the pallays, and when there were ceremonial dances he was banned altogether.

Old Koshi told him gently, "There are the gods of the blacks and the gods of the white man. There is the magic of Africa and the miracles of the Bible. These are our gods; we serve them and that is right. But the white man who serves the black gods has betrayed both his gods and ours. And in the end he shall die, forsaken by both."

Mullen had the sudden memory of Kate, the ceremonial knife of the Ashanti raised high above her head. He spoke quickly, "My mother—"

Koshi's hand signaled him to silence. The old man's eyes were veiled and wary. Mullen turned from him and afterwards he visited the pallays less frequently. But sometimes when the drums beat, he went out onto the lawn and waited. Once he saw Kate slip out too. He hid in the darkness and did not follow her when she passed. When he went in, he listened at Jonathan's door. He

243

heard Rodney laugh and knew that the chess game was still on.

Rodney's painting lacked precision and balance, but it had a primitive power. He used masses of color effectively and his blurred, broken lines gave a sense of movement, almost of violence. His portrait of Shamey Lady was his best work. She made up his cabin each day and, as she went about her tasks, he had studied her. Despite her years in Jamaica, there was still a wildness about the girl. The deep-set eyes were haunted by memories of Africa and there was the constant suggestion of flight in her movements. Rodney had painted her with a scarlet bandana twisted about her head. He had captured the perfection of her black skin with its slight blue tinge and he had managed to convey the sense of restless power, of dormant anger that lay within her.

Rodney hung the portrait on his wall and Mario came to see it. Rodney had taken an instant liking to Mario. The same power that he had found in Shamey Lady was present in her husband—but in Mario this power was leashed, held in control to be used when he wished. There was a quiet confidence in him, a sureness of purpose, an inward peace.

Kate had come to the cabin as Mario was leaving. Rodney saw the look that passed between them—the cold withdrawal in Mario's eyes, the slight mockery in Kate's smile. Kate had asked again, "Why do you bother with the Negroes? Why do you not try something more ambitious?"

Rodney laughed. "I'm trying to learn what is inside of them. I understand people better when I have painted them. At least I think I do."

Kate remained silent, watching him. Then she said softly, "In that case, I'd like you to paint me."

He hesitated. "I don't think I should care to try. You see, I must have some knowledge of what I paint. I have none of you. Your face is calm but you are not. Your beauty is a mask."

"You have a vivid imagination. But a woman likes to be considered—shall we say—enigmatic. I am flattered. Perhaps if you paint me, you will understand me better.

244

I'll be waiting for you this afternoon when you have finished with Mullen's studies."

That afternoon Mullen had learned that Picon was staying with Koshi in his cabin outside Baraçong and he had persuaded the old man to teach him some of the almost forgotten leggoes—the choruses around which the Negroes sang impromptu tunes as they worked in the cane fields. He talked eagerly of Picon, never doubting that Rodney would share his adventure. Rodney wavered as he looked at the boy's flushed face—after all, there was no reason why he should be at Kate's beck and call.

He said slowly, "I'd planned to paint."

Mullen's head jerked up in surprise and there was hurt and resentment in his eyes. Rodney was stirred to an anger which he himself did not understand. "Damn it all, I was hired as a tutor not a nursemaid."

Mullen stared incredulously and his lower lip began to tremble. He jumped up quickly and ran out of the cabin.

Rodney followed him to the door and called his name but Mullen did not stop. Rodney was disgusted with himself—with his impulse to hurt the boy. "The damned Jamaica heat," he growled, but he knew that he was only making excuses for himself. The thought of being alone with Kate filled him with excitement. The first day he had seen her he had felt the blood tingling in his face. There was something bold and reckless about her, yet there was a great warmth. The White Witch they called her and he could understand that—she did not belong in the world of the planters, the bookkeepers, the petty government officials. No wonder they made up fantastic stories about her. He did not believe for a moment that she had connived in the kidnapping of Sir William Elgin, nor that she took part in the Ashanti sacrificial ceremonies. Still there were things he could not understand. When he had protested Hodge's brutal flogging of the slaves, she had only smiled indulgently and told him that Hodge knew best how to handle the incorrigibles. And once when Mullen was ill she had refused to call a doctor and had prepared a concoction of native roots and herbs.

Rodney threw himself down on his bed, trying to drive away all thoughts of Kate or Mullen. He closed

245

his eyes but no matter in which way he turned his thoughts, they soon came back to Kate. He got up and boiled himself a pot of the strong Jamaica coffee. He would take his easel up to the top of Pinchback Mountain, he determined. He collected his kit and his canvas and started out through the sugar cane, but after a few steps, he stopped.

He started back toward Rune Hall slowly, but by the time he reached it, his heart was pounding. . . .

The rain beat a steady tattoo on the dried banana leaves of Koshi's roof. Picon strummed his quartro and sang in his cracked, slurred voice:

> "Oh me went up de stairs
> An' de door done lock
> An' me take out de wood
> An' me bus' de darn lock."

Mullen squatted in the corner, his arms about his knees. He joined in the chorus because he knew it was expected of him, but he could not get interested in the music.

> "Iron bar! Iron bar!
> Iron bar! Iron bar!
> Tra-la-la-la-la."

Mullen had spent every afternoon for a week listening to Picon chatting with Koshi, Mario and Shamey Lady. But his thoughts were constantly at Rune Hall. What had got into Rodney? Had he, Mullen, done something wrong?

> "Say me drink white rum
> 'Til me tumble down . . ."

Picon's voice trailed off. Mullen looked up in surprise. The old man made a movement with his hand, sweeping the bottle and glass from the table. They landed with dull thuds on the earthen floor. Picon sohuted, "Me through, gor-darm! Dis is no de day."

Mullen was suddenly aware of the tensions in the room. Mario and Shamey Lady were facing each other, their expressions blank. Koshi said softly, "Never mind." Mullen looked from one to another but none of them met his glance.

"What's wrong?" he asked.

Mario got up slowly, stooped and picked up the rum bottle. There was still some rum in it and he drank it. Finally he said slowly, "Shamey Lady's been forbidden to go to Rune Hall."

Mullen repeated the words incredulously. "But why?" he asked.

Mario did not look at him. "Your mother accuses Shamey Lady of setting Penney against her."

Mullen could think of no reply. He felt a restless stirring within him. Something was wrong at Rune Hall, yet he still had no idea what it was. His eyes moved about the room, seeking some sympathetic understanding. But none of them returned his gaze. He cried irritably, "There's something you're not telling me. What is it?"

Mario shrugged and sat down with his back to the boy. Mullen got up and went to Koshi. The old man looked down at his folded hands and did not speak. Mullen turned from one to the other, but all were silent. He went to the door and opened it. He took a step into the rain, hoping he would be called back, but there was still no sound. He closed the door softly and then, shivering, he began to run through the drizzling dampness.

The climb up Pinchback Hill was steep and slippery. Mullen was soon soaked and covered with mud. He ripped his clothing on the briars but he scarcely noticed. He could not think; he was driven on by a blind urge to get back to Rune Hill, to face Rodney Penney and force some explanation from him.

The rain came down in torrents as Mullen slipped across the lawn. He stood for a moment under the silk-cotton tree to catch his breath, then dashed for the safety formed by the arch of the wide windows of the great hall. He grasped the wrought-iron railing and pulled himself up. Kate was seated only a few feet from him. Her head was tilted back proudly, her hands folded in her lap. She wore a white gown threaded with scarlet at the

247

throat, and the ruby pendant which she loved was suspended from a gold chain about her neck. The immobility of her pose lent her an almost unearthly calm.

Mullen cried out softly but the heavy rain drowned out the sound. He could see Rodney now. The tutor stood before his easel, his forehead creased in a frown.

"It's no good," Rodney said, "you're sitting as though you were made of stone, Kate. How can I paint you when the face you show me is only a mask."

Kate's laughter tinkled. "I don't think you've tried to know me very hard, Rodney."

Rodney threw down his brush and walked to her. She looked up, her lips parted. For a moment Penney stood undecided, then turned away. Kate took his hand. "Rodney," she said, "are you afraid?"

"Afraid? Afraid of what?" he asked irritably.

"Afraid of yourself—to find out what you really are."

"I know what I am—a tutor, a notch above a servant. A man whom you can call and dismiss at will."

"Don't be silly, Rodney. Mullen couldn't get along without you. Rune Hall was dying until you came. You've given us all life and hope."

Penney swung about. "Kate—Kate," he cried. "I must —I must not—Kate, what shall I do? I want to be fair to Mullen—to Jonathan."

"What about me, Rodney?"

He put his hand out and the fingers touched her hair. Then with a swift movement his arms were about her and he pressed his lips against her neck. His body was wracked, as though with sobbing. Kate held him tight against her and her lips found his.

Mullen dropped back to the wet earth. He lay there, afraid to move, for many minutes. When he got up his face was white and strained. He went up the back stairway to his room. He stripped off his sodden clothing and rubbed himself until his body was glowing. He dressed again slowly, and when he was finished he tiptoed to the door of the room where Jonathan Minor lay.

He opened the door and peered in. Jonathan was breathing stertorously, his eyes closed. Mullen moved quietly across the room to the fireplace, above which two pistols rested on the mahogany mantelpiece. He took one down, examined it and thrust it in his belt. But when he turned, Jonathan Minor was no longer sleeping. The old man's eyes were directly on him.

"Mullen," he said, in a voice that was surprisingly strong. "Come to me, lad."

The boy moved obediently to the bedside.

"I've a mind what you're up to, lad, and 'tis no good. Quarrels cannot be settled with a gun."

Mullen was trembling and on the edge of tears, but he managed to stand erect. He said, "A point of honor is at stake, sir."

Jonathan did not smile. His thin hand reached out and pulled the pistol from Mullen's waist. "I do not doubt your honor, Mullen. But what of your opponent? Is he worthy of an honorable meeting?"

Mullen remained silent. Jonathan motioned to the chair. "Come sit by me awhile, lad. 'Tis seldom enough I have a chance to speak with you and that I must do. I'm an old man, Mullen, and I've no doubt that I'm to die soon. I've spent most of my life here in Jamaica and still there is not a man on the island that I can trust, so I must place my faith in you.

"I've a mind what you're up to with the pistol. 'Tis Penney—is it not? Do not judge him harshly, lad. If it were not he, 'twould be another. And I'm to blame and so are you. I've not the strength of loving Kate demands and you've not given fully of yourself. Your mother's a lonely woman, Mullen. She will always be lonely, always trying to fill the emptiness within her, never finding the way. But you, Mullen, can fill your life if you will. But not with a pistol—not with death. Another's death cannot bring you peace."

Mullen was unable to look at the old man. He kept his eyes on his hands and fought back the tears.

"I want you to make a promise, lad. Will you listen to what I ask? As I've lain here waiting for the end, I've thought of Ishbel. I've wanted her with me and I've written her to come. It was a mistake. There's danger for Ishbel here. I should not have asked this of her— but it is too late to turn back. Ishbel will come back to Rune Hall where she was born and there'll be none to take care of her save you. Elgin cannot be trusted and

Kate—" His voice broke off and he closed his eyes for a moment.

When he opened them he said, "Mullen, take care of Ishbel. See that no harm comes to her."

Mullen nodded. "I'll try, sir."

"That's a good lad. I'll rest more easily knowing the lass will not be alone." He struggled to a sitting position and tucked the pistol beneath his pillow. "You'll have no need of this, Mullen," he said, smiling. "And as for Rodney Penney, if you see him send him to me. I'd like a game of chess."

26

RODNEY PENNEY was drunk. He lay on his back and stared up at the ceiling of wattle and dob.

"Kate," he mumbled. "Kate."

He moaned softly. There was something that he had to do but he couldn't remember what. Oh yes, collect his gear and take it up to Rune Hall. No need for concealment—not after last night.

How long had Jonathan Minor known about him and Kate? Probably from the very beginning. As for Mullen —the boy had avoided him ever since the first day he had kissed Kate. The pose of tutor and student was a mere farce now. Mullen refused even to speak to him. God knew that he, Penney, hadn't intended matters to take this course. Oh, he had done a few rotten things in his time. He had knocked down the old beadle at Oxford. And there was a girl in London whom he didn't like to think about. But cuckolding the man who had befriended him—that was different.

He had not even played the man's part; it was Kate who had done the seducing. She had kissed him, comforted him, quelled his fears, lulled his scruples, laughed at him when he told her he couldn't take advantage of her. He flushed at the thought of the grotesque scene on the divan when, after kissing her again and again, he had pulled away from her. "It's all wrong," he had protested. "We must think of Mullen—of Jonathan."

Kate had run her finger up his arm and when he looked at her, her eyes were filled with mocking laughter. He kissed her again and felt the pressure of her body as she strained against him. Then she broke away and ran up the stairs and he had followed her.

In the darkness of her room he could not see her, but he could hear her breathing. She said softly, "Not here—not tonight." He turned to the door, then anger, shame and humiliation had churned up within him. He moved toward her and his groping hands reached her breasts. His fingers molded the soft contours of the bodice and touched the warm flesh above. With a sob, he began to rip at her clothing, to caress her wildly. She fought him away, but even as she did so, she laughed. He took her in his arms and forced her across the great bed. He would master her, he thought—make her his own; but when their passion was ended Kate was as cool as ever. She smiled at both his protestations of love and his self-recriminations and he realized that all the wild tumult of emotion that had taken possession of him had left her untouched.

The days that followed were miserable. Mullen sneaked off in the morning and stayed away until late at night. Rodney could not bring himself to face Jonathan Minor, and Kate was busy with her household duties. He stayed in his cabin and drank until dark. Then he went out in the cane field and waited for the sight of Kate on her balcony. Each night he swore that he would not go to her; each morning would find him in her room.

Kate had urged him to take one of the guest rooms at Rune Hall but he had refused. He clung to the cabin, even though Kate had sent Shamey Lady away and the place was uncared for. The cabin represented some independence, some slight degree of self-respect. But after last night pretense was useless. He was no longer his own master.

The soft scraping at Kate's door had come a little

251

after midnight. Rodney leapt from the bed, his first thought one of escape. Kate had only laughed. The knob turned slowly and a cold sweat broke out on Rodney's skin as he realized that, in the heat of his passion, he had forgotten to drop the bar in place. The heavy mahogany door swung wide. Jonathan Minor's gaunt figure, supported by a cane, could be seen against the pale light of the hall.

Kate lit the lamp and turned to face the old man. Their faces were both stolid as their eyes met. Jonathan looked from his wife to Rodney. His thin lips curved in a contemptuous smile. "What did she use to snare you with, my boy? 'Tis said Kate knows all the love philters of the Ashanti. Hashish and dried feces mixed with your chocolate? Or maybe blood, cut hair and the oil of the jonkra weed stirred up in your rice? Either one would do the trick."

Rodney had a mad impulse to protest, to flaunt his manliness. But the whole thing was absurd. Here he stood, half-naked and shivering in the damp night air, facing the sick husband of the woman who had made love to him, trying to think of some means, not of justifying himself, but of proving that his was the man's role.

Minor tried to speak again but a spasm of coughing shook his allennated frame. The cane slipped from his hand and clattered on the mahogany floor. The old man went down on one knee. Rodney hurried to him and Minor smiled grimly as he grasped the tutor's arm.

Rodney helped the sick man down the hall, back to his own room and into the wide bed, fighting the self-revulsion that nauseated him and aware of the ludicrous picture he made as, only partially clothed, he assisted the man whom he had cuckolded.

Minor's eyes met his and the old man gave a wry chuckle. "Ah, I've made a fool of myself. 'Twould be better had I pretended not to know. 'Tis not your fault, Rodney, nor yet hers, I guess. Kate's paying off an old score and I cannot say that I blame her too much."

Rodney went back to Kate's room and completed his dressing in silence, feeling unspeakably foolish. When he finished he went to Kate and there was pleading in his eyes that she would say something that would relieve the stupidity of the fiasco.

"Oh, go," she said irritably. "Just leave me alone."

He picked his way through the silent house and out through the back door. His chagrin changed to unreasoning anger. He would go back and kill the old man. No, that was insane—Minor had done him no wrong. The thing to do was get drunk.

He had done a thorough job and now he was sick. Maybe another drink would make him feel better. He fumbled for the bottle and found it. He raised it to his lips but it was empty. He threw it across the room and the sound of the splintering glass brought him momentary pleasure. He sat up and cupped his head in his hands. A step at the door attracted his attention. He looked up expecting to see Kate, but Shamey Lady was there.

She stood for a moment, her slim body outlined against the bright glare of the sun.

"Shamey Lady—what are you doing here? Didn't Kate tell you not to come here?"

The girl nodded. "I know, Mas' Rodney. But I had to come to you. I got to tell you to get away. Rune Hall is bad and the Witch is filled with evil. Go away while there is time."

Rodney stared at her. "How do you know these things?"

"The voice of our people whispers in the night. We know what the Witch does. We would flee if we could but we are bound to the island. That is not true of you. You can go."

Rodney staggered to his feet. "Why do you call her the Witch? What nonsense is this?"

"She is a witch," Shamey Lady said firmly. "Why do you think Jonathan Minor cannot walk? His ribs were broken, yes. But other men have recovered from worse injuries. She has put a spell on him. She will do the same to you."

As Shamey Lady talked she gathered his clothing together, stuffing it into his bags. "You will come with me?" she asked.

"Where?"

"It does not matter as long as you get away. Koshi will give you a place to sleep if you like."

Shamey Lady's body suddenly stiffened and her face turned gray. Rodney followed the direction of her eyes. Kate Minor stood in the doorway and Rodney wondered how much she had heard. Kate's eyes were blazing as she took a step toward the girl.

Shamey Lady cringed away from her. "No," she cried. "Don't do it to me. Don't put an obi on me."

Kate stepped closer, her arms at her side, her eyes wide.

Shamey Lady was shaking. She gave a little cry and slipped to the floor. Her body arched with pain. Her tongue came out and her teeth pressed against it until blood spurted from her mouth. She writhed in agony, beating the floor with her clenched fists.

Rodney clutched Kate's arm. "For God's sake, stop it."

Kate glanced at him. "I have done nothing," she said coldly. "It is the girl's own sense of guilt that has betrayed her."

Shamey Lady's body relaxed and she lay moaning softly. Rodney, still befuddled by the rum, stood over her.

There was a roar from the doorway and Mario charged into the room. He pushed Rodney aside and knelt beside the stricken girl. He picked her up in his arms and turned to face Kate. His dark eyes were filled with fury, but his tones were surprisingly soft.

"Koshi and I taught you what you know of obeah, for once we believed that you would use this knowledge to help our people. Instead you have made it serve your own selfish ends. The power is in you, but you have used it solely for evil. Now you have struck Shamey Lady. This is the end."

Kate laughed. "What do you intend to do, Mario? I know more of obeah now than either you or Koshi. You cannot harm me."

Mario shook his head. "You are mistaken. We have but to let the white man's law have its way. I shall go to the court and denounce you. I know every one of your crimes from the murder of Mannie Cousins to what you have done to Jonathan Minor."

"You would not dare. Any statement would implicate you and Koshi."

"It does not matter. There must be an end to this thing. You have destroyed the lives of all with whom you have come in contact."

"They will not believe you."

"Perhaps not, but there are many whites who will bear witness against you."

"Mario, don't be a fool. I've not hurt the girl."

Mario stepped to one side and carried Shamey Lady through the doorway. Rodney watched him striding through the cane. He turned back to Kate.

"Surely he cannot harm you," he said.

Kate's face was grim. "Maybe not. I dare not chance it. Get a horse and saddle it for me. I must reach Kingston quickly."

"What are you going to do?"

"Make charges against Mario first. Then whatever he may say will be taken as a desire to get revenge."

"But what charge can you make?"

Kate laughed. "There is only one that will stick, that no one will dare question, where there'll be no trial—rape."

"Kate, you can't do that!"

"I must. Will you saddle the horse or must I do it myself?"

Penney's hands were slippery with perspiration as he worked at the cinches, and nausea sickened him. Kate grasped the white mare's reins and thrust her foot into the stirrup.

"Wait," Rodney gasped, "I'm coming with you."

"There's no time, you fool. If Mario reaches Kingston before I do, they'll listen to him. There'll be trouble then, no matter what happens."

Rodney's hands dropped from the reins. Kate's quirt fell on the mare's flank and the animal leapt forward. Rodney watched until Kate reached the gate, then he started to saddle the gelding.

His trembling hands were awkward and the gelding moved restlessly. The animal reared twice and Rodney fell backward, narrowly escaping the raised foreleg. Minutes passed before he could quiet the gelding down.

When he tried to mount, the nausea took hold of him again and he was sick. By the time he reached the roadway, Kate's mare was long out of sight.

A crowd was already assembled in front of the courthouse when he arrived at the far end of the Parade. Even from here he could catch the sound of angry cries. At least fifty men were gathered around Kate's mare and others streamed in from the side streets. Kate's voice, sharp and clear, rose above the rest. Rodney caught the words "Mario" and "rape" and knew that he was too late to forestall Kate's accusations. The islanders might be suspicious of her and her mysterious powers, but she was a white woman and they would believe her.

Sydney Brandon mounted the steps and spread out his hands for silence. Throughout the years he had never ceased haranguing the loungers about the Parade and his constant topic was the perfidy of the freedmen. His voice trumpeted as though in victory. "Many a time have I told ye what the blacks o' Baraçong were like. Men o' Jamaica, shall we stand by and watch our women be despoiled?" The crowd roared "No!"

"Then who among ye will come to Baraçong? We'll find Mario there—" The mob drowned out his words with a shout of approval. Again Brandon signaled for silence, but as he did so, there was a stirring at the fringe of the crowd and men nudged each other and pointed toward a figure tumbling across the parade.

"Kate! Kate! Dinna do it, lass!" The shrill voice carried the length of the Parade. MacFeathers, his bald head shining, his bagpipes strapped across his shoulders, ran across the rutted ground toward Kate. "Lassie, lassie, dinna feed Mario to these John Crows."

" 'Tis the Scottie again," bellowed Brandon. "He fooled us once years ago with a cock and bull tale of Nigel. Shall he do it again?" He rushed down the steps and seized MacFeathers' shirt in his great hand. The mob surged about them and Kate's mare shied restlessly. Rodney leapt from his horse and tried to force his way toward Kate, but the crowd pushed him back.

Brandon's bellow rose above the uproar. "I ask ye

256

a second time, who will come wi' me to fetch the black bastard out o' Baraçong."

"Lead the way," someone shouted.

"That I will." Brandon broke loose and started to swagger down King Street. The mob swayed and half a dozen men took their place behind Brandon. The others turned to watch them and then followed more slowly. Kate's mare moved with the crowd. Then it whinnied and its forelegs rose high.

MacFeathers, who had been pushed to the ground by Brandon, was on his feet again. He stood before Kate, his hand raised as though in imprecation. He whirled as the horse towered above him and then staggered backward. A piercing cry rose, but the din of Brandon's followers cut it short.

Kate lashed at the mare's flank and twisted its bit. The crowd cleared about her. Without a look at MacFeathers, she rode past him toward Brandon. Only a few stragglers remained behind. The rest followed the procession.

Soon the Parade was deserted save for the man who lay in a crumpled heap beneath a tamarind tree near the courthouse stairs, and the two who knelt beside him. Rodney Penney saw the broken bagpipes in the roadway and a sudden wild anger seized him. He hurried forward and reached the stricken man just as Father Maholan rose from MacFeathers' side.

He said, "Father, he's not dead. He can't be."

The priest looked at him gravely. "I'm afraid he is. The mare's hoof caught him just above the heart." He knelt again and Rodney saw him make the sign of the cross.

His eyes turned to the third person. Mullen Cousins' face was white as he watched the priest. Rodney stretched out his hand to touch the boy but Mullen jerked away.

"Don't touch me," he said shakily. "I've seen you with her. And now—now my mother is a murderess. I can't even pretend I don't know."

The priest stood up slowly, his eyes on the boy. "That is true. Yet twice I have known Kate Cousins to save an innocent man from the mob. She has changed, but who may speak the words of blame. There are too many things we cannot understand."

While the priest was speaking, a carriage jolted across

the Parade. The coachman reined in the horses and Sir William Elgin stepped out. He looked down at Mac-Feathers and his lips pursed. Father Maholan told him the story quickly.

The Governor looked into the old priest's tired eyes. "Kate and Brandon leading a mob together," he said slowly. "That is something I thought could never happen. Kate always feared the man and hated him. Perhaps it was because she knew that in the end they would join together."

There was a moment of silence, then Mullen plucked at the priest's sleeve. "Father," he whispered, "what can I do?"

The old man looked at him with kindness. "Go to St. Clement's, lad, and wait for me there. It is a long time since you have been there, but there is still comfort to be found in prayer."

The boy nodded. As he started to walk away, Rodney Penney reached out and touched his arm. "Mullen," he said, "I'll not be going back to Rune Hall. As soon as I can find a ship I'll be leaving Jamaica. I'll not see you again. Do not think too harshly of me." The boy had been looking down at the ground as the tutor spoke. Now he raised his eyes until they rested on Rodney's outstretched hand. Slowly his own hand came up and he clasped Penney's as he had on their first meeting.

As the two others walked away in opposite directions, the priest and the Governor stood alone, looking at each other over the body of the tiny Scot. "Mario must be warned," Elgin said.

"There is no need for that." The priest raised his hand. "Listen." The soft insistent note of the dondo drum vibrated as though from the very earth. Then there was silence and the high confused wail of the abeng. "It has been attended to. But I am glad you thought of it. A few years ago you would not have cared, Sir William."

"That is true. Then there was room only for ambition. But I have watched Kate Minor. I have seen the wish for power escape from her control until it molded her into what she is. She has gone mad with it—rushing to her own destruction. And Because I have seen this, I have been able to curb myself. Father, is there no way of saving her?"

The priest spread his hands. "That I cannot say, Sir William. Each one must find salvation within himself. But I think it is best to leave her be. She has chosen her way. She has no need of you."

27

JONATHAN MINOR turned and twisted on the wide bed. The pain had been worse than ever the last few days. He was cold, yet his body was slimy with sweat. He wanted Kate but he would not call for her. He choked back her name as it took shape on his lips. His stomach muscles grew taut, and fire shot through his groin. He stiffened and a whimpering cry was wrung from him. He clenched his teeth and pressed down hard with his palms. Even now when the pain was almost unbearable, the shame of his crying out was uppermost in his mind.

Fat Dowsie appeared in the doorway with a tray of food. She uttered a low cry at the sight of him and limped to his bedside. The cramps eased off and Jonathan fell back exhausted, rivulets of perspiration trickling down his face. He looked up at Dowsie's flaccid cheeks and quivering lips and managed a weak smile.

"Don't be frightened, Dowsie. It has passed now."

The old woman shook her head. "I better git Doctor Gibbon. You need him bad, bad."

"No, Dowsie. Gibbie'll do me no good."

"Then Miss Kate—"

"No!" Jonathan surprised himself at the vehemence with which he spoke the single word.

Dowsie nodded her understanding. She fussed over the tray and poured broth from a pewter pitcher into a bowl. She said softly, "I made the broth me'self, Mas'

Jonathan. I seen no one come nowhere near it. You drink the broth. It'll be good for you."

Jonathan raised the bowl to his lips and sipped the almost scalding fluid. The pain had gone and it had left him strangely quiescent. He felt the pressing desire for companionship. "Dowsie," he said, "sit with me a while."

The Negress' eyes rolled. "I dassn't. She'd know."

"What if she does?"

"She told me not to stay."

Anger flared up in Jonathan but he could not speak ill of Kate to Dowsie. "All right, go then."

He watched the old woman as she waddled across the room. Her feet dragged as she put her weight gingerly first on one foot then the other. Jonathan crinkled his forehead in perplexity. Dowsie was getting along in years and she had a touch of the gout, but certainly she was not crippled as this. She had been at Rune Hall ever since he had bought the place and Jonathan was fond of her. The only trouble he had ever had with her was about Sam. Sam was a squat, ugly, lazy freedman who had a hut in Baraçong. Jonathan could never tell wherein Sam's fascination lay but Dowsie adored him and so did others of the Negro women. About once a month Dowsie would slip past the guards and go down to Baraçong to spend a night with Sam.

Jonathan had first learned of this dereliction on Dowsie's part years before when, as he was passing the cooling sheds, he had heard her pitiful wails. He rushed in and found her lying on the ground. Hodge stood over her, the ebony raised high. Dowsie's back and buttocks were already flecked with blood from the thorned branches. Jonathan grasped the overseer's wrist before he could bring the ebony down again. Hodge whirled, his face livid. But when he saw that it was Jonathan his manner became sycophantic. Self-righteously, he told the story of Dowsie's misdoings.

Jonathan laughed. "Why not let her go?"

"But she's Pye's woman," Hodge complained smugly.

Pye was the strongest of the field hands used to stud the women slaves. "Does Pye object?"

"No, it ain't that," Hodge admitted. "It just ain't right."

"Don't be such a sanctimonious cove," Jonathan snapped. Later he had given sharp orders to Hodge to cease his floggings and he had advised the sentries to pay no attention when Dowsie slipped past them.

Now as Jonathan lay in bed and watched the old Negress hobbling away from him, he sighed. He knew, now that he was no longer able to supervise the grounds, the floggings were being continued, but he did not think Hodge would dare to beat Dowsie.

He called to her and she turned back reluctantly. "Why are you so lame?" he asked. "Hodge hasn't been bothering you again, has he?"

Dowsie loomed above him and he was surprised to see round tears on her cheeks. " 'Tain't Hodge," she said, then added furtively, "I'm skeered."

"Scared? Of whom?"

Dowsie's fingers moved surreptitiously to make the fumbling sign of the cross.

"The Witch," she answered beneath her breath.

Jonathan was startled. He knew that this was the common name for Kate among the slaves, but none among them had ever used it before in his presence.

"What's the trouble—Sam again?"

"Yass, Mas' Jonathan, I been seein' him again."

"What has she done to you?"

Dowsie turned to the door and listened. There was no sound. She leaned over and took off her flat shoe. Driven through the sole was a sharp wooden peg coated with blood. Jonathan looked at it incredulously. "You don't mean she makes you wear this! You can't mean that!"

The old woman nodded dumbly. "She say she ebony me, I take 'em off."

Fury seared Minor's thin body. He rose on one elbow. "Kate," he shouted. "Kate!" His voice had lost its thinness and thundered through Rune Hall. He heard footsteps on the stairs, but by the time Kate reached him, the pain was with him again. Coughing wracked his frame and agony convulsed him. He writhed against the bed. A hand shot out to point at Kate and he mumbled words, and though they were meaningless, the anger and determination on his face were clear.

261

"Get back to the kitchen," Kate ordered Dowsie. Then she went to the sideboard and poured liquids and powders into a glass. She pressed the rim to Jonathan's lips. He shook his head at first but finally took a long gulp. He lay back on the bed. His labored breathing grew weaker until it was inaudible.

Kate looked down at him, her face calm, watchful. Then she whirled suddenly as there was a sound at her back. It was Dowsie. The old woman stretched out a trembling finger to touch Minor's face.

"I told you to go," Kate said coldly.

Dowsie twisted her head. Her lips were writhing in fear, but there was stubborn defiance in her eyes. "Mas' Jonathan be daid," she said. "I see you mix the poison for he."

Kate's face turned pale but her voice was steady. "He's dead—but the rest is nonsense. 'Twould not be wise to repeat such old wives' tales. You saw me prepare the medicine. That was all."

Dowsie shook her head. "Jonkra weed and whistling Tom be not for a sick man."

Kate moved forward threateningly. "Perhaps you'd like me to call for Hodges. He'll not spare the ebony now that Mr. Minor's not here to protect you."

Dowsie shrank away from her and began to whimper softly. Kate's voice was suddenly gentle. " 'Tis not the time for harsh words. Find Master Mullen and tell him to fetch Dr. Gibbon." Kate turned and walked to the sideboard. She waited until Dowsie's hobbling footsteps could be heard shuffling through the hall. Then she reached for a bottle, took it to the balcony and poured the brown liquid on the lawn below.

Michael Scott leaned across the turret tower of Rune Hall, peering through the spyglass. He straightened up and smiled at Mullen. "Ay, lad, 'tis the *Willow Queen* well enough. I can tell by the cut o' her."

Mullen took the glass from him and looked out across the open sea. Four sailing vessels rode the crested water close together. "They've played in luck not to meet the Yankees," he said.

"Right you are, lad. They must have taken a run far

to the south. The Yankees could outdistance ships like those on a fair run without a bit of trouble. Ah, wait 'til you see the *Foam*," he added reflectively. "She's the loveliest little craft you've ever laid eyes upon. Beautiful in her hull and rigging she is, but the dockyard riggers have fairly bedeviled her, at least as far as appearance goes. They've replaced the light rail on her gunwale by heavy bulwarks four feet high surmounted by hammock nettings of at least another foot. She used to float like a sea gull on the waves, but now she looks like a clumsy dish-shaped dogger. But she's fast, my lad, faster than any ship that flies the British ensign."

Mullen scarcely heard the older man's words. His hand was in his pocket where the letter from Ishbel Minor formed a crumpled heap. He did not need to read it again; he knew it by heart. This was the last letter that Ishbel had written to her father, informing him that she would be sailing in a fortnight aboard the *Willow Queen*. Jonathan Minor had handed it to Mullen just two days before his death. "I fear she'll not get past the Yankees. Had I known in time I would have tried to stop her. You'll keep your promise to me, lad, to see no harm comes to her if I'm gone before she arrives?"

Mullen had nodded. The summer of 1812 was filled with dangers for the English sailing vessels. Even before war had been officially declared, the American privateers had teemed into the waters of the West Indies. They were light and fast and their crews were hardy fighters. The tiny craft with only two or four guns could move in fast before the English ships could turn.

Mullen grinned ruefully. He had told himself that he hoped the *Foam* would seize the *Willow Queen*, for then he would be freed of all responsibility. He might even smuggle himself out of Jamaica, get to Cuba and join with the Americans. But he knew this was impossible. He was bound to Rune Hall with unbreakable chains. Kate was there and she would not leave—even though she was frightened. Kate was the very soul of Rune Hall. They shared together the sullen beauty, the forbidding calm, the sense of foreboding and danger.

Mullen shrugged and turned his thoughts again to Ishbel. He remembered the pale heart-shaped face, the fragile child's body, the soft voice. She would be a child no longer. She would be sixteen, nearly seventeen. Would she look like Rose? And what would she think of him? Would he seem crude to her, untutored? Well, what did it matter? He had made a promise to Jonathan Minor; he'd keep it as best he could.

He started at the touch of Michael Scott's fingers on his arm. The big man looked down at him. "The *Willow Queen* will be alongside o' Kerry's Jetty within the hour. Shall I go with ye, lad?"

"No," Mullen mumbled. "It's kind of you, but I'll find my way alone."

" 'Twill not be easy to tell the lass o' Jonathan's death."

"I'm thinking it will be right hard, but it must be done."

Scott's eyes lingered on the boy's face. "Is it wise to bring Ishbel here to Rune Hall?"

Mullen flushed and turned away. He knew what Scott meant. Kate's long silences, her spells of lashing anger, the hours she spent pacing her narrow balcony, had all given rise to new and wilder tales about her. Since Mac-Feathers' death she lived in complete isolation from the island folk save for an occasional visit from Lettie Parsons. Many of the slaves had run away and only Hodge's brutality had stopped an uprising on the estate. The work at Rune Hall had come almost to a standstill. The far fields had run to seed and two of the bolling houses remained idle during the season. Rumors claimed that poison had been placed in the vats and the company factors had found an excuse not to purchase their quota of rum and sugar from Rune Hall.

Mullen felt the anger rise within him as he descended the twisted turret stairs. He came to the wide staircase windows and jerked to a stop. A man was standing in the high cane, looking up at Kate's balcony. The man stepped back and disappeared amid the heavy green leaves. But Mullen had recognized him. He swore softly to himself. Why was Koshi here at Rune Hall?

All night long Kate had heard the drums, soft and fierce, beating in the high hills. The whistle of the abeng reached her ears but she could not distinguish the words. She knew the drums were calling her to the pallay of the

Ashanti, but she would not go. The drums were more and more insistent. Her knuckles were white as she clutched the railing. It would be so easy to walk out and meet the drums. She could place the obis in her cheeks and drink the opaque rum. The sense of lightness, of power would fill her body and she would stand before the Ashanti without fear.

But she must not go. She had turned her knowledge of obeah against Mario. She had flaunted the words of Koshi. Before the assembled Ashanti she had once declared herself the embodiment of Erzulie of the Red Eyes and they had knelt down before the altar. The blood of the white cock and the white goat had bathed her feet. But now she had given over Baraçong to the crowd of whites under Sydney Brandon. True, Mario had escaped to the Cockpit country, but Baraçong lay in ashes before the mob had finished. Tonight there would be a trial and they would place the curved knife of Oshunai in her hands. Kate had seen a Maroon woman plunge the knife into her breast and draw the blade out free of blood. The woman had been declared innocent of her alleged crimes and she had danced that night over the fiery embers and her skin had remained unblistered.

But Kate was not innocent. Once the knife was in her hands, the inexplicable power that took possession of the pallay would compel her to thrust it into her breast. Even now, the thought of it sent a pleasant tingling through her body. There would be no pain; only the ecstasy of sacrifice. It would be easy, so easy. She started to turn, but her hand still gripped the railing. She looked down at it for a moment, uncomprehendingly. Then she shivered and fell to her knees. Her other hand reached out and clasped the metal balustrade. The drum beats grew more and more commanding but she clung to the balcony, swaying back and forth for a while. After a time, she rose. She knew now that she was strong enough to resist the temptation of the drum.

It was the next day before Koshi came to her. She knew that he was there before she heard the rustle of the cane. For a moment he stepped into sight, but there was the sound of Mullen's feet on the turret stairs and Koshi slid back into the shelter of the great stalks. She waited until there was silence again. The old man pushed aside the cane and took a place on the lawn beneath the balcony.

Kate marveled again at the power that emanated from the slender body. He was dressed as a fieldworker in a battered hat, a faded blue shirt and loose trousers of Russian duck. As always his feet were bare. He had aged since she had first seen him in the Laughing Donkey, yet his skin remained as firm as mahogany. She looked down into the delicately lined face, examined the straight nose, the thin lips, the narrow arched cheekbones, the fringe of frizzly white hair. There was no sign of malevolence in the man; his expression was mild, almost kindly.

When he spoke, his voice was filled with sorrow. "The mystic rites of Africa have been open to you, my child. But you must forget what you have learned. I have come to warn you—"

Kate broke in, "To warn or to threaten, Koshi?"

"To warn. Already I have told you that the power of obeah lies within the person who practices it. The power can build or destroy the one within whom it rises. You have not listened, my child. You have let the evil take possession of you. Now you must cast out the power or it will destroy you. I cannot help you; you must do this thing alone. You must turn your back upon the rites of obeah or you will die. Forget its symbols; forsake its drugs. Above all, stay away from the pallays, for if you go again you will not return."

"Then what have I left? A barren house, an empty life, a legacy of hate. Is this all that the power of obeah had to give?"

"No. You chose the gifts, seeking out those which were material. Above all other things you wanted Rune Hall for Mullen. It is his. You have wealth. You have power too; enough so that at your word Baraçong was burned. The power has been yours to use as you wish. But now, it is greater than you. Do not employ the rites of obeah again. To violate this decree means death."

Kate cried out, "I will have one more thing—the love of my son."

The old man shook his head. "Obeah cannot give you this."

"It must."

"Take care. Remember my warning—"

"I am not afraid," Kate screamed, "I am not afraid."
But Koshi had gone. Kate saw Dowsie peering up at her
from the cookhouse, her eyes wide with wonder. Kate's
face grew hard and she went back into her room. Her
riding crop lay on the bureau. She picked it up and went
to the head of the stairs. She called Dowsie's name but
there was no answer. She started down the steps rapidly,
but at the landing she stopped. The crop fell from her
hand and she began to tremble.

A cry welled up within her. *"I am not afraid."* But the
words, as she said them, were only whispered.

28

KERRY'S JETTY was thronged with passengers alighting
from the *Willow Queen* and her sister ships. Even so,
there could be no mistaking the girl in the wine-colored
dress. The heart-shaped face, the auburn hair and the
large deep-set eyes were those of the child whom Mullen
remembered. But there was a vividness in her coloring,
a vivacity in her manner that surprised him. She was
taller than Rose had been and, although she was slender,
the soft curves of her breasts showed beneath her lace
bodice.

Mullen stood staring at her, almost forgetting the
mission that had brought him to the jetty. He saw other
men's eyes turn to her and caught the low exclamations
of a group of loungers near him. He colored and moved
toward the girl, feeling suddenly shy and awkward.

She was standing on tiptoe, scanning the crowd for her
father. At first she took no notice of him. He scowled
and cleared his throat. She glanced at him quickly, then
away. Her eyes came back to him and recognition lighted

her face. "Mullen," she cried, and took his hand in both of hers. "My father? Is he too ill to come?"

"He has not walked for a long time. Didn't you know?"

"No. He wrote that he had been sick—that was all."

"Ishbel," he blurted out, "it's not fair to deceive you. Yet I don't know how to tell you."

She looked at him and read the truth in his face. "He's dead," she said quietly.

Mullen nodded. He saw the tears come to her eyes. She turned from him and he put his hand on her arm. Emotions that were new to him welled up within him—the sudden desire to offer protection and the warmth of companionship.

"Ishbel," he called, "he asked me to take care of you."

She looked up at him and, despite her tears, a smile came to her lips. "Mullen, you were always good to me," she said. "Do you remember your collection of thunderstones? Do you still have them?"

Mullen let out his breath sharply. The girl had courage right enough. There would be no scene here at the jetty. He offered her his arm and she took it gently. He led her to where the carriage was waiting and helped her in. She sat facing him, her hand still in his, and acting on instinct, he raised the fingers to his lips.

When he took his place beside her she said, "Mullen, hold my hand tight. I mustn't cry—not before strangers."

He felt the slender fingers, cool and delicate, lying in his palm. He spoke awkwardly. "I hope that you do not consider me a stranger, Ishbel."

"No, it may sound odd but it has always been you I've remembered when I thought of Rune Hall. My father must have been a wonderful person, but I can only remember him as being frightfully tall and having a deep voice that frightened me. Mamma was like a delicate piece of china, lovely and flawless in her beauty, but not really alive. But you, Mullen—I always envied you. I used to watch you chase the wood slaves and wondered if I could ever run that fast. You told me stories too, about mummers, cockfights and a wonderful spider you called Anansi. I believed every word of them."

Mullen smiled at her. "Right you were, too, for every word was the solemn truth."

The carriage jostled off the paved street and began to bounce along the shore road. Mullen caught a glimpse of the dark mahogany forest on the near side of Pinchback Hill. He turned abruptly to the girl. "Ishbel, I'm not sure that I should take you to Rune Hall. It's a desolate place nowadays. Only Kate and I live in the Hall. Hodge and a young bookkeeper are the only other whites on the place. Many of the slaves have run away. We're even short on sentries. Perhaps it would be better for you in Montego Bay."

"It would be lonely. I want to be where my parents lived—and I want to be with you."

Mullen looked at his hands. "Kate is not well, she . . ." he hesitated, unable to think of the proper words to describe his mother; then he asked sharply, "Do you remember her, Ishbel?"

"Yes," she said and he felt her hand tremble in his. "Mullen, I know it's wrong, but I used to hate her."

"Why?"

"Because of something I know can't be true. Because I used to think she killed my mother. It's silly, isn't it?"

"Yes," Mullen agreed, "of course, it's silly." But he thought of Kate slipping a knife into Bard's hand. He thought of MacFeathers lying dead beneath the tamarind tree on the Parade. A chill crept through his body. He forced himself to laugh, but a new picture was forming in his mind—Kate standing at the sideboard, deftly mixing Jonathan Minor's medicine; Kate pressing the glass to the sick man's lips.

The carriage rolled through the wide gate and Mullen saw, with a surprised start, that his mother stood in the open doorway. A man was talking to her, but at the sound of the wheels on the gravel, he turned. Mullen flushed when he recognized Sir William Elgin. The Governor had not been in Rune Hall for several years. Mullen knew of Jonathan Minor's loathing for the man and suspected the truth, that Elgin had been forbidden the house.

Mullen was perplexed too by his mother's attitude toward Elgin. Whenever Kate met Elgin her manner changed, became more haughty, and yet Mullen sensed that they shared some secret which he could not understand. Why was Elgin here now? Was it to meet Ishbel?

Mullen felt a twinge of jealousy as he noted the Governor's immaculate attire, his bland, smiling features. Then he remembered that Elgin was Ishbel's cousin, guardian of the estate left her by his uncle, Stallybrass. As Elgin walked toward them with his hand outstretched he saw the heavy lines of weariness in the Governor's face, and his resentment changed to something akin to pity.

As Ishbel jumped down from the carriage, Elgin caught her in his arms and kissed her lightly. Then he held her at arm's length. "Ah, 'tis Rose all over again," he said laughing. "You are more like her than one can believe."

Mullen looked past them to his mother and sudden fear stabbed at his heart. Kate's face was calm but in the depths of her eyes anger and hatred burned. She saw Mullen's gaze upon her and she smiled. She stepped forward and greeted Ishbel graciously, tucking the girl's arm in hers.

Mullen watched as the woman and the girl walked up the stairs of Rune Hall. Their voices were gay, yet the fear would not leave him. He turned to Elgin, and saw the reflection of his own foreboding in the Governor's lined face.

Three months later Kate stood in the open window of the great hall and looked across the lawn. Mullen was lying on his stomach beneath the silk-cotton tree, reading aloud to Ishbel from a book of poems that Rodney Penney had once given to him. He stopped as a wood slave came near and put out his hand to capture the tiny lizard, but it darted away from him. The sound of their young laughter drifted up to Kate. She stood still, listening, her cheeks slightly flushed.

Footsteps echoed on the mahogany floor but Kate was unaware of the sound. Only when a hand touched her did she look up with a start. Sir William Elgin stood beside her. His face had lost its youthfulness and was lined and haggard. His skin had coarsened from the bright Jamaica sun and there were pouches beneath his eyes. The light raillery of his manner had changed to a studied cynicism. Yet the boldness, the self-assurance and much of his swaggering charm remained.

He followed the direction of Kate's gaze. Mullen was

helping Ishbel to her feet. The adulation in his eyes was unmistakable. The girl laughed and placed her hand beneath his crooked arm. They started down the pathway toward the slave quarters.

Elgin turned back to Kate. "They're a well-matched couple," he said slowly. "And Ishbel will be coming into a stack of money when she's married. They're young, Kate, but I'm thinking it's not a bad thing to have their futures settled."

Kate's eyes were sullen. " 'Tis only a passing fancy of the boy's. He's had no chance to meet other girls."

"Nor is he likely to here in Jamaica."

Kate stared at him angrily. "You're the girl's guardian, Sir William. Send her away. Jamaica is a place for the strong. The girl will be sick here. She may die, as her mother did."

Elgin lounged against the window frame. His manner was negligent, but his eyes were watchful as he thought of the way in which Rose had died. "Kate, why do you hate the girl so? She'll do Mullen no harm."

Kate said bitterly, "Rose took Jonathan from me. Now her daughter wants Mullen."

Elgin placed his hands on both her arms and looked into her face. "Kate, you never loved Jonathan Minor. You've never loved any man. You've only taken what men could give you—and hated them for the giving."

She tried to free herself from his grasp but he held her fast. "Kate, you and I are much alike. You had your eyes on Rune Hall; I had mine on the governorship. We both got what we wanted, didn't we, Kate? And little enough happiness it's brought us. Did you think I ever doubted that you bought Rune Hall with the money from my own ransom? I did not blame you. 'Tis the sort of thing I might have done myself. You're still young, Kate, and you're still lovely. Ever since that night in the Salamander, I've wanted you. Did you think I did not know how the knife came into Bard's hand? Aye, I did. Again it did not matter. I could not love a wishy-washy woman. I need one with the courage and the fire—even the ruthlessness—that will match those qualities within me. I love you, Kate. I want you to marry me."

Kate stood still now and her face was mocking. "Ah,

Sir William, do you mean to make the bound girl into the Governor's lady?"

"You know I cannot do that. But I've money enough to retire. We can go back to England. To the States. Wherever you wish."

Kate laughed suddenly. "Once Jonathan Minor thought me not good enough to be Mistress of Rune Hall. Now you offer me the sacrifice of your career to marry me—but of course you will not take me to Government House."

Elgin spread his hands. "Kate, it is not what I wish. It is simply a thing that cannot be done."

Her eyes blazed in sudden fury. "You would take my son from me—*and* Rune Hall. You would give them both to Ishbel. Then you would take me with you to laugh at me and mock me. Well, let me tell you. I will not leave Rune Hall. Do you hear? I will not leave. Take the girl away from here, Sir William. You spoke truly when you say that I am ruthless. Neither she nor you will take what is mine."

She wrenched away from him and her hand struck across his face. Elgin drew back and watched her as she ran up the stairs. The longing for her was still strong in him, but he knew that it was useless for him to follow. He turned back to the window. Mullen and Ishbel were returning along the circular path. Mullen stopped to pick a spray of flame vine and twisted it in the girl's dark hair. She looked up at him, her face alive and eager. He stooped to kiss her, but she turned so that his lips only brushed her cheek.

Sir William Elgin's face grew hard. He vaulted the low window ledge and strode down the pathway toward the youngsters. A sound attracted his attention and he glanced up. Kate was standing on her balcony. He stopped and their eyes met. He looked away toward Ishbel. How lovely the child was! She was much as Rose Stallybrass once had been, save that Rose had never been so animated, so obviously happy, so much in love.

Neither Ishbel nor Mullen had seen him. He knew that there was nothing he could say. He moved away from them and suddenly he felt old and, for the first time in his life, he was frightened.

29

EVEN IN THE FIRST FEW MONTHS of the war, the exploits
of the *Foam* had become legendary throughout the West
Indies. The tiny privateer, with a crew of only nineteen
men and armed only with two twelve-pound guns, was
the scourge of the proud English sailing vessels that
patrolled the sea lanes. The *Foam*, as Michael Scott wrote
in the *Jamaica Advertiser*, was the fastest vessel afloat in
calm water, but if she was once compelled to run before
the wind in heavy seas she would either capsize or fall
an easy prey to the British.

The Jamaicans cursed the *Foam* but, even as they did
so, they admitted a grudging admiration for the courage
and skill of her captain and her crew. Despite their aver-
sion to the Yankees, they admitted that Captain Morgan
came close to being a gentleman. Whenever the *Foam*
took a prize, the English were treated with punctilious
courtesy.

"Morgan has the daring of the devil himself," Scott
boomed at Mullen, and the boy nodded in agreement. The
Foam had sailed in sight of Kingston harbor more than
once and Mullen, standing in the turret tower of Rune
Hall, had followed her passage through his spyglass. The
long slender wands of the *Foam*'s masts had swung about,
as taut and stiff as church steeples. Mullen, watching,
had felt the tingling urge to adventure and instinctively
he allied himself to the Yankee cause.

Not that Mullen's life was lacking in richness, for he
had found a fresh and absorbing interest. The wandering
companies of American players had ceased coming to
Jamaica with the outbreak of the war. For a while the
theaters had closed, but at Mullen's instigation, a local
group was formed. Mullen, despite his youth, had picked

up enough information from the strolling players to direct the performances with considerable skill. Moreover, he played the leads in several plays which had entertained London audiences in past seasons. Ishbel too shared his enthusiasm for the theater and assumed minor roles.

It was during an intermission of *The Talkative Barber* that news came that the *Foam* had been taken captive. A heavy storm had caught the Yankee privateer by surprise and she had been forced to run before the wind with two English frigates in pursuit. The top-heavy little vessel had nearly foundered before she had struck her colors. The *Bayette Queen* was standing off Kingston Harbor at the moment with the *Foam*'s crew aboard as prisoners of war.

The lashing rain was almost spent by the time the play had ended. The local company had performed to a nearly empty house, and as Mullen helped Ishbel into the carriage, he felt disgruntled and discouraged. They rode in silence past the Parade and down King Street. Then the sound of shouting and the bright glare of oil lamps attracted their attention.

Mullen ordered the coachman to rein in the horses and he and Ishbel watched the straggling procession that marched along Harbour Street. Both guards and prisoners were drenched but, Mullen thought, it was perhaps the wisest time to lead the Americans to the prisoners' barracks. Sydney Brandon's demagoguery had whipped the Jamaicans into violence too often and the capture of the *Foam*'s crew would be too good an excuse for mob action.

Mullen felt Ishbel's hand upon his wrist. "Where are they taking them?" she whispered.

"To the barracks beyond Croom's place."

One of the prisoners stumbled past the carriage and, for a moment, he raised his head and looked directly into Mullen's face. Mullen stiffened with surprise and grasped Ishbel's wrist so tightly that she cried out.

"What is it, Mullen?"

"Nothing," he answered, "it was just that I thought I recognized one of those men. I must be mistaken. It can't be he. It can't."

Mullen leaned forward to give directions to the coach-

274

man, but his thoughts were in a turmoil. There was no mistake. He could never forget the round, brutal face of the man who had passed him. The last time he had seen Bard was in the Salamander Tavern. The seaman had just driven a knife into the heart of Gabriel Cousins and stood threatening Sir William Elgin. Then Rose Minor had come between the two men and the jagged knife had run the length of her hand and Bard had disappeared fleeing into the night.

A long time ago, Mullen had boasted that if he ever found the man who had murdered his father he would kill him. Well, now he knew where the man could be found. But was Bard really the murderer? It was Kate who had placed the knife in his hand.

Mullen shuddered and felt Ishbel at his side. He turned and looked into her face and was struck with the wonder of her delicate beauty. He drew her to him and, for the first time, she put her arms about him and pressed her lips tight against his in return. He clung to her almost with a sense of desperation and whispered her name again and again as the jogging carriage carried them to Rune Hall.

A pebble rattled against the jalousie. Mullen stirred restlessly, then sat upright in his bed. A second pebble skittled across the tiled floor. Mullen arose and moved cautiously to the open doorway of the balcony. A hunched figure was black among the dark shadows of the silk-cotton tree.

"Mullen," a voice called softly. The tones were familiar but Mullen could not place the voice.

He stepped out on the balcony and looked down. The figure moved out of the shadows and the moonlight fell on the face of Father Maholan. Mullen sucked in his breath with surprise.

"Father, is it you?"

The priest pressed a finger to his lips, signaling for silence. Then he motioned with his hand for Mullen to join him.

Mullen clutched the heavy vines that clung to the walls of Rune Hall and lowered himself to the lawn. Father Maholan drew him beneath the thick branches of the

275

tree. Mullen peered through the darkness but he could not see the priest's face. "What is it, Father?" he whispered.

"It is a strange thing that I have to tell you, my son. I have come with a message from your father. I dared trust no one to bring it."

Mullen thought at first that he had misunderstood the words. "My father!" he repeated. Did the priest mean Gabriel Cousins—or possibly Jonathan Minor? But both were dead. Perhaps he was using the word "father" to refer to another priest. He said, "I do not understand. My father died long ago."

"You are mistaken. Your father is living, Mullen. He is here in Jamaica. I have come to take you to him."

"Gabriel Cousins—he cannot be alive. I saw him buried."

"Gabe was not your father, my son. You were conceived before your mother's marriage. Perhaps I should not tell you these things, but you have a right to know. Your father was one of the men taken prisoner aboard the *Foam*. They have all been held at Croom's but last night he was able to escape. He has begged me to bring you to him. Will you go?"

Mullen shifted his weight from foot to foot. Now that his eyes had become accustomed to the darkness he could see the priest's white skin and deep-set eyes, but he could not read the expression on the old man's face. He spoke hesitantly. "This man—you say he is my father. How can you be sure? How can I know?"

The priest's voice was mlid. "I think he'll have no difficulty in convincing you once you have seen him."

"But Gabe. I always believed that Gabe . . ." Mullen hesitated, realizing that his own words were not completely true. Even as a small boy, he had not thought of Gabe Cousins as his father but more as a rough, rather uncouth companion. He had liked the tavernkeeper but he had never felt any nearness to him as he did with Kate. There were times when he hated his mother, but never was a time when he was not aware of the bond that linked them together. She was not only of his flesh and blood, she was of his soul and spirit as well. The evil that was in her was a part of himself and the greatness of her spirit that had shriveled through the years had

276

left in him barrenness and sterility so that there was no way in which he could express his love for her. Instinctively he knew that what Father Maholan told him was true and that the man whom he would meet must be his father, whom he would love or hate more than any man in the world.

"I'll go," he whispered. "Let me get some clothing. I'll go with you, Father."

Mullen was impatient as they walked the back pathways down Pinchback Hill. At first he flooded the old priest with questions, but Father Maholan was breathing hard and he only shook his head. "You'll meet him soon enough, my lad. 'Tis better he should tell you of himself than I."

"What is his name?" The old priest did not answer and Mullen reflected that whatever it might be, it was his own as well. Father Maholan was limping a little and leaning on his cane. Mullen, in his excitement, ran ahead and then came back to him.

"Easy, lad," the priest warned. "The soldiers and the sentries are all on the lookout. Do not arouse their suspicions, nor make them wonder what an old priest and a lad are doing on the streets this time o' night."

They passed through the fringes of the town and found a narrow path that twisted behind St. Clement's and up the far hill. They came to a lawn and Father Maholan stopped and listened. Mullen recognized the dark house that loomed before them. It was the Christian Steps.

A door opened silently and Lettie Parsons stood in the opening, shading a candle with her hand. The old priest slipped by her and, as the flickering light of the candle fell across his face, Mullen saw his lips puckered in a wry smile. Lettie put a fat arm about Mullen and gave him a warm hug.

"Do they ever guess I've your daddy here 'tis like they'll string me to a yardarm. Yet there be always a good reason why a mon walks quiet to the Christian Steps. Be it not so, Father?"

The priest's chuckle was drowned out by Lettie's hearty guffaws. "And you, my young cockalorum, sneakin' in me back door. There's many as come this way afore ye. But what would your Ishbel say, should she know where ye be? Answer me that, laddie."

Mullen felt himself blushing and was grateful for the darkness of the corridor. Lettie led the way up the back stairs and along a narrow hall. She rapped on the door and a rough voice answered her.

"Open up, the young un's here," Lettie called.

The door was flung open and a hulking figure was outlined against the light of the oil lamps. One arm was raised and a knife was clasped in a hairy hand. The man lowered his arm and grimaced at Lettie. Mullen looked up and his stomach turned to water. The round brutal face was that of Bard.

Mullen's fist clenched as he whirled on Lettie. "What is this? A jest? Have you gone mad—all of you?"

The brothelkeeper rocked with laughter and the tears streamed down her cheeks. "Ay, lad. 'Tis a shock we've given ye, but 'twas not meant so. Flummoxed I'd be me'self if I thought Bard were kin o' mine."

In the swift confusion Mullen had not seen the other man who stood quietly by the table in the center of the room. The light shone upon his hands but shadowed his face. He came forward and held out his arms to the boy. Mullen stood facing him, troubled and uncertain.

"Meet your father, lad," he heard Bard say gruffly. "Captain Percy Morgan o' the *Foam*. Ye've heard o' him no doubt, for there's no braver skipper ever sailed the Seven Seas."

Morgan led the boy to the wide mirror at the far end of the room and set the lamp before it. The resemblance between the man and the boy was striking. Morgan was a trifle taller and heavier and there were deep lines upon his face. Mullen was blond and Morgan dark. But the bone structure of the brow, the nose and cheeks was identical; so was the hairline and the long, narrow jaw. Their bodies were hewn from the same mold, though Mullen's was more finely chiseled.

Morgan looked into the mirror and grinned. "I'd had my doubts about ye, lad. Bard had told me I'd borne a son, but the man is such a scoundrel I'd no reason to take his word." His glance at Bard took the sting from his taunt. "If ye truly be my son, I'm thinking you like the cocks and will soon be taking to the sea."

Mullen nodded, unable to think of suitable words to greet this man whom he no longer doubted was his father. The old priest had slipped away in the confusion. Lettie Parsons brought two bottles of whisky and plopped them before the men.

Bard tossed the knife on the table and reached out for a bottle. Mullen's eyes flicked to the knife and he saw the cabalistic signs carved on the mahogany haft. He remembered the last time he had seen Bard, years before, crouched over the body of Gabe Cousins. Then Bard's heavy hand fell on his knee and brought him back to the present.

"Yer daddy be one o' the richest men o' Salem, Mullen, lad. In prize money alone, he's made a fortune, to say nothing o' what he's stored in Salem town. But money does a prisoner no good, to say nought o' a mon what dances from a rope's end. Ye've a right to be proud o' being the son of the Captain o' the *Foam* even from the wrong side o' the bed so to speak. But that's neither here nor there, lad. What we need o' ye is some help. Me neck aches a'ready from the thought o' being caught. But git us a sailin' vessel o' any kind—even a skiff, and the Captain an' me will soon be wi' the Yankees again."

Mullen turned his gaze from Bard to Morgan. The Captain nodded. "What Bard says is true enough. There's danger for all of us while I'm here on the island. Bard knocked out a guard and I'm afraid the blow was too hard. The poor man may be a-dying. The two of us cut out through the cotton fields and into the woods. We found sanctuary in St. Clement's for 'tis known that Father Maholan, like the good Irishman he is, has no fondness for the English. Still, perhaps it was wrong to place the old man in such danger. He brought us here to Lettie and though she's being paid well it will matter little if we're caught, for all of us will pay the piper."

He stopped and tamped his pipe. "Maybe 'tis not a kind thing for me to bring you here, lad. But I wanted to lay my eyes upon my son. Now that I've seen you I'm not thinking so well of myself for making you a party to this matter. It's like to make a pack of trouble for you."

Mullen's eyes glistened. "I'll find a ship even if I have to steal it from the fishing fleet. But it is a rough stretch 'twixt here and Santiago. Can you make it in a fishing craft?"

Bard waggled a hairy finger in front of the boy's face. "Do ye think there's a ship ye daddy canna sail? He's Captain Morgan o' the *Foam*, I tell ye."

A grin lighted up Morgan's face. "I've made the trip before from Kingston Harbor to Santiago and I doubt you could find me a frailer craft than the one I sailed in."

Bard broke in again. "Come wi' us, lad. Ye daddy can make a ruddy rich man out o' ye. Ye can have what ye will o' him, I'll wager. Perhaps it's an education at Harvard ye'd be a-likin', or I hear as how ye like the boards and grease paint o' the theater. There's none as can set ye up better than Percy Morgan."

"Bard is right in that. Come along with us and you can have what you want. Jamaica's no place for an up-and-coming lad. Come to the States. 'Tis still the land of opportunity."

Excitement raced through the boy at the thought of the adventures that might lie ahead. He remembered the stories told him by the strolling players about the great theaters in Boston and Philadelphia and New York, the bright lights, the rounds of applause. Reluctantly he shook his head. There was Ishbel to think of and, even now, he grew warm with the memory of her kisses. There was Kate too whom he dared not leave alone in Rune Hall. There was the Hall itself and those whose lives depended upon it. "No," he said slowly, "I cannot go."

Bard leaned close to him and the stench of the whisky was sour on his breath. "Is it a lass ye're thinking of? There be plenty a merry lady in the States will welcome the chance to while away a night wi' such a buckra boy as ye be."

Mullen shook his head again. Bard snarled. " 'Tis the murderous bitch as raised ye. May her soul rot in hell. Kate's a—"

Bard got no further. Morgan reached out and twisted the big man's jersey until it formed a ball in his hand. His other hand flicked out across the seaman's cheek. Bard gave a whimpering cry. His eyes were frightened.

"What care ye for what I say about her. Ha' ye forgotten Mannie Cousins?"

"Shut up," Morgan ordered.

"Ay, if that's what ye wish, Captain, but me and you is in this together like." Bard stretched out a shaky hand for the whisky.

Mullen rose and he and his father faced each other. Quick understanding passed between them. They might both hate Kate, but they had loved her, too. They might curse her silently, but no other would malign her in their presence. Neither knew the full hurt that she had imposed upon the other, but each recognized that she was an inseparable part of both.

Mullen spoke first. "Will you go without seeing her?"

" 'Tis best that way. Yet I loved her, son. That you must believe. One cannot make the past live again. 'Tis no good to try."

Mullen felt a lump in his throat. "I'll be going," he said, but there'll be a ship waiting for you by tomorrow night. I'll come to lead the way for you." He turned abruptly and strode out into the corridor. Bard followed him and grasped him by the arm. Mullen whirled defiantly, but Bard's face was friendly. "Ay, lad, be not thinkin' too hard o' me," he said. "I've done some rummy things in me day, but I'd no intent o' killin' Gabe Cousins. 'Twas as if the knife went into his body without me a willin' it. Look, lad, I've kept the knife with me all these years. Here it is, lad, take it. I reckon ye've more right to it than me."

Mullen felt the knife pushed into his hand and knew that in some strange way by the acceptance of it he had shrived himself of his hatred for Bard. He thrust the blade beneath his belt and covered it with his shirt. Without a word to Bard, he hurried through the hall.

At the foot of the stairs, Lettie Parsons was asleep on the divan. She opened her eyes at the sound of Mullen's footfalls, yawned and sat up. Mullen sat down beside her and she put fat arms about him. "Ah, what a cushy lad ye be, Mullen. Were I young enough, I'd need no guinea to love ye."

Mullen laughed. "Thank you, Lettie, for all you've done. 'Tis a big risk you've taken."

"And 'twas a good price I was paid; though not enough for a stretched neck."

Outside there was the clatter of hoofs on cobblestones and a sharp command. Mullen caught the words and knew that the man hunt for Bard and his father was on.

Lettie chuckled. "Out the front door and walk bold, me lad. There's many a young gentleman as leaves the Christian Steps this time o' the morning. Even if there's the look of guilt about ye, 'twill be likened to the cat as has just had a chunk out o' the canary."

Rune Hall lay quiet in the dazzling early morning sunlight. Mullen mounted the front steps quietly and slipped into the great hall. He drew up with a start of surprise as Kate turned from the open window. They stood facing each other in silence, and as they did so, they heard the sound of hoofs in the roadway. A moment later, Sydney Brandon's bawling voice shouted out. Kate went to the doorway and Mullen listened as Brandon relayed the news of Captain Percy Morgan's escape.

"Have ye seen sign o' him, Kate?" Brandon bellowed. "Ah, 'twould do my fingers good to get them about the Yankee's neck."

"I've no doubt of that," Kate retorted tartly—"had you a posse of men to back you up."

"'Tis no time for ye banter, Kate. I asked ye a civil question."

"And my answer is no. I know nothing of the whereabouts of Percy Morgan."

Mullen waited until Kate came back to the room. Her face was flushed and there was excited expectation in her manner. She came close to him but she did not touch him. She said quickly, "You have been to him, I know. I heard Father Maholan and guessed what was happening."

Mullen nodded, but said nothing. Kate seemed to be waiting for him to speak, but he could think of no words.

"Did he speak of me?" she asked at length. "Did he send any message?"

"No," Mullen answered. Then, as a spasm of pain passed across her face, he added, "But he struck a man who dared speak ill of you."

Kate's lips flickered in a frosty smile. "'Tis too late, I

guess, to think o' Percy Morgan. And yet—" she stopped and Mullen sensed some defeat and longing within her.

"Do you wish to see him?" he asked quietly.

Kate drew in her breath sharply and her hands went out to Mullen. "You are so much like him, Mullen. There are times you seem to be he. Perhaps I should have gone with him long ago. Perhaps that would have been right." Her hands came down about his waist and touched the heavy knife. She drew his shirt aside and uttered a strangled cry as she saw the carved mahogany haft.

"Where did you get it?"

"Bard gave it to me."

"Bard?"

"Yes. He's with Morgan. They escaped together."

Kate's face had turned white and she drew away from him. She spread out her hands before her and looked down at them. When she looked up again her eyes were blazing. "No, no," she cried fiercely. "I'll not see Morgan and he must not come here. Rune Hall is just for the two of us, Mullen. No one else must come and we must never leave. I could have gone away a long time ago, but I could not have taken Rune Hall with me."

Mullen stepped back, appalled by the wildness of her speech and the fierce possessiveness of her eyes. But she did not appear to notice. She stepped past him and hurried up the broad stairway.

Mullen stood motionless watching her. Then he loosened the knife from his belt and held it out in the sunlight streaming through the window. He was silent, thinking of Kate as he had seen her years before, pressing the knife into Bard's huge fist. Slowly he became aware of the sound of Kate's footsteps on the balcony above.

The touch of the knife was unbearable. For a moment he thought of hurling it out onto the lawn, but someone would pick it up and bring it back to him. Jonathan Minor's old desk was near. Mullen jerked open the bottom drawer and saw that it was empty save for a few scraps of yellow paper. He tossed the knife inside and kicked the drawer shut.

Then he heard his name called softly and looked up to see that Ishbel was watching him from the head of the stairs. He went to her quickly and took her in his arms and kissed her. They clung together, listening to Kate's restless, seemingly endless, pacing.

Mullen could hear the slap of the waves against the side of the sloop but already she was almost invisible. The sail had been stained black and she ran without lights. Only a shadow, narrow and angular, formed a moving patch of blackness against the dark sky.

A soft halloo echoed briefly across the water and Mullen raised his arm in a farewell salute which he knew could not be seen. He listened intently but there was no further sound from the bay. From somewhere in the city a pack of wild dogs ran barking through the streets. Closer at hand, there was the muffled tolling of a church bell, issuing out of the waters that covered the sunken city of Port Royal.

He walked through the white sand to the roadway. He whistled softly and a minute later, he heard the clumping of hoofs on the sandy bottom. Ishbel rode toward him, leading his gelding. She leapt from her horse and stood beside him.

"Shall we watch?" he asked. "We may catch a glimpse of them as they sail through Pike's Channel."

Ishbel took his hand and they walked together to the edge of the water. A cloud covered the moon and nearly obscured the harbor. Only the lights from the two brigantines moored at Kerry's Jetty shone through the darkness.

"Let's hope their luck holds," Ishbel murmured. "If the moon comes out before they reach the channel, there'll be a pursuit."

Mullen laughed. "Bard knows the inlets and—" he hesitated before using the term, "my father knows all the tricks of the sea."

He felt Ishbel's hand tighten on his. "Are you glad about your father, Mullen?"

Mullen was silent for a few moments. "In a way, yes. Yet it means something else that is incomplete."

"I like him," Ishbel said. "He seems so strong and self-reliant and there is something bold and a bit dashing about him too."

Mullen nodded in the darkness. He had had a half hour alone with Percy Morgan before they took the back trails to the bay. He heard his father's words again. " 'Tis no disgrace to leave a place behind when it has naught to offer you but unhappy memories and disgrace. I fled from Kingston once before, lad, and if you knew the reasons why you might be blaming me. I was scarce older than you, Mullen, and I'd made a bad mistake and was frightened. I guess you'd say I ran away. Be that as it may, I left. Sometimes it is the thing to do—clear out and start again. I've my doubts about how happy you are at Rune Hall and if the time ever comes when you wish a new start I'm hoping you and the lass will come to me. 'Twill not be flight to do so; it will be taking life in your own hands to start again with courage, hope and belief. Ah, lad, I may be sounding like the old priest. But how's a man to talk to his son?"

A few minutes later he had called for Bard, and the three of them had set out along the paths and alleys that eventually came out on the beach road that led to Baraçong and Port Royal. They crossed the road two miles out of Kingston and Ishbel was waiting for them. She had managed to pry the full story out of Mullen and had insisted on sharing the adventure. She had gone with him to buy the sloop and had helped him stain the sail. Later she had acted as sentry while the three men launched the sloop and set her rigging. There was little danger for her, Mullen was forced to admit, and her warning of impending search parties might well make the difference between safety and capture for the others.

At the crossing, he had presented Ishbel to his father. He watched anxiously, eager that each should please the other but, just the same, he had felt a sudden pang of jealousy at the warmth which passed between them. Later Morgan had said, "She's a fine lass, that one. Keep close to her. You'll go far before you meet another like her." Mullen's misgivings had disappeared quickly and when, at length, he had stood waist-high in the water and reached up for a final handclasp with Morgan, he had an even stronger sense of the man's kindliness than before.

Now as he stood beside Ishbel, peering into the impenetrable darkness, he felt her give a sudden start. She pointed upward where the glowing edge of the moon shone from behind a cloud. The warm breeze that had dried his clothing was now becoming fresher each minute. As they watched, the low hanging clouds were driven from the sky and the night turned clear and light. They waited breathlessly, scanning the bay for some sign of the sloop.

"Can they have cleared the channel?" Ishbel asked.

"There's not been time. They must be sailing close to shore, keeping to the shadows."

Even as he spoke, a dark form darted from the black line of the shore and was outlined against the pale sky. The single sail seemed incredibly fragile as it billowed out in the spanking breeze.

Mullen held his breath, expecting to hear a challenging shout or the report of a rifle. The tiny craft cleared the channel without a sound to indicate that she had been spotted.

"The guards must be asleep or drunk," he mumbled.

"Perhaps they mistook her for a fishing vessel," Ishbel suggested.

" 'Tis not likely at this time of night. I'm thinking 'tis too many mugs of grog they've taken aboard the *Bayette Queen*."

They clung together, still tense, expecting to hear the sounds of an alarm, but there were only the howls of dogs and the incessant clanging of the bell. The thick clusters of stars now spread a haze of light across the sky and it seemed almost a miracle that the sloop had escaped notice, but the minutes dragged on and Kingston continued to sleep. Mullen gave a sigh of relief and shifted his gaze from the channel to Ishbel's face, then cupped her chin in his palm and kissed her swiftly.

They ran back across the sand together to where their horses champed at their bits. Ishbel laughed as she mounted. "It's too beautiful a night to sleep," she challenged. "I'll race you to the fort."

The horses galloped along the bay road away from the town, and not until they reached Fort Royal did Mullen catch up to Ishbel. They turned and started back together, their lathered horses moving slowly side by side. They

286

chatted lightly as they rode and their laughter echoed along the beach.

Baraçong lay in their path. The Negro village was always dark and silent at night, the shacks boarded up against the night air and the intrusion of duppies or hags. But tonight there were lights in some of the cabins and the high-pitched sound of the death wail swept along the road. As the horses drew near, the wailing stopped. Shutters were drawn with sharp bangings and the flames of the candles were extinguished. Baraçong lay quiet and motionless. Mullen reined his gelding and looked about.

Only an old woman, bent and gnarled, stood in a doorway. She wore a stained gray kerchief over her head and it had slipped across her face so that all that was visible of her features was a single eye, loose gray lips and a jaw from which there sprouted a tuft of gray beard. Her bony hand was clenched in a fist and as she shook it above her she shouted words in Ashanti that Mullen could not understand. The malevolence of her face and voice startled him and he heard Ishbel give a sharp cry of fear.

But the old woman was not looking at them. She peered upward, her head thrown back so that she could see high up Pinchback Mountain.

Mullen followed the direction of her gaze. The turrets of Rune Hall cast long shadows down the sharp slope. The wide, arched windows reflected the shimmer of the stars and the full moon. A narrow balcony was plainly visible and a figure in white walked upon it. Mullen watched as Kate paced the length of the balcony and then turned back. Some strange trick of the moonlight as it was reflected against the walls of the old house spread out a pale green emanation behind her.

Mullen swore beneath his breath and swung about to face the old woman. She scuttled into her house and slammed the door. There was the grating of a bar as it fell into place. Baraçong was quiet again save for a child's frightened weeping.

Ishbel's horse shied suddenly and Mullen grasped the reins, but he did not meet her look. They started up the winding path to Rune Hall, but they no longer laughed as they rode.

287

BOOK FIVE

1815

30

MULLEN'S HANDS rested on the gray boards of the rotting fence that surrounded the Ashanti pallay. It had long been deserted, but he remembered when he had first found it and the night when he had watched the obeah ceremony from the high mahogany tree. Kate had come into the pallay that night and he had seen the curved knife of Oshunai cradled in her hand.

He peered about him searching for Mario. Fat Dowsie had brought him a message that morning that Mario wished to see him. Mullen was not surprised. Since the death of MacFeathers, the Maroons had depended more and more on Mullen to sound out the English. There was no one else whom they dared trust. Old Buddhoe loathed and despised Sir William Elgin and his retinue at Government House. As for the planters, they were under the domination of Sydney Brandon, and Buddhoe regarded them all as his sworn enemies.

There was still a price on Mario's head and he dared not come back to Kingston openly. But Buddhoe treated him almost as a son and often sent him with messages to Baraçong. On these trips Mario and Mullen met frequently and they had chosen the deserted pallay as a place that was safe from prying eyes.

Mullen knew that the Maroons had been hard hit by the summer droughts and that their food supplies were dwindling rapidly. Already he had pleaded with Sir William Elgin to send rice to Accompong, but Elgin's eyes had grown wary and Mullen judged that the Governor feared that any act of mercy would bring down upon him the wrath of the planters.

The snap of a twig interrupted Mullen's thoughts and he looked down the path to see Mario coming toward him. Mario smiled as he approached, but his eyes were serious. Without speaking, the two took seats beneath the mahogany tree. Mario lolled negligently with his back against the smooth trunk, but underneath his lazy manner he was tense and waiting.

Minutes passed without either of them breaking the silence. Finally Mario blurted out, "Mullen, your mother must leave Jamaica. You must make her go away. It doesn't matter where, so long as she goes."

Mullen gaped in surprise. He knew many of the wild tales that circulated about Kate. There could be no doubt that she was hated by the Negroes now, since she had led Sydney Brandon and his mob to Baraçong. Yet he doubted that any among them would dare use violence against her.

"I don't understand," he stammered. "What has happened?"

Mario avoided his eyes. "Another child died in Baraçong last night. He was bitten by a vampire bat in his sleep."

"But what has that to do with Kate?"

Mario still looked away. "They say her spirit flies at night in the form of a bat—that she sucks the life blood from our children."

"Surely you do not believe such nonsense?" Mullen retorted hotly. Anger brought circles of red to his cheeks.

"It doesn't matter much what I believe or don't believe. They believe it down in Baraçong. They're afraid of Kate. I tell you she's in danger. Make her leave Jamaica."

"I can't, not even if I would. Why, Kate's built her life around Rune Hall. 'Twould be easier to tear the place down with my bare hands than to make her go away. Besides, these stories are sheer fantasy. There are no such things as werewolves and vampires."

Mario smiled wryly. "I'll not argue with you about the werewolves, but there are vampire bats here right enough. Listen to me, Mullen; I know the bats are simply animals, but my people will not believe me. There have been bats in the islands since the beginning of time, but

292

recently they've increased. Even a mosquito netting will not protect you from them. The bats push in the netting until they touch flesh, and their teeth are small enough to bite through the holes in the net. You may not even wake up when they attack. There's no pain and only a small cut to show the bat has taken your blood. For a grown person, the bat is not dangerous; but for a child it is. Three babies have been killed by vampires in the last year. Our people are frightened and excited. It's the traditional belief that the vampire is the soul of an evil person—a soul that leaves the body and flies abroad seeking blood."

"But why do they think it is Kate? Surely there are many others on the island who have incurred their wrath."

"Kate alone among the whites has visited the pallays. She has openly boasted of her power of obeah. Others have been cruel but none so cruel as she. Did you know that she has driven spikes into the shoes of some of the women slaves? That she has flogged the men herself? That she ordered Hodge to pinch the breasts of a runaway woman with hot irons? And now she paces her balcony every night, so that all in Baraçong can see her. She was responsible for the burning of their town. It is little wonder that they blame her for all their other troubles. Get her away, Mullen. Get her away while there's time. If one more child dies by a vampire's bite, there'll be no stopping the Negroes."

Mullen sat in stunned silence. He had never before heard Mario speak with such vehemence. The idea of sending Kate away from Rune Hall was unthinkable, yet he knew that Mario was no alarmist. And some of the things he had said about Kate were true.

He turned to Mario. "Can't you explain to your people that bats are merely animals? Can't Koshi? The people trust him."

Mario shook his head. "Koshi holds himself to blame for all Kate's cruelty. He is angry and puzzled. He half believes that Kate is guilty. Besides this, there is another reason why we can do nothing. The people of Baraçong know that Kate has practiced obeah. They are afraid of her. If Koshi convinced them that she had no supernatural power, they would lose their fear, but not their anger. Our only way of keeping them away from Rune Hall is by making them believe that Kate has the power to protect herself and to work black magic against those who would injure her."

"What of Buddhoe? Can't he help?"

"Buddhoe is getting old and is nearly helpless. Nigel is taking over more and more power in Accompong. That is dangerous. Buddhoe has decreed that I am to be the next chief of the Maroons, but Nigel is already planning to oust me. Nigel is fanatical in his hatred for the whites and you must admit that he has reasons. Nigel is a black version of Sydney Brandon. He would use anger and hate to stir up trouble between whites and blacks. In the end, it is our people who will suffer most, but Nigel does not care. He is using the story of the vampire bats for his own ends. So there is more at stake than Kate's life—the peace of the island. You must persuade her to leave."

Mullen answered bitterly, "You know I can't. It's impossible." He stood up and crossed to the pallay. He stopped before the neglected altar, his thoughts in turmoil.

Mario followed him and swung him about. Mullen was surprised at the strength of the Ashanti's hands. "Mullen," he said, "one more thing I must tell you. When a person's soul flies at night, death alone cannot stop it. The vampire bat still lives on until—" He hesitated and dropped his hand.

"Until what?" Mullen demanded, almost truculently.

"Until a stake is driven through that person's heart."

Mullen shivered involuntarily. His eyes scanned Mario's face, but the other looked away. "What madness! Can you do nothing?"

Mario shook his head.

"Then take me to Buddhoe."

"It will do no good. He is very sick."

"He can restrain his people still."

"I doubt it, but I will take you if you wish. At least he may convince you that Kate should leave. And, Mullen—"

"Yes."

"You and Ishbel must go too. Rune Hall is a place of superstitious dread for the blacks, of pressing danger for the whites. Fear, anger, frustration, vengeance—these are not things that can be dispelled by reason. Buddhoe will tell you this and you must believe him."

Buddhoe lay dying. His wizened old face was lined; his cheeks hollow. His emaciated body was like a stick beneath the red covering. Yet he still wore the scarlet uniform jacket bedecked with tarnished gold braid, and the tricorn hat rested on the stool beside him.

The old man's eyes had darted from Mario to Mullen as they came into his presence. His tongue licked his gray lips and he extended a gnarled, shaking finger toward first one then the other. Words rattled in his throat but the jumble of sound that issued was meaningless.

Another figure stepped through the doorway and Mullen recognized Nigel. The huge Koramantyn glared at him, then beckoned to Mario. The younger man followed him from the room. A torrent of angry words arose but Mullen could not understand the heavy dialect.

Then Nigel spoke, his voice loud so that Mullen might hear. "Why you bring the white mon here? I was pimp to the whites because I had to be. You are white mon's pimp because you choose."

An inarticulate cry burst from the lips of the man on the pallet. His eyes popped and his lips were crusted with spittle. He tried to sit up but the effort was too much for him and he fell back. Mullen went to him and Buddhoe clutched his hand. The old chief's fingers were hot with fever but he was surprisingly strong. He began to whisper and Mullen leaned close to catch the words.

"Mario not Nigel. Mario must be chief. Nigel will destroy the Maroons."

Mullen nodded his understanding. Buddhoe closed his eyes, but his fingers were still tight on Mullen's hand. Mullen released himself as gently as possible and went to the room beyond. Neither Mario nor Nigel was there. He found water, filled a calabash and took it to Buddhoe. The old man looked at the water and shook his head. He tried to speak again, but no words came.

There was a babble of voices from outside and the sound of running feet. The cries of excitement mounted to a steady roar. Mullen looked at Buddhoe. The old man's eyes were open but he did not move. Mullen ran to the front of the house. In the clearing, which was called the Parade, men, women and children were jostling one another and shouting. Others were hurrying to join the agitated mob. Mullen hesitated, loath to leave the old man, yet fearful for Mario.

He returned to the doorway and saw that Buddhoe lay quiet. He sprinted down the path to the Parade. The crowd was more orderly now and they formed a huge ring. A hunchbacked Maroon traced a circle on the ground with a pointed stick. Within the circle, Nigel and Mario stood facing each other. Each had stripped to the waist and each was testing in his hand a long stick cut from the branch of a cannon-bail tree, the limbs of which have the hardness, the suppleness and the cutting edge of fine steel.

The hunchback darted back to the center of the ring. He stood with both hands raised, then he gave a loud cry and jumped to one side.

The two men approached each other, their sticks extended. When they drew close enough their sticks touched; then each leapt back a step. They stood tense, each waiting for the other to attack. The crowd was silent, breathing hard. Mullen pushed his way to the edge of the circle, but he dared not interfere or cry out lest he distract Mario and give Nigel a chance to strike.

Moments passed and still the fighters remained motionless. Muscles rippled in Nigel's knotted arm and his stick swayed slightly. His eyes were bright and his lips were drawn back against his gleaming teeth. His torso shone like burnished ebony. Even as he stood still, his body gave forth a sense of driving power, of tremendous strength temporarily held in check.

Mario was well-knit and lithe but he looked almost fragile as he crouched before the gigantic Koramantyn. His skin was lighter and his waist more narrow. His face was solemn; his eyes without expression. Mullen wanted to shout out, to stop the uneven combat, but he knew that to do so would place both himself and Mario in extreme danger. The watching Maroons had forgotten the cockpits of Jamaica and were living again in their African pasts. They would let no one stop the ceremonial battle for leadership.

It was Mario who struck the first blow. He darted forward and his stick formed a lashing arc. Nigel parried and the thin crack of the sticks sounded like a whip in the taut silence. Nigel raised his stick high and took a step forward, but before he could strike, Mario was moving in and Nigel was forced to counter the blow instead of attacking.

Mario weaved and circled, using his stick like a rapier. Nigel slashed at the dancing stick as though to wrest it from his adversary's hand. Sweat stood on Mario's body and drenched his breeches. Nigel grinned and stood his ground without wasting a single motion.

Then Nigel began his attack. His stick weaved in powerful arcs, flicking out only occasionally at Mario's ribs. Nigel moved forward step by step and Mario was forced to retreat. He came within an inch of the line, then whirled desperately and circled his opponent. Nigel's slow, relentless pursuit went on. He drove Mario back across the circle and again Mario danced away just in time. Nigel's face was savage. If possible he wished to force his opponent from the ring without a mark upon him. For if he succeeded, Mario could never live down the disgrace.

Mario strove to keep within the center of the circle. He tried recklessly to break through the big man's guard. He shifted his attack, striking now high, now low. Nigel countered the blows with apparent indifference. Again and again Mario was driven to the edge of the ring, but each time he escaped. But the strain of the battle was showing; his blows were weaker and he moved more slowly.

For the eighth time Mario was driven the full breadth of the ring. His heel was almost upon the line. The watchers crouched expectantly, ready to cry out if his foot passed across the edge. The circle had been drawn crudely and Mario was trapped by the uneven line. He glanced down, and as he did so, Nigel lurched forward. Mario took the full force of the blow with his stick and it was nearly torn from his hand. Nigel's weapon swung to the side and came sizzling straight at Mario's face. There was no retreat for the lighter man. He leapt high and the heavy stick cut deep into his ribs. He arched backward and his body slithered to the ground. Blood spurted from the wound. Nigel stood above him grunting.

The hunchback picked up Mario's stick from where it had fallen and handed it to Nigel as a token of victory. The big man raised the two sticks aloft and crossed them. The crowd let out a roar.

Mullen ran forward but Mario was already on his feet. The wounded man lurched sideways and Mullen caught him as he fell the second time. Mullen half carried Mario to Buddhoe's house and stretched him out upon a pallet. With dexterous fingers he probed the wound. There could be no doubt that two ribs were broken. Mullen bound them up as best he could and laid fresh John-John leaves on the open cut. Mario's eyes were closed and he appeared to have lost consciousness, but when Mullen had finished, Mario looked up.

"Buddhoe," he whispered.

Mullen nodded and went to the room where the old chieftain lay. Buddhoe was motionless and sudden fear shot through Mullen. He knelt at the old man's side and felt above his heart. He could find no beat. He tried for the pulse; there was none.

Mullen returned to Mario. The house was strangely quiet, though they could hear shouting at the far end of the Parade. Mario saw the distress on Mullen's face and asked, "Has he gone?"

Mullen nodded. Mario looked up at him, "Listen to me, Mullen, for I may faint again. Get me away from here. Get me into the Cockpits and leave me there. Then make you own way to Kingston. Nigel is top man now. Neither your life nor mine is safe. They'll be after us as soon as they learn that Buddhoe has died."

"I understand," Mullen answered softly. He crossed to the window and peered out. The Maroons had built a fire and were rolling out puncheons of rum. Nigel stood triumphantly on a raised platform and harangued the

298

crowd. Mullen slipped back to Mario and put an arm beneath him. Mario struggled to his feet.

They found the trail that led through the valleys to Nannie Town, but they climbed upward instead of down where they would be followed. Mario could not move fast and Mullen refused to leave him. They camped that night within half a mile of Accompong. All night long the fires sent up a red glow and they could hear the harsh cries of the Maroons.

Once the abeng whined across the mountainside. Mario listened intently. "It is the news that Buddhoe is dead and Nigel is the new chief." He hesitated. "It is a promise that the black man shall be avenged for his indignities —that Nigel is a warrior who will prove his worth."

31.

THE BRIGHT SUNLIGHT filtered through the lime trees of Government House and spread delicate traceries along the tiled walks. Sir William Elgin turned away from the girl who sat opposite him and looked out across the gardens. It was beneath one of these trees, he thought, where he had first held Kate in his arms. Jonathan Minor had taken her away from him even as Jonathan had taken Rose Stallybrass a few years earlier. Kate and Rose, he reflected bitterly—they had been the only women in his life. He wondered if anyone had ever realized how tenderly he had loved Rose. He doubted it. He had concealed his secret well. Not even Rose had suspected.

Rose had been so young when she married Jonathan. Elgin had watched over her ever since she had been a child, taking it for granted that he would marry her when she was grown. Then somehow Jonathan had snatched her from him before he had uttered a single word of love. Jonathan had never understood why Elgin hated him, wanted to destroy him. The older man had believed that Elgin had come to Jamaica simply to attach himself to Stallybrass, that ambition and greed set his goals. In part Jonathan had been right, but there had been another motive—the driving need to destroy the man who had married Rose. But in the end it was not Elgin who had accomplished that. Kate had done it for him.

When he had once met Kate, there was no longer need to conceal his love for Rose. The fragile love for the delicate girl had withered in the fire of passion that Kate had roused. Yet the memory of Rose was always sweet; while his love for Kate was shot with bitterness. Rose was the good in him; Kate the evil. And one could love evil, cherish it, hug it close to one, so that no other could see. That was the way he loved Kate—with the full knowledge that only grief and suffering could result—still jealously guarding the love, letting it fester until it had become a torment with him.

He sighed and forced his attention back to the girl who had brought up these memories because she looked so much like Rose. The girl who was Jonathan's daughter. The girl who was in love with Kate's son, the girl who had come to him for help.

"Confound it all, Ishbel," he burst out, "Mullen's all right. He's always mixing up with the Negroes, but he manages to keep out of trouble. Do you know what the young whippersnapper wanted me to do? Send three months' supply of rice to Accompong. Said the Maroons needed it and if I gave it to 'em it would stop them raiding the plantations. Poof! If you ask me, what Buddhoe needs is a whip on his back. If they'd only give me enough troops I'd go up to the Cockpits myself and wipe out the whole lot of 'em. The Maroons are up to no good and they'll always be a menace until they're exterminated, I've always said. But they'll not touch Mullen. They need a few whites like the lad to plead their cause."

"It's been so long and there's been no word," Ishbel protested. "Besides, Mario would not stay so long from Baraçong. Not now, when Shamey Lady is expecting."

Elgin's face grew red with anger and he shook a finger at the girl. "What do you know about Shamey Lady?

Have you been gadding about Baraçong again? Have I not warned you to keep away? Baraçong is no place for Stallybrass' granddaughter, for Rose's girl."

Ishbel laughed despite herself. "I'm thinking I'm safer there than among the ladies of Kingston. Their tongues are sharper than any knives, and laden with venom too."

Elgin looked at her and the anger faded from his face. "What would you have me do about Mullen?" he growled.

"Can't you send out a search party? He may have been hurt somewhere between here and Accompong."

"Do you know what would happen to the searchers? Well, I'll tell you. They'd be picked off one by one. 'Twould take an army to reach Accompong—and maybe they would never get there."

Ishbel shuddered. "But still you say Mullen is in no danger?"

"I honestly do not think that he is. As I've said, the Maroons trust him and he has served their interests well. Why should they harm him?"

Ishbel sprang up. There were tears in her eyes, but her face was stubborn. "If you'll not help me, I'll go to Koshi. There must be a way of finding out about Mullen."

Elgin forced her back into the chair and she was surprised by both the strength and the gentleness of his hands. "Listen to me, my dear. Mullen can fend for himself. I doubt that there's a white man in Jamaica who knows the trails and the people as well as he. But you— that's a different matter. I'll have no more of your running about even if I have to take you across my knee to stop it. Stallybrass made me your guardian and for once, at least, I'll have my say."

Ishbel stared at him defiantly and then tittered. "The role of stern guardian fits you well. What must I do— sit quietly at Rune Hall and twiddle my fingers? Shall I take up my needlework again? Perhaps Dowsie will teach me to bake confect cakes."

Elgin smiled, but there was no amusement in his eyes. "When the boy comes back marry him, Ishbel. He's twenty; you're nineteen—a good age for marrying. You should have done it a year ago and then the lad would not be gallivanting about the Cockpit country."

"It's not I who have caused the delay. You know that well."

"A woman can twist a man who loves her about her finger. And Mullen loves you right enough. I've no liking for what I see at Rune Hall. When you're married, make him take you away. And until you're married, say nothing of the date to Kate."

"Mullen will not have it that way."

"Mullen is a young fool. He cannot see his mother as she really is—and God forbid that he ever should. Kate hates you, Ishbel, and Kate's hatred is a dangerous thing."

Ishbel looked down at her hands. "She's always pleasant enough to me. Why do you say she hates me?"

"It's true. You're standing between Kate and Mullen whom she loves. You don't understand love like Kate's. It's a pagan love, possessive, demanding. There's nothing gentle about it. It's a consuming fire that destroys all that comes close. Kate's love for Mullen is her own torture and she clutches it close about her, scarring her flesh and her soul with it. There's no sharing a love like that. You're in her way. Ishbel, and there's no bounds to what she may do. The thought of your being at Rune Hall alone with her frightens me. Come and stay with me at Government House until things are settled."

Ishbel's eyes were wide with fear, but she shook her head stubbornly. "If I'm to marry Mullen, I must follow his wishes. It would look strange indeed if I left Kate alone at Rune Hall."

Elgin paced up and down the room. "Ishbel, I hate to think this, but it may be true that your life is in danger."

"What nonsense! Surely you do not think Kate would harm me!"

Elgin stood still, staring at the girl. How much like Rose she was! Once he had suspected Kate of poisoning Rose. He had told himself his suspicions were absurd. Had not Kate tended the sick woman with tenderness and affection? Certainly Rose had trusted her, even loved her. Yet he knew Kate was responsible for other deaths —Gabe Cousins, MacFeathers. He had heard rumors of how Mannie Cousins had died. And what of Jonathan Minor? No, Ishbel was not safe. But how could he make

302

her believe such monstrous stories when he could not quite believe them himself.

Ishbel had come close to him and her arms were about his waist. He realized that his face was beaded with perspiration and his hands were shaking. She said, "You're sick. Let me get you water—whisky."

"It's nothing. Ishbel, don't go back to Rune Hall."

"I must, and truly you do not believe these things. One evening in the Great Hall, I heard you tell Kate you loved her. You must believe in her goodness, her kindness, or you would not want her for your wife."

"You do not understand. I love in the same way that Kate does. I demand that the flames should burn me. I cherish the pain and the grief, even the evil of love. I must have the torture of possessing her." He looked up and his face was drained of blood. He saw the pity in Ishbel's eyes and could not even rouse himself to anger. "You think me mad that I should love so, but Kate has a power within her such as I have never seen in any other woman. She and I were once alive, twisted inside, ripped by ambition, distorted. Perhaps I saved myself from madness by watching her. I tell you there was greatness within Kate, but somewhere she took the wrong path and could not find her way back. Maybe it was when her father died, maybe long before. It does not matter to me. I love her."

Ishbel spoke softly. "Tell her. Tell her as you have told me. She will understand."

"No, never. Only Rose could have saved me from this."

"Rose!" Ishbel exclaimed. "My mother."

Elgin strode past her to the window. He stood staring sightlessly at the glass. Slowly he forced a smile to his lips and his eyes became bland, expressionless. He turned back to the girl and spoke softly. "Forgive me, child. I was ill and did not know what I was saying. Forget what you have heard."

Ishbel nodded numbly.

"Go back to Rune Hall tonight, if you must. I will come to you in a few hours. Maybe I will have word from Mullen. I'll send a deputy to Baraçong to see what he can learn. Now go, child. I've work to do."

They had spent weeks on the trail, making a wide half-circle westward. Mario's wound had not healed properly despite the daily application of the John-John leaves. There was a festering line of sores at the cut's edge and Mario was in constant pain. He could hardly eat the wild fruits and vegetables that Mullen brought him and he was so weak that he could scarcely walk. They had to travel slowly, cautiously, for even in the back trails, Nigel's scouts were searching for them.

They had hidden in the deep foliage of the Cockpits at night and listened to the message of the drums. Nigel was pleading with the slaves to throw off their chains and join him in the hills. Mullen believed that few would heed the bidding, for it was common knowledge that food and weapons were scarce at Accompong. Moreover, Nigel had not been tested as chief and he ruled by fear rather than trust. Nevertheless no black man would carry the messages to the whites. To do so meant certain, painful death.

When they finally came within sight of Rune Hall, it was late afternoon. They waited among the mahoganies for darkness. For Mario, the danger was still great. When he was well enough, he could plead his case in Baraçong and there were many who would champion his cause. But in his weakened condition, he would fall an easy prey to any of Nigel's men who were posted in the village. And should he be taken prisoner by the whites, almost certain death awaited him.

The cabin which had been Rodney Penney's was long deserted and the cane grew thick about the door. It was the safest place of which Mullen could think. He gave a sigh of relief when he had helped Mario onto the cot. The Ashanti was in a delirium of fever and Mullen knew that he must summon Koshi to tend him as soon as possible. But first he must let Ishbel know that he was safe.

His clothes were torn and matted and a scraggle of beard grew on his face. He scaled the wall to his own room and quickly shaved and changed his clothing. He peered in his glass and saw that only the thinness of his face and his sunken eyes disclosed the hardships of the trek.

He opened the door and stepped into the long corridor. He heard no sound of movement, but the great hall was brightly lighted. He tapped at Ishbel's door and a voice called for him to enter. He pushed the door open and stood on the threshold. A candle flickered on the table and, in its pale light, Mullen could see Ishbel lying on the wide bed. She tried to rise, but fell back, gasping for breath.

Kate had been standing at the bedside; she came forward, her arms outstretched. "Mullen, Mullen, 'tis time you came." She put her arm about him and kissed him, but he scarcely noticed her.

He went to where Ishbel lay and looked down upon her. She smiled a little and opened her lips. They formed his name, but he could hear no other word.

32

RUNE HALL was unnaturally still. Thin wisps of fog crept into the Great Hall through the open windows and seemed to deaden all sound. Even the chatter of the coachmen in the yard was muted. Mullen sat at the long, narrow mahogany table and his fingers drummed on its surface. From time to time he glanced at the man who sat opposite him, but Elgin did not lift his eyes. Instead he stared into his nearly empty glass. Mullen wondered at the heavy lines of weariness in the Governor's face. Elgin's skin was almost the color of ashes and his eyes were bloodshot.

A door opened upstairs. Mullen lifted his head and listened to the pompous voice of the doctor as he gave final directions to the nurse. Mullen disliked and distrusted Doctor Gibbon but he knew there was no more capable doctor in the island.

Footsteps clacked along the upstairs corridor and the doctor appeared at the head of the open stairway. Mullen sprang up and went to meet him. Elgin joined him at the foot of the stairs. Gibbon was nearly bald, round of face and round of body. His clothing was always rumpled, his manner harried. The doctor never admitted himself to be in doubt and he stated his opinions in a high-pitched, didactic voice that swept aside all objections.

Gibbon did not wait for Mullen's question. He said, "The girl's still asleep. I've told the nurse she's not to be bothered. Her condition is precarious, gentlemen, that I must admit. Yet she stands a good chance of pulling through if she is not excited in any way. It is hard to say what her illness is, but it is imperative that she have absolute quiet. Her pulse is faint and her heartbeat abnormally slow."

Elgin interrupted. "Can't we take her out of here, Gibbon? She'd be better off at Government House."

The doctor's eyes glittered angrily. "I tell you she could not stand the shock. I absolutely forbid any movement and refuse to take any further responsibility, Sir William, unless you fulfill my instructions. They are for complete quiet!"

Elgin shrugged and his eyes flicked to Mullen. Their glances met and each realized that his own suspicions were shared by the other. The doctor rambled on about pellets and purges. Neither of them listened to him. They were impatient for him to be gone, so that they could discuss with each other the steps that must be taken for Ishbel's safety. Yet even after the grating noise of the doctor's carriage wheels had faded away, they remained silent.

Finally Elgin lifted his head. "Where's Kate? Is she still in her room?"

"Yes," Mullen answered dully. "She's not left it since noontime." Then he blurted out. "We've got to take Ishbel away, no matter what Gibbon says."

"Do we dare disobey him, lad? Gibbie may be an old fuddy-dud, but he's practiced thirty years in Jamaica. He knows a lot more of medicine than you or I. He's told

306

us what the consequences of trying to move her may be. It's too great a risk to take."

"But Doctor Gibbon doesn't know about—about—" he halted at mentioning his mother's name, at putting his ugly thoughts into words.

Elgin laid a kindly hand on his shoulder. " 'Tis time we faced it, lad. Both you and I believe that Kate's done this thing to Ishbel. Maybe it's poison she's used. Maybe she's cast a spell. Who can say, if the doctor can't? Personally I think he's at a complete loss, though he'll not admit it. But be that as it may, I'll not take a chance on running counter to his orders, not with Ishbel's life at stake."

Mullen shook off the man's hand. "I can't stand this any longer. I'm going up to Kate. I'm going to accuse her to her face. I'm going to make her stop."

Elgin blocked his way. "No, Mullen, that's one thing you must not do. You would only frighten her, force her hand. She would strike quickly. No, you cannot add to Ishbel's danger."

"Shall we just wait?" Mullen asked shrilly. "Shall we let Ishbel die because we can't accuse Kate?"

"Easy, lad, easy. We may be doing your mother a grievous wrong. God knows I hope so. What we have to do now, is keep the two of them apart—for Kate's sake as well as Ishbel's."

"We can't do it forever. If Kate really wants to harm Ishbel, she'll have a chance sooner or later."

"The first job cut out for us is to see the girl through the night. One of us must keep constant watch outside Ishbel's door. I'll take the first watch for you're tired, lad. You can relieve me in three hours' time."

Mullen nodded for he did not trust himself to speak. He went to the table and poured a glass of whisky but did not drink it. He listened to the sounds of Elgin's feet on the steps and the scraping of a chair. He left the table and went to the stairwell and listened. The house was quiet. He returned to the table, picked up the glass, carried it to the low window and stepped out on the veranda.

The fog had grown thicker and Mullen had difficulty in finding his way through the cane field to Rodney's old cabin. He stopped outside and heard the hum of voices within. He tapped lightly. The door swung open a crack and Koshi peered out at him. Mullen pushed back the door and slipped through the narrow opening. The windows of the cabin were closed and the air was hot and foul. Mullen felt a wave of nausea course through him and fought it back. A single candle burned on the bedstand. In its flare, he could see Mario propped up on the cot, his eyes white and large, his skin gray.

Mario reached for the glass of whisky and took a great gulp. He grinned at Mullen. "That's better," he said. "Koshi says I'll be all right. I should be able to get along to Baraçong in a day or two." Then he added solemnly, "What of Ishbel? Has she been able to speak?"

"No. She's still in a coma." Mullen turned to Koshi and there was truculence in his gaze. "Koshi, you taught Kate all she knows of obeah. Do you think she has done this to Ishbel?"

The old man nodded solemnly. "It is true. Kate has done this thing. She was seen picking herbs at Maret and it is known that she built a sacrificial fire in the deserted altar of the mahoganies."

"If she is using herbs, there must be remedies. Do you know what she picked?"

"Every herb has its antidote, but there is none for the poison that springs from the soul."

Mullen's eyes flashed. "In God's name, this is no time to make riddles. If there is a way of curing Ishbel, tell me."

Koshi stepped back from Mullen and the candle flame lit his face. The skin gleamed like metal and the eyes were deeply shadowed. Mullen looked at him in wonder, for the face was suddenly transfigured as though by a malevolent mask. Koshi's voice was low-pitched and hollow. "Never again will I share the secrets of obeah with a white. She in whom I believed, has brought misery and degradation to our people. I have warned her not to practice obeah again. She has given no heed to my warning. But what I have said is true. Death is inevitable when the power that lies within obeah becomes stronger than the spirit of the one who invokes it. Kate will be destroyed by the evil she herself has summoned."

To Mullen, the old man whom he had known all his life seemed suddenly a stranger. He felt his skin grow cold despite the steaming heat of the cabin. Then anger at his own helplessness took possession of him. He took a step toward Koshi, his fists balled. "If you have a cure, tell me; if you have not, stop your prating."

Koshi did not move. His eyes rested on the boy's face. "Come to Baraçong tomorrow afternoon. I will do the best I can for you."

"Tomorrow may be too late."

"I can procure the ingredients no sooner. Now go, Mullen. It is not wise that you should remain here."

Mullen turned desperately toward the cot, but Mario's face was impassive. He strode to the door and yanked it open. A drift of air snuffed out the candle. Mullen stopped and peered back into the darkness, but there was neither sound nor movement. He thrust his way through the cane until Rune Hall loomed up in front of him. A dim light burned in Ishbel's window. Mullen stood gazing up at it for several minutes, then he skirted the cane field and hurried along the path that led beneath Kate's balcony. He took a post beneath the silk-cotton tree and waited. Once he thought he saw a flutter of white and heard the rustle of a gown. But he was not certain. For the fog was like cotton and the long, slender fingers of the acacias filled the night with whispers.

Halfway down the side of Pinchback Mountain, Mullen heard the shrieks of the women. They were high-pitched, piercing, and he was uncertain whether they were of anger or sorrow. As he stopped to listen the cries died down, then sprang up again louder than before. He scrambled down the rocks, scraping his hands in his hurry.

A stone ledge jutted out of the mountainside just above Baraçong and he could look down on the village streets and back yards. The Negroes were gathered in the tiny square. Some of the women lay on the ground moaning; others seemed to be striking at the earth with brooms and sticks. The heavy yellow dust swirled about them, concealing their movements. Beneath the sound of the screams was a low monotonous chanting.

Mullen lowered himself to the roadway and walked

quietly toward the square. Men lounged against the sides of the cabins. They spat and cursed but paid no attention to him, for their eyes were turned to the center of the square where the women formed a crude circle, screaming and flailing with their brooms.

A woman turned away and fell upon the ground, moaning. For the first time, Mullen could see what lay in the middle of the circle. An iguana, nearly eight feet long, was tied securely to four posts. Red ropes bound the giant lizard so tightly that it could only jerk and shudder and lash feebly with its tail. The silvery body was coated with dust and blood. The jaws were open, held into place by interlaced red ropes.

Sticks and brooms were not the only weapons used against the defenseless animal. Some of the women swung shoes attached to long strings and others dug at the iguana's sides with sharp, three-prong, metal forks. Mullen shuddered as he saw that the great lizard's tongue had been sheared off and lay in the dust in front of it.

Mullen knew the superstitious fear and dread of the natives for the iguana. The Negroes believed that the great lizards were carriers of evil and it was their custom to whip the reptiles in order to purify them before using them for food. There were times too, when a white person hated by the island Negroes would be tried by proxy in the person of an iguana. Articles of clothing belonging to the accused would be draped about the animal's body; it would then be given the white person's name and it would be flogged with whips and long red ribbons. Later the iguana might be hanged or roasted alive. If the accused should be guilty of the crimes, it was believed that he would eventually suffer the tortures inflicted upon his effigy.

Now amid the senseless shrieking, Mullen heard his mother's name and the phrase "De White Witch" repeated over and over. A long wailing cry came from the far end of the square. The women fell silent and dropped back from the iguana. An enormously fat woman approached the beast. Her face was black and flat; her nostrils wide; her lips thick. Her arms were like tree trunks; the skin rough as aged bark. The woman stripped a red bandana from her head and wound it around a

310

stick of ironwood. She raised it high, shouting, "Witch, yo done drink de blood o' our people. Yo suck de blood and fly far, far."

The stick came swirling down and struck the great lizard on the side of the head. *"Whun,"* screamed the woman. *"Whun,"* chorused the crowd.

Again the old woman raised the stick. "Witch, le' be our chilers. Stay in Rune Hall and le' us be." The stick struck again and the cry of *"Whun"* echoed along the roadway.

She raised her stick for a third blow, but as she did so her eyes met those of Mullen. She screamed and her eyes seemed to pop from her head. She pointed the stick, like a long maledictory finger. "De witch's spawn he be here wid us. He de blood o' de vampire. Kill he."

Silence came to the crowd as one by one they turned to Mullen. Their eyes were veiled and watchful and their lips moved in imprecation. Mullen glanced about and saw that the men had moved up quietly so that a half circle of them blocked off his retreat. Mixing with the freedmen of Baraçong were a number of Maroons and these men Mullen recognized as Nigel's henchmen from Accompong.

He stood, waiting quietly, fearful lest any movement on his part might precipitate an attack. The eyes of the Negroes filled with hate. Mullen realized with a sickening lurch of terror that the men were inching toward him, slowly closing in the circle. He stifled the impulse to run, to try to crash through the encroaching circle. It could only mean death. He searched the square for some friendly face, but though these were men he had known most of his life, their faces were set in grim lines of enmity. Sam, old Dowsie's paramour, was among them but Mullen knew that, even if he wished, Sam had little influence with the men. Mullen looked about wildly for Koshi and as he did so he heard a stir at the fringe of the crowd.

Koshi had come up behind the old woman with the stick. He took the stick from her and thrust her aside. He stood facing Mullen over the body of the feebly struggling iguana.

"Koshi," Mullen cried. "Thank God!"

"Call not me name," the old man shouted and Mullen

was surprised, even then, to hear the thick patois of his speech, rather than his customarily clipped inflections.

"What is happening? I don't understand. You know I came as your friend."

"Last night de witch torment us again in de form of de vampire. She suck de blood from one o' us chiles. She leave de curse o' death wid us. De chile dies and de witch has de taste o' de blood in her mout'."

"Koshi, what are you saying? You know such things cannot be true. Why do you speak patois? Why do you rouse your people to hatred?"

"What I say be true. I ha' seen de witch and seen her handiwork. I know de way of de vampire and de way o' Kate Minor."

"Stop this, Koshi. Don't you see where it will lead?"

"Go," Koshi screamed. "I will protect you if you go quickly. But go! Go now!"

"I've come for the herbs you promised."

"I'll gi' yo' nothing now. De witch ha' brought death to Baraçong for de last time. No longer will she fly among us sucking de blood o' our young. De time has come. Speak nothing; only go."

Mullen whipped about and walked swiftly past the men who were closing in upon him. A Maroon growled and stepped toward him, brandishing a club. Koshi called out sharply and the man hesitated and drew back again. When Mullen reached the dusty roadway he walked rapidly, keeping his eyes ahead, fearful of looking back. The steep pathway that led up the mountainside cut the rocks ahead of him. He pulled himself over the wooden barrier and scuttled along the stony pass. In a few minutes he reached the ledge and peered down at Baraçong. The crowd was still silent and their faces were turned toward him.

Koshi stood where Mullen had left him. His legs were spraddled and the thin stick of ironwood was still in his hand. As Mullen looked down, the foreshortened figure of the old Negro seemed thick and squat and the shoulders broad. Mullen turned quickly and again started the sharp ascent.

His breath was coming in gasping sobs when he finally reached Rune Hall. He scaled the wall and leapt down

312

onto the lawn. For a moment he waited uncertainly, looking up at Kate's empty balcony; then he turned to the cane fields and made his way to Rodney Penney's old cabin. The door was ajar. He pushed it open and called Mario's name. There was no answer. When his eyes were adjusted to the darkness, he saw that the blanket on the cot was crumpled and an empty glass lay on the floor. Other than these there was no sign of Mario.

In a panic, he rushed back to the main building. He heard fat Dowsie singing in the cookhouse, but otherwise the cloak of silence that had settled down over Rune Hall remained unchanged. He climbed the stairs quickly to where Sir William Elgin kept watch before Ishbel's door. Elgin sprang up at the sight of Mullen's wild face and torn clothing.

"Good God, lad. What ever has happened to you? You look as though you'd seen a ghost."

Mullen choked for breath. "Ishbel, is she all right?"

"The nurse was out just a moment ago. The girl's condition is unchanged. She's breathing a bit more freely."

"Have you seen Kate? Has she tried to come near Ishbel?"

"No. Kate's stayed in her room. I've heard nary a sound from her since you've left. But what is wrong? Tell me, lad."

"Last night another child died in Baraçong—bitten by a vampire. They're blaming Kate for it."

"A vampire! Ridiculous."

Mullen's voice rose in hysteria as he poured out the tale. "I'm afraid they'll come to Rune Hall," he cried. "They might try to kill Kate. And Ishbel is in danger."

"Hush, lad," Elgin warned. "You'll disturb the lass and frighten Kate."

"You're mistaken, William." It was Kate who spoke. Both men looked up, startled to find her close at hand. Her face was calm and her voice even. "Neither Mullen nor the blacks can frighten me." She put out her hand as though to touch Mullen but he moved aside and stepped past her to Ishbel's door. He opened it softly and went inside.

Kate's eyes burned with anger as she wheeled toward

Elgin. "You and Ishbel have turned my son against me. You intend to take him away from me and leave me alone. You'll not do it. He is mine and Rune Hall is mine. No one shall stand in my way."

Elgin's face was drained of blood and he looked old and haggard. "My God, Kate, I do not want to believe the nonsense I've heard about you, though I'd love you even if I knew it all to be true. Still, you must have done something to the girl—drugged her or cast a spell upon her. I saw Rose die this way, and Jonathan too. Now you have brought the wrath of the Negroes down upon you —attending their drazzons, pretending to practice obeah, walking on your balcony at night until all Baraçong is frightened of you. Kate, 'tis no time for pride. You heard Mullen's story. Let us all leave Rune Hall as quickly as we can. If the blacks come we'll all be helpless. The Negro sentries will not protect us and there is no time to reach Kingston for help."

Kate did not appear to listen. Her face was calm, her eyes gently mocking. "So now you believe I'm a witch, William. You're mistaken; 'tis Ishbel who has bewitched both you and Mullen to think evil of me. As for the blacks, let them come if they dare. I know more of the power of obeah than they. I will make them run from Rune Hall as though they had the devil's whips upon their backs."

"This is madness, Kate. You are driving yourself insane with your herbs, your drugs, your incantations and Lord knows what else. Yes, you have frightened the Negroes for years. But now their hatred has grown stronger than their fear. Kate, I love you and because I do I beg you to go to Kingston and place yourself under the protection of my deputies."

Kate's expression remained impassive. "I really think that you believe I have drugged the girl."

"If you have, release her, Kate. For your own sake —for Mullen's love, do her no more harm."

Suddenly Kate blanched and her lips quivered with anger. "There is a power stronger than drugs. A power that knows neither time nor space. Shall I let the girl cling to Mullen, wrap herself about him, rob him of his love for me? Shall I watch him be destroyed by Ishbel,

314

as Jonathan was destroyed by Rose? No, that I will never allow. And the power to prevent it is mine."

Elgin's arms encircled her. "Kate, my love. Forget this hate. Start living again—with me."

Kate pulled herself free and her hand lashed sharply across Elgin's face. There was madness in her eyes. She whirled and ran to her room. Elgin listened as the bar of the mahogany door fell in place. His face was gray save for the mark of Kate's fingers. He touched his cheek with a shaking hand. Then he went to Ishbel's door. Mullen stood watching over the sleeping girl, despite the nurse's silent protestations. Elgin called to him softly.

"Mullen," he said, "Kate will not leave Rune Hall and we dare not move Ishbel. I was a fool not to have brought deputies with me but I had hoped to keep this whole thing secret. It is too late for that now. Find Hodge as fast as you can. Send him to Kingston to get a guard for the Hall. Brandon will be the best man to see. Syd can get a group together quickly. Hurry, Mullen, it's turning dark already. If there are Maroons in Baraçong, they are there to start trouble. We may not have much time."

33

HODGE SPRAWLED ON A RUMPLED BED in the overseer's quarters. He was snoring loudly. One arm hung loosely over the bed's side so that the fingers dangled just above an upturned bottle. The other arm was flung across a naked slave girl who slept beside him. The air was foul with the stench of whisky and sweat.

Mullen called the overseer's name and shone the oil lamp in his face. Hodge only muttered without opening his eyes. Mullen pummeled the big man with his fists until Hodge sat up, grumbling and cursing. The black girl woke too and she began to whimper. Hodge looked blearily from Mullen to the girl. He reached out and smacked the girl resoundingly on the buttock. She cried out and drew the stained blanket over her. Hodge turned his truculent gaze to Mullen.

"What be the idea? Can ye not leave a mon be to take his rest and his bit o' sport when the day's work be done?" he grumbled.

Mullen fought down his anger at the man's insolent manner. This was no time for quarreling. As quickly as he could, he told the overseer of the danger that Rune Hall might be raided. Hodge leered and drew the back of his hand across his wet mouth. " 'Tis a pretty piece they'll be makin' o' Kate, do they lay their hands upon her. 'Tis no loose paps she has like Connie Abbott."

Mullen's fist clenched but he turned away quickly. He ran to the bookkeeper's cabin. Bailey had heard the noise and was standing in the doorway. Mullen looked at Bailey's yellow face and emaciated frame and wondered if it would not be best to tell the bookkeeper to stay clear. Still, the man might be able to use a gun even if he did so with a shaking hand. Mullen gave him hasty directions. The bookkeeper's mouth fell open; and he took a step backward and reached for an open bottle on the table. He tilted it to his lips and choked until the tears streamed down his cheeks. Mullen watched him in disgust. As he turned, he saw Hodge start down to the stables.

Mullen raced along the twisting path that led through the cane fields. Darkness was closing in rapidly and already the high cane cast deep purple shadows on the earth. The green stalks ahead of him rustled. Mullen jerked to a stop. He leveled his revolver and gave a cry of warning.

"Mullen," a voice whispered. "It's Mario. Come into the cane where I can talk with you without being seen."

Mullen brushed aside the stalks and stood beside the colored man. He was impatient to get back to Ishbel and he questioned Mario sharply.

"I've just come from Baraçong," Mario told him. "There's trouble brewing tonight. Nigel is in the village and he's had a puncheon of rum opened. The people are excited that a child has died again and Nigel is whipping them up to violence. Nigel has many enemies among the Maroons, but if there's open fighting he'll stay in power. He's the best warrior among them. He knows that. He'll do anything he can to provoke bloodshed."

"Can't Koshi stop him? He's still head man in Baraçong."

Mario's voice was grim in the darkness. "Koshi is a medicine man, the most powerful in the island. I have seen him walk through fire unscathed, heard his voice when he was far away, watched him drive sickness from a woman for whom the white doctor had given up hope. But Koshi believes that Kate's spirit has taken the form of a bat and come to Baraçong. He is a sad man tonight for he feels responsible for Kate. He always loved her. You know that. He taught her much of obeah and now he believes himself to be punished for betraying its rites to a white. I cannot tell what he will do."

Mullen listened restlessly. His eyes were on the dimly lit window of Ishbel's room. "Will they come tonight?" he asked.

"I'm afraid so."

"Who will lead them? Nigel or Koshi?"

"I truly do not know. If Koshi comes there is hope that no harm will be done. But Nigel cares only for killing."

Mullen placed his hand in Mario's and clasped it hard. "I must get back. We have had so little time to prepare for danger. I got back from Baraçong only a few minutes ago. We have sent for a guard but meanwhile Elgin is standing watch alone."

"If Koshi comes do not resist him."

Mullen scarcely heard, for he already had started to run toward the Hall. He leapt up on the veranda and pushed open the glass doors. Elgin was at the foot of the stairs, a pistol held grimly in his hands. When he saw Mullen his face creased in a harsh smile.

"What of Hodge? Has he gone?"

"Yes, but the man's so drunk I doubt he can keep his saddle. I ordered Bailey to come to the Hall but it's more likely he'll run out on us. Perhaps it's as well. Little enough good the bookkeeper will be to us."

"How about the servants? Are there any we can trust?"

"None. Not to the extent of firing on their own people, though I doubt that they'll join against us. A few years ago it might have been different. But between Kate and Hodge, they've little reason to give us loyalty."

The two men faced each other. Elgin, tall, still erect, his face gray, lined and tired. Mullen, wiry and boyish, his hair in disarray, his shirt ripped open over his thin chest. A smile flickered across Elgin's face and Mullen grinned. Neither need fear weakness in the other.

A door creaked and both men started, but it was only Dowsie with a tray of food and steaming coffee. Mullen went to her. "You'd better leave, Dowsie," he said gently. "There may be trouble here tonight."

Dowsie's eyes rolled and her lips were loose, but she shook her head vigorously. "De odders gone, but I stay. Here me place, Mas' Mullen."

Mullen squeezed her arm. He remembered he had not eaten since morning. He drained a cup of the scalding coffee and gulped down bread and cold meat. He turned to Elgin. "It's easy to get up on the balconies. One of us should guard the upstairs corridor; one the hall."

Elgin nodded. "I'll stay here."

Mullen ran up the stairs quietly. He listened before Ishbel's door. No sound came from within. He fought the impulse to enter the room. It was best that Ishbel should remain undisturbed. He went down the corridor. He could hear Kate's footsteps moving steadily back and forth. Could she be on the balcony? A door opened behind him. He whirled about and saw the nurse standing in the doorway of Ishbel's room. Her face was white and frightened. She beckoned and he went to her.

"A figure in the cane," she whispered. "I saw it clearly—a black man. He's down there now."

Mullen followed her into the room. Ishbel lay with her eyes closed, breathing faintly. He went with the nurse to the window and peered out. The sky was overcast and a light wind whipped the cane stalks. He could hear the dry rustle of the heavy leaves, but nothing else. Perhaps Mario had passed this way, or one of the servants anxious to quit Rune Hall.

"Mullen," the cry came very softly from the bed. He

318

spun about. Ishbel's eyes were open and there was a faint touch of color in her cheeks.

He went to her, leaned across her bed and touched his lips to her forehead.

"What has happened?" she asked. "I feel so strange. As though someone were holding me so that I can't move."

He could think of no words to say to her. He put his hand over hers, and in a few seconds she closed her eyes again. He was leaving the hall unguarded, he realized. He forced himself away from the bed and returned to the corridor.

He went to the head of the stairs but he could not see Elgin. He called Elgin's name in a low voice but there was no answer. He started down the stairs cautiously, his pistol drawn. He reached the foot and there was still no sign of the older man.

He stopped and listened. There was only the night sounds—the rustle of wind in the cane, the muted tattoo of a tamarind tree knocking against the turret, the chirr of insects. "Elgin," he called more loudly, "Elgin!" The name echoed against the mahogany walls, whispered and died.

He stood listening. The great hall seemed to grow larger and the night sounds to urge him to action. Perhaps Dowsie could tell him where Elgin had gone. He crossed the length of the hall, moving warily, his pistol in readiness. He opened the window to see if the cookhouse was lighted. The heavy drapes of red velvet billowed about him and then there was a sound like the shuffling of feet.

He swung about, but even as he did so an arm encircled his throat. He opened his mouth to cry out, but strong fingers cut off his breath. The pistol fell from his hand and went skittering across the floor. The man who held him laughed and he looked up into the face of Nigel.

The huge Koramantyn's forehead was beaded with sweat and his teeth gleamed white against his black skin. He laughed aloud as he thrust the rope from the curtain into Mullen's mouth. Mullen struggled but he was helpless in the big man's grasp. He was choking for breath and ripping pains seared his chest.

"Do not hurt him."

Mullen heard the order and recognized Koshi's voice, but Nigel held him so tightly that he could not twist about to see the old man. Nigel's face filled with anger and his arm jerked upward so that he lifted Mullen from his feet. The Negro gave a powerful thrust forward. Mullen fell to his knees and rolled over, but before he could struggle to his feet, his arms were pinioned behind him. He tried to shout a warning, but the rope gagged him and cut his lips so that the cry was little more than a gurgle.

When Mullen looked up again, Koshi stood before him. "Do not struggle," he ordered quietly. "We mean you no harm. We have come to take the curse from our people, not to injure the innocent."

Mullen gazed about him. The great hall was slowly filling with Negroes. They moved in from the entrance to the cookhouse; through the veranda windows, from the servants' quarters. The huge front door was thrown open and still others entered. Mullen recognized most of them. The free men and women of Baraçong, the slaves from Rune Hall, a scattering of Maroons.

The Negroes were quiet. They shuffled their feet awkwardly and looked away from Mullen. Their faces showed more of fear than anger; yet there was stubborn resolve in their manner. Mullen saw that Elgin, like himself, was gagged and that his arms were held securely by two Maroons. Elgin's forehead was bruised and there was blood on his hair and face. He lurched forward but his guards jerked him back so sharply that Elgin's face was twisted with pain.

Dowsie was standing among the women. She was whimpering softly. When Mullen looked at her she tried to go to him, but the women on either side held her. Outside there was the sound of a scuffle and Mullen had a minute of hope, thinking that help might be coming. Instead, Sam and a Maroon appeared in the door, with Bailey between them. The little bookkeeper could hardly stand and he was gibbering with fright.

Sam spoke and Mullen noted that it was Koshi whom he addressed. "Us found he in de cane." He grinned

320

broadly. "Had a gun on he, but he too skeered to pull de trigger."

Koshi regarded the bookkeeper with contemptuous eyes. "Leave him be. He'll make no trouble." . .

The two Negroes released the man's arms and he slid to the floor moaning. Nigel strode toward the fallen man, but Koshi blocked his way. Nigel stopped, facing the old Ashanti. Koshi made no movement, but looked full into the younger man's face. "These be my people. They will obey me," he said quietly.

Nigel's hands twitched and a grimace distorted his face. He turned and looked at the men and women. He spoke to them in Maroon dialect. His voice rose in anger; then changed to pleading. The Negroes listened stolidly. When he was finished there was silence. Then the answer to his plea came from an old woman. Mullen recognized in her the hag who had stood above the iguana that afternoon. She said calmly, "No—Koshi. He de leader."

Others spoke the name, saying it quietly, "Koshi."

Nigel's eyes glowed bright, and the muscles of his arms knotted, but he spread his hands in defeat and stepped back into the circle.

Koshi walked into the cleared space before the stairs. He stood gazing at his people. He raised his arms above his head, then brought them down slowly to the level of his shoulders. The fingers pointed directly in front of him. The hands moved, scarcely perceptibly, in a widening arc.

As Mullen watched, it seemed to him that the man grew larger until he towered high above the others. Mullen strained against the arms of the man who held him, but sickening pains shot through him. He closed his eyes and when he opened them again, Koshi seemed far away and his voice was faint.

"My people, we have not come to kill, but to scourge the evil that lives among us. We do not seek revenge; we only ask to be left in peace."

"*Yeh doojoo.*" The answer come softly.

Koshi turned and knelt. From the gray bag at his belt, he took out charcoal. Slowly, carefully, he drew the interlacing circles and the cabalistic sign of the cock's print. He reached into the bag again and brought out a handful of sand. He dropped it grain by grain until ninety-nine grains had fallen. Then he took a lime, slit it in half and squeezed the juice upon the pile of sand. As Koshi worked, the candles and the oil lamps were quietly extinguished, save for two that were placed on the lowest step.

Koshi rose and his long shadows swept the length of the hall and fell across the watchers. His voice boomed out and echoed through the long corridors.

"Kate Minor, we have come to cleanse the evil from you. Stand before us, false Erzulie."

Again Mullen struggled, but the arms that held him were like metal bands. The breath was forced out of his body and blackness swept over him. He shook his head and the room came into focus again. Kate stood at the top of the stairs. The lamp in her hand spread light across her breasts, her throat and face. It highlighted the cheekbones, threw deep shadows about the eyes, made her hair shine like burnished metal. She wore the white gown in which Rodney Penney had once painted her. The red threads at the neck seemed drops of blood and the ruby pendant flashed scarlet.

The crowd sighed and a ripple of fear passed through the hall. Mullen felt his own heartbeat quicken, for the woman at the top of the stairs was no longer his mother, but a stranger possessed of an exotic beauty.

She spoke and her voice was rich, strong and calm. "You call me false Erzulie, Koshi, and in that you lie. How often have I proven my power in the pallays. Did you not boast among your people that you taught me the secrets of obeah? Let them know now that that is not true. My power is greater than yours and for that reason alone you have stirred up your people to hate. You are the high priest of the Ashanti, but I am Erzulie. Those who defy me shall be destroyed."

When Koshi answered her his tones were sad, filled with grief rather than anger. "We do not deny that you have learned many of the secrets of obeah. We had hoped that you would learn them well to bring peace and comfort to our people. But you cared only for the evil. You learned how to brew herbs and used your knowledge to poison. You learned to cast spells and used your knowledge to kill. You learned to separate the spirit from the

322

body, but the spirit was contaminated by the wrong that you had done. You have demanded the blood of our people. That you shall have no longer."

Kate looked beyond Koshi to the shadowy figures in the Hall. Her voice rose in harsh command. "Leave, leave at once. You do well to fear me. Are you fools enough to believe this old man can harm me? The doors of your homes are not strong enough to protect you. Your pallays will be circled with fire, your drazzons ridden by death. Do not arouse my anger for if you do so, none among you can stop my vengeance."

The Negroes stirred restlessly and looked at one another, but none among them left his place. Then a woman shouted, "She de White Witch. She kill me pickn'y. She mu' die." The crowd took up the cry. "Kill her. Kill de White Witch."

Kate's voice rang out above the uproar. "Are you such fools that you place your trust in an addled old man? Koshi, throw out the dolos bones if you dare and I will fling them into the faces of this scurvy crew of yours." She stopped and waited for silence, then spoke portentously. "Those whom the bones touch will swell with poison 'til their limbs burst open. They will die. I say that they will die. Do you dare throw out the bones, old man?"

Koshi did not turn but spoke softly. "My people fear you no longer. I will throw the dolos bones, but you will not pick them up." He reached for the sack in which the dolos were kept. He opened it and rattled the bones in his hand. Then he tossed them lightly so that they landed halfway up the high, steep flight of stairs. They struck with a dull thump on the thick carpet runner and one of them bounced and rattled on the polished mahogany.

Kate raised her hand and took a single step downward. The crowd sucked in their breaths and drew back. Koshi called, "Kate, look at me."

Kate stopped and smiled slightly but her eyes avoided the old witch doctor's face. He mounted the bottom step and called her name again. The crowd grew taut, waiting, uncertain.

Again Kate took a step downward, but the lamp in her

hand wavered and this time she touched the rail with the tip of her fingers.

"You are afraid," Koshi called softly. "You dare not look into my face. You dare not reach for the bones." He took another step, bringing them closer.

Kate stared at him. Her face was still impervious, defiant, and her eyes still flashed, but her body seemed to stiffen gradually and her fingers curled tightly about the rail.

Step by step she descended and Koshi matched her moving upward. Kate's movements became slower, more awkward. The smile was fixed on her lips, her face was white and her eyes glazed. Finally only the step on which the dolos bones rested lay between them.

Koshi's whisper echoed through the silent hall. "Kate, you cannot pick them up."

Kate's lips moved but there were no words. Slowly, stiffly, she bent forward. Her fingers spread out and touched the nearest bone. Then her mouth opened in a scream and she pitched forward. She clutched at the stair carpeting. It ripped loose and wound about her as she hurtled down the stairs. The lamp in her hand smashed against the balustrade and the burning oil soaked the runner. Flames licked at the carpet. The two lamps at the foot of the stairs were wrenched loose. The flaming oil splattered against the velvet portieres and the wide tapestries were soon sheets of fire.

Kate writhed in the runner, unable to free herself. Tongues of flame licked at her face and hair. Rune Hall echoed with the screams of the Negroes as they trampled over one another rushing for safety. The windows were flung open and the brisk breeze swirled the flames against the woodwork and carried them high into the rafters.

Nigel leapt forward. He held in his hand a long pole, sharpened at the end to form a stake. He jumped upon the flaming carpet that bound Kate, regardless of the fire licking at his feet. He stood poised above her, his mouth open in a wild savage cry, the stake ready to plunge into her body.

Mullen struggled against the arms that held him, but they dragged him back to the door. But as his guards stopped to stare at Nigel, he wrenched himself free. The curtains beneath which his pistol had fallen were on fire, but he reached beneath them and felt the hot metal of the barrel on his hand. He raised the pistol to fire but when he pulled the trigger there was no report. One of the Negroes kicked it from his grip. Mullen heard Nigel scream *"Babawah"* and he knew that the stake was meant for Kate's heart.

In desperation, he remembered that knife that Bard had given him and that it was in the drawer of Jonathan Minor's desk. He rolled across the floor and yanked the drawer open. The knife seemed to leap from his hand. Above the crackling flames, he heard Nigel give a startled cry. Then the giant Koramantyn's body jerked and straightened out. The stake fell from Nigel's grasp and his big hand touched the carved mahogany handle of the knife, striving to pull the blade from his chest. Then he bent over slowly and crumpled to the floor beside Kate.

A moment later Elgin had thrown himself across Kate, smothering the fire with his body and beating at her burning hair with his bare hands.

"Ishbel," Mullen cried, "Ishbel." He rushed to the stairway but it was a solid mass of flame. He buried his face in his arms and took a step forward, but the searing heat drove him back. A hand clutched at him and he saw that Mario was beside him. "In back, Mullen," he called. "We must get Ishbel out. Come."

Mullen shot a single glance to the top of the stairs. Koshi stood there, his arms outspread. The old man cried out but Mullen could not hear his words.

Mullen, with Mario beside him, sprinted to the cookhouse entrance, but already the light pine boards were ablaze and the wood of the stairway was burning like a bonfire. Beneath his bedroom window, Mullen grasped the thick vines and pulled himself up to his narrow balcony. When he flung open his door he found that the corridor was filled with smoke but the fire whirled upward through the turret towers. Mullen lurched down the hall, trying to hold his breath. The smoke blinded him and he nearly collided with Koshi and the nurse. The old man grasped Ishbel close to him, her face against his chest. Mullen took her hurriedly from Koshi's arms and carried her back to his balcony. The nurse was beside him and between the two of them they lowered Ishbel to a point where Mario could reach her and prevent her fall. The nurse climbed down, supported by the thick vine, and Mullen turned around to speak to Koshi.

The old man had gone. Mullen called his name but there was no answer. He rushed back through the corridors. Momentarily the breeze whipped the smoke clear and the blazing stairway was visible. The Ashanti witch doctor was at the head of the stairs; slowly, resolutely he walked into the mounting flames. There was the sound of the rending of wood as the stairs collapsed. Great swirls of sparks flew upward and the roar of the fire was deafening. Mullen rushed back to the balcony. Mario stood beneath him holding Ishbel. As Mullen clambered down to the lawn there was a volley of shots.

The nurse had brought a blanket and she spread it on the ground amid the shadows of the silk-cotton tree. Mario whispered, "Quick, Mullen, I must leave. Brandon and his men are here."

Only then did Mullen realize that the sound of shouts, of carriage wheels and pistol shots were mingling with the crackle of flames and the breaking of glass. A group of men were already rounding the hall and, at the sight of Mario, they cried out hoarsely. As Mario dove for the safety of the cane, Mullen heard the whirr of a bullet. Sydney Brandon and Hodge ran up. Brandon leveled a revolver at the fleeing man. Mullen threw himself at the big man and forced him arm down. Brandon snarled and cursed and tried to wrench his arm free, but Mullen clung to him.

"Be ye mod, mon? Ye've let the nigger get away."

Mullen whirled away from Brandon and knelt beside Ishbel. She looked at him. Her eyes showed fright, but for the first time since her sickness they were bright with understanding. "Something has happened to me," she whispered. "I'm better. It's as though the cords that were binding me had been cut. I can raise my hands. I think I can walk."

Mullen glanced from Ishbel to the nurse. "It's best she should be quiet," the nurse said. "Maybe Doctor Gibbon has come with the men."

"If he's here, I'll find him," Mullen promised. He

brushed his lips against Ishbel's cheek, then rose and ran to the front of the house. Carriages clogged the driveway, and horses, frightened by the fire, whinnied and pawed the earth. Men milled about the smoking building, shouting and cursing. The flames were beginning to die down, but red tongues still licked at the mahogany ceilings and crept along the giant rafters. The smoke billowed up through the turret towers and formed grotesque patterns against the dull sky. There were repeated flashes of gunfire in the cane fields and an occasional scream of pain.

A body lay in Mullen's path and he nearly stumbled over it. He looked down to see a Maroon who had been caught by the crowd and beaten to death. Another Negro lay nearby. Many of the whites whom Hodge had rounded up were drunk. Their voices were coarse, filled with the lust of killing. Mullen forced his way past them toward the front of the great hall where a knot of men were standing. They gave way before him and he saw that Kate lay on a blanket on the ground. Mercifully the carpet had partially protected her face and throat but the whole lower part of her body was hideously burned. Nigel's stake had missed her heart, but it had ripped her breast and blood was clotted over her bodice. Elgin crouched beside her. His face and hands were red and blistered but he appeared oblivious to the pain. He clasped one of Kate's hands tightly and he repeated her name over and over.

Father Maholan knelt on the opposite side of Kate. Mullen caught the mumble of Latin phrases and knew that the old priest uttered the words of extreme unction. Kate's eyes had been closed but when Mullen approached she opened them as though sensing his presence. She looked up at him calmly and her lips curved in a soft smile. She tried to speak but her voice was so low that Mullen could not hear. He stooped beside the priest.

"Mullen," Kate whispered. "At least I have always loved you. Help me—make the cross."

He took her hand in his and guided it to shape the holy cross. Kate sighed and turned her head. Her eyes closed again, but her face remained calm. Father Maholan plucked at Mullen's sleeve. "It's over, lad," he said gently. "She has died within the Faith."

Mullen's eyes were stinging and his throat was clogged. He forced the numbness from his body and rose. "Where is Gibbon?" he asked. "Has he come?"

"The doctor can do no good. It is too late."

"I know. But Ishbel needs Gibbon. Why isn't he here?" In his anxiety, Mullen was almost shaking the old priest.

A firm hand fell on his shoulder and he looked up into the stern face of Michael Scott. "Easy, lad," Scott cautioned. "Gibbie'll be here in a minute. We've been scouring the town for him, but we've found him at last at the Christian Steps. Here's Lettie's carriage now if I'm not mistaken."

A carriage caromed through the gates of Rune Hall and its wheels grated on the gravel drive. A halloo echoed across the lawn and a woman's voice shrieked, "Kate, me love, where be ye?" Lettie Parsons, monstrous in lavender silk, leaned from the carriage door. Father Maholan went to her and took her hand. "Kate's gone, Lettie," he said gently. Lettie screamed and the priest added sharply, "There's no time for vapors, Lettie. We've a sick girl here and Elgin's badly burned."

Doctor Gibbon had dismounted from the far side of the carriage. He came forward stiffly and asked fussily, "Where's the Governor?"

Elgin stepped forward. "Never mind me, Gibbie. Get to Ishbel. She needs you. Mullen will take you to her."

Mullen led the way. The priest, the doctor and Michael Scott followed. Elgin hesitated, then turned on his heel and walked back to where Kate lay. He knelt and took the covering from her face. He rose slowly, his eyes fixed on Kate.

Lettie Parsons came up beside him. She put both hands on his arm. She said hoarsely, "Ah, she was a cushy one, was Kate. Sometimes she seemed hard but there was that about her that always turned me water-trembly inside."

Elgin remained motionless. The hard muscles of his jaw drew into knots and his fingers dug into his palms.

"Don't judge her harshly, William," Lettie said more softly. "There was many a mon whose love she accepted, but never yours. Why was it so? She tried to tell me more than once, but 'tis a hard thing to explain. Perhaps 'twas because love meant pain and suffering and grief to Kate. And the love of you was more than she could endure. Ah, ye do not know a woman's heart, William. Ye do not know how fiercely a woman like Kate turns upon the one she loves, lest the love destroy her, tear her apart, cause her to lose herself in it. If Kate did not love ye, 'twas 'cause she did not dare. Ye were the only one had more strength than her and she was not one to give in. 'Tis strange words from the like o' me and I know, but 'tis a lucky mon ye be that Kate's love for ye was no weak thing. I'm thinking 'tis still alive and 'twill always be with ye."

34

THE THICK PARCHMENT SCROLL was spread on the table between the two men. Sir William Elgin dipped his quill into the ink. Linen bandages still covered the burns on his hand so that his fingers moved stiffly as, with elaborate care, he signed his name to the bottom of the document. He looked up, smiled and passed the quill to the man opposite him.

Mario's eyes ran over the scroll, although already he knew its terms by heart. The treaty granted twenty-five thousand acres of land to the Maroons, complete sovereignty, the promise of essential foods and other supplies, the dignity of an independent status. In return, the Maroons guaranteed to stop all depredations in the countryside, to enter into negotiations with the English officials for the return of slaves guilty of criminal acts who sought sanctuary in Accompong, and to restrain any member of the colony who might prove dangerous to the welfare of the island. Mario nodded and scrawled his name beside that of the Governor.

When Mario had finished, Elgin quietly handed him a second legal paper. Mario read it quickly; it was an order for the arrest of Sydney Brandon on three charges: those of inciting to riot, beating freedmen and violating the Civil Properties Act. Mario looked up and his lip curled slightly. "No jury of whites will convict him," he said slowly.

Elgin shrugged. "That may well be true, but I know Brandon well and this will curb his demagoguery. If it should fail, there are other charges that can be brought against him. I can assure you that you'll have no more trouble from the man."

He held out his hand and Mario grasped it. Elgin said evenly, "This must be an end of fear and distrust, for both my people and yours. That is why I have asked you to meet me alone, that I may pledge my personal word that there will be no further expeditions against Accompong, nor will your men be molested in other parts of Jamaica. I have no fear of the Maroons under your leadership, Mario. The raids will stop and the sentries can be withdrawn from the plantations."

Mario answered simply. "The Maroons have wanted peace, but that could not come while men like Brandon and Nigel held positions of power."

Elgin turned from him and walked to the window that overlooked the gardens of Government House. Without looking back, he said, "Mullen wishes to see you. He and Ishbel will be leaving for America in a few days. If it were not for the lad, I would not have trusted you in this way, Mario. He has pleaded your cause well."

Elgin waited at the window, watching Mario as he walked down the shaded path to the bench where Mullen and Ishbel sat together. He saw Mullen's face, flushed with happiness as he rose to greet the young Maroon chief and he heard the tinkle of Ishbel's laughter. For a moment his hand rested on the wooden frame, then he sighed and drew the jalousies tight.

Sister Madeleva stooped to arrange the flowers that lay upon the unmarked grave in the grounds of the Convent of the Immaculate Conception. She remembered the night twenty years before when Father Maholan had come to her to ask her to take in the destitute girl who had been living at the Christian Steps. How attentively the girl had seemed to listen as the sisters sang the Salve Regina; yet even then Sister Madeleva had noticed her face as the Ashanti drums beat in the hills.

A few days later Kate had run away; but she was back at the Convent now and this time she would stay. Father Maholan had brought her again to Sister Madeleva and asked that she be buried within the convent grounds. "I know the ways of the Ashanti," he said sadly. "There will always be pestilence, sickness and death among them. The bats will still fly and the lizards find their way into the cabins of Baraçong. And when a legend has started there is no end to it. They will say that Kate still walks among them and brings evil to them. There are those among them who would seek Kate out and, even in death, drive a stake through her heart. Only here will her grave be safe from desecration."

Sister Madeleva had nodded even though she had not fully understood. Yet somehow the grave within the garden brought her comfort, and when at night she heard the pulsing beat of the drums, she thought of Kate Minor and the passionate desire for life she had once glimpsed in Kate's eyes.

Captain Flynn of the *Hickory* stood before Mullen and Ishbel. His wide grin showed solid teeth stained with tobacco. His eyes shone blue and clear in his weather-beaten face. A servant had led him into the garden of Government House a few minutes previously and now, as he waited for Mullen to slit open the envelope he had brought, Flynn chuckled and said, "There's none as see you could doubt you're Percy Morgan's boy. Ah, I've known him since he was a lad like yourself. Save for the coloring of you, there's no more difference than two peas."

Mullen read the note swiftly. His eyes sparkled with excitement and he reached for Ishbel's hand. "He's done even more than he promised," he said exultantly. "He's arranged for me to join up with Lewis Hallam's troupe

331

They'll be touring all winter from Falmouth to Charleston. There's no better actor in America today than Hallam."

Flynn laughed. "The *Hickory*'ll be sailing with the tide tomorrow at nightfall. Can you make it, lad? I'd like to be the one as takes you to your dad."

Mullen's face fell. " 'Tis the night before we planned our marriage. We've booked passage on the *Vallery Queen*."

"Ah, you canna tell me Father Maholan will not up the date, and if he refuses, well, it's the Captain's right to tie the wedding knot. I may be a bit rusty on the words, but they're written down on the flyleaf of me Bible. I can read 'em well enow—what do you say, lad? Will you rob an old man of his pleasure?"

Mullen turned to Isabel questioningly and read her answer in her glistening eyes. He held her tight and pressed his lips to hers.

Captain Flynn chuckled. "I've no need for further words. We'll be waiting for you on the *Hickory*. I'm thinkin' it's a happy man that Percy Morgan will be once I've seen you safe to Salem."

From the roof of Government House, Sir William Elgin could look down over the sweep of Jamaica Bay. The setting sun streaked the gray waters of Slyke Sound with gold and a spanking wind billowed the sails of the *Hickory* as she veered out to the open sea. He watched until the slim sailing vessel was out of sight, then he turned and his eyes sought out Pinchback Hill and the scorched, gray turret towers of Rune Hall. He hesitated only momentarily, then he walked back across the roof and down the steep flight of stairs that led to the ground floor.

Outside he could hear the wind in the lime trees, but he did not look out. Instead he went to the inner room which he had forbidden even the servants to enter. He lit the lamps with a steady hand and then went to the massive mahogany desk and poured himself a glass of whisky. He stood staring down at it and then he slowly turned until he faced the far wall.

Rodney Penney's portrait of Kate Minor hung there. Her eyes seemed to look down at him and her lips were smiling. Elgin's heart beat more quickly as he studied the portrait. The firm lines of Kate's breast and throat, the high cheekbones, the rounded forehead, the coloring of eyes and hair were all as he remembered. But the sense of urgency in her, the driving ambition, the anger at life, the torment of frustration were missing. It was strange, Elgin thought, that Penney should have painted her thus, for it was as though he had foreseen how Kate's face would look in the last moments of her life. That could not have been true, of course. It was simply that Penney had stripped her of all that he himself could not understand and, in so doing, he had given to Kate the simplicity, the kindliness, the natural generosity that should have been hers.

Elgin took his drink to the wide leather chair and sat down. It was almost a miracle, he thought, that the portrait had escaped with so little damage. One corner had been charred and the painting smudged with smoke, but Michael Scott had worked over it until these things scarcely showed. Fortunately the portrait had hung in the front hallway and the huge mahogany doors had swung back to protect it. Elgin had found it the day after Rune Hall had been gutted by fire. He had asked Mullen for the right to keep it and the boy had consented without comment. Perhaps Mullen was a bit like the portrait, Elgin reflected. In some strange way he too had escaped the holocaust of passion, hate and fear that had destroyed the lives of so many whom Kate's life had touched. Perhaps it was because Mullen too had doors to protect him—his love for life, his love for the theater, his love for Ishbel.

Elgin raised his glass to his lips and looked at Kate. He gave a salute and drank. He listened for a moment to the stirring of the breeze in the branches of the lime trees. Somewhere, far away, he heard the soft tinkle of laughter and he thought of Ishbel and Mullen. It was right that they should go; life was just beginning for them. As for himself, his place was here. He knew that he would never leave.

THE END

THE BEST OF BESTSELLERS
FROM WARNER BOOKS!

THE BEST OF BESTSELLERS
FROM WARNER BOOKS!

WITHOUT FEATHERS by Woody Allen   (89-035, $1.95)
A major N.Y. Times bestseller; Woody Allen's funniest book since *Getting Even*. This new collection of short pieces and plays "crackles with droll remarks . . . mixing the comic with the cosmic"— Hartford Courant

GETTING EVEN by Woody Allen   (88-244, $1.50)
Getting Even is the first collection by one of America's last serious humorists, Woody Allen. *Getting Even* represents Woody Allen as psychologist, historian, philosopher and sex maniac. "The funniest books I've read since *Portnoy's Complaint*."
—The National Observer

ROUGHING IT EASY by Dian Thomas   (89-119, $1.95)
A great new idea book for camping and cooking—the best book ever published on America's fastest-growing leisure activity! More than 130,000 copies in print in the trade edition! Crammed with diagrams, drawings and photographs, many in full color, and "just bursting with practical, inventive solutions to everyday and special camping needs."—Family Weekly

MAN IN BLACK by Johnny Cash   (89-086, $1.95)
A "moving and often punishingly honest reading experience" (Publishers Weekly) in which Johnny tells the true story of how he was saved from drugs by his religion. **16 pages of photographs.**

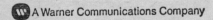 A Warner Communications Company

Please send me the books I have checked.

Enclose check or money order only, no cash please. Plus 35¢ per copy to cover postage and handling. N.Y. State residents add applicable sales tax.

Please allow 2 weeks for delivery.

WARNER BOOKS
P.O. Box 690
New York, N.Y. 10019

Name ....

Address ....

City .... State .... Zip ....

_____ Please send me your free mail order catalog